**Lynne Graham** lives in Northern Ireland and has been a keen romance reader since her teens. Happily married, Lynne has five children. Her eldest is her only natural child. Her other children, who are every bit as dear to her heart, are adopted. The family has a variety of pets, and Lynne loves gardening, cooking, collecting antiques and is crazy about every aspect of Christmas.

Addicted to daydreaming and romance from a young age, **Angela Bissell** suspects she was destined to become a writer although she did travel a convoluted career path on her way to authordom. Like many an intrepid Kiwi she also travelled the world, backpacking through Europe, Egypt, Israel, Turkey and the Greek Islands before settling for a time in London. Now she lives back home in New Zealand, never taking a day in her beautiful country for granted and loving the challenge of pursuing her writerly dreams.

Mills & Boon novels were **Julia James'** first 'grown up' books she read as a teenager, and she's been reading them ever since. She adores the Mediterranean and the English countryside in all its seasons, and is fascinated by all things historical, from castles to cottages. In between writing she enjoys walking, gardening, needlework and baking 'extremely gooey chocolate cakes' and trying to stay fit! Julia lives in England with her family.

# Confessions

# Confessions of the Mistress

LYNNE GRAHAM

ANGELA BISSELL

JULIA JAMES

MILLS & BOON

First Published in Great Britain 2022
By Mills & Boon, an imprint of HarperCollins*Publishers*
1 London Bridge Street, London, SE1 9GF

www.harpercollins.co.uk

HarperCollins*Publishers*
1st Floor, Watermarque Building,
Ringsend Road, Dublin 4, Ireland

CONFESSIONS OF THE MISTRESS
© 2022 Harlequin Enterprises ULC.

*The Italian's Inherited Mistress* © 2018 Lynne Graham
*A Mistress, A Scandal, A Ring* © 2018 Angela Bissell
*Carrying His Scandalous Heir* © 2017 Julia James

ISBN: 978-0-263-31796-1

MIX
Paper | Supporting
responsible forestry
FSC™ C007454

This book is produced from independently certified FSC™ paper to ensure responsible forest management.

For more information visit: www.harpercollins.co.uk/green

Printed and Bound in Spain using 100% Renewable electricity at CPI Black Print, Barcelona

# THE ITALIAN'S
# INHERITED MISTRESS

## LYNNE GRAHAM

# CHAPTER ONE

'THAT'S IMPOSSIBLE... I don't believe it!' Alissandru Rossetti erupted from his chair in the midst of the reading of his brother's will, rigid with outraged disbelief. 'Why the hell would Paulu leave that little slut anything?' he demanded of the room at large.

Fortunately, his mother, Constantia, and the family lawyer, Marco Morelli, were the only parties present because all attempts to contact the *main* beneficiary of the will had proved fruitless. Disconcerted by that revealing word, 'main', Alissandru had merely frowned, thinking it would be just like his late brother Paulu to have left his worldly goods to some do-good favourite charity. After all, he and his wife Tania had died together and their marriage had been childless and Alissandru, his twin, had no need of any inheritance, being not only the elder twin and owner of the family estate in Sicily but also a billionaire in his own right.

'Take a deep breath, Alissandru,' Constantia urged, well acquainted with her surviving son's sizzling temper. 'Paulu had the right to leave his estate where he wished and we do not know that Tania's sister is deserving of so unpleasant a label.'

Alissandru was pacing the small legal office, a form of behaviour that was distinctly intimidating in a confined space because he was several inches over six feet tall, a lean, powerful figure, dressed in one of the elegant tailored black suits he favoured. That funereal colour had earned him the nickname 'The Raven' in the City of London, where his aggressive and hugely successful business instincts were famous, as befitted a renowned entrepreneur in the new technology field. Pacing that office, he reminded the family lawyer of a prowling tiger penned up in a cage.

*Not* deserving? Alissandru thought in outrage, recalling that little red-headed teenager, Isla Stewart, at his brother's wedding six long years before. At barely sixteen years old, she had been rocking a sexually provocative outfit, parading her nubile curves and shapely legs in a clear sexual offer to the highest bidder, he reflected in disgust. Later that day too, he had seen her emerging from one of the bedrooms in a dishevelled state, only moments before one of his cousins left the same room, straightening his cuffs and tidying his hair. Obviously Isla was just like her sister, Tania, who had been brazen, wanton and dishonest.

'I was not aware that Paulu was in any form of contact with Tania's sister,' Alissandru admitted curtly. 'No doubt she pulled the wool over his trusting eyes as easily as her sister did and wheedled her way into his soft heart.'

Very real grief fractured Alissandru's hard driven

drawl as he spoke because he had loved his twin a great deal and could still, even six weeks after the helicopter crash that had claimed the lives of both Paulu and Tania, not quite believe that he would never ever speak to him again. Even worse, Alissandru could not shake the guilt of knowing that he had been powerless to *protect* his brother from that designing harpy, Tania Stewart. Sadly, Paulu's last years had been deeply unhappy, but he had refused to divorce the sleazy underwear model he had married in such haste, believing that she was pregnant…only, surprise, surprise, Alissandru recalled cynically, *that* had proved to be a false alarm.

Tania had gone on to destroy his brother's life with her wild extravagance, her shrewish tantrums and, finally, her infidelity. Yet throughout those excesses, Paulu had steadily continued to adore Tania as though she were a goddess amongst women. But then, unhappily for him, Paulu had been a gentle soul, very caring, loyal and committed. *As unlike Alissandru in every way as day was to night.* Yet Alissandru had treasured those stark differences and had trusted Paulu in a way he had trusted no other living person. And although he was enraged at his conviction that yet another Stewart woman had somehow contrived to mislead and manipulate his brother into drawing up such a will, there was yet another part of him which, sadly, felt *betrayed* by his sibling.

After all, Paulu had known how much the family estate meant to Alissandru and yet he had left his home on the Sicilian estate and all his money to Tania's sister. A lottery win for the sister, a slap in the face for

Alissandru even though he knew his brother would have sooner cut off his hand than hurt him. Paulu, being Paulu, however, could never have dreamt that so tragic an accident might take both his and his wife's lives together, clearing the way for Paulu's sister-in-law to inherit what should never ever have become hers.

'Paulu visited Isla a few times in London during that period that…er…' Contantia hesitated, choosing her words with particular tact '…that he and Tania were separated. He was fond of the girl.'

'He never mentioned it to me!' Alissandru bit out explosively, his dark eyes flashing and his lean, darkly handsome features clenching hard at the image of yet *another* Stewart woman having woven her seductive, cloying charm over his impressionable brother in pursuit of profit. Paulu had always been a soft touch for a sob story, Alissandru conceded grimly.

Speaking for himself, however, Alissandru had never been that foolish. He liked women but women *loved* him, hunting him like a rare breed because he was rich and single. In his younger days he had heard every sob story going and once or twice, in his inexperience, had even fallen for such ploys, but it had been years since he had been that naive or imprudent. These days he chose his lovers from his own stratum in society. Women with their own wealth or very demanding careers were a safer bet for the kind of casual light affair in which Alissandru specialised. They understood that he wasn't ready to settle down and practised the same discretion that he did.

'Knowing how you felt about Tania, Paulu wouldn't

have mentioned it,' his mother pointed out gently. 'What will you do?'

'Buy Paulu's house back from her...what else?' Alissandru pronounced with an angry shrug at the infuriating prospect of having to enrich a Stewart woman yet again. How many times had he paid Tania's debts to protect his brother and shield him from her insatiable demands? But what else could he do in the present? Tania was dead and buried and her sister had not even bothered to attend the funeral, all attempts to contact her directly at her last-known address having failed. That fact alone really said it all about the weak bond between the sisters, didn't it?

'We'll have to track Tania's little sister down,' Alissandru breathed in a raw driven undertone of menace.

Isla blew on her frozen fingers, the gathering wind chilling her face below her woolly bobble hat as she fed the hens in haste and gathered the eggs. She would have to bake to use them up, she thought cheerfully, and then she immediately felt guilty for having a happy thought when her only sister and her brother-in-law were dead.

And even worse, she wouldn't even have *known* that it had happened, had not a kind neighbour driven over a week earlier to break that tragic news in person. Her aunt and uncle, who owned the Highland croft in Scotland where Isla was staying, but who were currently visiting her aunt's family in New Zealand, had read on the Internet about the news of Paulu and Tania's death in a helicopter crash. They had immediately contacted their neighbour and had then phoned to ask if Isla wanted them to come home so that she could travel out to Italy.

But what would have been the point in that trip when she had already missed the funerals? Isla asked herself heavily. It was the great sadness of her life that she had never got to know her only sibling. Of course, they had grown up apart and Tania had been ten years older, and Isla was the daughter who was an unplanned and not very welcome late arrival following their father's premature death. Their mother, Morag, already struggling to survive, had headed down to London with Tania to find work while accepting her own mother's offer to take care of her new baby until such time as the little family of mother and daughters could be reunited.

Only unfortunately that reunion had never happened. Isla had grown up in the same Highland croft as her mother had with grandparents who were effectively her parents. Morag had made occasional visits at Christmas, gifting Isla with vague memories of a soft-faced woman with red curly hair like her own and a much taller, leggy, blonde sister, who even as an adolescent had blossomed into a classic beauty. Tania had left home at a very young age to become a model, and not long afterwards Isla's mother had passed away from the kidney complaint she had long suffered from. Indeed, the first time Isla had communicated directly with her sister had been when Tania phoned the croft to invite Isla to her wedding in Sicily.

Isla had been embarrassed that her grandparents

were not also being invited but the elderly couple had insisted that she go alone because Tania was generously offering to pay for her kid sister's travel costs. Being fair-minded people, her grandparents had also pointed out that Tania had never had the opportunity to get to know *any* of them and that they were all next door to being strangers even if they were bound by blood.

Isla still cringed at the memory of how out of her depth she had felt attending that opulent wedding with all its important moneyed guests and of the unpleasant experience she had suffered when cornered by a predatory older man. But, worst of all, the longed-for connection with her only sibling had signally failed to materialise from her visit. Indeed, Tania's attitude to life in general had shocked Isla.

'No, you can thank Paulu for your invite,' Tania had breezed. 'He said I had to have *some* family member present and I decided a teenager was a far better bet than the boring old fossils in the croft Ma used to rattle on about. I'm moving *up* in life with this marriage. I don't want poverty-stricken relatives with a thick Scottish brogue reducing my status in our guests' eyes!'

Tania had merely been outspoken, Isla had decided forgivingly, the product of a liberal and far less old-fashioned upbringing.

'That girl ran wild,' her grandma had once insisted. 'Your mother couldn't control her or give her enough of what she wanted.'

'But what *did* Tania want?' Isla had asked in her

disappointment after her sister's wedding when there had been no mention of the sisters ever meeting again.

'Och, the only dream that one ever had was to be rich and famous.' Her grandma had chuckled. 'And by the sound of the wedding you described, that pretty face of hers got her exactly what she always wanted.'

Only that hadn't been true either, Isla reasoned wryly, recalling her next meeting with her sister several years later, after she too had moved down to London. Her grandparents had died within weeks of each other and her uncle had taken over the croft. Her uncle had urged her to stay with them but, after months of having helped her grandmother nurse her grandfather while he was dying and still sad over the loss of them both, Isla had believed that she needed to move out of her comfort zone at the croft and seek independence.

'Paulu misrepresented himself,' Tania had insisted with scorn after announcing that she had left her husband and the marital home. 'He can't give me what he promised. He can't *afford* to!'

And shortly after that, Paulu had come to visit Isla in her humble bedsit to seek advice about her volatile sister. A lovely, lovely man, she thought sadly, so much in love with Tania and so desperate to do whatever it might take to win her back. Her eyes stung as she thought that at least Paulu *had* got the love of his life back before their deaths, *had* reclaimed that happiness before fate had cut their respective lives brutally short. She had liked Paulu, had actually got to know him much better than she had ever got to know her sister.

Had Paulu followed Isla's feisty advice on how to

recapture Tania's interest? She supposed she would never know now.

In the snug croft kitchen, she fed the turf fire and shed her outdoor layers with relief. She loved being at the croft, but she missed her city social life with friends. Living where she had grown up meant that even a cinema trip to Oban required extensive planning and a very long drive. In another few weeks, though, she would be heading south again, her promise to her relatives fulfilled. Her aunt and uncle were lovely people; however, they were childless and had nobody but Isla to rely on if they wanted to leave home. It was over twenty years since her aunt had last visited New Zealand and Isla had been happy to help to make that dream come true, especially when that request had come at a time when the café where she had long worked as a waitress was closing and the rent had gone sky-high on her bedsit.

Her uncle's sheep and hens couldn't be left to take care of themselves, especially not in winter or when bad weather was expected, she reflected, casting a nervous glance out at the grey laden sky: heavy snow had been forecast.

She still smiled while watching her dog, Puggle, daringly nestle his tiny body in beside her uncle's elderly and increasingly deaf dog, Shep, the collie who herded the sheep. Puggle adored heat but the little dog was Isla's most impractical acquisition ever. Abandoned on a road somewhere near the croft, he had turned up shivering and starving the week Isla had arrived and she didn't know how on earth she was going to keep him when she returned to London, but his perky little wagging tail, enormous eyes and ridiculously huge ears had sneaked into her heart before she'd known what was happening. He was a very mixed breed with perhaps a dash of chihuahua and poodle because, besides the ears, he had a very curly coat but he also had very short legs and odd spotty black-and-white colouring. Regrettably, it seemed nobody was searching for him because she had notified the relevant authorities and had heard nothing back from any source.

The noisy sound of a helicopter overhead made her frown because the sheep hated loud noises, but she already knew, having checked, that the herd was safely nestled in the big shelter in their pasture, their reading of the temperature as good as any forecaster's. Minutes later, when she was brewing a cup of tea, she was startled when Puggle began barking seconds before two loud knocks thundered on the sturdy wooden front door.

Assuming it was her uncle's nearest neighbour, who had kindly been keeping an eye on her in the isolated croft, Isla sped to the door and yanked it straight open, only to fall back in shock.

*It was him...* Alissandru—Paulu's brother—the insanely *hot* and gorgeous twin who had knocked Isla for six the first time she'd seen him when she was a naive teenager. There Alissandru was, inconceivably, on the croft's doorstep, jet-black hair ruffling in the wind, dark eyes set below level ebony brows, flawless classic features bronzed by a warmer climate. A strikingly beautiful male, Isla had thought at that wedding while he stalked about the place like a brooding volcano, emanating the most extraordinary intensity of emotion. But Tania had *hated* Alissandru, she reminded herself ruefully, blaming Alissandru for everything that went wrong in her marriage to his brother.

Alissandru focussed on his quarry, Isla, dressed unexpectedly in a long tatty sweater and gym pants, not even shoes on her tiny feet. A woman down on her luck, he decided instantly. Why else would she be back in the family home in the back end of nowhere? An explosion of red curls tumbled down to her slight shoulders, eyes the same purplish blue as violets huge against the porcelain perfection of her skin, her full plump pink lips slightly agape. Another beauty like her evil sister, Alissandru reasoned, refusing to react in any way to the sudden surge of desire. He was a man with all a man's physical weaknesses and responding to a lovely face and beautiful hair was simply proof of a healthy libido, nothing to beat himself up about.

'Er… *Alissandru*?' she questioned incredulously, doubting her recognition because his arrival was so very surprising. They might have been linked by their siblings' marriage but she had never actually spoken to Alissandru before because he had regally ignored her at that long-ago wedding.

'May I come in?' Alissandru demanded imperiously, stifling the urge to shiver even in the black cashmere overcoat he wore over his suit.

Isla remembered her manners and stepped back, muttering, 'Of course…of course. It's freezing, isn't it?'

Alissandru scanned the humble interior, unimpressed at the sight of the one large cluttered room that acted as kitchen, dining and living area. Yes, definitely down on her luck when she was living in such a dump. Some man had probably got wise to her and thrown her out, he thought without hesitation. He was quite sure that the news of her inheritance would make her day and it galled him to be the one forced to make that revelation.

'Er… I was just making tea. Would you like a cup?' she asked hesitantly.

Alissandru flung his handsome dark head back, leaving her uneasily aware of how tall he was below the low ceiling above. His seemingly dark eyes flared to a vivid gold that was stunning below the lights she had on to combat the winter darkness that folded in so early in the day this far north. Unable to stifle the need, she stared, transfixed by those amazing eyes, gloriously fringed and accentuated with spiky inky lashes. Hurriedly, she turned her attention to making a pot of tea, every brain cell scrambled by his appearance into sheer stupidity as she grasped what she should have been saying first.

'I'm so sorry about your loss,' Isla muttered uncomfortably. 'Paulu was a very special person and I liked him a great deal.'

'Did you indeed?' Alissandru flared back at her, eyes sparking bright as the sun in his darkly handsome features, an oddity in his stance and intonation that struck a wrong note. 'Tell me, when did you start sleeping with him?'

In total shock at that offensive question, Isla froze. 'I beg your pardon?' she mumbled as she made the tea with her back turned to him, thinking she must have misheard him.

'I asked you when you began sleeping with my brother. I'm genuinely curious because guilt would explain a lot,' Alissandru admitted grittily, wishing she would turn back round again because he wanted to see her face.

*'Guilt?'* Still very much at sea as to what could possibly have brought Alissandru Rossetti to her door to abuse her with such horrifying enquiries, Isla gave up on the tea-making and flipped round. 'What on earth are you talking about? That was a disgusting question to ask me about the man who was married to my only sister!' she snapped back at him, colour flushing her triangular face, the colour of both anger and embarrassment.

Alissandru shrugged a broad shoulder as he took off his heavy coat and draped it over the back of a chair at the kitchen table. 'It was an honest question. Naturally, I'm curious and I can't ask Paulu.'

A slight quiver in his accented drawl attracted Isla's attention to the reality that Alissandru had been hit very hard by the loss of his twin, much harder than she had been hit by the loss of a sister she had only met on a handful of occasions. Alissandru Rossetti was grieving, and her anger dwindled a little in response to that awareness.

'I don't know why you would even think to ask me a question like that,' Isla admitted more levelly while watching him as though he were an unexploded firework still fizzing dangerously.

Paulu had once told her despairingly that Alissandru could not comprehend the love that Paulu had for Tania because he had never been in love and lacked the emotional depth to even fall in love, but Isla, at only her second look at Alissandru, thoroughly disagreed with that belief. In Alissandru, Isla saw a highly volatile male who literally *seethed* with emotion, every flashing tautening of his features, every spark of brightness in his extraordinary eyes telegraphing that reality.

He stood poised there below the stark light above him, blue-black hair gleaming with the gloss of expensive silk, the smooth hard planes of his flawless face the colour of bronze and doing nothing to hide the strength of his grim jaw line or the angle of his arrogant aristocratic nose, while the faint shadowing of stubble growth darkening the skin round his mouth only highlighted the sensuality of his chiselled lips. Heat mushroomed inside Isla, increasing her discomfiture.

So, she genuinely *didn't* know about the will? Did he look that stupid?

Alissandru tensed, hating the role forced on him by circumstance, wide shoulders straightening, long, powerful legs bracing with instinctive distaste. 'I asked that question because in his will Paulu left everything he possessed in this world to *you*.'

Isla's lips fell open in disbelief and she stared back

at him in silence for several seconds before stumbling into speech again. 'No…no, he couldn't have done that…for goodness' sake, *why* would he have done that? That would be crazy!'

Alissandru hitched an unimpressed ebony brow. 'And you're still trying to say you didn't have sex with him? Not even when he was getting friendly with you while he and Tania were separated? I'm sure only a purist would condemn you for loosening the knicker elastic at that point when he was legally *almost* a free man…'

Isla finally unfroze with those deeply offensive and aggressive words still echoing in her incredulous ears. She marched over to the door and dragged it wide, ushering in a blast of icy air that made Alissandru Rossetti shiver. 'Get out!' she told him fiercely. 'Get out and never come near me again!'

Impervious to the command, Alissandru merely laughed. 'Yes, let's take the gloves off, *cara*. Let me see the *real* Isla Stewart!'

Puggle was growling soft and low and circling Alissandru's feet while being ignored.

*'Out!'* Isla said again with biting emphasis, blue eyes purple with fury.

Still as a granite pillar, Alissandru surveyed her with cynical amusement, much as though he were watching an entertaining play. Maddened by that lack of reaction, Isla grabbed up his fancy overcoat and pitched it out of the door onto the frozen ground outside. *'Leave!'* she repeated doggedly.

Alissandru shrugged again with blatant unconcern.

'I have nowhere to go until the helicopter comes back to pick me up in an hour's time,' he told her.

'Then you should work at being a politer visitor. I've had enough of you for one day!' Isla replied with spirit. 'You're the most hateful man and I'm finally seeing why my sister loathed you.'

'Do we have to bring that whore into the conversation?' Alissandru asked so smoothly she almost missed the word.

And Isla just lost it at that point. Her sister was dead and she deeply regretted that fact because it meant that she could no longer hope to attain the relationship she had longed to have with Tania. His lack of respect for the departed was too much to be borne and she rushed at him, attempting to slap him, getting caught up instead by two powerful arms that held her back.

'You bastard…you absolute bastard!' she shouted at him in tears. 'How dare you call Tania that when she's gone?'

'I said it to her face as well. The married man she deserted Paulu for was neither the first lover she took nor the last during their marriage,' Alissandru informed her smoothly, and then he released her again, pressing her firmly back from him as though even being that close to her was distasteful. 'Tania slept more often with other men than she did with her husband. You can't expect me to sanctify her memory now that she's gone.'

Isla lost every scrap of colour at those words and backed away in haste from her visitor. *Was it true?* How could she know? Tania had always done what she *wanted* to do, regardless of morality or loyalty. Isla had recognised that disturbing trait in her sibling and had refused to dwell on it, telling herself that it was none of her business because she had been keener to see similarity rather than a vast gulf of understanding stretching between herself and her sister.

'Paulu would've told me,' Isla muttered in desperation.

'Paulu didn't know everything that she got up to but *I did*. I saw no reason to humiliate him with the truth,' Alissandru confessed harshly. 'He suffered enough at her hands without me piling on the agony.'

And the wild defensive rage drained from Isla in that moment. What on earth were they doing? Fighting over a troubled marriage when both parties had since passed away? It was insanity. Alissandru was grieving, she reminded herself reluctantly, bitter as hell about his twin's need for Tania when clearly he himself—in his brother's shoes—would have dumped Tania the first chance he got. He was not a forgiving man, not a man capable of overlooking moral frailties in others.

'Oh, go and fetch your coat back in, for goodness' sake!' Isla urged him impatiently. 'We'll have tea but if you want to stay under this roof you will not insult my late sister again...*is that clear?* You have your view of her but I have my own and I will not have you sullying the few memories I have of her.'

Alissandru studied her set face. It was heart-shaped, full of determination and unconcealed exasperation. In all his life no woman had ever looked at Alissandru

Rossetti as Isla did at that moment. As if she was thoroughly fed up with him and being the bigger person in her self-control and practicality. Her bright eyes challenged his, her head at a defiant angle as she awaited his response. Alissandru retrieved his coat. *Per Dio*, even inside the house he was cold!

An odd little creature, he reasoned as he scooped up his coat with a frown. No glamour, no grooming, no flirtation or fawning either. He didn't *drink* tea! He was Sicilian. He drank the best coffee and the purest grappa. It was, however, possible that in a temper he had been ruder than was wise in the circumstances, he conceded grudgingly. He had a very bad temper. He knew that; everyone knew that about him and made allowances. She didn't, though—she had talked down to him as though he were an angry, uncontrollable child. He was enraged by that little speech she had made; Alissandru's lean dark features froze into icy proud immobility and he stepped back indoors to head straight for the smoking fire. On his passage there, however, something bit at his ankle and he bent down with a Sicilian curse to smack away the little animal with the sharp teeth set into his leg.

*'No!'* Isla thundered at him, charging across the room to scoop up the weird little dog but only after slipping a finger into its mouth to detach its resolute teeth from Alissandru's silk sock and the bruised flesh beneath. 'Puggle's only a puppy. He doesn't know any better.'

'He *bit* me!' Alissandru snarled.

'You *deserved* to be bitten and bitten *hard*!' Isla

told him roundly, cradling the strange little animal to her chest as if it were a baby. 'Stay away from him.'

'I don't like dogs,' Alissandru informed her drily.

Isla dealt him an irritated glance. 'Tell me something that surprises me,' she suggested just as drily.

Huge ears set wide above his curly head, Puggle rested big round dark eyes on his victim from the safety of Isla's arms and if a dog could be said to smile, Puggle the puppy was smiling.

# CHAPTER TWO

CLAD IN HIS COAT, Alissandru lowered himself reluctantly into a chair by the kitchen table. The silence was uncomfortable, but he refused to break it. It didn't help that he had never been so cold in his life or that Isla was still running around in bare feet and clearly much hardier in such temperatures than he was. His body wanted to shiver but, macho to his very fingertips, he rigorously suppressed the urge.

Watching Isla's quick steps round the small kitchen area that encompassed a good half of the claustrophobic low-ceilinged room, he absently and then more deliberately found himself taking note of the surprisingly full curves that rounded out the unflattering clothing she wore. Her sister Tania had been tall and model-thin but, being both small in height and curvy at hip and breast, Isla had a very different shape. The sort of shape Alissandru much preferred in women, he acknowledged grudgingly, momentarily becoming rigid as his body found something other than the intense cold to respond to while he struggled to curb that male weakness.

Even so, his response didn't surprise him because Isla was beautiful, even if she was rather less flashy and far more of a natural beauty than he was accustomed to meeting. She wasn't ever going to stop the traffic, he reasoned with determination, but somehow she constantly drew a man's attention back to the delicate bones of her face, the vivacity in her eyes and the sultry fullness of lips that would inspire any man with erotic images. *Any* man, Alissandru told himself insistently, noting the fine scattering of freckles across her fine cheekbones, even more naturally wondering if she had any anywhere else.

His mobile phone rang, uncannily loud in the silence.

'My goodness, you get reception here!' Isla exclaimed in surprise. 'You're lucky. I have to drive a mile down the road to use my mobile.'

The call was a welcome interruption, however, throwing Alissandru out of a rare moment of introspection and thoughts that thoroughly irritated him. He leapt upright and pulled out his phone with the oddest sense of relief at that sense of being connected with *his* world again. But, unfortunately, the call brought bad news and sent Alissandru straight to the window to stare out broodingly at the big fluffy snowflakes already falling and drifting as the wind caught hold of them.

'The helicopter can't pick me up until tomorrow,' he breathed grittily, annoyance and impatience gripping him. 'Blizzard conditions will hit this evening.'

'So, you're stuck here,' Isla concluded, wondering

where on earth she was supposed to put him because there was only one bedroom and one bed and no sofa or anything else to offer as a handy substitute. Usually when she stayed her uncle and aunt borrowed an ancient sofa bed from their neighbour and set it up downstairs for her use but in their absence she had been sleeping in their bed.

'Is there a hotel or anything of that nature around here?' Alissandru enquired thinly.

'I'm afraid not,' Isla told him ruefully, setting his tea down by his abandoned chair. 'We'd have to drive for miles and we could easily get trapped in the car somewhere. We don't go out unless we have to in weather like this.'

Alissandru expelled his breath in a hiss and raked agitated long brown fingers through his luxuriant black hair. 'It's my own fault,' he ground out grimly as he swung back to her, his lean, strong face grim. 'The pilot warned me before we took off about the weather and the risk and I didn't listen.'

With admirable tact, Isla compressed her lips on the temptation to remark that she wasn't surprised. Alissandru Rossetti had a very powerful personality and she imagined he rarely listened to the advice of others when it ran contrary to his wishes. Evidently, he had wanted to see her today and no other day and waiting for better flying conditions hadn't been an option he was prepared to contemplate. Now his impatience had rebounded on him.

'You can stay here,' Isla announced wryly. 'And I'm sure we're *both* absolutely thrilled by the prospect.'

An unexpected glimmer of amusement flared in his eyes, lighting them up with pure gold enticement. Isla wondered why nature had bothered to bless him with such beautiful eyes when most of the time they were hard and cold with sharpness and suspicion. She shook away that bizarre thought and instead tried to concentrate on what she could defrost from the freezer to feed him.

Alissandru sat back down and manfully lifted the mug of tea, his mother's training in good manners finally kicking in. But even as he did so he was wondering if he should simply have asked for coffee because he had never before been in a situation, aside of his brother's marital problems, where he was forced to make the best of things that were bad. He supposed he was very spoilt when it came to the luxury of choice because the Rossetti family had always been rich. It was true that Alissandru's business acumen had made his nearest and dearest considerably wealthier, but he still had to look back several generations to find an ancestor who had not been able to afford the indulgent extras of life. The tea proved not to be as horrible as he had expected and at least it warmed him up a little.

'Where will I sleep?' Alissandru enquired politely.

Isla rose in haste. 'Come on, I'll show you,' she said uncomfortably, leading the way up the small twisting staircase.

Alissandru's gaze flickered over the three doors opening off a landing the size of a postage stamp. 'That's the bathroom,' she told him, opening up one of the doors. 'And this is where you'll have to sleep,' she added tautly, opening up a room that was rather larger than he had expected and furnished with a double bed, old-fashioned furniture and a fireplace.

'Where do you sleep?' he asked.

'This is the only bedroom,' Isla admitted, sidestepping the question. 'There used to be two but my uncle knocked them into one after he found out that they couldn't have children. He felt the empty bedroom next door was a constant reminder they didn't need.'

The arctic chill in the air cooled Alissandru's face. 'There's no heating up here,' he remarked abstractedly, wondering how on earth anyone could live with such a privation in the depth of winter.

'No,' she conceded. 'But I can light the fire for you,' she offered, biting her lip when she saw him struggle to kill a shiver and recalling the heat of the Sicilian climate, as foreign to her as extreme cold appeared to be to him.

'I would be very grateful if you did,' Alissandru said with unusual humility.

Isla thought ruefully of all the to-ing and fro-ing up the stairs carting logs and coal and stiffened her flagging resolve. He was a guest and she had been brought up to believe that, if it was possible, guests should be pampered.

'I'll go for a shower…if there's hot water?' Alissandru studied her enquiringly, recognising that there was nothing he could take for granted in such a poor household.

'Lots of hot water,' Isla assured him more cheerfully. 'But you have no luggage so let me see if there's something of my uncle's that you could borrow,' she added, heading for the chest of drawers by the window.

'That won't be necessary,' Alissandru asserted, his nostrils flaring with distaste at the thought of wearing another man's clothing.

'My uncle wouldn't mind and he's tall like you,' Isla argued, misinterpreting his response and assuming that he had sufficient manners not to want to be a nuisance. She rifled through several drawers and produced a pair of worn jeans and a husky sweater that looked as though it had seen better days before the last world war, settling both items on the bed. 'You'll be more comfortable in these than in that suit. I'll go downstairs and sort out something for dinner.'

'Thank you…' Alissandru forced out the words. 'Considering what I said when I arrived, you've been surprisingly kind.'

A delicate coppery brow raised as she spun back to look at him. 'I don't think you consider what you say very often,' she admitted with a sudden spontaneous smile of amusement that lit up her heart-shaped face like a glorious sunrise. 'And you're completely out of your depth in this environment, which makes me more forgiving. I was just as ill at ease in your home in Sicily.'

'*Dio mio…* I thought we made you welcome.'

A tide of colour rose up beneath her fair skin, making Alissandru study her in fascination and move several steps closer to stare down at her.

'Oh, my goodness, of course you did. I stayed in a wonderful bedroom and the food and everything was incredible,' Isla babbled, belatedly conscious that she might have sounded rude and unappreciative of his hospitality and alarmingly aware of his proximity because he was so very tall and powerfully built. 'But it wasn't my world and I was a fish out of water there. I'd never even been abroad before, never seen a house like yours except on television…you know, everything in your home was unfamiliar…and rather unnerving, to be honest.'

Alissandru scanned the tiny pulse flickering wildly just above her delicate collarbone and he wanted to put his mouth there. He was convinced that her heart was hammering out the same fast nervous beat because naturally she recognised the heightened sexual awareness that laced the atmosphere between them. *Of course*, she did, he told himself cynically. She was twenty-two, no longer a teenager, precocious or otherwise, and an adult woman in every sense of the word. With that thought driving him, he lifted a hand to tilt up her chin, gazing down into startled dark blue eyes and the surge of pink suddenly brightening her cheeks. She blushed. When had he last met a woman who blushed? It was simply that fair skin of hers, doubtless telegraphing the existence of the same erotic thoughts that were currently controlling him.

Would she, wouldn't she? Alissandru asked himself but he rather thought the answer to the suggestion of sex would be yes. He always got the answer yes from women, couldn't remember when he had last been rejected, and the chemistry between him and Isla Stewart was indisputable. He didn't like it, indeed he despised it, but the same powerful drive that had hardened him to steel with arousal was what kept the human race alive and it was appallingly hard to resist for a man unaccustomed to having to deny such a normal urge. He pictured her spread across the bed with its ugly patchwork duvet set…pale and lush and pink and *freckled*? Sex would be one useful way of keeping warm and it would provide entertainment into the bargain, Alissandru rationalised with ease.

Alissandru slowly lowered his handsome dark head, giving her time to retreat. But Isla was frozen into immobility, disturbingly preoccupied by the tightening of her nipples and the low pulse of heat thrumming at the centre of her body. Once or twice before she had experienced such glimmerings of awareness with other men but the attraction had always vanished the moment they actually touched her, convincing her that the fertile scope of a woman's imagination had to explain a lot of encounters that were later regretted. Yet now, when her every cautious instinct with his sex urged her to back away from Alissandru, sheer curiosity kept her where she stood because she wanted, inexplicably *needed*, to know if it would be the same with him.

And he kissed her cheek and her temples and brushed his mouth with astonishing gentleness across hers in an exploratory sortie. 'Tell me now if you want me to stop.'

Isla quivered inside her skin, entrapped by feelings she had never felt before, her body alight from those fleeting caresses, the sudden heat in her pelvis making her squirm. And the *scent* of him that close… Oh, dear heaven, how did she describe that faint evocative scent of cologne and musky masculinity that made her positively quiver with powerful awareness?

'Do it,' she heard herself urge wantonly, and the breathless sound of her own voice shook her.

With a smothered laugh, Alissandru crushed her parted lips beneath his own and sensual shock engulfed her because with one passionate kiss he inflamed her, and her hands lifted to curve round his neck to steady legs that had turned bendy as straws. He scooped her up against him with a strength that initially disconcerted and then, ultimately, thrilled her. His tongue darted into her mouth, flicked, dallied, twinned with hers and extraordinary sensation exploded throughout her body, switching it onto an altogether higher plane of response. A choked little sound escaped low in her throat, and he set her down and stepped back from her, so aroused by that hoarse little noise she had made in the back of her throat that he had to call a halt.

'I need that shower. I've been travelling all day, *gioia mia,*' Alissandru intoned thickly, hot golden eyes locked to her flushed and embarrassed face. 'Now I look forward to the evening ahead with anticipation.'

And with that unanswerable assumption that Isla knew full well that she had encouraged, he vanished into the bathroom. Her bare feet slapped down the stairs in a hasty retreat and she caught a glimpse of herself in the mirror at the foot, hair a messy bonfire of curls, her face hot enough to fry eggs on.

Why *had* she encouraged him? A foolish thing to do when he had to stay the night and was the kind of man

accustomed to easy, casual sex. At the wedding, Tania
had gossiped about Alissandru's many affairs and even
though Isla knew she shouldn't have listened, she had
because at the age of sixteen she had been mesmerised
by his looks and commanding charismatic presence.
But she was twenty-two now, she reminded herself
ruefully, and supposed to be beyond such silliness.
Even so, she couldn't lie to herself. When the opportunity had presented itself, she had grabbed at it and
him, desperate to know what it would feel like when
a man of his smooth sophistication and high-voltage
sensuality kissed her. And now she knew and she also
knew it would've been better had she not found out.

He knew how to kiss—he really, *really* knew how
to kiss—but of course they weren't going to take it any
further. She was related to Tania and he had hated her
sister, it seemed, as much as her sister had hated him.
No, nothing more would happen, she told herself, striving to feel relief at that conviction instead of shamelessly disappointed. As Tania had once said, her kid
sister needed to get out there and find a life, but Tania
had been so much more confident and experienced,
freely admitting that she much preferred the company
of men to women.

Isla, however, had been raised with Victorian values that tripped her up when she tried to fit into the
real world. Most of the men she had met or dated had
expected sex the first night, and those that hadn't demanded sex as though it was a right hadn't appealed
enough to her for her to experiment. And then there
had been her off-putting *first* experience of male sexual

urges, she conceded, recalling in disgust the older man who had followed her up to Tania's bedroom and cornered her at that Sicilian wedding. Ill equipped to deal with such an incident back then, she had been frightened and revolted when he'd tried to touch her where he shouldn't have and that episode had, for years, made her very wary of being alone with men.

She had stayed a virgin more from lack of temptation than for any other reason, however, hoping and trusting that eventually the right guy would come along. But her brain knew very well that Alissandru Rossetti would *never* be that guy. He had hated her sister and was clearly predisposed to be prejudiced against Isla as well. Alissandru would be the last man alive likely to offer Tania's kid sister a relationship.

Apart from anything else, Alissandru didn't *have* relationships with women. He wasn't looking for one special woman or commitment. He wasn't interested in settling down. Catching herself up on that revealing thought train with a mortified wince, Isla crept reluctantly out into the teeth of a gale and driving snow with the coal bucket while scoffing at her own foolishness. Alissandru kissed her once and *she* started fretting about their lack of a future as a couple. How ridiculous! He would run like the wind if he knew! Her grandma had raised a young woman out of step with the modern world, imprinting her with a belief pattern that others had long since abandoned.

And Alissandru would be the worst possible man for her to experiment with, she told herself impatiently. No, she would light a fire in the bedroom for him, cook him a hot meal and keep her distance by dozing in an armchair overnight. If she had roused his expectations of something more than a kiss, and she was convinced that she had, she would make it clear that nothing was going to happen. And with the options a man as gorgeous as Alissandru had in his life, that disappointment was hardly going to break his heart. In fact, it was much more likely that Alissandru had only come on to her in the first place because she was the *only* woman available. Her nose wrinkled. His apparent attraction to her suddenly no longer seemed flattering.

Isla trundled kindling, coal and logs upstairs and lit the bedroom fire while listening to the water running in the bathroom. There would be no hot water left for her use: he must've emptied the tank. The back burner in the fire was efficient at heating the water but Isla was trained to spend no more than ten minutes under the shower.

Warm for the first time since arriving in the frozen north of Scotland, Alissandru dried himself vigorously with a towel and stepped out onto the icy landing in his boxers, passing on through into the bedroom at speed where the flickering hot flames of a very welcome fire greeted him. In his eagerness to reach the warmth of the fire, he forgot to lower his head to avoid the rafters above and reaped a stunning blow to his skull. He groaned, teetered sickly where he stood for a second or two and then dropped like a falling tree to the wooden floor.

Isla heard the crash of something heavy falling overhead and stilled for an instant. Alissandru must've dropped something or knocked something flying. She rolled her eyes and got on with chopping the vegetables for the stew she was preparing, thinking that at least Alissándru had finally dragged himself out of the shower. The quicker she got the casserole into the oven, the sooner they could eat.

What had Alissandru knocked over? Her brow indented because there was very little clutter in that room and nothing that would make a noise of that magnitude when it fell, unless it was the wardrobe or the chest of drawers. Suddenly anxious, Isla called his name up the stairs and waited but no answer came. Compressing her lips, she went up and through the ajar door saw Alissandru lying in the middle of the floor on his back. He was naked apart from a pair of black cotton boxers. With a stricken exclamation, she sped over to him, horrified to register that he was unconscious. What on earth had he done to himself?

She touched a bare brown shoulder, noting how cold he was, and she jumped to her feet to drag the duvet off the bed and wrap it round him. That small step accomplished, she carefully smoothed her fingers through his hair and felt the smooth stickiness of blood as well as a rising bump. She released her breath in a short hiss and raced back downstairs to lift the phone and call the local doctor.

Unfortunately, the doctor was out attending a home delivery but the doctor's wife, a friendly, practical woman whom Isla had known since childhood, was able to tell her exactly how to treat a patient with concussion and warn her what to expect. Out of breath, she hurried back to Alissandru's side, relieved to see the flicker of his eyelids and the slight movements that signified his return to consciousness.

'Alissandru…?' she murmured.

His outrageously long black eyelashes lifted and he stared at her with a dazed frowning look. 'What happened?'

'You fell. I think you bashed your head on something.'

'Hellish headache,' he conceded, lifting his hand and trying to touch his head. He was noticeably disorientated and clumsy and she grasped his hand before he could touch the swelling.

'Lie still for a moment until you get your bearings,' she urged. 'I'll bring you painkillers when it's safe to leave you.'

Alissandru stared up at her, the blur of her face slowly filling in on detail. He blinked because her hair looked as if it were on fire in the light cast by the flickering flames. Her mop of curls glinted in sugar-maple colours that encompassed every shade from red to tawny to gold. Her blue eyes were full of anxiety and he immediately wanted to soothe her. 'I'm fine,' he told her, instinctively lying. 'Why am I on the floor?'

'You *fell*,' she reminded him again, worried by his confused state of mind. 'Can you move your legs and arms? We want to check that nothing's broken before we try to get you up.'

'Who's *we*?'

'You and me as a team,' Isla rephrased. 'Don't nitpick, Alissandru. What a fright you gave me when I saw you lying here!'

'Legs and arms fine,' Alissandru confirmed, shifting his lean, powerful body with a groan. 'But my head's killing me.'

'Do you think you could get up? You would be more comfortable in the bed,' she pointed out.

'Of course I can get up,' Alissandru assured her, but it wasn't as easy as he assumed and Isla hoped because the instant Alissandru began to get up, he was overtaken by a bout of dizziness, and Isla struggled to steady him when he swayed.

But he was too heavy for her to hold and he slumped back against the bed for support, shaking his head as though trying to clear it and muttering something in Sicilian that she suspected was a curse. 'I feel like I'm very drunk,' he acknowledged blearily, bracing himself on the mattress to stay upright.

'You'll feel better when you're lying flat again,' Isla declared, hoping she was right while her brain spent an inordinate amount of time struggling to process his near nudity at the same time as guilt that she had noticed that reality attacked her conscience.

But there it was, a near-naked Alissandru was a shockingly eye-catching sight, particularly when Isla had never seen a flesh-and-blood man in that state close up. Of course, she had seen men in trunks at the swimming pool but had never found her gaze tempted to wander or linger on those men, but when it came to Alissandru, dragging her attention from the corrugated expanse of his muscular abs and powerful biceps was a disconcerting challenge. Was it because she knew him? Simple feminine curiosity? Her face burning, she moved forward to help him turn around on unsteady feet and climb into the bed.

But what looked easy turned out to be anything but and in her fear of his falling again she got pinned between him and the bed and safely manoeuvring him down onto the mattress involved a considerable amount of physical contact that drenched her in perspiration and embarrassment. Finally, she managed to get Alissandru lying flat but by that stage she was painfully aware of the tented arousal beneath his boxers that all that sliding against his near-naked bronzed body had provoked. She pounced on the duvet still lying on the floor and flung it back over him with relief.

'No, you lie there and don't move. Don't touch your head either,' she instructed. 'I'm going downstairs to get painkillers for you and the first-aid box.'

Alissandru gave her a dazed half-smile. 'Bossy, aren't you?'

'I'm good in a crisis and this is a crisis because if it hadn't been for Dr McKinney's wife I wouldn't have known what to do with you,' Isla admitted guiltily. 'First chance I get, I'm going to do one of those emergency-first-aid courses that are so popular now.'

'I'll be fine,' Alissandru asserted, unwillingly impressed by her genuine concern for his well-being.

Tania would have kicked him while he was down and taken advantage of his vulnerability any way she could but Isla's only goal was to take care of him to the best of her ability. He rested his aching head on the pillows with a stifled groan, feeling trapped, knowing in frustration that he didn't dare even stand up when his balance was so out of sync. His vision was blurred as well, only slowly achieving normal focus. He should have told her that he had done four years at medical school before his father's death had made his dropping out of university inevitable. Neither his brother nor his mother had been up to the demands of taking control of his father's business enterprises. Alissandru had had to step in and take charge and if, at the time, he had loathed the necessity of giving up his dream of becoming a doctor, he had since learned to love the cut and thrust of the business world and revel in the siren call of new technology worthy of his investment.

Isla returned with a glass of water and a couple of pills. 'Don't know if they'll help,' she said ruefully, trying to prop pillows behind him to help him sit up.

'Might take the edge off it.' Alissandru drained the glass and slumped back down again. 'I want to sleep but I know I shouldn't sleep for long.'

'I didn't know that until the doctor's wife told me that I had to keep checking on you, waking you up if necessary to work out whether you were getting worse. But if the helicopter couldn't pick you up this evening, I'm not sure how the emergency medics could get through either,' she told him ruefully. 'Lift your head.'

Isla knelt beside him, skimming cautious fingers through his luxuriant silky hair and swabbing away the blood, finally spotting the cut and tracing the swelling beneath. 'It doesn't look like it needs stitches but it's still bleeding a little. You could have a fractured skull,' she warned him. 'Try to stay still. I'm going to get dinner into the oven and then I'll come back up.'

'Could you put the light out?' Alissandru asked. 'It's hurting my eyes.'

Isla switched off the bedside lamp and fed the fire to keep it burning. Before she left the room she glanced back at him where he lay in the bed, his dark eyes reflecting the golden heat of the firelight at her. He didn't look right to her lying so still and quiet, his innate restless volatility suppressed.

She finished the casserole and put it on to cook before laying a tray. That achieved, she went up to check on Alissandru. He was awake and watching the fire.

'I'm supposed to ask you stupid questions now like what day it is and who the British Prime Minister is,' she confided.

Alissandru responded straight away with the answers. 'There's nothing wrong with my brain. It's just working slower than usual,' he told her lazily and he stretched out an arm and patted the vacant side of the bed. 'Come and sit down and keep me company. Tell me about you and Paulu.'

Isla went stiff and stayed where she was, belatedly recalling the inheritance he had mentioned and feeling very uncomfortable at the thought of her late brother-in-law having left her anything. 'We were friends. While he and Tania were separated he came to see me several times to talk about her, not that I could tell him much because I didn't know her that well,' she pointed out tautly. 'I liked your brother a lot…but I assure you that there was nothing sexual between us.'

Lifting his tousled head several inches off the pillows, Alissandru shrugged a bare brown shoulder in fluid dismissal. 'It would've explained a great deal if there had been,' he commented.

'There *wasn't*,' Isla emphasised flatly.

'I'm not going to apologise,' Alissandru warned her. 'It was a natural suspicion.'

Isla gritted her teeth, swallowing back a rude remark about his lack of faith in standards of family behaviour and the kind of people he must know to harbour such a sleazy suspicion. He was a hard, distrustful man and she wasn't going to change that reality by arguing with him. 'Paulu would never have been unfaithful to my sister.'

Alissandru compressed his wide sensual mouth. 'More's the pity.'

'I'll bring dinner up when it's ready,' she said stiltedly, burrowing into the hot press on the landing to find fresh clothing for herself and heading into the bathroom for a shower.

She found it *so* hard not to rise to Alissandru's every pointed comment, but she was determined not to lose her temper with him again. It had scared her when she'd lost her temper to the extent she had earlier because she had flown at him like a shrew and tried to slap him. He had brought out a side of her she didn't like. Being that out of control was frightening.

She dried herself on a very damp towel and pulled on her fleece lounging set, which also doubled as pyjamas on the coldest nights. Coloured grey, the set was sexless and unrevealing. In any case, she was con-

vinced that Alissandru's accident had banished any
raunchy expectations she might have awakened by
succumbing to that kiss. Thankfully they had moved
way beyond that level now, she reasoned, scolding herself for the tiny pang of disappointment that made her
heart heavy.

She had only once envied her sister, Tania, and that
had been when she'd recognised how much Paulu *loved*
Tania, regardless of her capriciousness. Always popular with men, however, Tania had simply accepted her
husband's devotion as her due.

But nobody had *ever* loved Isla the way Tania had
been loved.

Tania had been the apple of their mother's eye but
Isla had barely known the woman and their father had
died before she was born. Her grandparents had been
both kind and loving but she had always been conscious that she was an extra burden and expense to
two pensioners, who had worked hard throughout their
lives with very little material reward.

Alissandru's momentary interest had sent Isla's
imagination rocketing and made her body fizz with
new energy because that kiss had been just about the
most exciting thing that had *ever* happened to her. And
wasn't *that* in itself a pathetic truth? she told herself
with self-loathing.

# CHAPTER THREE

WHILE ISLA WAS keeping busy in the kitchen and setting a tray, Alissandru lay back bored in bed and wondered why Isla had yet to ask him *what* she had inherited from his brother. Was that a deliberate avoidance tactic calculated to impress him with her lack of avarice? But why would she want to impress him? After all, regardless of Alissandru's feelings, she *would* receive that inheritance. Her attitude, however, was an anomaly and Alissandru didn't like anomalies. He flatly refused to accept that Tania could have a sister who wasn't greedy. His sister-in-law had craved money the way a dying man would crave water or air.

And moving on from his inflexible conviction that Isla had to be a gold-digger like so many other women he had met, he thought about that kiss and wondered what insanity had possessed him. Tania's sister, *so* inappropriate a choice. But she tasted like strawberries and cream, all the evocative flavours of a summer day and sunlight. Alissandru frowned darkly, forced to recognise afresh that his brain had yet to recover its normal function. That blow to the head had done more damage than he appreciated when his sharp-as-a-tack logic was failing to filter out such a fanciful comparison. Isla was curiously sexy and that was it, no need to be thinking about tastes and flavours, he told himself irritably.

*Stupendously* sexy, he adjusted, the ready stirring at his groin provoking him to greater honesty. He didn't understand why, he simply recognised that the minute she touched him, or indeed got anywhere near him, he reacted with an almost juvenile instant surge of excitement. A woman had never heated him up so fast or with such ease and it bothered him, because no way was he in the market for an affair with Tania's sister.

Isla brought in the tray, watching as Alissandru dragged himself up against the pillows to accept it. His bronzed skin gleamed in the firelight, accentuating a honed and very muscular physique straight out of a woman's fantasy. Her face burned and she wondered if she should be searching for a pair of her uncle's pyjamas to offer him. But wouldn't that make her look like a prude? It was her bet that Alissandru routinely wore little in bed.

'What on earth are you wearing?' Alissandru enquired as he accepted the tray, his brows drawing together as he studied the furry fabric top and loose bottoms to match.

'It's warm.'

'Where's your meal?' he asked.

'Downstairs,' she admitted stiffly.

'*Per carita*, Isla!' Alissandru exclaimed. 'It's boring up here alone.'

The tip of her tongue slid out to moisten her dry lower lip, discomfiture gripping her. 'I'll bring mine up,' she finally said, feeling a little foolish over her determination to avoid him simply because he made her feel uncomfortable.

She sank down on the side of the bed beside him, both flustered and harassed by the amused glance he flung her as she slowly lifted her legs up after her to balance the tray on her knees. So, it was a *bed*, no need to make a silly fuss about that when there was no chair available, she instructed herself in exasperation.

'You still haven't fully explained your connection with Paulu,' Alissandru remarked softly.

Isla gritted her teeth on her fork. 'We became friends…he was upset about his marriage breaking down and I tried to advise him on how to get Tania back.'

'Good to know who I have to thank for that final mistake,' Alissandru commented drily.

'You need a filter button before you speak,' Isla told him tartly.

'Share with me the advice you gave him,' Alissandru urged.

She turned her head to look at him and, unexpectedly, her heart softened. She recognised the glow of curiosity in his eyes for what it was: a kind of hunger to know and understand *anything* about his twin that he had been excluded from, and naturally Paulu had not shared his eagerness to reclaim his estranged wife with a brother who had probably cheered at her departure.

'Paulu was behaving like a stalker. He was send-

ing Tania emails, texts and showering her with invitations and it wasn't getting him anywhere. Tania was
annoyed he had followed her back to London,' Isla admitted ruefully. 'She told me the marriage was over.'

'So, what changed?'

'I don't know for sure because, apart from a text
from Paulu telling me they were giving their marriage
another go, I didn't get to see either of them again,'
Isla confided ruefully. 'But I had warned Paulu to stop
chasing her and to back off and give her some space.
She took him for granted...you see.'

'*Sì,*' Alissandru agreed grimly.

'But at the same time, Paulu was Tania's security
blanket, her safe place, and I suspect that if he did
show a little backbone and she started to fear that she
truly was losing him for ever, she might think again.'

'It's the eighth wonder of the world that Paulu and
I shared the same womb,' Alissandru intoned. 'We
barely had a thought in common.'

'You were twins.'

'Fraternal. I inherited more of my father's traits but
Paulu didn't have an aggressive bone in his body.'

'He had much more important gifts,' Isla cut in. 'He
was kind and loving and generous.'

'*Sì, very* generous,' Alissandru sliced in darkly, setting his tray down and welding his broad shoulders to
the headboard in physical emphasis of his exasperated sarcasm. 'If he hadn't almost bankrupted himself
*treating* Tania to her every wish before he married her,
he wouldn't have got himself into so much financial
trouble afterwards.'

Isla set down her tray as well, her heart-shaped face troubled. 'Is that what you always do? Take the gloomy view?'

'The truth can hurt and I don't avoid it,' Alissandru assured her.

'But what you're refusing to see is how *happy* Tania made your brother. You may not have liked her, but *he* adored her and I'm so grateful they got back together before they died,' Isla confessed emotively. 'How happy was he the last time you saw him?'

Unimpressed by her sentimental outlook, Alissandru thought back to his last meeting with his twin. Ironically, only days before the helicopter crash, Paulu had been full of the joys of spring, striding into Alissandru's office to cheerfully announce that Tania was willing to try for a baby. Alissandru had been taken aback by the unashamed depth of his brother's desire to have a child of his own because it was not an aspiration that had ever entered Alissandru's head. No, for Alissandru, having a family featured only in some far distant future and it was not something he felt any need to consider before he even reached his thirtieth birthday.

'He *was* happy,' Alissandru admitted grudgingly, and even as he uttered those words he felt some of the weight of his grief slip free and lighten his heart. Suddenly he realised what a comfort it was to look back and recognise that his twin's last months had been joyful because he had reunited with the love of his life and together they had been planning a more settled future.

Isla turned to study him, her wide blue eyes full of understanding and compassion. 'And doesn't that make *you* feel better? I know it makes me feel better.'

That truth was so simple it positively shrieked at Alissandru but he had not seen that truth for himself and in a sudden movement he snaked an arm round her and pulled her close.

'*Grazie*…thank you,' he breathed in a hoarse tone of relief, his eyes hot liquid gold with naked emotion.

He had such beautiful eyes, she found herself thinking again, and the spiky black lashes surrounding them only boosted their appeal. And as she gazed up at him he lowered his dark head and crushed her soft mouth under his, sending a wave of such hopeless longing snaking through Isla that she shivered with the effect of it.

'You're cold,' Alissandru assumed, lifting her onto his lap to throw back the duvet and then shift her beneath it and back into his strong arms.

Spontaneous laughter shook Alissandru's body as he held her. 'You feel furry like a teddy bear,' he confided unevenly. 'Is there really a woman underneath the fur?'

Taken aback by both his boldness and his amusement, Isla winced. 'I didn't want to be wearing anything provocative around you.'

'It's definitely not provocative,' Alissandru assured her, long fingers smoothing her soft curls back from her face. 'But then I only need to look at you to want you, *mia bella*.'

Sentenced to stillness by that startling admission,

Isla gazed up at him, barely crediting that she was in his arms in a bed. Could it be true that she attracted him to that extent? Even though he had despised her sister and had revealed, with his accusation about Paulu, a worrying bias against her likely character as well?

'Stop thinking so hard,' Alissandru urged her, a fingertip smoothing the frown line forming between her delicate brows.

The heat of his big powerful body filtering through her lounging pyjamas made her feel warm and secure. He actually wanted her. Alissandru Rossetti *wanted* her and somehow that made Isla feel less alone. But then, at the age of twenty-two she had lost every living person who had ever mattered to her and she often felt alone. Her uncle and aunt were one of those couples so content to *be* a couple that they rarely invited visitors and, although they always assured her that she was welcome, Isla was not comfortable inviting herself.

'Are you warm enough now?' Alissandru enquired silkily, a hand sliding beneath her top to splay across her midriff.

Her breath snarled up in her throat at the feel of his big hand against her skin. She couldn't think straight and an instant of panic claimed her because she had never been in such an intimate situation with a man. Her brain whirred at a frantic pace because she knew that Alissandru would expect sex. And why not? another little voice chimed in the back of her head. Why not? *Why shouldn't she?* She was finally with a man who made her heart beat so fast she felt breathless.

And shouldn't that be celebrated rather than denied or suppressed?

'Yes…you're as effective as an electric blanket,' she told him awkwardly.

Alissandru dealt her an incredulous look from glittering dark eyes and then his wide sensual mouth curved and he laughed again. 'Never heard that one before.'

And Isla knew it was the moment where she should mention her lack of experience because he obviously hadn't a clue, but pride silenced her. He would think she was a freak still being so innocent at her age and she didn't want him thinking *that* of her, much preferring that he should assume that she was as casual about sex as she had been told he was.

'I feel at peace for the first time in weeks,' Alissandru admitted reflectively. 'What you said about Paulu being happy…it helped.'

'I'm glad,' she whispered, lifting a hand to trace her fingers down over his stubbled jaw line, appreciating the masculine roughness of his skin and the dark shadowing that accentuated his beautifully shaped mouth.

'*Maledizione…ti voglio…* I want you,' Alissandru breathed in a raw, driven undertone, his body hot and taut from even that glancing caress.

His sensual mouth ravished hers, sending a shower of sparks flaring low in her belly, and he shifted against her, letting her feel the hard thrust of his readiness in the cradle of her thighs. The pressure of him at the junction of her thighs electrified her, making her almost painfully aware that that was where she really needed to be touched. He leant back from her to lift her top up over her head and she gasped in surprise, only just resisting the urge to cover her exposed breasts.

The cold air pinched her nipples, and she flushed all over as he gazed down at her hungrily.

'It's a sin to cover those,' Alissandru growled, curving a reverent hand to a lush breast crowned with a pouting pink nipple and dipping his head to savour that peak with his mouth.

Her brain in a wild whirl, Isla felt her back arch of its own volition and her pelvis tilt up as heat surged between her legs. He toyed with her other breast, tugging at the sensitive crest until her head fell back, her neck extending as the storm of her response grew stronger. She had never felt anything so powerful before, had not known her body had the ability to feel anything that intense. And then before she could even catch her breath, Alissandru was divesting her of her pants and prying her thighs apart to bury his wicked mouth there instead.

Shock consumed Isla and she parted dry lips to protest. Of course, she knew what he was doing but it was not something she had ever thought would appeal to her, at least until Alissandru applied his tongue to the most sensitive spot on her entire body and a spectacular wave of sensation engulfed her. And the tide of sensation built and built as he entered her with his fingers until she was writhing in response, agonised gasps torn from her parted lips, and for a split second as that explosive peak of pleasure gripped her she saw stars, jerking and out of control, blissful cries wrenched from her lips.

Alissandru grinned down at her with outrageous satisfaction. 'I love a passionate woman,' he told her thickly. 'You match me every step of the way.'

Isla was in a daze of shattered satiation as he shifted lithely over her and lifted her legs to increase his access to her still-thrumming body. She was reeling with disconcertion at what he had done and what she had felt and even then she was questioning what they were doing when he was supposed to have concussion.

'Do you feel all right?' she asked abruptly.

'In a few minutes I will feel one hell of a lot better,' Alissandru asserted with unquenchable certainty, and she felt the powerful surge of him against her swollen entrance.

There wasn't time for her to tense because he sank into her with raw energy and suddenly he was where she had never felt anyone before and he was thrusting deep and hard. She flung her head back and squeezed her eyes tightly shut as discomfort mutated into a sharp stab of pain but not a whisper of sound escaped her. The instant she registered that the worst was over, her body made her more aware of other sensations, stretching to accommodate his invasion and the deeply satisfying burn of him where she ached for more. And once he set up a fluid rhythm, deep down inside her muscles began to clench and tiny ripples of growing need assailed her.

'You are so tight and hot,' Alissandru growled thickly, dark eyes sheer gold enticement in the firelight casting flickering shadows across the walls and the bed.

Her hips rose to meet his because finally she was part of something, fully involved and sentient and wanting, *wanting* so much she could hardly contain it. The driving need to reach the same plateau again consumed her as he speeded up, his every lithe invasion feeding her hunger while her heart raced insanely fast. The tension inside her knotted and knotted ever tighter until he sent her flying again and the wild excitement and hot, sweet pleasure rolled over her again in wave after wave, leaving her limp and weak as he shuddered over her with his own release.

'That was spectacular,' Alissandru muttered raggedly in the aftermath, rolling off her but carrying her with him and keeping both arms wrapped around her so that she sprawled on top of him, drenched in the hot, already familiar scent of him.

And she had no regrets, Isla recognised in a stark instant of clarity as she pressed her lips sleepily to a broad brown shoulder. Alissandru had made her feel truly *alive* for the first time in months and she felt gloriously relaxed and warm and safe. More troubled thoughts tried to nudge at her but she was far too sleepy to let them in. There would be time enough in the morning to consider what she had done but, just at that moment, she didn't want to torment herself with what she couldn't change.

He was attracted to her but he would never love her. Well, that was life, she told herself drowsily, giving with one hand, taking with the other. It still struck her as better than what she had had before.

\* \* \*

She woke up very early and slid out of bed, flinching at the tenderness of her body. She tugged out the case below the bed with care, careful not to make too much noise as she extracted warm clothes to take into the bathroom with her. But she didn't leave the room until she had taken her fill of looking at Alissandru while he slept. His face was roughened with dark stubble, his black hair very dark against the bedding while the long golden sweep of his muscular back was a masculine work of art. Carelessly sprawled across the bed, he looked utterly gorgeous and impossibly sexy. He was out of her league, *totally* out of her league, she told herself as she washed and dressed in the bathroom, hurrying downstairs to let out the dogs and feed the hens.

She would also have to take some hay out to the sheep in their shelter because the snow was probably too deep for them to forage. Wrapped up against the cold, she took care of the livestock first, trudging through the snow to the barn for the hay and driving the old tractor as close to the pasture as she could get so that she could heft the hay into the sheep shelter with greater ease.

By the time she finished her chores, however, her shoulders and back were aching and she was breathing heavily and hoping the snow wouldn't last long because snow made everything twice as much work.

When she walked back indoors, it was an intense relief to shed her outdoor clothing and let her face and hands defrost close to the fire she had banked up the night before, and which she now revived. Steps

overhead and the creak of the stairs warned her that
Alissandru was about to join her, and she turned her
head with a shy smile, not quite sure how to greet
him in the light of day and reality. Like a lover? Like
a friend? Like a relative? There was no etiquette rule
that covered what had taken place between them the
night before.

'Isla…' Alissandru came to a halt at the foot of the
stairs and studied her, his lean, strong face clenching
hard. 'We have to talk.'

'I'll make breakfast,' Isla proffered readily, keen to
make herself busy and pretty much unnerved by the
grim brooding expression tautening his dark devastating features. He had put his suit back on and, even
unshaven, he looked like a super-sleek businessman
again, expensive and detached.

'Thank you, but I haven't got time for breakfast…
perhaps a coffee?' Alissandru suggested smoothly.
'The helicopter is picking me up in about fifteen minutes. Where were you?'

'Feeding the sheep and the hens,' she explained,
putting on the kettle, shaken that he was leaving so immediately while anxiously wondering what he planned
to talk about. Puggle was showing a worrying tendency to prowl around Alissandru's feet while growling threateningly and she shooed him away.

Having ignored the dog's ridiculous moves entirely—for how intimidating did something barely six
inches tall think it could be—Alissandru withdrew a
folded document from the pocket of his suit jacket,
straightened it out and settled it down on the table.

'The details of your inheritance. All you need to do is contact the solicitor and give him your current address and you will receive your bequest. Paulu, I should warn you, also left you his house in Sicily on the family estate…if you are agreeable, I would like to *buy* that back from you as it should stay with my family.'

Isla studied him in dismay, disconcerted that he had plunged straight into the impersonal matter of his brother's will. 'I'll think about that,' she murmured, playing for time, barely able to comprehend the concept of becoming the owner of a property abroad when she had never owned a house before. But she did receive his strong hint that he didn't want her using that house on the Rossetti estate and that made her feel uncomfortable and distinctly rejected.

With hands that shook a little with nerves, she prepared coffee for them both. She had shared a bed with Alissandru last night and that was no big deal in the modern world, she reminded herself firmly. She needed to wise up and expect less. Alissandru only had a few minutes before he had to leave and naturally he would be keen to get the business aspect of Paulu's bequest dealt with first.

'Do you want to discuss the sale of the house now?' Alissandru asked quietly, watching her like a hawk, hopeful she would grab at that option and agree an immediate deal.

For someone dressed like a homeless waif, she contrived to look astonishingly pretty, he acknowledged reluctantly. The cold had forced colour into her cheeks and blown her vibrant hair into a wild curly mop. She fiddled with a stray curl nervously and her sparkling dark blue eyes clung to him. Alissandru studied his coffee instead, keen to move on fast and without fanfare from his monumental error of judgement the night before. He had made a mistake, well, in truth, *several* mistakes, but there was no need to dwell on that unwelcome reality.

'No, let's leave the house aside for the moment,' Isla suggested unevenly, sitting down opposite him. 'I'm sure all that can be dealt with at some more convenient time.'

'Isla…?' Alissandru hesitated. 'Last night was a blunder on my part.'

'A…blunder?' she framed and then paled. 'You mean, a mistake?'

Alissandru lifted his chin in acknowledgement. 'I wasn't playing with a full deck. The concussion and the discussion we had about my brother put me in a weird frame of mind.'

Isla stiffened. 'You kissed me *before* you bashed your head. Are you saying I took advantage of you when you were vulnerable?' she asked in angry mortification.

Dark colour edged Alissandru's high cheekbones and he flung her an incredulous glance. 'Of course not. I'm saying that I was confused and unable to think clearly. Bearing in mind your sister's history with my family, it was very unwise for us to blur those lines with sex.'

Isla was frozen to her chair, feeling very much as though he had punched her in the stomach without warning. He was pairing her with Tania, who was, sadly, dead and buried but also Tania, whom Alissandru had loathed. In fact, he was backtracking so fast from their intimacy it was a wonder he wasn't succumbing to whiplash.

With as much dignity as she could contrive, Isla shifted an offhand shoulder.

'Whatever,' she said as if his about-face meant absolutely nothing to her. 'Do we really need to talk about this?'

Alissandru's lean dark features shadowed and hardened. 'I'm afraid that we do because I didn't take precautions with you. That's what I meant when I said I was…er…confused. That is an oversight I have never made before and, although I'm quite sure you are on the pill and safe from any risk of pregnancy, I want to assure you that I'm regularly tested and clean,' he completed with icy precision.

Isla could feel the colour draining from her face because the danger of conception or indeed infection had not crossed her mind even once, which seemed to underline how very stupid she had been to impulsively succumb to temptation. The man she had given her virginity to hadn't even noticed her lack of experience and now he chose to simply assume that she was taking contraceptive precautions to facilitate her non-existent sex life with other men. She didn't want to disabuse him on that score because the idea of him worrying that she *could* conceive struck her as even *more* humiliating. And just at that moment, she felt almost overwhelmed by the crushing hurt and humiliation Alissandru was already inflicting on her.

Alissandru was conscious as he watched her turn the colour of the ash scattered on the hearth that he had used all the wrong words because he still couldn't concentrate, couldn't find the words that usually came so easily and smoothly to his lips with a woman. Something about Isla was different and he was different with her too, and that acknowledgement freaked him out.

'I shouldn't think there's much risk of conception from one sexual encounter,' Alissandru asserted confidently, while wondering why she wasn't reassuring him that she was fully protected from such a danger.

'I shouldn't think so,' she mumbled in careful agreement, burning her tongue on the hot gulp of coffee she forced down her clenched throat.

Overhead, the noise of a helicopter intruded, and Alissandru sprang upright with alacrity while Puggle bounced and barked. Alissandru couldn't *wait* to get away from her, Isla interpreted, a sinking sensation of shame over her own conduct gripping her tummy.

'I'll leave my card in case of any…complications,' Alissandru said as he shrugged into his cashmere overcoat at speed and slapped a business card down on the table. 'And the offer for the house will be made in due course. Naturally, it will be a most generous offer.'

*Naturally*, Isla echoed dizzily inside her head. Only there was nothing natural about anything that had happened between them, she reflected painfully. She didn't believe that waitresses and billionaires regularly got together in the same bed but then what did she know? What did she know about *anything*? she asked herself in sudden anguish, realising that ignorance was anything but bliss when naivety could leave her open to such dreadful humiliation.

'I wish you well in the future,' Alissandru murmured coolly on the doorstep.

And she wanted to bury him deep in a snowdrift, but not before she punched him hard for rejecting her in every way that a woman could be rejected. He had hammered nails of fire into her self-esteem, puncturing her pride on every possible level. But then he wanted to be sure that there was no misunderstanding, wanted to be sure that she would not use his phone number for anything other than the direst emergency.

Alissandru didn't want to *see* her again, didn't want to *talk* to her again, really didn't want *anything* more to do with her at all. Only he had clumsily contrived to put those facts across as politely as he could.

And Isla had no plans to disappoint him, assuring herself that she would sooner be publicly whipped than even glance in his disdainful direction again.

# CHAPTER FOUR

ISLA LIFTED THE wand to check it with an unsteady hand. And there it was, what she had most feared to see: the positive pregnancy result that confirmed that she had conceived a child with Alissandru Rossetti. Perspiration beaded her brow and her tummy muscles winced in dismay.

He wouldn't like that news, he wouldn't like that at all, wouldn't be expecting it either if she went by the tone of their final conversation. Of course, he had assumed that she was taking birth-control pills and that the risk of pregnancy would therefore be minimal. Well, he had been wrong and did it really matter how *he* felt about this particular development?

A couple of months ago, following that night they had spent together at the croft, such a discovery would have filled her with sheer panic, Isla acknowledged ruefully, but her life had changed out of all recognition since then. How? Well, first and foremost Paulu Rossetti had left her a very generous amount of money. She was already making plans to sign up at a further education college to remedy the lack of qualifications

that restricted her in the job market. She had been
forced to drop out of school as a teenager to help care
for her grandfather because her grandma hadn't been
able to nurse him alone. She had always hoped to go
back to school some day to pass the exams she had
missed. However, the revelation that she was expecting a child altered everything because even though she
could still study while pregnant or as a single mum,
her head spun at the amount of organisation it would
require and she baulked at the prospect of putting her
baby into someone else's care.

After all, Isla very much wanted her baby. In fact,
a warm glow spread inside her at the mere thought
of the precious burden she carried. Her baby would
give her a family again, and wouldn't that be wonderful? Not to be alone any more? To have her child to
focus on and look after, to have a seriously good reason for everything she did in the future? And that she
could warmly accept its accidental conception was
solely down to Paulu Rossetti's generosity and thought-
fulness. Had her sister even known what was in her
husband's will? She didn't think it would ever have
occurred to Tania to leave her kid sister anything if
she passed away first. Of course, Tania had never had
much of her own and what she had had she'd spent on
designer clothes and the like.

A week after that snowbound night, when Isla had
still been feeling very depressed about having slept
with Alissandru, her uncle and aunt had returned from
New Zealand. After spending a fortnight on the rick-
ety old sofa bed her relatives had borrowed for her use,

and catching a bad bout of flu, Isla had been ready to leave. Although she had missed a period by that stage, she had not been unduly concerned because the flu had left her run-down. Only when her menstrual cycle had failed a second time had Isla realised that she needed to buy a pregnancy test, and by then she had flown back to London, encouraged by the fact that her inheritance had given her options. Instead of worrying about where she would stay or how she would afford to stay anywhere without an income, thanks to Paulu she had the luxury of choice. Her friend Lindsay had announced that Isla and Puggle could stay in her flat with her for a while because her flatmate was away on a training course.

Paulu's bequest had included far more money than Isla had ever dreamt of receiving, and no sooner had Isla asked her Scottish solicitor to contact the Rossetti family's solicitor than a ridiculously generous offer had come through to buy Paulu's house back from her. But Isla was, as yet, in no hurry to sell the house and the discovery that Alissandru had got her pregnant had only complicated the situation.

Isla wanted to *see* the house where Paulu and her sister had been living. She wanted to go through Tania's possessions and keep a few sentimental objects to remember her sibling by. And the knowledge that her baby would be a Rossetti had also made her reluctant to immediately sell the house on the family estate. Not that Alissandru would want her there or even visiting, she conceded uncomfortably, but her baby would have rights too, she reasoned, and might well appreciate that connection to his or her Sicilian heritage. No, selling the house, totally breaking that connection, wasn't a decision to be made in haste, she reasoned ruefully…regardless of how Alissandru felt about her owning part of his precious family estate.

So, now what did she do about Alissandru? She would *have* to tell him that she was pregnant because he had the right to know, but she wasn't looking forward to breaking that news because she was convinced that it would be a deeply unwelcome announcement. Alissandru didn't want anything more to do with her, so the news that they would be linked for ever by a child could only infuriate him. But there was nothing she could do about that, so Alissandru would just *have* to deal with it.

Before she could lose her nerve, Isla pulled out her phone and called the number he had given her.

'Alissandru?' she queried the instant she heard his dark deep drawl answer with an impatient edge. 'It's Isla Stewart. I'm sorry to have to bother you but I have something to tell you.'

At the other end of the line, Alissandru had tensed. 'You want more money for the house?' he assumed, stepping away from the conference table he had been seated at, jerking his head in dismissal at his staff as he stalked into his office next door, tension stamped in every angular line and hollow of his darkly handsome features.

'It's nothing to do with the house,' Isla admitted. 'I haven't made a decision about that yet.'

'Why not?' Alissandru cut in edgily.

'Because I've just found out that I'm pregnant and right now that is all I can think about,' Isla confided reluctantly.

A freezing little silence fell at the other end of the line. Alissandru was reeling in silent shock because he had not once considered that possibility and when it came at him out of nowhere, he froze, stunned by her announcement. How *could* she be pregnant? Was it even his? What were the odds?

'I don't understand how this has happened,' Alissandru murmured flatly.

'Well, I've done my duty by telling you and for the moment we can leave it there,' Isla told him, eager to conclude the call. 'We've got nothing to discuss.'

'If what you claim is true we have a great deal to discuss,' Alissandru contradicted harshly.

'Why on earth would I lie about being pregnant?' Isla snapped.

'I don't know, but your sister *did*,' Alissandru told her with ruthless emphasis. 'But be assured that even if you turn out to be having triplets, I'm unlikely to offer a wedding ring.'

Isla sucked in a deep steadying breath. 'Since I'm well aware of your habit of saying exactly what enters your mind and because I have better manners than you have, I will just ignore those comments,' she responded tartly. 'But allow me to assure you that I *am* pregnant, you *are* the father and I wouldn't marry you if you were the last man alive!'

'I will arrange for you to see a doctor first and we will move on from there.'

'I'm ready to move on past you *right now*, Alissandru!' Isla flashed back, so angry she could barely vocalise.

'I will call you back once I've made arrangements,' Alissandru countered grimly and finished the call.

Isla was pregnant? How could that be? Why hadn't the contraceptive pill worked? And why would she have waited weeks to tell him? It seemed like a long time since that night they had spent together. In a rage, Alissandru slammed his phone down on his desk. What an idiot he had been that night to fall into the trap of having unprotected sex! He had run an insane risk and incredibly he had done it with Tania Stewart's sister. Of all the worst possible women to have got entangled with, why had he succumbed to her?

Over the past two months, Alissandru had repeatedly relived that night. Waking or sleeping, he just couldn't seem to shake free of those memories of Isla. The sex had been phenomenal. That was why he couldn't get that night with *her* out of his head. Clearly, he was more driven by his libido than he had ever appreciated and the knowledge that he was guilty of that fatal flaw, that demeaning weakness, had turned him off casual sex and other women. He had not been with a woman since that night, which was probably even unhealthier, he reasoned rawly.

*Pregnant!* Was it possible? Of course it was possible, but it was equally possible after several weeks that even if Isla *was* pregnant the child would ultimately turn out not to be *his* child. Dragging in a shuddering breath of restraint, Alissandru called his lawyer to ask for advice and only after that enlightening discussion, and in a much cooler frame of mind, did he organise a medical appointment. He requested Isla's address by text and informed her that he would pick her up the next morning at nine and accompany her to the examination.

Isla gritted her teeth and told him that he would be waiting outside the door if there was to be any medical examination. She gave him the address, though, reasoning that once he was satisfied that she was telling him the truth they could move on and she would need to have nothing more to do with him. After all, she didn't need his financial help, did she? Paulu had left her comfortably off, giving her the means to raise a child as a single parent. While she was pregnant, she would attend classes and study, she decided, making the most of that time before she sought employment again. Many women were successful working mothers and so would she be.

Another worry now clawed at her, though. Was it *true* that Tania had claimed to be pregnant at some stage of her relationship with Paulu? Was that, in fact, why she and Paulu had married as Alissandru seemed to think? And even if it was true and Tania had made an understandable mistake in assuming that she was pregnant when she was not, why was Isla's word now being doubted and why was she expected to hang her head in shame for her sibling's error?

Suddenly, Isla knew exactly what she would be saying to Alissandru in the morning and none of it would be polite, she thought furiously. How could she have slept with a man like that? He was horribly suspicious and distrustful of women. Not to mention unreasonably biased against Isla because of the blood in her veins. She would be the mother of Alissandru's child. How the heck could they ever establish a civilised relationship as parents on that basis? The guy was a living nightmare! Nobody halfway normal could handle him! Her poor sister was dead and he was *still* holding Tania's past actions against her.

Lindsay, a pretty blonde with tough views on men, had an entirely different take on Isla's situation. 'Of course, you need Alissandru's financial help.'

'I don't,' Isla protested.

'Paulu left you a lovely nest egg but it's not going to keep you or a child for the rest of your days. Not unless you flog that house in Sicily as well and invest the proceeds,' Lindsay pronounced. 'And the child is his child, as well…why shouldn't he pay towards his child's upkeep? That's his duty.'

'He assumed I was on the pill.'

'But he didn't ask you if you *were*, did he? You both took the risk and it didn't pay off, so you're not any more responsible for this development than *he* is,' Lindsay completed roundly. 'Stop beating yourself up about it.'

But Isla was tormenting herself because she felt very guilty that on a secret level she was *pleased* to be pregnant and already excitedly looking forward to becoming a first-time mum. Family was what she cared about most and finally she was going to have a family again. At the same time, even the sound of Alissandru's voice on the phone had warned her that *he* was angry, bitter and unhappy about the prospect of her being pregnant with his child. How could she feel anything other than guilty in the circumstances? Another woman might have been willing to consider a termination or adoption but Isla wasn't prepared to consider either of those options.

In the morning, she got up early, ate a good breakfast and donned a winter-weight jersey dress, teaming it with knee-high boots, items recently purchased with her newly affluent bank account. She questioned why she was making that much effort for Alissandru and decided that pure pride was motivating her, because Alissandru had rejected her on every possible level after the night they had spent together. She needed the comfort of knowing she looked her best in Alissandru's radius.

The bell buzzed through the empty flat, Lindsay having long since left for work. Isla used the peephole and undid the chain, standing back as she opened the door. Alissandru stood there, six-feet-plus inches of volatile brooding male.

'Will you come in for a moment?' Isla asked politely.

'The traffic's bad and we don't want to be late.'

'If you want me to go anywhere with you, you have to come in first,' Isla delivered without hesitation, wondering how he could look so gorgeous early in the morning and yet be a total irredeemable toad beneath the surface sophistication.

Wide sensual mouth flattening with annoyance, Alissandru skimmed grim dark golden eyes over the flushed triangle of her face. *Sì*, he reasoned angrily, *already* he could feel the dangerous pull of sexual attraction. The dress cupped the full swell of her magnificent breasts to perfection and hinted at her gloriously curvaceous hips while the boots accentuated legs that were surprisingly long despite her diminutive height. Isla could cover herself from head to toe and screen every atom of bare flesh and still look like a total temptress with her pink sultry mouth, sexy curves and sparkling violet-blue eyes. She didn't look remotely pregnant to him but then she wouldn't be showing yet, would she? Alissandru knew virtually nothing about pregnancy and at that moment, his ignorance galled him.

'Why do you want me to come in?'

'I want your full attention and I don't want to stage an argument with you while you're trying to drive,' she confided.

'I have a driver,' Alissandru slotted in icily. 'And I do not see what we have to argue about.'

Isla raised a dubious coppery brow. 'Your attitude? It *stinks*. I'm not my sister. I don't look like her and I don't think I behave like her but you can't seem to see that. Getting pregnant after a one-night stand is worrying enough without me feeling that I'm constantly up against your irrational prejudice against me.'

'I do not suffer from irrational prejudice,' Alissandru declared in a stubborn tone of denial.

'Sorry to be the one to tell you but you *do*,' Isla replied quietly. 'I can accept that you didn't like my sister and that it's too late now for you to change your mind about her, but you *have* to accept that I'm a different person. Stop comparing us and being suspicious of my every move because this baby I'm carrying doesn't need that tension in the air between us.'

'Mr Welch will tell us if you *are* carrying a baby but we won't know if it's mine until the child is born. DNA testing can be done while you are pregnant but it *could* compromise your pregnancy, so I'm prepared to wait for that confirmation until after the birth,' Alissandru informed her, looking very much as if he was expecting a lofty round of applause for that consideration. 'May we leave now?'

'You didn't listen to a word I said, did you?' Isla exclaimed angrily. 'Well, maybe you didn't listen but you can sit down and think about your prejudice later, can't you? I'm tired of dealing with it.'

'The car's waiting,' Alissandru murmured, standing back for her to precede him, careful to be courteous as advised by his lawyer. Arguing with Isla, who was potentially the mother of his child, would be unwise. He needed a plan and then he would deal with the whole situation. *Irrational prejudice?* What was she talking about? She was Tania's sister and naturally he distrusted her. That was *not* unreasonable, he told himself squarely.

The limousine impressed Isla to death but she refused to reveal the fact, sinking into the opulent cream padded upholstery and looking out at the traffic as if she travelled in such style every day. Not a word passed either of their lips until they entered an elegant waiting room to await the appointment he had arranged. When Isla's name was called, an argument broke out when Alissandru stood up, as well.

'No, you can't come in with me. This is private. You can speak to the doctor afterwards with my permission, but you are *not* coming in with me!' Isla warned him furiously, her cheeks infusing with hot colour as the other couple waiting across the room stared at them as though they had escaped from a zoo.

Impervious to such self-consciousness, Alissandru settled glittering dark golden eyes on her. 'I wish to accompany you.'

'I said no, Alissandru, and *no* means *no*!' Isla bit out angrily as she stalked off and left him behind.

Fizzing with pent-up energy and frustration, Alissandru paced the floor. Of course, her pregnancy would be confirmed. He wasn't expecting to discover that she had lied about that, but the real question was whether or not it was *his* child she carried and he wouldn't have the answer to that question for months to come.

Isla found Mr Welch friendly and professional. He confirmed that she was pregnant and seemed a little surprised that she had not experienced any textbook signs of pregnancy like dizziness or nausea. 'Of course, it's very early days,' he added comfortably. 'Now that you know for sure, you'll probably start feeling small effects very soon.'

It was a little embarrassing having to ask the doctor to speak to Alissandru separately, but Isla kept a smile on her face and did so, returning to the waiting room just as Alissandru was called. He was gone for longer than she expected and returned, looking taut and serious, to usher her back out to the limousine.

'So, not a false alarm,' he remarked as the limo moved back into the traffic.

'I'm to come back for a scan in a couple of weeks,' Isla told him brightly, determined not to be affected by Alissandru's mood.

'Do you have any idea why the pills you were on failed?' he asked flatly.

'I wasn't taking any pills,' Isla admitted baldly, keen to get that misunderstanding out of the way. 'You assumed that I was, but I wasn't.'

Alissandru shot her a startled glance. 'In other words, we were entirely unprotected that night.'

Isla nodded stiffly. 'Yes, and I'm as much to blame as you are for not appreciating the risk that we were taking.'

Faint dark colour edged Alissandru's sculpted cheekbones, accentuating the bronzed hollows beneath and the perfect bone structure that gave his face such masculine strength. He was a twin but he and Paulu had not looked much alike, Isla acknowledged. Paulu had been slighter in build and much more boyish in his looks.

'Why weren't you taking any contraceptive precautions?' Alissandru prompted, his wide sensual mouth taking on a sardonic slant.

'I wasn't having sex so there was no need for me to consider precautions,' Isla revealed, lifting her chin, refusing to succumb to her embarrassment. She had had sex with Alissandru, she reminded herself in exasperation. There was no excuse for such prudishness now that she had conceived.

A frown line indented his brow. 'You *weren't*?'

Isla jerked a slight shoulder in a dismissive shrug. 'You were the first…and you didn't notice, but that's all right. To be fair, at the time I didn't want to draw your attention to my lack of experience.'

Alissandru had lost colour below his Mediterranean tan and his stunning dark eyes had narrowed, his black lacelike lashes almost tangling. 'You're telling me that you were a virgin?' he pressed in disbelief.

'Yes, and the sooner you accept that and that this child can *only* be yours, the happier we will both be,' Isla responded doggedly. 'Telling yourself that this child may be someone else's is simply wishful thinking—'

'I refuse to accept that you were a virgin,' Alissandru interrupted in a raw undertone.

Tranquil in that moment as a garden pond, Isla gazed steadily back at him. 'I expected that reaction. You learn everything the hard way. However, I've done what I had to do. I've told you. But I *can't* change the way you think. You can drop me home now and we can talk again after the baby's born.'

Her tone of careless dismissal set Alissandru's perfect teeth on edge. 'Whether the child is mine or not, I will be much more involved before the birth than you seem to expect.'

'I don't think so…not without my agreement. And you won't be getting that. I don't need the aggravation. I want to make plans and look forward to my baby.'

*'Look forward?'* Alissandru incised thunderously.

Isla gave him a sunny smile, refusing to conceal her feelings. 'Yes, I'm very excited about this baby and I won't pretend otherwise.'

Mindful of his temper, Alissandru breathed in deep and slow. She was delighted to be pregnant, openly admitting it. Was she one of those women he had read about who just decided to have a child and went out and picked a man to do the deed? He gritted his even white teeth. Even if she was, what could he do about it? He was in a situation in which he couldn't win. An unwed pregnant mother held all the aces. He would be damned if he did help her because the child might not be his, and damned if he didn't because if he didn't help her now, he could be denied access after the child was born because his child's mother would hate him.

*The child.* He remembered how much Paulu had longed for a child, and his heart clenched painfully. Paulu would've celebrated such news and their mother would've been ecstatic at the prospect of a grandchild. Alissandru didn't know how he felt beyond shocked, frustrated and bewildered. He studied Isla from below his lashes, recalling that night in astonishing detail for a person claiming concussion as an excuse for mental confusion. A virgin? He had never been with one. It was true that she had done nothing that implied a higher level of sexual skill. It was also true that he had had to utilise more power than usual to gain access to her squirming little body.

Feeling strangely breathless and hot, Alissandru dragged his smouldering gaze from her and focussed on a leather-clad leg instead. *He had parted those knees.* Hard as a rock and uncomfortable, he shifted position, angling his long, lean, powerful body back into a corner. Yes, it was possible she had been a virgin. Tania's sister a virgin at twenty-two years of age? Surprising but not impossible, he reasoned doggedly, battling his arousal with all his strength.

Isla watched Alissandru, wondering what he was thinking about, wondering if she should even *want* to know. She was on edge in his radius, unable to relax while recalling everything she had worked hard at trying to forget. His touch, the feel of him over her, inside her, the seething, storming excitement of his every movement. He had made her ignite in a blaze of elation and pleasure that still haunted her at weak moments. An ache stirred at the heart of her, warning her that even remembering that night was dangerous. But there he sprawled, effortlessly elegant and infuriating and still breathtakingly beautiful, from the blue-black fall of hair he wore rather longer than was fashionable to the broad shoulders and powerful muscular torso that even the fanciest suit couldn't conceal.

'We could talk over an early lunch at my town house,' Alissandru suggested, startling her out of her reverie.

'I don't think we have anything to talk about at present,' Isla said in surprise.

'That's where you're wrong,' Alissandru asserted without hesitation.

'I wish I could say that that declaration surprises me…but I can't,' Isla said ruefully. 'You always think you're right.'

# CHAPTER FIVE

ALISSANDRU'S TOWN HOUSE lay off a quiet, elegant Georgian square. It was a family-sized house, not at all the ritzy single-man accommodation Isla would have expected him to inhabit and, when she commented, he confided that he needed a spacious property because his family stayed with him when they were visiting London.

'My mother likes London for shopping and so do my cousins. She usually brings company with her.'

An inner shudder of recoil assailed Isla as she recalled Alissandru's cousin Fantino, who had cornered her in that bedroom in Sicily and assaulted her. Not that she had recognised it as an actual assault at the time, being young and ignorant of such labels. Tania, after all, had dismissed the incident as a misunderstanding and had angrily warned a distraught Isla not to kick up a fuss over what had happened and spoil her wedding day. Did Fantino come to London? Was Alissandru close to him? The men were about the same age. Suppressing her wandering thoughts, she pushed the matter and that unfortunate connection back out of her mind again.

Alissandru showed her into a contemporary dining room decorated in fashionable shades of soft grey and tucked her into a comfortable chair. 'Would you like a drink?' he enquired.

'No, thanks. Alcohol is off my menu for the immediate future—better safe than sorry,' she quipped.

'I didn't know. In fact, I don't know anything about pregnant women apart from the fact that they put on weight and get very tired,' Alissandru admitted wryly. 'And I only picked up that from listening to my cousins' complaints.'

His honesty disconcerted her. She watched as an older woman brought in a tray and set plates out for them. It was a light meal, exactly what she preferred at present because, although she had yet to feel sick, her appetite had dwindled and she had lost a little weight.

'You said that we had to talk,' she reminded him as she sipped at her water. 'What about?'

'About me getting involved in all this,' Alissandru specified. 'You're behaving as if you want me to step back and stay out of things until after the birth.'

Isla glanced up, her violet eyes troubled. 'That *is* what I want.'

'That won't work for me,' Alissandru countered bluntly. 'I'm opening a bank account for you to take care of your expenses. Who are you living with at present?'

Isla flung back her shoulders. 'A friend, but it's only a temporary arrangement. I'll need to find my own place. Alissandru... I really don't need your financial help, not when I have what Paulu gave me.'

'I *have* to contribute,' Alissandru spelt out resolutely.

'Even though you're not convinced that this is your child?' Isla snapped in exasperation.

'Even though,' Alissandru confirmed without hesitation. 'I also intend to cover all your medical expenses and, with your agreement, accompany you to any important procedures…such as the scan Mr Welch mentioned was coming up. You can't ask me to stand back and act like this has nothing to do with me. If this is my child I need to take an interest and take responsibility, as well.'

Isla swallowed hard on the flood of disagreement rising to her lips. Alissandru was very much a man of action and she could hardly fault him for stepping up to demand a share of the responsibility. He didn't want to be excluded. He didn't want to stand on the sidelines hearing stuff third-hand from her. But his wish to get involved contravened her earnest need to shut him out. Not very charitable, she scolded herself, not very fair. He had rejected her but he was not rejecting the possibility of their child. He was trying to do the right thing and if she denied him, it would only increase his distrust.

Playing for time, Isla toyed with her food. 'I understand what you're saying but I don't need your money.'

'Allow me to contribute towards your expenses. I want you to have the very best medical care and decent accommodation. I don't want you worrying about the future.' Brilliant dark golden eyes rested on her. 'I *must* help. That's not negotiable. I need to be supportive. I won't interfere in your life, but I will be there in the background.'

Somewhat soothed by that reference to his staying in the background, Isla sighed. 'I suppose I can hardly say no. I will keep you informed but I don't want anything else to do with you. I don't think that you can expect any warmer welcome from me after the way we parted in Scotland.'

'I don't want to upset you in any way,' Alissandru told her. 'But I do need to be part of this situation.'

Travelling back to the office, having dropped Isla home, Alissandru took stock at a more leisurely and reflective pace than was usual for him. He was imbued with the energetic conviction that he had plans to make, a *lot* of plans. First and foremost, he needed to find somewhere comfortable and with good security for Isla to live because at present she wasn't staying in one of the safest areas of the city. Where she lived was a priority, he reasoned. And Mr Welch had impressed on him that she also needed a healthy diet so he would organise some sort of food service or delivery, as well.

A baby. If it was a little boy, it might be a little like Paulu, he reasoned, startling himself with that thought. Or why not a little girl with Paulu's sweet nature? He didn't care either way and his mother would be ecstatic with either possibility, for Constantia Rossetti was still struggling to cope with the loss of her son. A baby would be something positive to focus on and ultimately a comfort to them all.

As long as it was *his* child…

But why would Isla lie on that score? He had warned her that he wouldn't marry her because naturally he couldn't forget the disaster of his twin's hasty marriage with Tania. Tania had wanted a rich husband much more than she had ever wanted a child. Isla, on the other hand, needed persuasion before she would even accept Alissandru's involvement and financial support during her pregnancy. She hadn't snatched at his offer for Paulu's house, either.

Maybe she was playing a long game and trying to impress him, although it was hard to see what she could gain from denying her legal right to have his support. Maybe he *was* too jaded after Paulu's experience to see the wood for the trees, he conceded uneasily, frowning at the mere suspicion that he could deserve Isla's accusation of irrational prejudice. Regardless, however, he was already beginning to see a much more positive angle to the baby scenario.

His interest had been caught, and was that thanks to Paulu, as well?

'What's it all for?' his twin had demanded that day in Alissandru's office when he'd admitted his own desire for a child. 'Who have you built this empire for? You already have more than you could spend in a lifetime. Wouldn't you like a son or daughter to leave it all to?'

And Alissandru had laughed, deeming that a question for the future, not the present, only now everything had changed and it was amazing how priorities could rearrange themselves in the aftermath of loss. Paulu was gone and there was nothing he could do about that, but a child would give him a fresh focus. A child would need teaching and guidance and love. Alissandru suddenly smiled at the prospect. A baby just might be exactly what he needed...

Two days later, Isla lay in bed mulling over her final conversation with the father of her child. It wasn't so much that Alissandru wanted to be part of the situation, more like he wanted to *take over*. He had already sent her details of three London properties he owned, inviting her to move into any one of them at his expense but, although it was a very lavish offer, Isla didn't want to become Alissandru Rossetti's kept woman. At the same time she only had a week to find somewhere of her own to live because Lindsay's flatmate would be returning soon. It would be easier to accept Alissandru's offer but the easy way wasn't always the wisest way, Isla acknowledged uneasily.

But she *knew* that the child she was carrying was *his* child even if he did not and it would not be as though she would be taking advantage of his generosity. He had also organised an early scan for her with Mr Welch and she had wanted to turn down that offer too, but she was too eager to see her baby for the first time, even if it was only the size of a pea. Alissandru also knew how to tempt a woman, she conceded ruefully, but could she face a scan at which he would undoubtedly expect to be present, as well? she asked herself. She would only be baring her stomach...

In the early hours of the following morning, Isla wakened to a cramping pain that made her wince. She sat up in bed, a sensation of dampness between her thighs stirring anxiety. When she realised that she was bleeding she started to panic. Was she losing her baby? What had she done wrong? Hadn't she looked after herself well enough?

Lindsay calmed her down and rang the emergency helpline, herding Isla into clothes and then into a taxi to take her to hospital. Her friend told her all sorts of soothing stories about false alarms and minor complications and Isla managed to hold herself together while they sat for hours waiting their turn in the hospital waiting room, surrounded by a mass of other anxious people.

In the end it took very little time for her to be dealt with. A doctor told her gently that if she was suffering a miscarriage nothing could be done to stop it happening and that such an experience was much more common than she realised in early pregnancy. Isla sat frozen to her seat as if a sudden movement might provoke a more serious crisis. Ushered into another room, she was prepared for a scan by a radiographer. Suddenly the kind of scan she had earlier been so much looking forward to receiving harboured a more menacing vibe.

The wand moved smoothly over her still-flat tummy, and Isla was barely breathing as she strained without success to see something recognisable as a baby on the screen. When the woman stopped and reached for her hand, Isla knew what was coming because the radiographer looked so sad for her.

'I'm so sorry. There's no heartbeat. It's not a viable pregnancy,' she said quietly.

A junior doctor saw her next. Isla was in shock: her baby was dead. Her wonderful beautiful baby was gone as if it had never been. Her surroundings suddenly seemed to be stretching away from her and she couldn't concentrate on what was being said. The doctor pressed medication into Isla's limp hand while Lindsay sat beside her not even trying to hide her tears, but Isla couldn't cry. Her eyes stayed dry while a great gulping sob of anguish seemed to be trapped somewhere in her throat, making it a challenge to breathe or speak.

'I'm so sorry,' Lindsay whispered in the taxi on the way back to the flat. 'This has happened to a couple of my friends at work. It's why some women won't tell anyone that they're pregnant until they're past the first trimester. That's the danger period…'

Isla nodded vigorously, striving to be strong and stoic, reluctant to subject her friends to the tears penned up inside her. 'It could have been the flu I had,' she mumbled.

'It could have been any of a dozen things.' Lindsay sighed. 'Do you want to talk about it?'

But, suddenly, Isla felt that there was nothing left to talk about. Talking wasn't going to bring her baby back and she had already kept Lindsay out of bed for half the night, she reflected guiltily. Her poor friend still had to go into work in the morning and she was already exhausted. Assuring Lindsay that all she wanted to do was sleep, she went back into the bedroom. Her first real thought was that she would have to tell Alissandru and that he would be pleased. Not that he would dare to *say* it, she assumed bitterly, but he had seen their baby as an undesirable complication and now that their baby was no longer on the way, he could only be relieved.

Unfortunately, Isla wasn't relieved because the whole cosy future she had envisaged around that precious baby had suddenly been cruelly taken from her and she didn't know what to do next. That was scary when she had felt so confident about managing everything after she first realised that she was pregnant. Now the floor of her world had suddenly vanished and she was fighting just to stay afloat.

The next morning, she agonised at length over the need to contact Alissandru. She couldn't face phoning him, saying those wounding words out loud about her baby and, midmorning, she sent him a text bluntly telling him that she had had a miscarriage.

In receipt of that unexpected message, Alissandru stared at his phone and felt sick. A *miscarriage*? How had that happened? Suddenly he was full of anxious questions.

'Something wrong?' one of his directors asked, and Alissandru glanced up, only then registering that his companions were regarding him expectantly.

'I've had bad news,' Alissandru admitted soberly. 'If you will excuse me…'

Isla's news had blindsided him even more than the announcement that she was pregnant. One minute they were having a baby, the next…? It was dead. He stared out of his office window, fighting the feelings engulfing him just as he had fought them when he'd learned that Paulu had died. He had to be strong, he *always* had to be strong because other people relied on him to be that way. When it had been Paulu, his mother had needed him, but now Isla needed him more because Isla had *wanted* that baby. *Their* baby, he adjusted, reluctant to credit any other option in that moment. He remembered Isla's glorious smile as she'd admitted how much she was looking forward to becoming a mother and he lost colour, his eyes prickling. She *had* to be devastated. He rang her immediately.

'Isla, it's Alissandru.'

'I've got nothing to say to you,' she framed woodenly.

'I got your text and obviously I want to see you and talk to you. I'm very sorry.'

'Are you?' she questioned doubtfully.

Anger flared in Alissandru's dark golden gaze. 'Of course I am! I'd like to come round and talk to you.'

'No, thanks,' she cut in immediately. 'I don't want to see you.'

'Have you had proper medical treatment?' Alissandru asked worriedly.

'Yes. I'll be fine,' she told him stiffly.

'Obviously, it wasn't meant to be,' Alissandru said heavily, raking long fingers through his tousled black hair in a gesture of frustration because he honestly didn't know what else to say to her. Words were empty. Words wouldn't change anything. He didn't want to mutter meaningless platitudes the way people did when they were faced with a difficult situation, nor did he feel that he could dare admit that he was upset, as well. Because she would *never* believe him, never believe that he too was full of regret for what was not to be.

He had warmed up to the idea of the baby just a little *too* late, he acknowledged grimly. The baby had been a surprise and he wasn't good with surprises. He had never liked the natural order and routine of his life being changed or threatened. Predictably the advent of a baby would have altered many things and he had resisted that prospect to the best of his ability, until he'd defrosted enough to concede that a baby could just be the best thing that had ever happened to him.

*It wasn't meant to be...* Isla flinched from that crass and demoralising assurance that cut to the quick. No, in Alissandru's rarefied world, billionaires did not have babies with former waitresses. Now, mercifully for him, if not for her, the real world had intervened, and no such baby would be born and the status quo would be preserved. Of course, he was relieved and fatalistic about her miscarriage. He hadn't wanted their baby in the first place, could hardly be expected to cry crocodile tears now that there was no longer a baby to worry about. Unlike her he hadn't learned to love their child, hadn't even begun to accept that the baby she carried *was* his child.

A bitterness as cutting as a knife slashed painfully through Isla and she finished the call. Without even thinking about it, she blocked Alissandru's number on her phone because she didn't want to be forced to speak to him again, *ever* again. That connection was finished for ever, severed by fate. She would never have to see him again, never have to speak to him again, never be hurt by him again. Eyes wet, she discovered that that was no comfort whatsoever.

The following morning, Lindsay got a call from her parents and grimaced through the conversation while offering repeated apologies for being unable to change her own plans.

'What's wrong?' Isla prompted.

Lindsay grimaced. 'My parents' friends are going on a round-the-world trip and they had a house-sitter organised to look after their pets. Now the house-sitter has cancelled and Mum and Dad are trying to put together a group of us to look after their house and their animals. I feel awful for saying no but I'm not prepared to use up my leave sitting in the back of beyond looking after dogs and cats,' she confided guiltily.

Isla, petting Puggle, who was turning into a lapdog, given to sleeping across her feet and nestling in her lap at every given opportunity, looked thoughtful. 'Could *I* do it? The house-sitting, I mean?'

'You?' Lindsay queried in surprise.

'Well, if I could bring Puggle with me, I'd be glad to get away for a while. I mean, I have to find somewhere to live anyway and the change, a little breathing space, would do me good while I decide what to do next.'

Lindsay frowned thoughtfully and warned Isla that her parents' friends lived in a converted farmhouse down a long track in Somerset and that it was a very quiet area. After a few minutes, however, she called her parents back and before Isla could even catch her breath it was all arranged and she was agreeing to travel to Somerset at the end of the week to meet the Wetherby family and receive their instructions before they departed. Isla breathed easier at the prospect of leaving London and Alissandru far behind her. A change of scene and the time and space to make practical plans were exactly what she needed, she told herself urgently.

*It wasn't meant to be...* His words haunted her but where Alissandru was concerned there were no sad thoughts of what might've been in Isla's troubled mind. His rejection had been brutal and blunt. She had been a mistake, a mistake he regretted, and the miscarriage and his reaction to it had drawn a final line under that reality.

And yet she had been drawn to Alissandru Rossetti in a way she had been drawn to no other man. That bothered her, seriously bothered her. Admittedly he was gorgeous but she had been aware of his prejudice from the outset and should've protected herself better, holding back instead of surrendering to the fierce attraction between them. She had believed that she could be totally adult and blasé about sleeping with him and she had been devastatingly wrong in that assumption because Alissandru had ultimately hurt her more deeply than anyone had ever hurt her. She was not as tough as she had believed and was now even more painfully aware that she had to get tougher.

When Alissandru turned up that evening, Lindsay tried to head him off, but when he became icily imperious with her unfortunate friend, Isla gave up listening behind her bedroom door and emerged, bitterly conscious that she looked a mess.

'Alissandru...' she said flatly.

He had never seen her so pale, her freckles stark

across her porcelain skin, her violet eyes dull and haunted. He had to tighten his hands into fists not to reach for her, not to try to offer the physical comfort that he knew would be offensive to her. 'I don't want to crowd you, but I thought you might want to talk,' he reasoned quietly.

Bitterness flashed through Isla, sharp and painful and unfamiliar, for such bitterness did not come naturally to her. 'We have nothing left to talk about,' she told him curtly.

Alissandru looked amazing...*of course* he did, breathtakingly elegant in a dark designer suit that was exquisitely tailored to his lean, muscular physique. He emanated energy and authority in vibrant waves, the smooth planes of his high cheekbones taut below his incredibly expressive dark golden eyes. Such stunning eyes, now telegraphing the kind of guilt that was unwanted because she knew as well as he knew that he hadn't wanted their baby and that any offer of sympathy was sheer hypocrisy on his part. Yet the sheer pulsing zing of his dark, sizzling, sensual allure still filtered through that awareness, mocking her failing self-discipline as every skin cell in her body fired with wanton renewed energy.

'Why don't we have dinner and discuss that?' Alissandru murmured hoarsely, his tension increasing as she stood there, her delicate face colouring with much-needed warmth, lighting up her sad eyes and accentuating her fragility.

'I'm leaving London in a couple of days, so there'd be no point,' she declared. 'I'll let you know what I decide to do about Paulu's house once I've thought stuff over.'

Alissandru was startled by the truth that he had genuinely forgotten about the house. 'I'm not such a bastard that I'd trouble you with that matter *now*,' he argued in a vehement undertone. 'Where are you going to stay?' he pressed curtly.

'That's my business,' Isla assured him, half closing the door. 'Goodnight, Alissandru.'

Where the hell was she going? Would she be safe there? Would someone be looking out for her? Looking after her? She looked like hell! With difficulty, Alissandru suppressed his concern, acknowledging that it was time for him to move on. He could hardly force Isla to talk to him or to listen to him. He had walked away from her in Scotland and now he had to do it again. He could not understand the wrenching sense of loss attacking him or the sensation that something in his world was very wrong. 'I'll stay in touch,' he breathed in a driven conclusion.

Good luck with that, Isla thought wryly, knowing she was not about to unblock his number on her phone. Alissandru Rossetti was in the past now and only wounding memories would result from any further contact from him. She had to find a new focus in life, she told herself urgently, and embrace her future alone.

# CHAPTER SIX

ISLA EXPERIENCED JOY for the first time in many weeks when she first saw the glorious cherry trees that lined the imposing private road that led up to the Palazzo Leonardo. Great foaming swathes of white blossom hung low above her hire car, making her feel as though she were driving through a tunnel of bridal lace.

It was a hot day, hotter than she had naively expected in spring, and she recognised familiar sights in every direction she looked on Rossetti land. Her visit at the age of sixteen had filled her with more memories than she had ever cared to recall. Although it had been her only trip abroad, Fantino's assault had distressed her and made her reluctant to dwell on her recollections of her visit to Sicily.

The Rossetti family lived in a very grand home but the place where their ancestors had chosen to build was quite simply magnificent. A lush green grove of natural woodland covered the hills behind the ancient *palazzo*, which presided over a wonderful patchwork carpet of lemon and orange groves, olive trees and vines. It was still very much a working agricultural estate, and Paulu had run the estate for his brother.

Stiff with considerable nervous tension, Isla parked on the gravel fronting the sprawling property. She had to call at the *palazzo* to pick up keys and directions for Paulu and Tania's house but it would only be polite to greet Paulu's mother first and offer her her condolences and some explanation for her arrival. Constantia Rossetti had been very kind to Isla when she had attended her son's wedding and, since Isla was planning to live in Paulu and Tania's home for at least a few weeks, she wanted to be on good terms with the older woman.

As far as Isla had been able to establish, Alissandru was still in London. The fact that she had lost Alissandru's child or that they had ever got close enough to even conceive a child was a secret, she thought gratefully, a secret known only to the two of them. Not that Alissandru had been grieving, she conceded ruefully. An Internet search of his recent activities had shown him attending a charity function with a beautiful but severely underdressed blonde on his arm. Was that sort of woman the type he went for? Skinny as a twig and showing off all of her flat chest?

Clutching a wriggling Puggle tightly beneath one arm, for Isla did not dare to leave him unattended in the hire car when he was still so disposed towards chewing anything within reach, Isla hit the modern doorbell. The bell was somewhat comically overshadowed by the giant wooded metal-studded double front doors that provided the main access to the *palazzo*.

A manservant greeted her and without hesitation showed her through the echoing main hall out into the delightfully feminine orangery, which was decorated in classic pale colours. The entire wall of glass, which overlooked a courtyard garden, had been pushed back to allow the fresh air and sunshine from outside to percolate indoors. The single occupant, a tall digni-fied woman with greying hair swept up in a chignon, stood up with a quiet smile.

'Isla… I can hardly believe that you're here with us again,' she remarked warmly.

'I'm so sorry that it's taken me this long to visit,' Isla murmured, offering her condolences and a brief explanation for her failure to attend the funerals. 'But I wanted to see the house.'

'Of course, you did,' Constantia commented sym-pathetically. 'I haven't been back since…er, the crash, although I have ensured that the house was kept clean. Nothing has been touched or changed. I want you to know that. Everything is exactly as it was when they left that morning.'

'I'll go through my sister's stuff,' Isla proffered hur-riedly. 'And perhaps Alissandru would like to take care of his brother's things when I've left again?'

'Is this only a flying visit?' the older woman asked as a tray of tea was brought into the orangery, and in response to her inviting gesture Isla took the seat be-side hers, feeling ridiculously like a schoolgirl in the older woman's dignified presence.

'I'm afraid I don't know. I haven't made up my mind about what I'm going to do next,' Isla told her, her cheeks warming a little with self-consciousness as she thought of the short-lived secret interlude she had had with Alissandru.

'Oh, what a dear little dog!' Constantia carolled, stroking Puggle beneath his chin and urging Isla to let him down to explore while she explained that her pug had died the previous winter and she had not yet had the heart to replace him.

The older woman was friendly and welcoming, although tears were visible in her eyes more than once as she reminisced about her son, finally squeezing Isla's hand and apologising for her emotionalism by saying, 'It's such a treat to talk about him to someone.'

'But don't you and Alissandru talk?' Isla had asked before she could think better of that personal question.

'Alissandru doesn't like to discuss such things,' his mother admitted wryly.

Puggle scrambled up onto Constantia's lap with the insouciance of a dog who knew how important humans were to his comfort. Fed crumbs of chocolate cake, he quite naturally refused to get down again, and when the older woman offered to look after him for Isla, to let her get established at the house and do some shopping, Isla didn't have the heart to take him away again when she could see that Puggle's easy affection was a comfort to her hostess.

An estate worker called Giovanni was summoned to guide her to the house, which Paulu had extended and modernised to please her sister, who had initially described the property as a 'horrible, dark, dank, cobwebby hole of a place'. There wasn't even a hint of darkness about the building slumbering in the warmth of midmorning, brilliant sunlight reflecting off the sparkling windows and accentuating the cheerful yellow shutters and the plant pots that sat around the front door. It looked so peaceful that it made Isla's heart ache when she reflected that the house's previous owners would never live there again.

Scolding herself for that sad thought, she let herself into the hall and then froze in the porch doorway at the sight of a little stool covered with leopard-print fur fabric and dripping with cerise crystal beads. It was outré, ridiculous, very, very much to her flamboyant sister's taste, and she knew she would never part with it yet it was so out of keeping with Paulu's murderously tidy and conservatively furnished and decorated study. Two very different people, Isla acknowledged, and yet in the end they had made their relationship work with both of them making compromises to achieve a better fit.

Tania must've loved him, Isla decided, seeing no other reason for her sister to agree to live in a quiet country house far from the more sophisticated amusements she enjoyed. Her eyes wet with tears, she walked through the house, peering into cupboards and standing feeling like an intruder in doorways. Everywhere she spotted flashes of her extrovert sister's personality. It was there in the bright colours, the marital bedroom awash in cerise pink and white lace like the ultra-feminine lair of some cartoon princess. She closed the door on that room, telling herself that she would start going through stuff in the morning while choosing a guest room for her own occupation. The room was still furnished with antiques and it had plain whitewashed walls. It had always been the estate manager's house, Paulu had once told her, and presumably that was one good reason why Alissandru wanted it back again. Obviously he had to have a property to offer to his twin's replacement.

She supposed her only real option was to sell the house back to Alissandru. If she hoped to buy a house in England she would have to sell, and maintaining a second home abroad would be far too expensive. Even so, that didn't mean she couldn't first enjoy a few weeks vacationing in Sicily on a beautiful private estate. Alissandru wouldn't like her being here in *his* brother's house on *Rossetti* land, though…well, what was that to her now and why should she care that she was an unwelcome visitor?

Her thoughts were interrupted by the arrival of one of the *palazzo* staff laden with food to fill her empty fridge, and they even prepared a meal for the evening, sparing her the pressure of having to go on an immediate shopping trip. Isla smiled, charmed by Constantia's welcoming kindness. At least she didn't have to worry about how Alissandru's mother felt about her arrival.

Almost two months spent mostly alone in a comfortable old farmhouse had gone a long way towards restoring Isla's peace of mind. Walking dogs and feeding kittens had kept her fully occupied. She would never forget the baby she had lost, but that first punishing weight of grief had eased. Worrying about what to cook for her next meal had been the summit of her problems in Somerset, but even there she had become disturbingly aware that she still harboured a great deal of anger and bitterness towards Alissandru. That was *why* she couldn't forget him, that was why she had regularly scoured the Internet for references to him, gleaning facts and figures and a list of glittering business triumphs, all of which had utterly failed to shade in the nuances of his complex and volatile character.

After an early evening meal, she ran a bath for herself and borrowed a silk robe from Tania's wardrobe because she had neglected to pack one. After she had bathed she would drive back up to the *palazzo* to collect Puggle, who would surely have worn out his welcome by then or eaten his way out of house and home. Always hungry, he was a greedy little monster of a dog for all his small size, she acknowledged ruefully as she settled into the deliciously warm water.

She was drifting close to falling asleep in the cooling water when she heard the loud knocking on the front door, and with a groan she sat up, water sloshing noisily around her. Who on earth could it be? Had Constantia sent someone down with Puggle? Roughly towelling her dripping body only semi-dry, she grabbed up the robe and threw it on, grimacing as it clung to the damp parts she had missed with the towel. Barefoot, she sped down the wooden stairs.

Alissandru was in an ungovernable rage. He had flown home unexpectedly, walked into his own home and had been unceremoniously bitten by a nasty little animal he had believed to be hundreds of miles away in another country. As his mother had cooingly picked up the vicious little brute to check that he had not hurt his teeth, Alissandru had been fit to be tied but his brain had been firing on all cylinders in shock that Isla could actually be in Sicily, in his brother's house, on *his* estate.

And that startling, baffling revelation had enraged Alissandru, who liked everything spelled out in clear black-and-white predictable terms. Isla had *refused* to see him, *refused* to speak to him, refused even to take his phone calls, and yet without even giving him a warning she could take up residence in Paulu and Tania's house barely a quarter of a kilometre from him. How was he supposed to feel about that? Obviously they were going to see each other on the estate and was she planning to flaunt her hostile attitude to him here at his home? Was this why she hadn't agreed to sell the house? Had she always planned to show up in Sicily and make his life uncomfortable?

Her hand closing the lapels of the iridescent robe as it tried to slide open at her throat, Isla opened the door. 'Sorry, I was in the bath,' she began breathlessly before she saw who it was. Typically, Alissandru was sheathed in a tailored black suit that only emphasised his towering height and broad, muscular build.

In a maddening instant, Alissandru was confronted head-on by everything he had tried to forget about Isla: the triangular face dominated by huge dark blue eyes, her vivid mop of tousled curls springing back from her pale brow in a contrast that intensified the porcelain clarity of her skin. For Alissandru it was as though everyone else he met was depicted in monotone grey and only Isla was shown in full colour. Even worse, for the first time ever he was seeing her scantily clad and the idea that anyone else might have witnessed how the

thin fabric of her robe clung wantonly to her voluptuous curves incensed him. He could see her nipples,
the slenderness of her waist, the pronounced curve of
her hips, and the hardening swell of arousal at his groin
was painfully familiar.

'Alissandru…' Isla framed stiltedly, staring out at
him wide-eyed as though he had risen cloven-hooved
and fork-tailed out of the cobblestones behind him, her
heart jumping behind her breastbone in shock.

And yet she had *known* she would see Alissandru,
had known they could hardly avoid each other on his
family estate and that her arrival would infuriate him.
The golden blaze of his eyes, so bright in his lean,
darkly devastating face alerted her to his mood and
she took a cautious step back. 'I thought you'd still be
in London.'

'I always come home now at weekends if I can,'
Alissandru admitted. *'Per l'amor di Dio*…what are
you doing here?'

In receipt of that question, a little inner devil overpowered Isla's caution. 'I have every right to be here.
This is *my* house,' she pointed out, lifting her chin.

Alissandru compressed his beautifully shaped mouth.
'It is, but you know that I wish to buy it from you.'

Daringly, Isla turned on her heel, turning her back
on him while leaving the door open because she was
determined not to politely invite him in. 'I don't owe
you any explanations about why I'm here.'

Behind her she heard the front door snapping shut.
'Did I say that you did?' Alissandru growled like a
grizzly bear.

'If I give you enough rope, you'll soon hang yourself,' Isla forecast witheringly. 'I know you don't want me here.'

'When did I ever say that?' Alissandru demanded, following her into the open-plan lounge with its sunken seated area and flashy built-in bar topped by a glittering disco ball, which was so out of place with the rest of the house.

Isla flipped round, her robe flying momentarily open to reveal a sleek stretch of pale pink inner thigh and a slender shapely knee. His mouth ran dry at the sight while he recalled the satin-soft smoothness of her skin.

Isla frowned, hating the way he was staring at her. 'You didn't need to say it after you made it clear that you didn't want anyone outside your family owning any part of this estate.'

'I won't apologise for that conviction,' Alissandru argued in frustration as he squared up to her, wide shoulders thrown back, long, powerful legs braced. 'The estate depends on the properties we own. We house our employees. Your ownership could lead to all sorts of complications. You could decide to rent it out, bring in strangers, turn it into some kind of business, argue about rights of way.'

Unimpressed by that parade of evidently dire possibilities, Isla folded her arms and stared back at him. 'I'm not planning to do any of those things… *Satisfied?*' she prompted.

'You know that's not what I'm trying to say.'

'I just want you…*gone!*' Isla surprised herself by

throwing out her arms in angry emphasis of that fervent wish.

'Couldn't you have warned me that you were intending to come here?' Alissandru demanded imperiously. 'Or would that common courtesy have crossed the line that says I have to be the bad guy in your every scenario?'

Isla gazed back at him, her attention locked to his lean, strong features and the raw tension stamped in the set angle of his jawline, the flare of his nostrils and the anger smouldering like an unquenchable fire in his stunning eyes. 'Well, you pretty much are the bad guy in every scenario…and let's not pretend that you make much effort to be anything else!' Isla slammed back at him furiously.

Alissandru froze as though she had slapped him, colour leaching from below his bronzed skin. 'You're talking about the baby, aren't you?' he prompted curtly.

Isla barely knew what she was talking about but that very personal question knocked her back on her heels and she rested disconcerted eyes on him. 'No, I'm not, I'm really not.'

'What else am I to think when you say I'm the bad guy in every situation?' Alissandru pressed between clenched teeth.

'Well, when aren't you the bad guy?' Isla demanded. 'You were certainly the bad guy as far as my sister was concerned.'

'No. Even when she made a pass at me, I kept it to myself,' Alissandru bit out with suppressed savagery.

Isla shot him an incredulous look. 'You're not serious?'

*'Che diavolo!'* Alissandru exclaimed wrathfully, swinging away from her in an angry movement that revealed that that admission had slipped out of him in temper. 'It's true that it happened but it's not something I intended to tell you about. But if you think about it, it makes perfect sense. I was rich and very much the twin Tania would have preferred to marry and until she got to know me better she saw herself as irresistible.'

Isla swallowed hard, wincing for her sister at his admission, wishing he hadn't told her that salient fact, but she could remember Tania telling her that if she put her mind to it she could get *any* man she wanted. And Alissandru would have overshadowed Paulu to such a degree that Tania had eventually succumbed to temptation, Isla gathered unhappily. Alissandru might have been Tania's brother-in-law but he was also as flawlessly beautiful as a black-haired warrior angel in a stained-glass window. Even more gilded by his great wealth, her sister had unwisely decided to make a play for him.

'Drop the subject,' Alissandru urged curtly. 'It is a distasteful one. I am sorry I spoke so freely.'

Yet in a strange way, Isla was not sorry, for she felt as though she had finally learned exactly what lay behind Alissandru's loathing for her sister and her sister's loathing for him. Alissandru would never have forgiven such disloyalty to his twin while Tania would never have forgiven or forgotten such a rejection.

'You made me into the bad guy when you lost the baby,' Alissandru breathed in a fierce undertone. 'You closed me out, ran away—'

'I did *not* run away!' Isla launched back at him in furious rebuttal. 'I just needed a change of scene. And I didn't close you out, either…you were already on the outside!'

'Because I was too honest and I admitted that I wasn't sure the child you had conceived was mine?' Alissandru fired back at her. 'I didn't realise that you were a virgin. Blame that on the passion or my concussion…whatever you like. I didn't notice anything different. Blame me for the assumptions I made concerning birth control, too.'

'Oh, I already have,' Isla said tartly.

'But in the absence of proof of whose child it was, I assumed there was room for doubt and that you could even have been pregnant before you slept with me,' Alissandru intoned grimly. 'I'm a cynic. I won't apologise for the way my mind works but I am naturally suspicious when it comes to protecting my family or myself. I tend to assume the worst and act accordingly. But I was upset too when we lost our baby.'

Isla froze. 'Don't you dare tell me a lie like that!' she flared.

Alissandru swallowed hard. 'Regardless of what you think, for you to continue holding my innate caution against me even after I have done everything possible to be supportive is unjust.'

'Is it really?' Isla flung at him thinly as he lounged back against the ugly bar, effortlessly sleek and elegant in his designer suit, utterly untouched by the maelstrom of emotions that had tormented her for weeks. 'You ran as far and as fast as you could get from me in Scotland! You hated my sister! You accused me of sleeping with your brother! How do you expect me to feel about you?'

Alissandru breathed in deep and slow like a marathon runner readying himself for a race but Isla knew he was struggling to hang on to his temper. 'I didn't *run*,' he grated.

'You couldn't handle the fact that you had spent the night with Tania's sister! You assumed I was a gold-digging slut even though I was a virgin.'

'Your behaviour…the way you were dressed…at my brother's wedding led me to make certain ill-judged assumptions about the level of your innocence,' Alissandru bit out grudgingly.

An angry flush mantled Isla's cheeks. 'I didn't have much choice about what I wore that day. Tania told me she had a dress for me and I had to wear it because I had nothing else,' she admitted stiffly. 'It didn't fit and it was far too revealing but she said I had to wear it because it matched her silver wedding gown.'

That simple explanation irritated Alissandru more than it soothed because even he could not ignore the unreasonable bias that he had evidently formed against Tania's sister the very first time he'd laid eyes on her. He waited for her to say something about her behaviour that same day, something that would explain what she had been doing in a bedroom with his cousin Fantino, but when she said nothing more, his lean, strong face hardened. He had misjudged her but she was no angel and why should she be? A woman who could make him want her even when she was clad in furry fabric was obviously more of a temptress than even he had been prepared to acknowledge.

'Time for you to go,' Isla told him feelingly, colliding momentarily with smouldering dark golden eyes that left her short of breath and almost dizzy.

He was making her remember that night in Scotland and she couldn't stand that. The feel of his mouth on hers had created a chemical explosion that raced through her entire body, the magic sensuality of his hands had utterly seduced her. She had realised instantly why she had never been tempted into bed by any other man. Nobody had ever made her feel as he had.

'I'm not leaving until we have something settled about the house,' Alissandru intoned stubbornly.

Isla cocked a delicate coppery brow. *'Seriously?'* she jibed. 'You storm in here at nine o'clock on a Friday evening, force me out of the bath and demand that we do a deal about a house that I'm not even sure I want to sell yet? Do you think that's reasonable?'

Alissandru angled his arrogant dark head back, his lean, powerful body acquiring a stunningly insolent air of relaxation. 'I'm not in a reasonable frame of mind. I'm never in a reasonable frame of mind around you,' he murmured thickly.

'And why is that?' Isla prompted dry-mouthed, her skin prickling with sudden awareness, wicked heat darting up between her thighs.

His eyes, framed by slumberous black lashes, glinted like liquid gold. 'Because every time I see you I want you and that's all I can think about.'

'You did not just say that,' Isla whispered shakily, her face burning.

'Tell the truth and shame the devil,' Alissandru challenged huskily. 'All I want to do right now is rip that robe off you and sink into you over and over again…'

Isla trembled like a leaf in a high wind, fearful of being torn loose. *'Stop it!'* she told him fiercely.

'No,' Alissandru countered softly. 'When you came here, you knew this was going to happen. Deal with the consequences.'

Isla dealt him an aghast look. 'That is absolutely untrue.'

'You want me,' Alissandru traded without hesitation. 'You may not like it but you want me every bit as much as I want you.'

'You walked away!' Isla reminded him furiously.

'I had to force myself to do it and it didn't work. You've spoiled me for other women,' Alissandru husked, shameless eyes ranging over her with a stormy sexual promise that she felt bite to the very marrow of her bones. That look made her shiver. He emanated a shocking mixture of bold challenge and assurance.

She watched like a hypnotist's victim as he uncoiled his lean, rangy body from his lounging stance and moved forward. She couldn't breathe for excitement, couldn't move for fear of breaking his dangerous spell. He reached for her, all potent male and confidence, and he lifted her right up into his arms.

'We'll talk about the house tomorrow,' he told her. 'Once this is out of the way, we'll stop fighting.'

Was that true? she wondered weakly as he carried her up the stairs with the same ease with which he might have carried a doll. One more time, she reasoned wildly, clutching at his conviction that it would free them both from temptation.

'We mustn't… We *shouldn't*!' she protested more frantically as he identified the room she was utilising and strode through the door.

'We're not hurting anyone,' Alissandru grated with finality.

And it was true, she realised. As far as she knew nobody could be hurt by them being together. In any case, who would even know? As her brain careened madly from stop to go and then back to almost panic-stricken indecision, Alissandru kissed her with searing heat, forcing her lips apart for the scorching possession of his tongue. Something clenched hard deep down inside her and she started to tremble again, her head falling back, her lips parting, and the impatient drum beat of arousal pounded through her slender body like a storm she knew she had to quench.

# CHAPTER SEVEN

*WHY AM I doing this?* Isla asked herself as she looked up at Alissandru in the dim light filtering up from the hallway. And it was so simple she could've screamed at the answer when it slotted neatly into place inside her head. She *wanted* him, just the way he had said she did; she couldn't control the craving, couldn't drive it out of her treacherous body, either. That craving was there, simply there, and it rewrote in an instant everything she had ever thought she knew about herself.

He yanked loose the sash on the robe, spreading it open slowly as he leant over her, unwrapping her with a care that suggested she was a very precious parcel. She didn't cringe the way she had at the croft, didn't try to hide herself, either. Instead, she listened to the catch in his breath and watched his face as he looked at her breasts with fierce appreciation. His hands lifted to cup the full swells, his thumbs rubbing at the swollen pink peaks as he stole another kiss, and her hands plunged into his luxuriant hair, fingers filtering through the silky strands and then dropping to his shoulders, unsuccessfully trying to come between them to pull at his jacket.

'I know… I know,' Alissandru ground out in similar frustration, backing away to unceremoniously yank the jacket off and tug at his tie with thrilling impatience.

Isla lay there, all of a quiver with heat and desire, just watching him undress. They had made love in virtual darkness at the croft and this time she was hungry for the details and curious. He tossed condoms on the bedside table and their eyes met, his defensive, hers troubled and evasive, and he came down beside her and kissed her again then as if his whole life depended on it. Breathless, Isla squirmed at the sleek, hot, heavy weight of him and then she arched as his mouth closed over a swollen nipple, drawing on the sensitised tip until she felt as though fire raced between her breast and her pelvis, stoking the slow burn of need rising between her legs. It was an ache, a sweet, hollow ache she couldn't bear.

'Touch me,' Alissandru said urgently, carrying her hand down over his hard, flat stomach.

And for a split second she froze, unsure of herself, afraid to do it wrong, and then she connected with the hunger in his intent gaze and she jerked as if he had lit a touchpaper inside her because it was the same hunger that drove her. Her hand stroked down the length and breadth of him. He felt like satin wrapped round steel but was infinitely more responsive, arching hungrily up to her touch.

Isla pressed him flat and lowered her head, closing her lips round him as she stroked, listening with helpless feminine amusement and satisfaction to the hoarse sounds and the ragged Italian words she dragged from him. A little more and he was dragging her up to him again, driving her lips apart with the hunger of his, twining his tongue with hers and delving deeper until she writhed against him, glancing into quite deliberate friction with the hard length of him.

'I intended to go slow but I can't wait. *Madre di Dio*, *bella mia*…what are you doing to me?' Alissandru groaned, sliding teasingly against the tender flesh at her core.

Without even thinking about what she was doing, Isla tilted up her hips to receive him, and he began to slide home with a sinuous circling of his lean hips and then he froze and yanked himself back from her again to reach for the condoms by the bed.

'What is it about you?' he exclaimed in raw disbelief. 'I almost forgot again and I swear *never* to make that mistake again!'

For a split second, Isla froze. *That mistake…* Their baby. Of course that was how he thought about that episode, and how could she blame him? An unplanned pregnancy with a woman he'd only intended to spend one night with? A big drama and a source of stress he could naturally have done without and he would be as keen as she to ensure that that oversight was not repeated. She could not understand why that sensible fact should make her feel so unbearably sad.

'I'm so sorry,' Alissandru grated as he came back to her and captured her reddened mouth hungrily with his. 'It won't happen again.'

That sensual assault unfroze her and mercifully threw her back out of her unhappy thoughts. She could think of nothing but Alissandru as he drove into her with potent energy and an unashamed groan of satisfaction, thrusting home to the very heart of her and sending such a jolt of stark pleasure through her that she cried out, her face warming in the aftermath. Sensation gathered with his every slick invasion, the tightening bands of muscle in her pelvis increasing the waves of excitement gripping her.

'Don't stop...oh, please, don't stop!' she gasped at the height of a spasm of pure bliss when her very existence seemed to depend on his next virile lunge and her heart was thumping so hard and fast she was breathless.

She hit the heights even faster in an explosive climax that threatened to jolt the very bones from her body, so all-encompassing was the experience. Sweet paroxysms of exquisite pleasure eddied out from her exhausted body and cocooned her in melting relaxation.

Alissandru cradled her in his arms, shell-shocked in the aftermath. Just as in their very first encounter, sex with Isla was sublime but he wasn't going to think about that, wasn't going to question anything, *anything at all*, he instructed himself grimly. A kind of peace, a peace that had evaded him for long torturous weeks, enclosed him.

'I didn't even ask you if it was okay...us making love again.' Alissandru registered that omission in dismay.

Isla sighed. It was fine, nothing left to worry about.

* * *

He awoke in the early hours and for an instant could not even work out where he was, and then he looked down at Isla and began to slide out of the bed, making a real effort not to disturb her. If he woke her, she would fight with him about something and then everything would go to hell again, he thought grimly. No, he would be discreet and tactful, even if neither trait came naturally to him, but he was getting better, wasn't he? He hadn't even mentioned being bitten by the rabid midget dog, had he? He would return home before he was missed and he would send Isla flowers and possibly something sparkly, because she didn't seem to own any jewellery beyond a watch and he wanted her to know how very much he appreciated being forgiven for his past excesses and awarded a second chance.

Isla woke up in a cocoon of contentment and then turned over and found Alissandru gone. She jumped straight out of bed, checked the bathroom and downstairs and realised with an angry stab of disbelief that he had walked out on her *again*…as if she was nothing, as if she was nobody, a one-night stand he could dismiss as soon as dawn folded in!

It was a painful moment of truth for Isla.

Alissandru had used her for sex. But hadn't she used him, too? She freshened up in the shower, her body tender and sensitised beneath her fingertips, and she thought of how he had woken her somewhere in the darkness of the night and made love to her again slowly and silently, but still with that dangerous, exhilarating edge of wildness that seemed to drive his passionate nature. Afterwards he had held her close, and she had felt sleepily, unquestioningly happy and secure.

Why did he have that effect on her when he had already done more to damage her self-esteem and hurt her than any man alive? Did her brain switch off when he was around? Did she have so little pride?

In the light of day, coming to terms with what had happened between them challenged her. She had wanted him and he had wanted her and it had seemed gloriously, wonderfully simple the night before. They weren't hurting anyone else, he had pointed out, but what about how *she* was being hurt? Losing their baby had already hurt her more than enough for one lifetime. Sleeping with Alissandru again would complicate their relationship even more.

Why wasn't she dealing with the reality that she had developed more feelings for Alissandru than was safe in such a scenario? He only wanted sex. Maybe that volatile temper of his spurred his lust for her but lust didn't amount to much, did it? It wasn't feelings, it wasn't caring…

Was that what she was looking for and had hoped to find with him? When she was at the point of tearing her hair out by the roots with frustration over her distinctly confusing reactions to Alissandru, Constantia arrived at the front door with Puggle.

Isla was as wreathed in blushes as a shamefaced teenager at being confronted by Alissandru's mother the morning after the night before. She invited the older woman in for coffee, apologised profusely for the messy kitchen and grabbed a tray to carry the cups out to the pretty terrace that overlooked a rather over-grown garden at the back of the house. Once there she concentrated on practicalities and asked if there were any local charities who might welcome a donation of clothes and things. Constantia was very helpful, and she asked Isla about her friendship with Paulu, visibly relaxing over the freedom to talk about her late son.

'Your sister made my son very, very happy,' the older woman said quietly. 'At times she also made him very unhappy but I am grateful for the happiness he did find with her.'

'Did you get to know Tania well?' Isla asked curiously.

'No. I was her mother-in-law and she was wary of me, fearful that I might be the interfering type. I've never been in this house before,' Alissandru's mother confided, startling Isla. 'Your sister would never have invited me in. She guarded her privacy fiercely.'

'I didn't get to know her well at all because she wasn't the confiding type and I can hardly blame her for that when I was so much younger,' Isla conceded ruefully.

'She was very independent, possibly because she was making her own living from an early age,' Constantia remarked reflectively. 'Alissandru and Tania clashed from day one but that was inevitable with them both being such strong-willed individuals.'

'I clash with Alissandru, too,' Isla heard herself confess and then was stunned that she had spoken so freely.

'That won't do him any harm.' Constantia's smile was warm with amusement. 'Alissandru always thinks he knows best. He was the same in the nursery…bossy and bold.'

'And quick-tempered?' Isla prompted helplessly.

'Oh, yes,' Constantia agreed. 'But the flipside of that was that he was also very honest and responsible. Paulu would've lied sooner than admit he had done something wrong but Alissandru was always fearless.'

When the bell went, Isla was mulling over that conversation while she guiltily cleaned the kitchen she had ignored the night before, but only because of Alissandru's unexpected arrival, she reminded herself wryly.

She went to the door and received an exuberant arrangement of white flowers, all ready for display in a sparkling crystal vase. She didn't need to read the card in the foliage but she opened it with compressed lips, scrutinising Alissandru's initials with reluctant amusement. He was being *very* discreet because there was no message or proper signature to reveal the identity of the sender.

When the bell went a second time, she was filling bin bags with Paulu's and Tania's clothing while carefully checking pockets or bags for anything that should be retained. This time it was a man in a chauffeur-driven car who formally presented her with a gift-wrapped shallow box, clicked his heels with military precision and climbed back into the car. Once again she found an initialled gift tag and she rolled her eyes, ripping open the package with little ceremony as she stood in the kitchen, which was flooded with sunlight. A disconcerted look on her face, she flipped open the shallow jewellery case and the blinding sparkle of the diamond necklace within knocked her for six. She lifted it out, stunned by the shimmering rainbow glitter of the row of diamonds, and rage engulfed her in a flood.

Alissandru thought he could give her diamonds after spending the night with her? Some sort of pay-off—a don't-ring-me-I'll-ring-you cop-out on decent behaviour? Well, he could take a flying jump off the edge of the planet!

She leapt into the hire car, Puggle accompanying her, and drove up to the *palazzo*, powered on the fuel of fury alone. The manservant, Octavio, whom Constantia had confessed ran her son's household with the efficiency of the former soldier he had been, ushered her in and, when she requested Alissandru, escorted her at a stately pace along a corridor where he knocked on a door for her and then departed.

'*Avanti!*' Alissandru called.

Isla plunged over the threshold with the eagerness of a cavalry charge, stopping dead one foot in the door to press it closed behind her while glowering at Alissandru, who was seated behind a laptop at his desk.

'Isla!' he exclaimed as though she were a welcome, if unexpected, visitor.

He lunged upright, black hair untidy above startlingly bright dark golden eyes, a smile curving his sculpted mouth. He wore faded jeans and an open black shirt and was visibly in weekend relaxed mode. 'To what do I owe the honour?' he asked, feasting his attention on the vision she made in a rather shapeless grey linen shift, which should in his opinion have looked dowdy but which inexplicably merely set off her wonderfully vibrant hair and eyes and accentuated the grace of her slender limbs.

Unfortunately his dark deep voice, which was utterly seductive in the darkness of the night hours, acted on Isla like a flame thrower. 'Thank you for the flowers,' she told him curtly. 'But no thank you for the jewels!'

As she slapped the jewel case loudly back on his desk, Alissandru stiffened and frowned at her, dark brows pleating, stunning eyes narrowing beneath his curling fringe of black lashes. '*Cosa c'è che non va?* What's wrong?' he demanded, taken aback by her mood.

'If you spend the night with me, you don't pay for it with diamonds!' Isla informed him with fierce pride.

'It wasn't a payment, it was a *gift*,' Alissandru contradicted with emphasis, studying her with frowning intensity, wondering how something so simple could be interpreted as something so wrong.

'I don't want gifts *that* expensive!' Isla fired back at him. 'I won't accept them.'

'Duly noted,' Alissandru said drily. 'But does a poor choice of gift really demand this vehement a refusal?'

Isla bridled, reluctant to go into what had made her so very angry, determined not to betray herself in such a way. 'You offended me.'

'Obviously,' Alissandru conceded, marvelling that he had once believed she was a carbon copy of her infinitely more avaricious sister. 'But it was a gift, a small sign of my appreciation for the night we shared.'

Isla gritted her teeth. 'Staying around for breakfast would have been better received.'

'But that would have been indiscreet and I did promise you discretion,' he reminded her silkily. 'If I'm home before dawn, nobody notices, but a later return attracts witnesses and I wasn't sure that you would be comfortable with a more public unveiling of our intimacy.'

Hot colour washed Isla's face in a slow, burning and very uncomfortable flush, because she didn't want anyone on the Rossetti estate knowing about that 'intimacy'. 'I want last night to remain a secret,' she told him without hesitation.

'Not a problem,' Alissandru agreed carelessly, stooping down to snatch up the document case that Puggle had dug his teeth into, contriving to lift both document case and dog together into the air.

Moving forward, Isla hurriedly detached Puggle and gave him a sharp word of reproof when he growled at Alissandru. 'Give him some food and he'll stop trying to bite you.'

'What about discipline? Training?' Alissandru suggested in wonderment. 'Wouldn't that be more sensible?'

'Food is quicker and easier, but if I don't watch out he's going to get fat.' Isla sighed.

Alissandru broke up a scone lying on the untouched tray to one side of his desk and dropped a chunk of it in front of Puggle. The little dog pounced on it with glee. There was good reason for Alissandru's generosity. He didn't fancy having to evade Puggle's sneak attacks at night in Isla's house.

'Coffee?' he proffered in the awkward little silence that had fallen.

'No, not right now. I'm busy clearing the house and, since it's not something I really want to be doing, I'd sooner get it done and finished,' Isla admitted in a rush, turning away in an uncoordinated circle, wanting to escape, wondering how he had managed to turn the situation on its head so that she felt as though *she* were the unreasonable one. 'I wondered what to do about Paulu's desk and personal effects.'

'If there's nothing you want I'll send someone over to collect them and bring them back here,' Alissandru said gravely. 'His desk is probably stuffed with estate paperwork and I should have that passed over to the new manager in case there's anything of interest.'

'Of course. Well, that's something sorted.' Isla wandered over to the window, which overlooked the wooded hills to the back of the house. 'I'm planning to stay here for a few weeks.'

'There's no pressure on you to make a decision about what you're doing or how long you're staying,' Alissandru hastened to declare, recalling how haunted she had been in the aftermath of the miscarriage and wondering how much of that regret she was still carrying.

'This is sort of a holiday for me before I get back to the real world,' Isla admitted.

'And what does getting back to the real world entail?' Alissandru asked, watching her as the sunlight gilded her hair into a multicoloured bonfire of curls, the pale perfect profile, the intense wariness of her stance as if she was waiting for him to say or do something she found objectionable and use that as an excuse to escape.

He had never met a woman like Isla before and to some extent it unnerved him because she was an unknown quantity. A woman who threw diamonds back in his face, *insulted* by them, he thought, marvelling at that lack of materialism. A woman who challenged him, stood up to him, went her own way regardless, unpredictable and in some ways as volatile as he was. An explosive combination. He gritted his teeth as the silence lay, his question unanswered.

'I'll probably go back to studying,' she confided somewhat grudgingly, as if giving such personal information went beyond the bounds of their relationship.

'Studying what?' he pressed, genuinely curious.

'I'd have to pass another course first but afterwards—assuming I'm successful—I think I'd like to go to university to do a paramedics course. I want something interesting, *active*,' she admitted, turning finally to look at him, her head tilting back because he was so tall.

'It would be challenging but I think you're strong enough to do it.' Alissandru stood there, his dark head at an arrogant questioning angle, his stunning dark golden eyes welded to her with intensity and a literal flame of heat ran over her entire skin surface, warming her within and without and in places she didn't like to think about. Her reaction was so instant it was terrifying and, feeling suddenly vulnerable, she turned her head away again and headed for the door.

'Oh,' she muttered, pausing on the threshold to

glance back at him. 'A little hint if you're not too proud to take it. Your mother's ready for another dog. She adores Puggle and I think she would love a new pet.'

And with that helpful little assurance she was gone like quicksilver. Alissandru frowned even as he got on the phone to organise an employee to pack up and collect the contents of his brother's study. Isla was thoughtful, kind and intuitive. A new puppy would indeed comfort his mother, whose need for company he had failed to fulfil. Constantia had seen his brother daily and missed him the most while Alissandru had always travelled the world on business. It was true that he was home a great deal more than he used to be, but his conscience twanged that it had taken an outsider to point out a possibility that he felt he should've thought of first.

On her return to the house, Isla made a trip to two local charity shops. She was thinking about Alissandru far more than she felt comfortable with and deeply regretting her loss of temper. She had overreacted; she *always* seemed to overreact to Alissandru. She had overlooked the reality that a diamond necklace might be a *huge* gift on her terms but that it was a much lesser thing to a man of his wealth. Even so, she thought ruefully, it was better to have returned such an expensive present and to keep the difference in their circumstances out of the equation before it threatened to muddy the water and he started thinking she was a gold-digger again. Or did he still secretly think that anyway? She rolled her eyes at her meandering ruminations. She had no idea what Alissandru *thought* because to a certain extent she had already taught him to watch what he said around her.

On her return, it was a relief to see the contents of Paulu's study being packed up and removed. From those personal effects, she chose only a framed photo of the couple together on a beach somewhere, their smiling faces a good memory she wanted to conserve as her own. That and a little gold locket that had once belonged to her mother and that silly stool were the only personal items that Isla wished to keep from the house.

With Paulu's former assistant helping, Alissandru tackled a job he had long avoided, feeling almost grateful for Isla's part in virtually forcing him into the task.

'This is…er, legal,' his brother's secretary told him, passing him a folded document, complete with a notary's seal.

Alissandru frowned down at the local notary's stamp, wondering why his brother had approached another solicitor instead of Marco, the family lawyer. He opened it up and was disconcerted to discover that the document was another will and, what was more, a will drawn up and duly witnessed more recently than the one the family lawyer had had.

And that later will *altered everything*, Alissandru realised in sheer consternation. Only weeks before his death his twin had changed his mind about how he would dispose of his worldly goods, clearly having had second thoughts about leaving his home to anyone outside the family. He had left everything, house and money as well, to Alissandru, and Alissandru almost groaned out loud. Why the hell had Paulu changed his mind?

Alissandru suspected that Isla's advice had helped his brother to win his wife back and, in that first instance of reclaiming Tania, gratitude had persuaded his brother to leave his estate to his sister-in-law, should both he and his wife die first. And then perhaps Paulu, an innate worrier, had begun to think about the risk of leaving such a will in his wake and the effect it could have on Alissandru.

Alissandru gritted his perfect white teeth. It had been wrong to leave the house away from the family estate but to leave that money to Alissandru instead had been an unnecessary gesture. *He* didn't need the money, but Isla *did*.

And how was Alissandru supposed to act to redress a situation that now threatened to become a messy injustice?

He would keep quiet. He would put the new will in the safe rather than lodge it with Marco Morelli, who would kick up a ruckus and, as the family lawyer, inform Isla immediately of the new will's existence. But was suppressing the new will in such a way illegal? Alissandru breathed in deep and slow. He didn't wish to break the law and, surely, it was *his* duty as Paulu's twin to ensure that his brother's last wishes were respectfully carried out?

He would lodge the new will with Marco and tell him that he did not wish it acted upon. Assuredly, as the main legatee, he must have the right to make that decision. He wanted Isla to keep the money, he only wanted the house and he was quite happy to *buy* the house back from her.

But what if Isla decided not to sell? Or chose to sell to someone else? The new will would be his safeguard, Alissandru decided grimly, a weapon only to be utilised if he was left with no other choice.

# CHAPTER EIGHT

'PLEASE JOIN US for dinner this evening,' Constantia argued, reading Isla's reluctant face with accuracy.

'It's a family do,' Isla pointed out as the older woman regarded her expectantly. 'And I'm not family.'

'Your sister was my son's wife and you will always be family,' Alissandru's mother assured her reproachfully.

'I don't really have anything suitable to wear. I'm sure you all dress up.'

'Only Grazia, Alissandru's friend, really dresses up, but then she *is* a fashion designer. A plain dress will be sufficient.'

'I'm afraid I didn't pack anything fancy.' Isla sighed, every muscle in her body tensing at the reference to Alissandru's 'friend' as she struggled to combat an overpowering urge to demand to know who Grazia was and what her relationship with Alissandru was. Secret relationships were all very well until such complications appeared, she conceded ruefully.

But liking Constantia as she did and reluctant to risk causing offence, Isla laid out her only suitable dress that evening and put it on. It was a typical little black dress that wouldn't have raised a thrill even in its fleeting glory days when she had bought it to wear at a work dinner. She went a little heavier on her make-up than she usually did, painstakingly using eye liner and more mascara than usual. Grazia? Who was Grazia? Fierce curiosity powering her, she drove up to the *palazzo* where a whole collection of cars was already parked.

Constantia made a point of introducing her to everyone and, truth to tell, although there was some very flashy jewellery on display, a lot of the women were wearing little black dresses although the majority were fancier than her own. Some of the faces were familiar from that long-ago wedding but mercifully there was no sign of Fantino the Perv, as she thought of Alissandru's cousin. Of Alissandru and his 'friend' there was as yet no sign, but then there was a burst of chatter at the foot of the huge reception room where they were gathered for drinks and Isla glanced towards the door to see their host make an entrance with a tall slender blonde garbed in a tangerine dress with giant raised shoulders and a plunging neckline. He liked blondes, she thought first, and then, he liked blondes who *clung* because his animated companion was hanging on to him so tightly it was as if she feared that he might make a break for freedom.

Isla's observations mushroomed the more she watched them. The minute anyone tried to get into conversation with Alissandru, Grazia intervened, occasionally stepping between him and someone else or hailing someone else across the room and tugging him in that direction. The blonde was very pointedly possessive. She talked constantly, demanding his attention, stroking his sleeve, at one point stopping dead to straighten his bow tie in a statement of familiarity that made Isla's teeth grit.

It was an uncomfortable show for Isla to be forced to watch when Alissandru had been in *her* bed with *her* the night before. Was she jealous? Overly possessive? she asked herself worriedly, disliking the shrewish tone of her thoughts. As for Alissandru, she could read him even better in the slight widening of his eyes when he saw her; he hadn't expected her to be present and he moved with his companion in every direction but Isla's, and by the time they all moved into dinner, Isla was angry at being ignored.

As they were passing through the big hall towards the dining room, Alissandru addressed her. 'Isla…my mother didn't tell me that you would be here.'

'It was kind of her to ask me,' Isla parried lightly, meeting Grazia's assessing dark eyes as Alissandru performed an introduction.

'So, you're Tania's little sister,' Grazia remarked. 'You don't look much like her.'

'No.' Accustomed to such comments when anyone had met Tania first, Isla merely smiled and added, 'Your dress is a wonderful colour…'

And that was all that was required to encourage Grazia to tell the tale of how she had found the material in a Moroccan silk market and imported it to make signature pieces for her most recent fashion show. They separated to find their seats and Isla was reasonably happy with the way the meeting had passed off. She hadn't scratched Grazia's eyes out. She hadn't slapped Alissandru across the face even though she was naturally wondering if he was sleeping with the beautiful blonde, as well.

Of course, she was going to wonder *that* when the woman was all over him like a rash, touching him with a level of familiarity that went beyond the usual definition of friendship. So, decidedly not just a platonic bond on Grazia's side, Isla decided, recognising that she was learning stuff about herself through Alissandru that she had never dreamt she would learn. She *was* the jealous, possessive type, she acknowledged with guilty unease. In fact, she found it very hard to look anywhere else in the room.

His mother should've warned him that Isla would be attending, Alissandru reflected impatiently, reading in Isla's stiff smiles and set little face all that he didn't want to see. Now she was furious with him, now she would be trying to throw him out of bed, her every suspicion aroused. The child they had lost had created a deeper bond between them but that extra layer both united and divided them, he conceded grimly. He cursed Isla's desire for secrecy and questioned how the hell he had strayed into so potentially chaotic an affair. In truth, he didn't know how he had ended up back in bed with Isla or why he had spent most of the day thinking about doing it again and revelling afresh in the hot, sweet welcome of her curvy body. Suddenly he was off-the-charts obsessed with sex for the first time since his adolescence and it had blinded him to every other consideration.

Isla was ridiculously unlike his previous lovers. She didn't look like them, didn't act like them, didn't think like them and was highly unlikely to respect his boundaries. Even more pertinently, those boundaries were set in stone: he didn't get attached, he didn't like strings or drama or plans for a future that stretched more than a week ahead.

'She's very jealous, isn't she?' Grazia whispered in his ear. 'She doesn't look the type to make a public scene, though.'

'What the hell have you been playing at?' Alissandru demanded grimly.

'I couldn't resist testing her out once you said she was here,' Grazia admitted. 'A woman who tosses back diamonds could be worth her weight in gold to a man like you.'

'What do you mean by a man like me?' Alissandru practically snarled back, so irate was he that Grazia was pot-stirring merely to amuse herself.

Grazia gave him a huge affectionate smile. 'Well, to be honest you've had it very easy with women. You click your fingers and they swamp you in attention, you ditch them and they still act like you're their best friend in the hope that you'll come back. And here you are having to *try* to impress a woman for the first time ever and she still won't even walk down the street in daylight with you,' she proffered. 'I think it's *precious*.'

'I shouldn't have told you about her.'

'Yes, but you didn't tell me *everything*, did you?'

Grazia said with a shrewd knowing look. 'I sense more of a back story than you're willing to share.'

'Mind your own business,' Alissandru advised her bluntly, thinking that that was one back story he would never share with anyone.

Isla stayed as long as was polite, cutting out after coffee and walking back out to her car with a sense of crashing relief that she had escaped the source of her discomfiture. Well, one lived and one learned, she reasoned with herself, and over the course of the evening Isla had learned that sex on its own wasn't enough for her. Alissandru was a womaniser and she couldn't say that she hadn't been warned, not only by Tania's gossip but also by his no-holds-barred rejection at the croft. Two people as different as she and Alissandru could only be a bad fit.

And that was *that*, she told herself as she removed her make-up and got ready for bed. She wasn't about to punish herself with regrets because it had undoubtedly been time she acquired some experience with men. And she had run through the entire range of emotions with Alissandru, from the heartbreaking loss of their child to the sheer joy she had discovered in his arms. He had been useful for that, at least, she thought ruefully. Useful for that but not for much else, she extended censoriously. A very off-putting example too, she ruminated, terrific for sex, useless in every other sphere.

The doorbell went. Isla stiffened and ignored it. It went again, shrill and sharp as if it was being jabbed by an angry hand, the noise provoking Puggle into staccato barks. Isla climbed into bed and reached for her book while wondering if she should've gone downstairs to speak to Alissandru. She just knew it was him ringing the bell. What on earth would she have said, though? Another argument would not improve matters, particularly when she would have to deal with him to sell the house. No, it was more sensible to move on and ignore him and that meant no more thinking about him, no more wondering, no more dreaming. It occurred to her that life was suddenly looking very dull indeed.

Alissandru, unhappily, had no experience of being ignored and it inflamed him. Isla blew hot and cold. He never knew what she would do next. If she wasn't shouting at him or blocking him on her phone, she was shutting him out, hugging the charmed circle of her privacy and all that made him want to do was invade it. A sensible man, however, would just go home again and leave her to stew, Alissandru reflected grimly. But Alissandru never turned his back on a challenge. He walked round to the side of the house and calculated his chances of climbing up onto the roof of the kitchen to make it into the bedroom where she had left the window open. *Go home*, logic advised, confront Isla, his volatile, stubborn nature urged. Yanking loose his bow tie to unbutton his collar, he cast his jacket over a shrub and tested a drainpipe for stability.

Isla heard a noise and looked up from her book. As she saw a hand come through the window to grasp at the sill she screamed so loud that she hurt her throat.

'*Per l'amor di Dio*...it is only I,' Alissandru drawled as he pushed the window wider and swung lithely through the gap, black hair tousled as he leant back on the ledge and stretched, long, lean black-trouser-clad legs extended.

In the blink of an eye, Isla transformed from terrified paralysis into raging-shrew mode. 'What the hell do you think you're doing? You frightened the life out of me!'

'You should've answered the doorbell,' Alissandru pointed out drily, studying her slumberously from beneath luxuriant black lashes.

'How the hell did you get up here?' Isla demanded, leaping out of the bed to peer out of the window into the darkness below. 'You climbed up? You stupid idiot! You could've been hurt!'

'But I wasn't,' Alissandru pointed out silkily, trapping her between his spread knees, big hands curving to her shapely hips. 'I don't like to boast but in my misspent youth I climbed Everest. And I'm very grateful to arrive and discover that you are not wearing anything furry...'

Isla froze, embarrassingly aware that, having taken her by surprise, Alissandru had caught her bare of make-up and wearing the shortie pyjamas she had packed for warmer nights in Sicily. Suddenly the fabric felt as though it were shrink-wrapped to her dampening skin, and she went red.

'Although you do have rather eccentric taste in lingerie,' Alissandru purred, his attention locked to the frog print on the pyjamas. 'I will buy you something much more to *my* taste.'

Isla brought her hands down abruptly to break the

spell, not to mention his hold on her hips, and she scrambled back into bed to say with as much cool as she could project, 'No, you won't be buying me anything *or* lingering to outline your fantasies. You're going to leave now…and sensibly, by the front door.'

Alissandru shook his dark head as if she had posed a question and sighed, stretching to loosen his shoulders, the front of his shirt rippling with the flexing fluidity of his muscles. Isla removed her attention from him quickly.

'What do you want?' she demanded tartly.

Alissandru dealt her a wolfish smile. 'I think you pretty much know what I want by now.'

Isla bridled. 'No. We're done.'

'Not as far as I'm concerned.'

'I didn't ask *you* how you felt about it!' Isla flung back at him in frustration.

'Why are you always angry with me?' Alissandru asked, frowning at her. 'I was your first, so I can't imagine there's a long line of bad guys who let you down in the past.'

'One of you is quite enough. Where did you stash your dinner date while you came here?'

'Grazia has gone home, probably laughing all the way,' Alissandru confided with sardonic bite. 'We've known each other from childhood as neighbours and friends. She's the sister I never had but I made the mistake of telling her about you before she arrived tonight, so she decided to play a game.'

'You told her about *me*?' Isla interrupted sharply. '*What* did you tell her about me? And since we're on a subject that *I* had no intention of raising, why does a woman you say you regard as a sister paw you like you're a cuddly toy?'

'To see if she could get a rise out of you…and drop me in it,' Alissandru told her with derision. 'She has an odd sense of humour, always did have.'

'What did you tell her about me?' Isla demanded accusingly.

'*Dio mio*… I didn't tell her anything too private… believe me,' Alissandru countered grimly. 'There are some stories you don't share and *that* tragedy is one of them.'

The worst of Isla's tension drained away and her eyes softened, acknowledging that that wounding memory was theirs alone.

'She was overdoing the flirtation so much that you should've realised that it was fake. Do you really think I would be with a woman who behaves like that with me in public?'

'I don't know. I haven't seen you in public with a woman before,' Isla pointed out woodenly, feeling foolish, feeling mortified by the explanation he was giving her and not really knowing whether to believe him or not. 'Oh, go home, Alissandru. I've had enough of you for one night.'

'But I haven't had enough of you,' Alissandru murmured huskily, beautiful eyes of pure mesmeric gold holding hers.

Perspiration broke out all over her and she swallowed hard, fighting the flush of heat uncoiling at her core with all her might.

'And tonight was a game changer,' Alissandru intoned rawly. 'If you and I were out in the open, I would've been with you tonight, *not* Grazia, so from now on—'

'*No!*' Isla cut in forcefully, second-guessing what he was about to say, her entire body freezing at the concept of their intimacy becoming public knowledge.

Everyone would know, she thought in horror. Everyone would think she was a slut to be sleeping with Alissandru five minutes after she arrived in Sicily and everyone would be a witness to her humiliation when it fell apart again. And what if somehow the story of the child they had lost came out? She turned cold to the bone at that fear because that memory was so very private. Her face suffused with angry colour because she knew what Alissandru was like, *knew* he didn't last longer than a couple of weeks with any woman, knew it would be foolish to imagine he would even last *that* long with her, a former waitress with no claim to fame or extraordinary beauty.

'Why not?' Alissandru asked silkily.

'I don't want people knowing,' Isla admitted without apology.

'Are you ashamed of me?' Alissandru studied her in angry fascination because he was used to women who wanted to show him off like a trophy.

Isla reddened. 'Of course not,' she muttered unconvincingly, still at war with her upbringing and the tenets that insisted sex was only really acceptable in a loving relationship. So, what did that make her? If she gave herself recklessly purely for pleasure? If she set her value so low she asked for nothing more? If other people saw those truths she would be humiliated, whereas what went on in private was strictly and literally her own affair.

'Either it's in the open or we're done here,' Alissandru delivered, rising fluidly upright, dark eyes glittering like golden blades.

Isla swallowed hard, unprepared for that direct challenge. It was an ultimatum as only Alissandru could make it. 'If we're out in the open where does that take us?' she prompted, playing for time.

'It may not take us anywhere,' Alissandru said bluntly. 'But at least it would be normal and I could share Sicily with you while you're here.'

'I'll think about it,' Isla muttered, plucking at the duvet with restive fingertips.

'Think harder, think now,' Alissandru instructed impatiently.

*While you're here.* A telling little comment. He didn't foresee them lasting for any appreciable length of time. But then, neither did she, so that was hardly a revelation. What did she have to lose? What did she most fear? *Losing him.* That revelation shocked her but it didn't change anything because either she chose to lose him now by choice or she faced losing him when she didn't want to in the near future. Did the baby she had lost make the idea of losing Alissandru more threatening? Was that why she felt so bonded to him? She liked that explanation. But wasn't it time she took a risk in life? Let up on the need to protect herself and broke the rules of her grandparents, who had grown up in a very different era?

'All right,' she pronounced tautly.

Alissandru shot her a wicked smile and dug out his phone, pressing a number and shooting a stream of liquid Italian into it. He tossed it aside and began to unbutton his shirt, a long riveting slice of bronzed muscular chest appearing. 'From now on, you'll let me buy you things.'

Isla cocked her bright head to one side, dark blue eyes gleaming in her flushed face. 'Alissandru? Quit while you're ahead,' she advised. 'You're supposed to be generous in victory.'

Alissandru leant down and hungrily ravished her soft pink mouth with his own, his tongue delving deep. 'No, that's when I move in for the kill, *bella mia*.'

He shed his clothes without taking his stunning eyes from her once and it made her feel as if she was the only woman on earth for him at that moment. One moment in time, she told herself, one moment to feel *that* special, was worth whatever the aftermath would cost her. This time she watched him strip without turning her gaze away in uneasy denial of her curiosity. And there he was, glorious as a Greek god, completely male, all hard contours of bone and sinew, sleek bronze skin beautifully encasing lean, powerful muscles. The prominence of his arousal made her mouth go dry and she no longer marvelled at the soreness that had taken days to ebb after their first night together.

He ripped off the frog-print pyjamas without ceremony and flung them across the room, studying her pale curves with immense appreciation, lowering his head to stroke a swollen pink nipple with his tongue. Her breath caught in her throat and she recognised the surge of slick heat at her core, her hips shifting, her body primed and ready.

'Who were you phoning?' she asked shakily.

'I was ordering breakfast for us here,' Alissandru told her, long fingers tracing the scattering of freckles across the slope of her breasts. 'I'm not sneaking out like a cat burglar before dawn in the morning.'

'*And* you'll be using the front door from now on,' she muttered breathlessly.

'As long as you answer the bell,' Alissandru qualified.

Isla sent him a glimmering smile of one-upmanship. 'Then you make sure you treat me well,' she murmured, running a possessive hand down over his flat stomach, finding him, watching him react, his lush black lashes sinking low over his vibrant eyes.

'I think I can promise that,' Alissandru husked, turning over to find the centre of her and establish his ownership with a sure expertise that made her writhe.

She found his mouth again for herself, arching up to him, needy in a way she had never allowed herself to be before, her entire body screaming for her to rush to the finishing line.

Alissandru loosed a hungry growl as she pushed against him, startled to register that he was struggling to hold on to his control because Isla's need for him set him on fire. It had never been like that for him. He was as disciplined with sex as he was with everything else in his life, but his desire for Isla was hard to quench. He flipped her over onto her knees and sank into her with a hoarse sigh of unapologetic pleasure.

Isla was so excited she didn't know which part of her was more inflamed. Her heart was thumping so crazily fast it was threatening to burst out of her chest. She was on a sensitised high of receptiveness. The throb at the tender heart of her was almost unbearable and then he was there where she most needed him to be and the intensity of that first forceful plunge sent her flying higher than the stars, her body clenching tight and exploding with scorching sensation, leaving her clutching at the metal headboard of the bed to stay in position.

But the sweltering heatwave of pulsating response only continued as he increased his tempo, grinding into her with an insistent power that drove her straight onto another high. The fierce paroxysms of pleasure blew her away until she finally collapsed under him, catching his cry of release as he hauled her to him in the aftermath, melding their hot, sweat-dampened bodies together with an intimacy that she found incredibly soothing.

'It's never been like this for me,' Alissandru breathed raggedly, burying his nose in the soft springiness of her strawberry-scented curls, feeling the slight weight of her on top of him, shaken to experience the first glimmerings of renewed arousal at the same time. 'We light up the sky.'

'You walked away from it the first time,' Isla could not resist reminding him, because she took everything he said with a large spoonful of salt, determined not to overestimate her worth in his eyes.

'We barely knew each other,' Alissandru reminded her wryly. 'And maybe I did twin you with your sister more than I should've done...'

In the darkness, Isla smiled at that grudging concession, which she had thought she would never hear.

'But nothing lasts for ever...particularly at our age,' Alissandru continued, to ensure that she didn't start thinking that their affair would be of the long-haul variety.

In silence, Isla gritted her teeth at that unnecessarily cool reminder. She didn't believe in fairy-tale happy ever afters. As a child she had continually dreamt that her mother would reclaim her and sweep her off to a more exciting life with her and Tania in London but it had never happened. In the same way as a teenager she had dreamt of the perfect man coming along and that hadn't happened, either. And then there had been the miscarriage and the loss of her first child. There had been few truly happy events in Isla's life and she was inured to disappointment. She preferred to concentrate on reaching more practical goals that would improve her life.

She would sell the house and get onto a course that would hopefully win her a place at university. As always work and effort would be what won her better prospects. With that thought in mind, she murmured drowsily, 'Relax, I'll be bored with you within a couple of weeks... You may be my "first" but you certainly won't be my last.'

The burn of hot liquid rage that flew up through Alissandru in answer to that forecast made him flinch. That was what he *wanted* to hear, he told himself decisively. It wasn't a rejection, or a criticism of his performance, it was only reality. In all likelihood he would get bored first, although he was anything but bored at that particular moment, he conceded grudgingly. There was no need to make a major production out of the discovery of great sex or imagine that it was anything more. No, the wiser approach was to make the most of any unexpected gift of pleasure and let the future take care of itself.

'I'm taking you shopping,' Alissandru announced at eight the following morning as he rifled through the wardrobe where she hung her few outfits. 'You haven't got enough clothes.'

'If you take me shopping you have to promise to keep your wallet closed,' Isla said quietly.

Alissandru ignored the proviso and tossed a plain white sundress on the bed. 'Come on, get up,' he urged impatiently. 'We're heading back to the *palazzo* for breakfast.'

'The *palazzo*? I thought you ordered breakfast to be delivered here?' Isla exclaimed in consternation, only halfway out of the bed. 'Besides, your mother's there.'

Alissandru groaned. 'My mother lives in her own entirely self-contained wing of the house and she would never dream of using the connecting door when I'm at home or I have a guest.'

Isla was unconvinced. 'But how will she know you have a...er...guest?'

'The staff will warn her.'

Isla sped into the bathroom, unnerved by the prospect of the staff that would report back to his mother, and then she scolded herself for worrying about something that was quite immaterial. Soon enough she would be leaving Sicily and only a vague memory because she was unlikely to ever return. What did it matter what anyone thought about her or her morals? Her grandparents had lived in a small tight-knit community where their reputation as a respectable family and the opinion of the neighbours had ruled their lives. Isla lived a much more anonymous life.

Alissandru noticed how Isla walked several steps away from him as if she were some chance-met stranger he had encountered on the drive and renewed irritation assailed him. He closed the gap and grabbed her hand to anchor her to his side, faint colour edging his cheekbones as she shot him a look of surprise. *Holding hands?* he derided. What the hell had he been thinking of? And how did he execute a smooth retreat?

Isla was disconcerted when Alissandru spun her close in full view of the *palazzo* and crushed her lips under his with all the enthusiasm of a man who had been held at bay for weeks. As he released her hand, she kissed him back, breathless and bubbling with sudden energy and happiness. She slid her hand shyly back into his before they headed for the front doors.

The dining room was a much smaller version of the room that had been used for entertaining the night before but, for all that, the table had been beautifully set with shining cutlery and beautiful crystal while Octavio was hovering beside a maid in charge of a large trolley.

'What do you usually eat for breakfast?' Isla asked casually.

'This morning I'm starving,' Alissandru confided with glinting amusement brightening his gaze as she coloured.

And Isla had to confess that, as soon as the silver domes were lifted on the cooked foods available, her stomach felt as though it were meeting her backbone.

Alissandru watched with satisfaction as Isla demonstrated the healthiest appetite he had ever seen in a woman and, having polished off a heaped plate, finished with a croissant and a cup of very rich hot chocolate.

'We have a busy day ahead of us,' he told her, lounging back in his chair.

'*We?*' she queried.

'It was your idea, so we're off to collect a puppy on the other side of the island where the last pug came from,' Alissandru told her. 'I could have had the dog delivered but there's a litter and I thought you should choose, being a doggy kind of person, unlike me.'

Isla's attention briefly strayed to Puggle, who was fawning at Alissandru's feet in the hope of another tit-bit. 'Are you starting to like him?'

'I'm afraid not. He's a shameless manipulator and a crawler into the bargain,' Alissandru told her in disgust.

Isla laughed. 'He doesn't care what you think as long as you feed him. He's a dog, not a human.'

The sound of her amusement animated the formal high-ceilinged room, bringing a warmer, lighter element into the atmosphere. Alissandru frowned at her as though she were a riddle he had still to solve. He could not recall a woman ever making less effort to impress him. She didn't flirt or pout to hold his attention; she was happy to disagree with him and perfectly relaxed in his company. That resistance to being impressed made her an intriguing combination and a challenge. And although he was always exasperated by women who were clingy, he was keen to see Isla make more of an effort to attract him. Was that because no woman had ever made him work so hard for approval before?

He didn't know and he didn't much care. He was content to live in the moment. Isla wouldn't be in Sicily for long and he would make the most of their time together, keeping their affair light, casual and fun until it reached its natural conclusion.

# CHAPTER NINE

'So, YOUR FAMILY has always been rich and privileged,' Isla gathered without surprise, for Alissandru's awe-inspiring self-assurance was an integral part of his character. 'My background is very different. I come from a long line of poor people. My grandparents on both sides were crofters and they barely scratched a living. My father qualified as an engineer and he might have done better if an aneurysm hadn't killed him in his early thirties.'

'Why did your mother's parents raise you? Where was your mother?' Alissandru interrupted, reaching for the wine bottle to top up her glass.

'Trying to work two jobs down in London and take care of Tania at the same time. There was no way she could've coped with a baby, as well. She had poor health—she had kidney disease. There was never really any hope of the three of us reuniting as a family and living together,' she pointed out wryly, covering her wine glass with her hand. 'No more for me. In this heat too much would send me to sleep.'

'I believe I could keep you awake,' Alissandru

teased, dark golden eyes settling on her with slumberous sensuality, sending warm colour flying up into her cheeks.

The remnants of a luxury picnic lunch spread in front of them, they were sitting in a meadow that gave them a bird's-eye view of the Rossetti estate. A lush green collage of flowering orchards and vines interspersed with the silvery foliage of the olive groves stretched across the fertile rolling landscape below them. That morning Alissandru had given her a tour of the entire estate and, although Isla did not feel she had been especially active, she was now feeling ridiculously sleepy. Drenched in sunshine and warmth, she stretched her shoulders, frowning as her bra cut into her ribcage while, confined within the tight bra cups, her tender breasts ached. Had she put on weight? She supposed that was perfectly possible when they had eaten out so often. Even when they ate in at the *palazzo*, meals ran to several courses and the food was rich.

But gaining a little weight wouldn't give her sore boobs, she reasoned ruefully. She had thought that was more likely to be linked to hormones and the failure of her menstrual cycle to return to normal and stay normal after her miscarriage. But how could she possibly consult a doctor here in Sicily about something so intimate when she didn't speak the language? In the same way she had baulked at asking Alissandru to organise birth control for her. All such matters could surely safely wait until she returned to London…although by then she would no longer have any need for birth control, she conceded with innate practicality.

Ought she be doing a pregnancy test? For goodness' sake, how could she be pregnant again? Apart from that one tiny moment her first night in Sicily with Alissandru, there had been no mishaps, no oversights. And yet sore breasts and absent periods were also the most common sign of pregnancy in a woman, she reminded herself worriedly, and there and then she decided that she would be perfectly capable of identifying a pregnancy-test kit in a Sicilian pharmacy. She would do a test simply to rule out that frightening possibility.

Alissandru rested back on one elbow watching her, wondering what she was thinking about that made her look so serious. He could barely credit that she had already been in Sicily for six weeks and that he had stayed with her that long, as hooked on the pleasure she gave him now as he had been at the outset. Six weeks had to be some kind of new record for him. But then Isla was intelligent and easy company and he had enjoyed seeing Sicily through her more innocent and less critical gaze. But when would the boredom, the itch to move on to fresh fields, kick in? He had also done the bare minimum of work since her arrival, an acknowledgement that disconcerted him.

Of course, that was what living in the moment entailed, he reminded himself bracingly and, since he hadn't taken a proper break in years from his workaholic schedule, it made sense to make the most of his time with Isla because she would not be in Sicily much longer. She had already applied to join an educational course in London, which started in the autumn. He assumed that she was planning to stay the summer, but he hadn't actually asked because he didn't want to give her the wrong impression, and looking that far ahead would definitely give her the wrong impression.

Isla lay down, her drowsy gaze welded to Alissandru's flawless bronzed profile, experiencing that revealing little kick in her pelvis that made her squirm, her body lighting up as if in search of him. That she couldn't imagine life without him now terrified her. Fleeting moments of happiness had always been the norm for Isla, but the kind of effervescent happiness that Alissandru gave her was an entirely new departure for her. She had not slept alone a single night since they got together and if business or travel intervened, Alissandru was not above joining her in bed in the middle of the night or even at dawn. Either she slept in his giant carved mahogany four-poster bed or he shared her far less ostentatious double at his late brother's house.

Recovering from being part of a couple and adapting to being alone again would be difficult for her. She had never imagined that togetherness developing when their affair began. She had assumed there would be days they wouldn't see each other, arguments when they rubbed each other up the wrong way and needed a break. But she had assumed wrong because she was with Alissandru round the clock and he didn't seem bored...*yet*. In addition, they had very few rows.

Dissension usually broke out when Alissandru tried to give her some ludicrously expensive gift and took offence at her refusal. He didn't seem to grasp that she didn't need presents to feel appreciated. She was much more impressed when he took the time to drive her up into some remote mountain village and walk her along narrow cobblestone streets to a tiny restaurant he had been told offered superlative but simple food, made of the finest, freshest ingredients. Or when he had taken her to see the Greek temple ruins in the beautiful valley at Agrigento even though he was not remotely interested in antiquity.

Yes, Alissandru was just chock-full of surprises, she conceded warmly. If he hadn't told her she would never have guessed that he had originally planned to be a doctor, but that he had abandoned his studies after his father's death because his parent had made some rather risky investments and the family finances had required a steady hand. That he had put his family's needs first had shown her how much caring he was capable of, and that he missed his twin every day was also a fact that touched her heart because, quite honestly, Alissandru had had very little in common with Paulu, yet he had still managed to love and value his brother.

'Just drop me at the house. I need to go to the pharmacy for…er…sun block,' she told Alissandru as she climbed back into his sports car.

'It's a five-minute drive into San Matteo. I'll take you,' Alissandru insisted.

And Isla thought about arguing and then worried that that would only draw attention to any purchase she made. Buying a pregnancy test was ridiculous, she told herself irritably. There was no way she could've fallen pregnant again. Even so, it was wise to rule out the possibility, however unlikely it was, she reasoned.

San Matteo was a pretty little town with a charming *piazza* surrounded by several cafés that overlooked the old church and the central fountain. Alissandru parked and said he would meet her at the bar next door to the pharmacy and she sped off. Recognising a pregnancy test on the shelf was not as much of a challenge as she had feared and she dug the package deep into her capacious bag and rejoined Alissandru with a smile on her face to enjoy a cold drink.

Driving past the *palazzo*, Alissandru glanced at the sleek car parked there and suddenly braked. 'Fantino and his mother must be here for lunch. Why don't you join us?'

Isla froze. 'Your cousin…er… Fantino?'

'*Sì*, you probably met them at my brother's wedding. I'm not particularly fond of Fantino but our mothers are sisters and close,' he explained wryly.

A chill ran over Isla's skin at the mere idea of even being in the same room as the man who had taken advantage of her youth and inexperience in a manner that had taken her months to recover from. 'No, thanks. I don't like Fantino.'

'You remember him?' Alissandru's voice emerged with an instinctive chill as he recalled what he had witnessed on the day of his brother's wedding. Reminding himself that Isla had been a mere teenager at the time, he just as quickly strove to forget the memory again.

'Yes, I remember him,' Isla responded woodenly. 'Just drop me back to the house…or I could walk from here if you like.'

His black brows drew together as he studied her pale, set face. 'What's wrong?' he prompted.

Isla breathed in slow and deep and then saw no reason to withhold the truth.

'Fantino assaulted me at the wedding.'

'Say that again,' Alissandru murmured more quietly.

'You heard me the first time,' Isla retorted curtly. 'I don't want to see Fantino or have anything to do with him.'

'That's a very serious allegation,' Alissandru pointed out harshly.

'Yes, and considering that he got away scot-free with what he did at the time, I don't feel any need to justify the way I feel now. Please take me home.'

Alissandru drove her back to the house in silence, his lean, darkly handsome features clenched with tension. 'We have to talk about this.'

Isla climbed out, her face still stiff. 'It's a little late in the day to talk about it.'

'And whose fault is that?' Alissandru shot at her, snapping the key for the front door from her nerveless fingers. 'If something happened between you at the wedding, we—my mother and I—as your hosts should've been made aware of it!'

Anger gusted through Isla in a heady wave as she stalked into the house, her vibrant curls bouncing on her shoulders, her dark blue eyes outraged. 'I made Tania aware of it and she said I wasn't to tell anyone else. Believe me, it happened! And it *wasn't* "between us", either. When a man assaults a woman, it *isn't* always a shared misunderstanding!'

'Tell me exactly what happened!' Alissandru urged her as she paced uneasily round the lounge.

'Tania sent me upstairs to her bedroom to fetch her bag and your cousin followed me. He tried to kiss me and he put his hand inside the neckline of my dress and tried to touch my breast!' Isla recounted with a helpless shudder of recollection. 'He said something disgusting and when I pushed him off me, he fell over the bed, which gave me the chance to get away. Of course, he was drunk and he thought it was all very funny and he started laughing. But I was scared and I was very upset. I was only sixteen, Alissandru... I'd never been touched before and I didn't know how to handle it.'

His eyes flared as golden as flames in his lean, strong face. The mere idea of Fantino touching sixteen-year-old Isla appalled Alissandru, most particularly because he had seen Isla leave that bedroom closely followed by his cousin and he had put entirely the wrong interpretation on what he had seen. The guilt of that shocking misconception hit him hard. He had caught a glimpse of a suspicious scenario and, instead of immediately being concerned about the welfare of a very young girl, he had assumed she had either been flirting or having sex and had done and said nothing. That awareness went right to the very heart of the prejudice she had accused him of harbouring, and in that instant he knew he could no longer deny that his low opinion of Tania had automatically encompassed her kid sister as well and had coloured his reading of the situation.

'I am so sorry that happened to you, but Fantino will be even sorrier!' Alissandru swore in a raw undertone, throwing back his broad shoulders. 'But I am also sorry that I did not intervene when I might have done that day.'

'How could you have intervened?' Isla questioned without comprehension.

'I saw you coming out of that bedroom. I didn't see your face, just your back view, and then I saw Fantino coming out some seconds after you. I'm ashamed to admit that I simply assumed you had been having some sort of sexual or flirtatious encounter with him. I didn't question it.'

It was Isla's turn to stiffen and stare at him in shock. 'You thought that at sixteen I would go into a bedroom with a man and have sex in someone else's house? How could you think that of me at that age?'

'I have little justification but I *did* think that,' Alissandru admitted reluctantly. 'From the minute I saw you wearing the low-necked dress your sister put you in, I decided that you were just like her.'

Isla groaned, suddenly seeing the whole history of her relationship with Alissandru rewritten in the blink of an eye. He was finally acknowledging that that prejudice had existed, though, and that was a relief, she told herself soothingly.

'I am sickened that you suffered such an experience in my home. You should've been safe there. You were very young. In the absence of a parental figure, it was my duty to look out for your well-being…and obviously I failed,' he bit out grimly. 'On the other hand, Tania was very wrong to persuade you to keep quiet about the assault.'

'Alissandru… I didn't know any of you and I couldn't have brought myself to share that story with anyone I didn't know well. I felt humiliated and embarrassed. Tania suggested I might've encouraged him in some way while I was downstairs,' Isla told him. 'But I hadn't even spoken to him when he followed me up to that bedroom.'

'Do you want me to call the police? A sexual assault is a sexual assault, regardless of how much time has passed.'

Isla stiffened. 'No, I don't wish to make an official complaint. I've put it behind me now but I wouldn't want to meet him again or be forced to pretend that what happened didn't happen.'

Alissandru nodded gravely, his dark golden eyes glittering pale like shards of broken glass below his black lashes. He was thinking of the family jokes told about Fantino's persistent approaches to any attractive woman available. Maybe that wasn't quite so funny now that Alissandru was seeing the other side of the coin and having to question his cousin's behaviour. It had never crossed his mind to look on Fantino as a sex pest but that now seemed more accurate. That he should've dared to frighten and distress a young guest in Alissandru's home was inexcusable. He was also thinking guiltily that he too had noticed Isla's attraction that day and had dealt with it less than honestly by telling himself that she was a shameless little baggage. But he would never have acknowledged that attraction to so youthful a girl, *never* have given way to it.

'What the hell was Tania thinking of when she silenced you?' he ground out on his purposeful path back to the front door.

Wincing, Isla looked pensive and wry. 'That it would've wrecked her wedding…and it *would've* done. Imagine the atmosphere it would've created if I'd publicly accused Fantino! I was a complete stranger in a foreign country and Tania was almost as unknown to your family as I was at that stage,' she pointed out ruefully. 'Would anyone even have believed me?'

'Certainly, I hope we would have.' Alissandru breathed in deep. 'But it will be dealt with now as it should've been then.'

'Why… What are you going to do?' Isla asked worriedly.

'Deal with Fantino,' Alissandru bit out wrathfully. 'What else?'

'So, you believe me,' Isla gathered.

'Of course, I do.'

A moment later, he had gone and once the sound of his car had receded Isla paced the wooden floor, amazed at how shaken up she felt after getting that episode six years earlier off her chest. *Finally.* Her shoulders slumped and she felt relieved that that horrible secret was now out in the open. Naturally, she hadn't shared the story with her grandparents, who would've been horrified. But she had also kept quiet because she had feared that if they knew they would not let

her travel alone again and back then she had still harboured the hope that the wedding invitation would lead
to other invites from her sister. Of course, that hadn't
happened and the sad repercussions of her encounter
with Fantino had lasted a lot longer. For years she had
been nervous of men, fearful of an assault coming her
way without warning, fearful that something she might
wear, say or do might attract such treatment. But she
had moved past that eventually, survived, she reminded
herself calmingly as she tripped over her bag, which
she had abandoned in the hall.

Recalling the pregnancy test in her bag, she pulled
it out. In the almost bare study, she lifted the diction-
ary of Italian words she had bought so that she could
translate the directions. Fortunately, the pictorial dia-
grams were more easily understood and she decided to
do the test immediately, rather than stress about it or be
forced to attempt to do it when Alissandru was around.

He had been very much shocked by her story about
Fantino, she acknowledged, but he would be a great
deal more shocked, she reckoned, if she was to conceive again. It wasn't possible, she told herself as her
heartbeat kicked up tempo. Her stupid hormones were
still out of sync after the miscarriage and she would
have to see a doctor when she got home again. Having
convinced herself that the test was a simple formality
to rule out an unlikely development, she went upstairs.

Fifteen minutes later, she was reeling in shock at
what was undeniably a positive pregnancy test. Having
returned her hire car some weeks before, she climbed
into the little runaround that had once belonged to

Tania and drove back to the pharmacy to buy a second test. Just to be on the safe side, she told herself. An hour later, she contemplated the second positive result and felt so dizzy and sick with nerves that she could barely breathe. After a few minutes she stood up and went to lie down on top of the bed and think.

Pregnant...*again*! How was she supposed to deal with the joy rising inside her and the quite opposite effect her news would have on Alissandru? How could it have happened when they had tried to be careful? Yet she knew that no contraception was foolproof. Her head swimming with confused feelings, she tried to imagine telling Alissandru *again* and immediately thought that maybe she *didn't* need to tell him this time, that maybe she should wait a few months to at least be sure she stayed pregnant.

She was, however, too sleepy to agonise for long and, while her conscience warred against keeping any secret from Alissandru, she couldn't help recalling the angst she had roused with her last announcement. Was she incredibly fertile? Was he? Would she manage to carry her baby to term this time around? Anxiety struck then and struck hard and she had to blank out her worries quite firmly before she could drift off to sleep, while telling herself that she would make decisions and worry about the consequences later.

The shrill noise of the doorbell woke her and, blinking sleepily, she scrambled up, stuffing her feet blindly back into the shoes she had kicked off while at the same time calling out to silence Puggle's frantic barks. She padded hurriedly downstairs and swung open the door on Alissandru, and that fast her cheeks burned and she ran an uneasy hand through her mussed curls.

'I have someone here who has something to say to you. It won't take long,' Alissandru murmured bracingly.

Isla spotted the car pulled up behind Alissandru's and stiffened in dismay as she spotted Fantino's weedy figure heading towards them. 'What does he want?' she hissed.

She didn't have to wait long to find out. Fantino had come to offer heartfelt apologies and regret for the distress he had caused at her sister's wedding and to insist that he would never do such a thing again. He made no excuses, offered no defence, merely concluding his awkward little speech with the assurance that he would be making a big effort to improve his behaviour. Isla studied the bruising and swelling on his thin face and swallowed hard, recognising that he had taken a beating and guessing by the granite-hard set of Alissandru's jaw that he had been the one to administer it. Jungle justice, she thought ruefully, but if it stopped Fantino in his tracks the next time he saw an attractive woman and made him think twice, she had no quarrel with the punishment.

She accepted the apology and watched Fantino jump back into his sports car with a curled lip.

'He will stay away from the estate while you're here,' Alissandru assured her.

'Did you have to beat him up?' Isla asked uncomfortably.

'I had to get the truth out of him...and I did,' Alissandru countered levelly, unable to explain even to his own satisfaction what had ignited the sheer rage that had gripped him once he'd got his hands on Fantino. The concept of anyone laying a single finger on Isla without her permission had incensed him. The awareness that she might not be his cousin's only victim had made him even angrier and determined to keep a watch on Fantino to ensure that he kept his promises to reform.

'I didn't want any violence, and your mother must've been very upset by all this,' she muttered ruefully.

'A generation back, a man could've been killed for any action that could damage a woman's reputation. Community disapproval controlled bad behaviour. My mother is only upset that you did not feel you could trust us with the story of what happened to you that day,' Alissandru explained grittily. 'Now, if you are in agreement, let us bury this matter.'

Isla nodded vigorously. 'Yes.'

'I have a fundraiser for a children's hospice that I support to attend this evening,' Alissandru told her. 'Will you accompany me?'

'If it's black tie, I have nothing to wear.'

'Grazia has already offered to provide you with a suitable dress,' Alissandru cut in. 'She'll be present tonight and would like to see you again. She is probably planning to ask you at least a hundred nosy questions.'

Isla looked up into his lean, darkly handsome face and tried to face telling him what she knew she had to tell him and she lost colour and dropped her head.

'Thank her for her offer. It's a very generous gesture, but I'm afraid I'd prefer to spend a quiet evening here.'

'You've had a distressing afternoon,' Alissandru conceded reluctantly, studying her with his shrewd gaze, picking up on her pallor and the shadows of strain below her eyes, wishing he could give her thoughts a more positive turn, wishing that Fantino's sleazy behaviour hadn't cast a pall over their day, for there was no denying that it had with Isla looking so drawn and fragile.

'A quiet evening and a good sleep will do me good,' Isla declared with a forced and brittle smile.

'How important is it that you sleep alone?' Alissandru asked bluntly, a long forefinger tracing the ripe curve of her lower lip. 'Because I don't sleep so well without you…'

Her dark blue eyes flew wide, her heart thumping at the smouldering appraisal he was giving her. It sent wicked little tingles coasting through her, started up a hot, needy throb at her core. *Because I don't sleep so well without you…* That was a statement that threw her heart wide open, filling her with dangerous warmth and an almost overpowering desire to throw herself into his arms. He was going out without her but he still wanted to spend the night with her.

Alissandru bent his dark head and kissed her, savouring the softness of her lips and the sweetness of her instant response, fierce arousal threatening his self-control and just as quickly unnerving him. You can go *one* night without her, he told himself irritably. You're *not* an addict. Why was everything with Isla so blasted complicated? He thought of Paulu's second will, which he had lodged with Marco, and suppressed a heavy sigh. He had felt foolish when Marco had erupted in approval of that discovery on the family's behalf when he knew he had no intention of having the contents of that second will actioned. Should he already have explained that decision to the family lawyer? But admitting that he was in a relationship with Isla had struck him as too private a revelation to make to one of his employees. If further explanation was required in the future, he would deal with it then, he thought in exasperation.

'I'll call you tomorrow,' he told her abruptly, releasing her to stride back to his car.

Isla stood there a few seconds longer, wondering what had happened, wondering why he had changed his mind about joining her after the fundraiser. She wandered back indoors, feeling strangely unsettled by her recollection of the sudden detachment that had momentarily frozen Alissandru's lean dark face, banishing his usual smile. Maybe he was getting tired of her, maybe he was only just beginning to realise that, she reasoned.

And how did that make her feel? As if the roof was about to fall in, she acknowledged guiltily, taken aback by the awful hollow sensation that filled her when she thought of Alissandru walking away from her. She had got attached, hadn't she? Seriously attached in spite of all the signs that he was not in the market for any kind of commitment. And even worse, now she was pregnant and that fact was more important than her feelings or his.

Isla walked around the house, busying herself with tidying up while she pondered her dilemma. There was really no avoiding the obvious. Alissandru had always been honest with her and she owed him the same honesty. A couple of hours later, her nerves nibbling at her in painful bites, she showered and changed and drove up to the *palazzo*, trying not to ask herself how it would feel when she saw angry resentment and regret in Alissandru's face when she told him she had once again conceived. As ever impervious to mood, Puggle danced at her heels, eager to see Constantia or Alissandru, both of whom could be depended on to feed him.

As she mounted the steps, a thickset older man emerged and hesitated. 'You must be Tania's sister, Isla,' he guessed as he extended his hand. 'I'm Marco Morelli, the Rossetti family lawyer.'

Isla tensed at the explanation. 'I suppose you'll be getting together some papers for me to sign,' she remarked, thinking of the legalities of selling the house back to Alissandru. She had already nominally agreed to sell the house back to him but the sticking point was that she was only willing to accept market value while Alissandru seemed to think that it was somehow his duty to pay very generously for it.

The older man frowned and shook his head in grave dismissal. 'No…there's nothing. A mistake that none of us could know *was* a mistake is already being rectified. Now that the new will has been lodged, it is merely a question of sorting out the tangle Paulu left behind him. I am sorry you have had this experience.'

Isla had fallen very still. '*New* will?' she queried breathlessly.

'Alissandru said that he would explain it all to you.' Marco Morelli checked his watch and sighed. 'Unfortunately, I have another call to make and I can't go into the complexities of a more recent will turning up and reversing the original right now, but if you have any questions, I would be happy to answer them for you at my office. Perhaps tomorrow...or the next day?' he prompted helpfully.

'So, there's nothing for me to sign,' Isla managed to gather, striving to act normally rather than betraying the reality that she had been dealt a body blow.

'No, once you return the inheritance the matter is fully concluded,' he assured her cheerfully. 'I know Alissandru wishes to compensate you for this most regrettable confusion but, to be frank, he owes you nothing because he was no more aware of the second will's existence than anyone else. I persuaded him that he had to have the will lodged legally with the courts if he wanted to avoid further complications.'

The older man bid her good day and hurried back to his car, leaving Isla standing there like a stone statue.

Slowly, very slowly as if her very bones ached, she retraced her steps to Tania's car, Puggle lagging behind her. She knew she couldn't face Alissandru at that moment. She had to gather herself, work out what to do next...aside from repaying what she owed. It was as if her life were a deck of cards that someone had tYhrown up into the air and now everything had changed radically.

Her independence, her plans, everything she had depended on was being torn away. Just her bad luck, as the lawyer had said. From somewhere, Alissandru had obtained another will and, within it, Paulu had presumably left his worldly goods to his brother instead. Isla was shattered. She remembered the contents of Paulu's desk being taken away and surmised that that was most likely where the second will had been found. Even she knew that a more recently dated will would take precedence over an earlier one. But Alissandru had seemingly learned about that will *weeks* ago!

Yet he still hadn't told her. The house was already his yet he was even now determined to *buy* it from her. Why? Because he *pitied* her. Her self-esteem squirmed as though it had come into contact with something very nasty and hurtful. And she was hurt, seriously hurt that he had not told her about that second will as soon as he became aware of its existence.

Knowing that Alissandru had seen her sister as avaricious, she had made a big effort to keep Alissandru's wealth out of their relationship. Pride had demanded that she stand on her own feet and Paulu's legacy had made it possible for her to do that. But now that financial security had vanished. And, even worse, it left her broke and in debt to Alissandru because everything she had spent in recent months, after being given access to Paulu's money, had not been *her* money to spend. How was she ever going to repay that money?

Thank goodness she hadn't spent like a lottery

winner, she thought heavily. Her native caution with money had meant that she was careful, but she had spent a fair bit of money simply travelling to Sicily and had been living off it ever since. How could he not have told her about the second will?

It had been a lie of omission. Feeling sorry for her, Alissandru had kept quiet. He had planned to virtually pay her off by paying for a house he already owned and he would never have told her the truth because he would've let her walk away with his brother's money. And now she was pregnant and she was going to cost Alissandru even *more* money. She would be the financial liability he had never wanted.

Hot tears of mortification burning the backs of her eyes, she entered the house that was no longer hers and went upstairs to pack. She would return to London. What else could she do? She had to find herself some way of making a living again, at least until the baby was born. But no way was she about to tell Alissandru about the baby now face-to-face, not with this horrible financial bombshell engulfing her at the same time. She felt devastated and humiliated and taking herself quietly away seemed like her only dignified option.

She would write Alissandru a letter. That way, he could curse and storm when he found out that there was to be another baby. He wouldn't be forced to be polite; he wouldn't be forced to hide his true feelings. Once the dust had settled on that revelation, she would get in touch with him again.

She went online to see how soon she could get a flight to London but ran into difficulties when it came to travelling with Puggle. Travelling with a dog across Europe could not be done without foresight and planning. Puggle had to receive an injection several days prior to travel and she would need to arrange that first. Constantia would take him, Isla thought ruefully, but when would she ever be able to return to Sicily to reclaim him? Furthermore, leaving her dog with Alissandru's mother would entail making explanations she had no desire to have to make.

Writing a letter to Alissandru took Isla hours. After several failed attempts, she decided to keep it simple. She admitted that she had found out about the second will and that she had no alternative other than to vacate the house. She made no promises of repayment because, with neither a home nor employment awaiting her in London when she finally got there, there was little point in talking about what she couldn't deliver. She wrote about the baby in bald terms and assured him that she would get in touch once she was settled again.

Hearts didn't really break, she told herself firmly as she walked out of the house with Puggle confined in his carrier. She would recover…*eventually*. Alissandru had not encouraged her to fall in love with him. He had been quite clear from the outset that they were simply having a casual affair. Now she needed to concentrate on finding a local veterinary surgeon and somewhere she could stay with a dog in tow.

# CHAPTER TEN

ALISSANDRU DROVE HOME from the fundraiser and the whole way he assured himself that he was giving Isla a night of unbroken sleep. But his foot hovered over the brake as he reached the *palazzo* and failed to connect, ensuring he drove on in the direction of his twin's former home. Isla had had an upsetting day and it was natural that he would want to check on her to ensure that she was all right, he reasoned ruefully.

The house was in darkness, which he hadn't expected because it wasn't late. Anxious now, he banged on the door, wondering if she had fallen asleep, and, when even that failed to rouse her, he dug out the key he had always had but neglected to mention and stuck it in the door. He called out her name, switched on lights, frowned and took the stairs two at a time, striding into her bedroom to find it empty. Where was she? The dog was missing, as well.

Obviously she had gone out. Was she with his mother? Since his mother had got the puppy, she had been communicating regularly with Isla about dog training. As if Isla could tell anyone anything about dog training, Alissandru reflected wryly. He called his mother to ask if she had company and, while she was telling him that she had not, he finally noticed the letter lying on the bed with his name printed on it.

As he read the first paragraph, which mentioned her unexpected meeting with Marco, he froze and he cursed. When she referred to her having left, he wrenched open the wardrobe door so roughly it almost fell off its hinges. It was empty. *Per l'amor di Dio…* Isla had *left* him. Alissandru was stunned into momentary paralysis. He hovered in the centre of the room and tried to entertain the concept of Isla being gone. No, he wasn't addicted to her, maybe a little obsessed…occasionally. Isla *gone*.

The shock of that knowledge made him sit down on the side of the bed because his legs turned weirdly weak. He returned to the letter with renewed interest and then reached the section about the baby on the way again and suddenly, in the midst of his turmoil, Alissandru was smiling. What was it about them? They got together and five minutes later…hey, no complaints, Alissandru reflected abstractedly, enthusiasm at the prospect leaping through him. Isla was going to have *his* baby. Obviously they were meant to be. It wouldn't have happened again, he reasoned, if the fates hadn't intended it so.

Alissandru smiled, temporarily in a world of his own, and then he unfroze. Isla had walked out on him when she *needed* him. He couldn't live with that awareness. In fact, it filled him with panic. Where was she? How was he to track her down? Could she have flown out of Sicily already? Should he go to the airport first?

His mobile buzzed, and he snatched it up.

It was Grazia and he only answered it because, if he didn't, Grazia would simply keep on ringing and ringing.

'Alissandru…' he breathed harshly.

'Have you lost anything? Or should I say anyone?'

'How do you *know* that?' Alissandru demanded rawly.

'Because I've found what you lost by the side of the road, complete with a yappy little dog.'

'By the side of the road?' Alissandru exclaimed, leaping upright in consternation.

'The getaway car broke down,' Grazia said succinctly. 'I drove past them on the way home, had to practically force Isla into my car. What have you been doing, Alissandru?'

'I screwed up,' Alissandru bit out in a roughened undertone.

'Well, they're at my house and I'm off to my parents' for the night. Keys in the usual place. Admit it… I'm the best friend you've ever had.'

'You're the best friend I've ever had,' Alissandru recited breathlessly as he practically ran down the stairs, slammed through the door, flung himself into his car.

'Now stop right there and *think*,' Grazia urged as he fired the engine. 'You don't go in cold and without knowing what you're going to say.'

'I know. I know exactly,' Alissandru told her boldly, and he did know, just the same way as his twin had once told him he knew, only it had taken an awful lot longer for the truth to hit Alissandru.

But the truth had hit him at remarkable speed when he'd walked through that empty house and the prospect of spending even one night without Isla had hung over him like a thunderclap of doom.

Emotionally speaking, Isla was all over the place. She had had the strength to walk away and then Tania's car had broken down halfway between the estate and San Matteo. That was when the floods of tears had engulfed her. That was when everything going wrong had just combined into one giant heavy rock grinding her down, squeezing the life out of her. But above all had been the screaming sense of having left part of herself behind, as well.

She *loved* Alissandru Rossetti. She hated him for feeling sorry for her and neglecting to tell her about the will, but he was still the father of her baby and the man she loved. When Grazia had stopped and initially offered her a lift into town, Isla had had no choice but to accept the offer, and when she had asked if Grazia knew anywhere she could get a room for the night with a dog, Grazia had informed her that there was only one place. And she hadn't explained until she'd pulled up outside a beautiful, newish-looking, modern detached house outside town that the only place that would take a dog for the night was *her* house.

Practically pushing Isla through the front door, Grazia had then shown her up to an en-suite bedroom, urging her to get into something comfortable while telling her that the kitchen was full of food and to make herself at home.

Puggle had required no such encouragement. He had curled up in a basket in the kitchen with Grazia's elegant little grey whippet, Primo, and gone straight to sleep, the trauma of being pushed into his transport carrier gratefully left behind him.

Isla had showered and put on her pyjamas. She wasn't hungry and she wasn't sleepy either and the prospect of watching Italian television when she couldn't speak the language had little appeal. When she heard the front door opening, she assumed it was Grazia returning from wherever she had rushed off to, and she stood up. The sight of Alissandru walking through the door was a total shock and her eyes flew wide.

'How did you know I was here?' she gasped.

'Grazia. She knew I'd want to know. I owe her a massive thank you,' Alissandru bit out harshly. 'How could you just run off like that? What on earth possessed you?'

'What else could I do in the circumstances?' Isla hurled back. 'How did you think I'd feel when I found out about the second will? Where was it anyway?'

'Paulu's assistant found it in the contents of his desk… Look, sit down. You shouldn't be getting all riled up,' Alissandru framed jerkily, shaken to look at her and appreciate that she was carrying his child again, even more shaken by how that made him feel. It made him feel better; it made him feel that he had a future again.

'Why shouldn't I be getting all riled up?' Isla asked combatively. 'You withheld vital information from me. Information that I had a right to know.'

Alissandru yanked loose his bow tie and undid his collar while expelling his breath slowly. He didn't look as knife-sharp elegant and self-contained as he usually did. His black hair was untidy and lines of strain bracketed his mouth. He stared at her with glittering golden eyes. 'Where were you going when the car broke down?'

'I was hoping to find a hotel that would take Puggle but Grazia said there wasn't one that she knew of and brought me here. Then she just disappeared.'

'She's gone to her parents' for the night,' Alissandru explained and he stalked round the room, stopped to shrug and then looked at her again. 'How was I supposed to tell you about the second will? I knew it would wreck all your plans. I knew it would make you leave Sicily and that you wouldn't accept my financial help. I didn't *want* you to leave.'

'I'm leaving,' Isla told him, dry-mouthed. 'I have to deal with this situation and get on with my life. I may be pregnant but I'm not living off you unless I'm forced to.'

'*Expect* to be forced,' Alissandru muttered half under his breath while scooping up Puggle and ruffling his curly head with a wry apology for not having a treat for him. 'You see, if you're Puggle, life is simple. He trusts and likes the people who feed him.'

'I don't need you to feed me, Alissandru,' Isla said drily, while watching in surprise as he stroked her dog. 'When did you start liking him?'

He set the dog down. 'I wouldn't go as far as saying I like him yet, but he's yours and that makes a difference. He accepts me, I accept him.' He glanced at her through the tangle of his long black lashes, golden eyes bright as sunlight. 'I *want* this baby… I really, really *want* this baby. By the time I warmed up to the idea of the first baby, it was gone.'

'I didn't know you'd warmed up,' Isla whispered shakily, thoroughly disconcerted by what he had declared.

'You didn't give me the chance to tell you,' he reminded her. 'You just shut me out after the…miscarriage. I didn't think you'd believe me if I told you how I felt or that I was grieving, too. It was a loss to me, as well. I'd started looking forward to becoming a father, seeing the whole situation in a very positive light. But what restricted me back then doesn't restrict me now.'

Her brow furrowed as she tried to accept that he had felt much more than she had given him credit for when she'd miscarried. But she could not doubt the sincerity in his eyes or the husky emotion lacing his words. 'What restricted you?'

'I still had you all tangled up with Tania inside my head back then. I didn't trust you, didn't really know you. That's all changed,' he pointed out.

'Yes. But after the miscarriage, you said that it wasn't meant to be, and that really upset me,' she admitted unevenly. 'I assumed you meant that people like you and me, from such different backgrounds, don't have children together.'

His ebony brows pleated. 'Of course, I didn't mean that. I'm not a snob. I don't rate people by how much money they have.'

'You did me,' she reminded him helplessly.

'Tania cast a long shadow,' he said ruefully in his own defence. 'And I received a bad first impression of you. I didn't want to make the same mistake Paulu had and get involved with the wrong woman. That's why I left the croft so fast that morning. I wanted to stay longer. I wanted to spend time with you and that shocked me. I thought I'd soon get over it but after you, I didn't want other women. You spoiled me for them. I've only been with you since that first night.'

Genuine joy unfurled inside Isla at that unexpected assurance. She had wondered, of course she'd wondered whether he had been with anyone else before she came to Sicily. The discovery that he had only been with her made her feel much more secure. That he wanted their baby as well and was willing to openly acknowledge the fact warmed her down deep inside.

'When I stood in that empty house tonight, I was devastated that you were gone and I knew then that I loved you and that nothing but marriage would satisfy me this time around.'

It was quite a speech and it shook Isla where she stood. She blinked and swallowed hard and when she looked again he was still studying her as if she was the only woman in the world for him. 'You love me? You want to marry me?'

'You once said you wouldn't marry me if I was the last man alive. I hope I've risen a little higher in your estimation since then,' he confided with entirely surprising humility as, to her shock, he got down on one knee.

'Marry me, Isla,' he urged. 'I do love you, more than

I ever thought I could love any woman. Unfortunately you came into my life when I wasn't expecting you but having you in my life means everything to me and I don't want to lose you.'

Absolutely gobsmacked, Isla stared down at him without words, in such shock that she was reeling. 'You really love me?'

'I started falling for you the first night but I didn't realise why I couldn't forget you. So, will you marry me? I'm starting to feel like a bit of an idiot down here!' he told her drily.

'Of course, I'm going to marry you,' Isla informed him with newly learned confidence as she hauled him up to her with greedy hands. 'You love me, you want me, you want our baby…that's the biggest surprise of all!'

'A piece of you, a piece of me, maybe even a dash of my brother or even Tania,' Alissandru pointed out with only the faintest flinch at that final possibility. 'How could I not want my child? It took me a long time to get here, Isla, but now you've got me, you're not going to get rid of me again.'

Isla stood in the strong circle of his arms, trying to compute how life could travel from being totally horrendous to totally wonderful in the space of minutes, and not doing very well. 'I don't want rid of you,' she mumbled shakily, and then the tears were coming, cascading from her eyes as though she had taps behind them.

And Alissandru grabbed her up in a panic and sank down on the sofa holding her. 'What's wrong?'

'I'm j-just s-so h-happy!' Isla stammered apologetically through her tears.

'But you're crying,' Alissandru said gently as though she might not have noticed.

Isla gave an inelegant sniff. 'I think it's my hormones. I think it's being pregnant.'

Alissandru was bewildered. 'So…you're happy? You're *definitely* going to marry me?'

'Obviously.' She gulped. 'You're not usually this stupid.'

'I've never been in love before. Never been with a woman who would dare to call me stupid, either,' Alissandru admitted with a spontaneous laugh.

'Well, of course, you're going to be stupid sometimes,' Isla told him briskly, having finally mastered the tears dripping down her face. 'But, you know, you're not the only one who fell in love this spring. I love you too, but this time I thought we were only having an affair because you kept on hinting that we weren't going to last for ever.'

'That was the last dying strands of the single guy trying to stay free,' Alissandru told her with wry amusement in his gaze. 'Paulu told me once I didn't know what love was and he was right. I would forgive you just about anything…but now don't take that as an invitation,' he added with his usual caution.

'Are you really happy about the baby? How do you think it happened?'

'I haven't got a clue and don't care. I'm just delighted that it has,' Alissandru confided with warmth glowing in his level dark golden eyes.

'I'm scared that something will go wrong again,' Isla confided in a rush.

'We both are, but at least we're together now and *together* we can handle anything,' Alissandru said with confidence. 'I've got you and a whole future with you waiting for me...and I've never been happier in my whole life than I feel at this moment.'

That was quite a declaration from the once cynical love of her life and Isla rested her head back against his shoulder, struggling to accept that such wondrous happiness could finally be hers. 'I love you,' she whispered, stroking a fingertip along his shapely upper lip. 'And we're going to be incredibly good together.'

Alissandru smiled down at her with such tenderness in his beautiful eyes that her heart squeezed tight as the hold she had on him. This man with all his emotion would love strong and true, she sensed, thinking of his care for his own family. They had travelled a rocky road to their happy ending but they had both learned a lot on the journey. Her whole life was now opening up into a new dimension and the knowledge that she was no longer alone was a great source of joy to her. Alissandru and a baby too, she thought blissfully...

Almost four years later, Isla presided over a Christmas spent in London in their town house, which was filled to capacity with dogs and children. Indeed, Alissandru was talking about looking for a larger house as a London base.

'I just don't know how you've managed to acquire

four of them so fast,' Grazia pronounced, eying the four children surrounding Constantia with astonishment. 'Thank heaven, I'm only having one,' she added, patting the swell of her stomach beneath her highly trendy mint-green dress.

'Two sets of twins adds to the count,' Isla pointed out with amusement sparkling in her eyes, for Grazia, who had become a dear friend, had only married the year before and motherhood was entirely new to her. Entering an environment cluttered with the paraphernalia of *four* young children was more than a little daunting for her.

Gerlanda and Cettina had been born first—identical twins, dark haired and blue-eyed, two very lively little girls now three years old. Luciu and Grazzianu were non-identical boys and still babies, one noisy and demanding like his father but with red hair, the other quieter and more contented and dark. They had truly planned their third pregnancy although they hadn't planned on a second set of twins.

Isla's favourite photograph of their wedding sat near the fire, ring-fenced by a guard to protect the children. It showed her gorgeous traditional wedding dress, which had been nowhere near as trendy as poor Grazia had wanted to make it but had been everything that Isla had dreamt of, which was exactly as it *should* be, Grazia had said of a bride's gown. Her uncle had given her away at their beautiful Sicilian summer wedding and it had been a wonderful family day, her relatives as welcome as the Rossetti clan could make them.

It was hard for Isla to credit that she had been married to Alissandru for almost four years. While she was pregnant with the girls she had done the London course she had wanted to do to complete her education to her own satisfaction. That achieved, she had discovered that she was happy to be a stay-at-home mother with a bunch of kids and dogs because she liked to be available when Alissandru was at home. He didn't travel as much as he once had and he was always home at weekends and holidays, she thought fondly, watching Alissandru lift his youngest son in his arms and talk with apparent confidence about his feeding schedule. As if *he* had anything to do with it, Isla ruminated with amusement. They had a nanny to help and Alissandru got more involved with the fun side of parenting like bathtime and bedtime and buying toys. My goodness, could that man buy toys!

That had possibly been the biggest surprise of their marriage, Isla conceded with a tender smile. Alissandru adored kids, adored her being pregnant and wanted more. And she had told him no, four was *enough* and he would just have to content himself with four.

They spent most of their time now in Sicily and Isla could speak the language, although she made a fair number of mistakes, which she could depend on Alissandru to always correct. Sometimes, she thought ruefully, he was the most annoying man and yet if anything, after four years, he owned even more of her heart than he had at the outset of their marriage. He treated her as if she were as fragile as glass and tried to protect her from anything that he deemed prejudicial to her state of mind.

He strode over to her, clutching Grazzianu to his chest like a well-wrapped parcel. 'He's ready for his nap.'

As he bent his dark head down to her she saw the devilment in his gaze and knew that the only person ready for a nap was Alissandru and it *wasn't* a nap he meant. She collected Luciu from his adoring grandmother and they took the babies upstairs to the nursery to settle them into their cots.

'I... I just wanted to give you this,' Alissandru confessed, surprising her as he loved to do, wrapping a diamond necklace round her throat like a choker and fixing the clasp before she could object. 'You thought I meant sex,' he said piously, as if such an idea would never have occurred to him.

'It's not even Christmas Day yet!' Isla exclaimed, ignoring that crack.

'I love buying you stuff. I love that you can't say no now, *mia bella*,' Alissandru confided, tugging her close to his lean, powerful frame.

'I have more diamonds than I know what to do with,' she muttered repressively, thinking of the king's ransom in jewellery he had given her and the shelves and shelves of glorious handmade silk and lace lingerie, which she was willing to admit that she enjoyed wearing. 'But thank you very, very much,' she whispered, because she knew it was his way of showing how much he loved her and that she couldn't change him and wouldn't have changed him even if she could have done.

'But you're the most precious diamond of all,' Alissandru intoned huskily. 'I just adore you.'

And Isla smiled with the tremendous warmth that had attracted him from the very first time he saw that smile, he acknowledged thankfully. She was the centre of his world and all the sunshine in it, and the idea that he might have walked on by and missed out on what he had found with her still terrified him in retrospect.

'And you know you're loved…or you ought to,' Isla informed him, kissing that smoothly shaven jaw line, which was as far up as she could reach, thinking how different he felt unshaven as he had been at dawn and as hot and rampant as only Alissandru could be and making her equally so.

'I like to be told occasionally,' Alissandru countered, taking a stand.

'Why don't I *show* you instead?' Isla whispered, watching those stunning eyes of his light up with alacrity and smiling even more.

* * * * *

# A MISTRESS,
# A SCANDAL, A RING

## ANGELA BISSELL

This book is dedicated to the memory of Susan Chapman, aka Lily Shepherd, an amazing lady who faced her final days with strength, grace and tremendous courage.

She will be sadly missed and fondly remembered by her friends in the romance writing community.

# CHAPTER ONE

'YOU MUST LEAVE NOW, *senyorita*.'

Jordan Walsh tipped her head back, and back some more, until she stared into the face of the uniformed security guard who towered over her.

'I'm not leaving,' she told him, making no move to vacate the chair she had occupied for over two hours in the waiting area of this vast marble foyer.

The big man's eyebrows beetled together. 'You must go. The building is closing.'

The building was the Vega Tower—a great big steel and glass monolith that rose from the heart of Barcelona's thriving business district and dwarfed everything around it. It had cost one point two billion US dollars to construct, had taken two years and three months from foundation to completion, and comprised forty-four floors of bustling head office activity for one of Europe's largest and most successful multinational conglomerates.

Jordan was well acquainted with these facts because she had picked up the glossy hardbound book titled *The Vega Corporation: Sixty Years of Success* off the low table beside her and, out of sheer boredom, read the entire thing from front cover to back. Twice.

'I'm not leaving without an appointment to see Mr de la Vega,' she said.

This was not news to the security man. She had made the same request on her arrival, and again an hour ago when it had become obvious that his call to the CEO's assistant had garnered no result.

'He is not available.'

'Which is why I want to make an appointment,' she explained with exaggerated patience. 'So that I can see him when he *is* available.'

'It is not possible,' the man said, and with that he clamped a giant hand around her upper arm and hauled her to her feet.

Jordan gasped. 'Wait!' She braced her legs to resist, her flat rubber-soled shoes giving her feet a much-needed moment of purchase on the shiny marble. 'You're not seriously going to manhandle me out of the building?'

'I am sorry, *senyorita*,' he said, but the sidelong glance he sent her didn't look apologetic so much as…pitying.

She bristled at the implication of that look. It wasn't difficult to guess what he and his colleagues behind the desk were thinking. A man as wealthy and powerful as their boss must have an abundance of female admirers and hangers-on, and his staff were no doubt required to act as gatekeepers on occasion.

But Jordan was no jilted lover or wannabe mistress. 'Please,' she persisted, hating the desperate note that crept into her voice. 'Can you just call his office one more time?'

Somebody must still be up there. Sure, it was almost six-thirty p.m., but didn't working hours in Spain differ from the norm at home? And hadn't she read an online article just yesterday in which the CEO was quoted as saying he not only worked long hours himself, but expected key members of his staff to do the same?

But the guard shook his head. 'Call tomorrow,' he said.

Jordan felt the sharp bite of frustration in her belly. She'd already phoned the day before, and the day before that. Each time she'd been stonewalled by the CEO's uppity assistant. Which was why she had trekked across the city in the stifling mid-August heat this afternoon and shown up in person.

She planted her feet and locked her knees, but her strength was no match for the guard's. He started walking and she was forced to stumble along beside him, clutching her tote bag and the shreds of her dignity as he marched her towards the automatic sliding glass doors.

Her heart lurched. A few more steps and she'd be out on the street, back to square one.

The glass doors parted before them, letting in a blast of hot air, and she thought of the envelope in her bag—the letter she'd carried ten thousand miles across the globe—and a crushing sense of failure engulfed her.

All because she couldn't find her way to the top of this imposing corporate fortress to see one man.

Her body stiffened in protest. 'I'm Mr de la Vega's stepsister!' she cried out, and the guard pulled up short, surprise making his grip slacken just enough so she could wrench herself free.

Around them the cavernous foyer came to a standstill, the other security personnel behind the desk and the few office workers making their way to and from the lifts having paused and fallen silent in the wake of her outburst.

A tidal wave of heat swept up her body and into her face. Doing her best to ignore the curious stares, she levelled her gaze at the guard and said quietly, 'I'm sure neither his assistant—nor you—would like to inform him that you've turned me away.'

The man rubbed the back of his neck, his face screwed up in a grimace of indecision. Finally, he said in a gruff voice, 'Please wait.'

He returned to the desk to make a phone call and two minutes later a tall, elegant woman wearing a sleek navy shift dress and high heels emerged from a lift. She looked to the guard, who steered her in Jordan's direction with a tilt of his head.

Jordan saw the woman give her an assessing, narrow-eyed once-over before striding across the marble floor towards her.

'Ms Walsh.' Her tone was cool. 'Mr de la Vega is extremely busy, but he is willing to give you ten minutes of his time.'

Her English was accented, but good, and Jordan recognised the voice at once. She was the assistant who'd screened her phone calls and refused to give her an appointment.

Jordan forced a smile and resisted asking if Mr de la Vega was sure he could spare a *whole* ten minutes from his extremely busy schedule. Instead she offered a gracious, 'Thank you,' but the woman had already pivoted on a spiked heel and started back across the foyer, leaving Jordan to follow.

The guard held the lift doors open and then boarded with them, taking a position at the rear as they hurtled upwards to the forty-fourth floor.

Jordan's heart raced and her hands grew clammy. After all the careful thought she'd put into this, the endless days of agonising indecision, the time spent working out what she'd say when…*if*…this moment came, she hadn't expected to feel quite so nervous.

But then it was no small thing she was about to do. She had no idea how Xavier de la Vega would receive her. How he'd react. She wasn't sure how she'd react herself in his position.

She cast a critical glance at her reflection in the highly polished panels of the lift doors. In a sleeveless white blouse, khaki capris and a pair of comfy shoes, she looked plain and unremarkable next to the tall, stunning Spanish woman. Her one feature worthy of note—her long, copper-red hair—was pulled into a high, no-fuss ponytail, and the tinted moisturiser she'd rubbed into her skin that morning was the closest thing to make-up her face had seen in weeks.

The lift doors opened and all thoughts of her appearance were swiftly forgotten as she followed the other woman into a large suite of offices. They walked along a wide corridor and she was conscious of the guard trailing close behind them, of thick carpet underfoot, high walls hung with expensive artwork and a hushed atmosphere. But the escalating flutter of nerves in her belly made everything else a blur.

And then they entered a big corner office and every shred of her attention was snagged and held by the man sitting behind the massive oak desk.

Jordan had seen photos of him online. Not many, mind you. Unlike his younger brother, of whom there were literally hundreds of photos scattered across the Internet, Xavier de la Vega appeared to value his privacy. But as her breath caught and her hands inexplicably shook she realised those two-dimensional images had not in any way prepared her for a personal, up-close encounter with this devastatingly handsome man.

*And his eyes.*

Grey…just like Camila's.

Her throat thickened and she had to swallow hard and blink fast to contain her emotion.

He stood, and she was struck by his height. Six foot at least, which surprised her. Her stepmother had been tiny, her figure perfectly proportioned but petite. By the time Jordan had turned sixteen she'd easily been able to rest her chin on top of Camila's head when they'd hugged.

He walked around the desk and she saw that everything about him, from his neatly cropped black hair to his tailored grey suit and expensive-looking leather shoes, was immaculate. Even the full Windsor knot in his tie looked as if it had been flawlessly executed.

He had an air of authority about him—and something else she couldn't quite pinpoint.

Arrogance?

Impatience?

Her gaze went to the hard line of his jaw and then up to his high, intelligent forehead and slashing jet-black eyebrows.

Yes, she concluded with a touch of unease. This man

looked as if he had little tolerance for weakness or compromise.

Suddenly she was conscious of the silence blanketing the room. Of the fact that he was returning her scrutiny with hard, narrowed eyes. He didn't smile. He didn't even step forward and offer to shake her hand in greeting. Which probably wasn't a bad thing, given her hands now felt as damp as soggy dishrags.

His attention shifted to his assistant. '*Gràcies*, Lucia,' he said, his voice deep and rich and undeniably masculine. 'Leave us, please.'

He looked to the guard and said something in Spanish—or perhaps he spoke in Catalan, since she'd read that he spoke both languages fluently, along with English and French—and she tried to pretend her knees hadn't just gone a little weak. She loved the romance languages, and despite his forbidding demeanour there was something indescribably sexy about the way Xavier de la Vega spoke in his native tongue.

The guard responded, but whatever he said it only drew a terse, dismissive word from his boss, and he quickly joined Lucia in vacating the room, closing the door on his way out.

Those grey eyes—a shade or two darker than Camila's, she realised now—settled on her again.

'My staff are concerned for my safety.'

It wasn't the start to their conversation she'd anticipated. She blinked, confused. 'Why?'

'They believe you might pose a threat,' he elaborated, watching her closely. 'Do you, Ms Walsh?'

Her eyes widened. 'A physical threat, you mean?' The notion was so preposterous a little laugh bubbled up her throat. 'Hardly.'

'Indeed.' His tone and the way his gaze raked over her, as though assessing her physical capabilities, implied that he too considered the idea ludicrous. 'Are you a journalist?' he asked abruptly.

'No,' she said, trying to ignore the disconcerting pulse of heat that fired through her body in the wake of his cursory appraisal. 'Why would you think that?'

His penetrating gaze locked onto hers. 'Journalists have a tendency to get creative in their attempts to access whomever they're pursuing.'

She frowned. 'I'm afraid I don't follow.'

'You claim to be my stepsister.'

'Ah...' She felt her cheeks grow pink. 'I can explain that...'

'Can you, Ms Walsh?' His tone was hard. 'Because the last time I checked my parents were still happily married—to each other. To my knowledge, neither of them is hiding additional spouses or secret stepchildren.'

Her blush intensified. She had expected this to be tricky. It was why she'd put such careful thought into what she would say and how she'd say it if she ever got the chance. But now that she was here and he was standing before her, so much more imposing in the flesh than she'd imagined, she couldn't recall a single one of the sentences she'd so painstakingly crafted in her mind.

She swallowed. 'Um... Maybe we could sit down?' she suggested.

For a long moment he didn't move, just stood there staring at her, eyes narrowed to slits of silver-grey as if he were debating whether to have her thrown out or let her stay. Finally, just as her composure teetered on the brink of collapse, he gestured to a chair in front of his desk.

Relief pushed a smile onto her face. 'Thank you,' she said, and noted that he waited until she was seated before sitting in his own chair.

It was a simple, old-fashioned courtesy that made her warm to him a bit—until he opened his mouth again.

'Start talking, Ms Walsh. I don't have all evening.'

The smile evaporated from her face. *Good grief.* Was he

this brusque with everyone? Or only with strangers who dared to ask for a piece of his precious time?

She sat up a little straighter and said, 'Jordan.'

'Excuse me?'

'My first name is Jordan.'

He drummed the long, tapered fingers of his right hand on the top of the desk, then abruptly stopped, curling his hand into a loose fist. 'Your accent—is it Australian?'

'Yes. I'm from Melbourne.'

She paused, took a deep breath, then opened her tote bag and pulled out her red leather-bound journal. She undid the clasp and lifted the cover. The sealed envelope and the two photos she'd carefully tucked inside the journal were still there, safe and sound.

'Until recently I lived there with my stepmother.' She picked up one of the photos and held it out, her arm extended across the desk. 'Camila Walsh.'

He glanced at the photo, but no flicker of recognition showed on his face. Jordan didn't know why that should disappoint her. Of course he wouldn't recognise her stepmother.

But her eyes...

Could he not see they were *his* eyes?

'Her maiden name was Sanchez,' she added. 'She was originally from a small village north of here.'

'Was?'

A stillness had come over him and Jordan hesitated, all the doubts she'd thought she'd laid to rest suddenly rearing up again, pushing at the walls of her resolve. For the past ten days she'd ridden a wave of certainty, firm in her belief that what she was doing was not only the right thing but a *good* thing.

After weeks of feeling lost and alone, adrift, with no job, nothing and no one left in the world to anchor her, she'd booked her flights to Spain almost with a sense of euphoria.

'She died six weeks ago.'

Somehow she managed to say the words without her voice wobbling. She lowered her arm and stared down at the photo of her stepmother.

'I am sorry for your loss.'

She looked up. The sentiment in his deep voice had sounded genuine. 'Thank you.'

Her gaze meshed with his and the intensity of those sharp, intelligent eyes made her breath catch in her throat. She shifted a bit, unsettled by her escalating awareness of him. He was so handsome. So compelling. She couldn't take her eyes off him. And that preternatural stillness in his body... It was disconcerting, making her think of the big, predatory cats in the wildlife documentaries her dad had loved to watch.

She took another deep breath, in through her nose, out through her mouth, the way Camila had taught her to do as a child to combat stress. He was waiting for her to speak— to spell out why she was here. Did he already have an inkling? She searched his face, but the chiselled features were impassive, giving nothing away.

Adopting the tone she often used at work when a mix of practicality and compassion was required, she said, 'Camila was your birth mother.'

The statement landed between them like a burning stick of dynamite tossed into the room. Jordan braced herself for its impact, her whole body tensing, but if Xavier de la Vega was even mildly shocked he hid it well.

'You have proof of this?'

She blinked at him. It was such a cool, controlled response—far less emotional than anything she'd expected— but she counselled herself not to read too much into it. At twenty-six years of age, and after five years of working as a trauma nurse, she'd seen people react in all kinds of ways in all sorts of life-altering situations. Often what showed on the surface belied the tumult within.

She slid the other photo from her journal across the desk

to him. This one was older, its colours faded, the edges a little bit worn.

He leaned forward, gave the photo a cursory glance, then drew back. 'This tells me nothing,' he said dismissively.

Jordan withdrew her hand, leaving the photo on his desk. 'It's you,' she said, and it gave her heart a funny little jolt to think that the tiny, innocent baby in the photo had grown into the powerful, intimidating man before her.

His frown sharpened and he flicked his hand towards the photo, the gesture faintly disdainful. 'This child could be anyone.'

She reached forward and flipped the photo over. The blue ink on the back had faded with time, but Camila's handwriting was still legible. 'It says "Xavier",' she pointed out, and waited, sensing his reluctance to look again. When he did, she saw his eyes widen a fraction. 'And the date of birth underneath… I believe it's—'

'Mine,' he bit out, cutting her off before she could finish. He sat back, nostrils flaring, a white line of tension forming around his mouth. 'It is no secret that I am adopted. An old photo with my forename and my birth date written on it proves nothing.'

'Perhaps not,' she conceded, determined to hold her nerve in the face of his denial and the hostility she sensed was gathering in him. 'But my stepmother told me things. Details that only your adoptive parents or your birth mother could know.'

His eyes darkened, the grey irises no more than a glint of cold steel between the thick fringes of his ebony lashes. 'Such as?'

Her lips felt bone-dry all of a sudden, and she moistened them with her tongue. 'Thirty-five years ago Regina Martinez worked as a housekeeper for your parents,' she began, carefully reciting the details Camila had shared with her for the first time just a month before she had died. 'She had an eighteen-year-old unmarried niece who fell pregnant. At the time, your parents were considering adopting a child after your mother had had several miscarriages. A private adoption was arranged, and soon after you were born—at a private hospital here in Barcelona which your parents paid for—they took you home.'

And the young Camila had been devastated, even though she had done the only thing she could. The alternative—living as an unwed mother under her strict father's roof in their small, conservative village—would have heaped as much misery and shame on her child's life as on her own.

Knowing first-hand how it felt to be genuinely unwanted by one's biological mother, Jordan hoped Xavier would see Camila's decision not as an act of rejection or abandonment, but one of love.

She waited for him to say something. It was perfectly understandable that he might need a minute or two to process what she had told him. Something like this was—

'What do you want, Ms Walsh?'

Her thoughts slammed to a halt, the question—not to mention the distinct chill in his voice—taking her by surprise. 'Excuse me?'

'Money?'

She stared at him. 'Money?' she echoed blankly.

His gaze was piercing, the colour of his eyes the dark pewter of storm clouds under his lowered brows. 'It is common knowledge that my family is one of the wealthiest in Spain. You would not be the first to claim a tenuous connection in hopes of a hand-out.'

*A hand-out?* Her head snapped back as if he'd flung acid at her face. She gripped the edges of her journal, shock receding beneath a rush of indignation. 'That is offensive,' she choked out.

'Quite,' he agreed. 'Which is why I will ask you again—what do you want, Ms Walsh?'

Jordan felt her heart begin to pound. How on earth could this arrogant, imperious man be her stepmother's son?

Camila had been a kind, gentle soul, who'd always looked for the best in people despite the heartbreak she'd suffered early in her life.

Jordan looked at the envelope she'd placed with such reverent care between the pages of her journal. She'd carried the envelope halfway around the world and not once had she been tempted to snoop inside it. The letter it contained was private, sacred—the precious words of a dying woman to her son.

Lifting her chin, she looked him in the eye, letting him know he didn't intimidate her—that she had nothing to feel ashamed about. She held up the envelope. 'I came here to give you this.'

'And what is "this"?'

'A letter from your birth mother.'

'Camila Walsh?'

'Yes—your birth mother,' she reiterated.

A muscle worked in his jaw. His gaze flicked to the photo that lay face-down on his desk, then back to her. 'A claim which is, at present, unsubstantiated.'

Jordan let her hand fall back to her lap, her frustration so great she wanted to slap her palm against the top of his desk and demand to know why he was being so bloody-minded. Instead, she clamped her back teeth together and waited for the impulse to pass.

She was not someone who flew off the handle at the slightest provocation. She might have been saddled with her mother's unruly flame-coloured hair but she hadn't, thank goodness, inherited her fiery personality.

Suddenly she felt as cross with herself as she did with him. Why hadn't she been better prepared for this kind of reaction? Had she imagined that because she and Camila had been close she would automatically feel some sort of instant kinship with this man?

Sadly, she had. She'd tucked her grief away in a safely locked compartment of her heart, donned those silly rose-coloured glasses she should have learnt to distrust years ago, and set off on her mission to deliver Camila's letter and scatter her ashes in the homeland she'd left thirty-three years before.

It was the final thing Jordan would be able to do for her stepmom—for the woman whose love and kindness had helped to heal the wound Jordan's mother had inflicted years earlier with her abrupt, unapologetic departure from her daughter's life.

And, embarrassing though it was to admit it, Jordan *had* built up a little fantasy in her head—imagining herself striking up a friendship with Camila's son, having a kind of stepsibling relationship with him—which, now that she was here, seemed totally laughable.

This was not a man she could imagine having such a relationship with. Girls did not look at their brothers and feel their skin prickle and heat or their mouths go dry.

He wasn't even the sort of man she liked. In fact he was everything she *dis*liked. Arrogant. Superior. Unfeeling. A self-appointed demigod in a power suit, ruling his kingdom from the top of his gilded tower.

And Jordan knew all about men with god complexes, didn't she? She'd dated a surgeon whose ego was the size of the Sydney Opera House and then—even worse, because she should have known better—she'd moved in with him and decided she was in love.

Jamming the brakes on her runaway thoughts, she focused on the cold, handsome face of the man in front of her and made a snap decision. 'I don't think you're ready for this letter, Mr de la Vega.'

And in that moment she knew *she* wasn't ready to relinquish it—because what if he didn't treat it with the respect it deserved? What if he threw it away without even reading it?

Stiffening her resolve, she tucked the envelope into her journal, then tore out a blank page from the back, pulled a pen from her tote bag and scribbled down her mobile number. 'I'll be staying at the Hostel Jardí across town for a few more days and then I'm travelling to Mallorca and then Madrid.' She put the piece of paper on his desk. 'If you want to reach me, here's my number.' She bundled her things back into her tote and slung the strap over her shoulder. 'Thank you for seeing me, Mr de la Vega.' And she turned to go.

'Ms Walsh.'

His deep, commanding voice brought her to a standstill and her heart leapt with hope. Had he had an epiphany? Realised, perhaps, that he'd behaved abominably?

Breath held, she turned back...and her heart landed with a heavy thud of disappointment.

He was standing, arm extended, holding out the photo she'd left on his desk—the one of himself as a baby. 'You forgot this.'

Releasing her breath, she shook her head. 'It's yours. Keep it—or throw it away. Up to you.'

She continued on to the door, and for a few agonising seconds her nerveless fingers fumbled with the handle while her nape prickled from the unsettling sensation of his gaze drilling into her back.

But he didn't call her name again. Didn't attempt to stop her.

As she walked past his assistant's desk and the stunning Lucia half rose out of her chair, Jordan held up her palm. 'I can see myself out, thanks.'

Her chest was so tight it wasn't until she stepped onto the street forty-four storeys below that she felt able to draw a full, oxygen-laden breath into her lungs again.

But as she set off across the city no amount of deep breathing could lift the weight from her heart.

*Damn him.*

What was she supposed to do now with her stepmom's letter?

# CHAPTER TWO

'I'VE LOCATED THE PAPERWORK,' said Roberto Fuentes, long-time solicitor and a trusted friend to the de la Vega family for over forty years. He paused, and a ripple of disquiet ran beneath the surface of Xav's iron-clad self-control.

Xav rose from behind his desk, his mobile pressed tightly to his ear. Three short strides brought him to a thick wall of glass—one of two floor-to-ceiling panes that afforded his office in the Vega Tower a panoramic view of the sprawling, sun-baked metropolis below.

He stared blindly out at the cityscape, his body bristling with impatience under the impeccably tailored lines of his charcoal-grey suit. 'And?'

'Your birth mother's name was Camila Sanchez.'

The first cold prickles of shock needled over his scalp, even though the solicitor only confirmed what he already knew in his gut was true.

He raised his left arm and leant his palm against the window, needing to steady himself.

He didn't suffer from vertigo, or a fear of heights, but suddenly the sheer drop on the other side of the glass to the city street over forty storeys below induced a wave of dizziness.

'Xavier—?'

'I heard you, Roberto.' He backed away from the window and returned to his desk. 'Was she related to anyone in my parents' employ?'

Another heavy pause. 'With the greatest respect, Xavier... I really would feel more comfortable if you had this conversation with Elena and Vittorio. They've always said—'

'No.' He cut Roberto off. He knew what his parents had always said.

*'We love you. Nothing will ever change that.'*

And in thirty-five years nothing ever had. Not even the unexpected arrival of his younger brother, Ramon, the 'miracle baby' the doctors had told his mother she'd never have.

His parents had also told him that if one day he decided he wanted to trace his biological family they would support him in that quest. He'd never chosen that path, but he knew that if he had they would have stayed true to their word.

Because Vittorio and Elena de la Vega were good people. Good parents.

Xav had worked hard over the years to make them proud. Worked harder still to prove to those members of the extended family who'd never accepted him as one of their own that he was worthy of the de la Vega name.

As a boy, seeing how the veiled barbs and sly taunts upset his *mamá* had made him even more determined to prove he was just as good as, if not better than, any of *them*.

Years later, he still faced the same insidious prejudices—but now he had the pleasure of rubbing his detractors' noses in his unrivalled success.

No. Despite the solicitor's discomfort, Xav would not involve his parents at this point. He would shield them. Protect them. At least until he understood what—or rather *who*—he was dealing with.

He sat down at the handcrafted oak desk that had been handed down from father to son, along with the role of Chief Executive, through four generations of de la Vega menfolk over a span of more than sixty years.

'This conversation remains strictly between you and me,' he said. 'Are we clear?'

'As you wish,' the older man said, resigned but respectful. 'Just a moment…'

Xav heard the sounds of papers being shuffled before Roberto spoke again.

'Ah… I remember now. Miss Sanchez was the niece of your parents' housekeeper at the time. The adoption was private, the paperwork drawn up through this office.'

Xav was silent a moment, his mind processing. Assimilating. Finally, he said, '*Gràcies*, Roberto. I appreciate your help—and discretion,' he emphasised, and then he ended the call and immediately made another.

The security specialist the Vega Corporation kept on retainer answered on the first ring. 'I just emailed the dossier through to you,' the man said without preamble.

'Any red flags?'

'None. A couple of parking offences, but nothing more serious. She's single, a qualified trauma nurse currently unemployed. Presence on social media is sporadic and low-key. Mother lives in North America. Father's dead—and, yes, he was married to a Camila Walsh, nee Sanchez, now also deceased.' He paused. 'Without knowing what your specific concerns are, I'd say she's pretty harmless.'

Xav twisted his lips. Any man who believed women were harmless was a fool. He knew from experience they weren't. It was why he'd taken exceptional care in choosing his lovers over the last decade—and why he was being equally judicious in choosing a wife.

'And the surveillance?' he asked.

'We've still got eyes on her. She was at a dance club till one a.m. She hasn't left the hostel yet this morning.'

Xav narrowed his eyes. Jordan Walsh was an unemployed *party girl*? 'Keep me apprised of her movements.' He tapped his keyboard to bring his computer screen to life. 'I'll let you know if I need anything further.'

He put his phone down, located the email in his inbox and opened the attachment. The first section of the document covered basic stats—name, age, marital status, occupation—and included a photo: a full-colour head-and-shoulders shot that had probably come from one of her social media accounts. She was smiling into the camera lens, giving the illusion that she was smiling straight at him, and just looking at the image gave him the same visceral gut-punch reaction that he'd experienced last night when she'd walked into his office.

Right before she had turned his world on its head and then stalked out.

Over the years he'd met hundreds of beautiful women, had slept with a select few, but never had he been so immediately or powerfully arrested by a woman's looks before.

Her colouring was striking, with a head-turning combination of Titian hair and extraordinary hazel eyes which were a fascinating blend of green and gold. Her features were strong and symmetrical, with bold cheekbones, a straight nose and a wide, generous mouth.

Not pretty by conventional standards, perhaps, but stunning nevertheless.

Abruptly he sat back, irritated at his unusual lack of focus. Jordan Walsh's looks, however remarkable, were irrelevant. She was a problem to be handled—that was all. One he needed to contain until he understood what threat, if any, she posed. Just as his feelings about his birth mother would have to be shelved and examined at a later stage. He didn't have time for distractions. He had a global corporation to run. A multimillion-dollar acquisition to negotiate—a major deal that at least one member of the board would relish seeing him fail to close.

He opened the drawer where he'd shoved the photo and the piece of paper she'd left on his desk last night. He picked up his phone to punch in the number she'd written down, but then suddenly changed his mind, slipped the paper and his phone into his jacket pocket and stood.

In the anteroom outside his office he paused by Lucia's desk and checked his watch. It was ten-twenty a.m. 'I'm heading out,' he told her.

Her heavily made-up eyes blinked as if he'd said something unintelligible. She glanced at her computer screen.

'But…you have a ten-thirty meeting with the Marketing Director.'

'Reschedule it. And arrange for Juan and Fernando to meet me with the car downstairs straight away.'

Lucia gaped at him, nonplussed. 'And your video call with Peter Reynaud at noon?'

'I'll be back in time for that,' he said, because he had to be. His intended acquisition of Reynaud Industries took priority over everything.

Buttoning his jacket, he turned to go.

Lucia shot up from her chair, her expression vaguely panicked. 'But where are you going?'

'To deal with a problem,' he replied, and strode towards the lifts, leaving his wide-eyed, slack-jawed secretary staring after him.

Barcelona was basking in the heat of a blazing sun beneath a glorious blue sky when Jordan emerged from the hostel just before eleven a.m. She'd risen late and then lingered over breakfast, chatting with a Canadian guy and a young German couple who'd wanted to ask her a bunch of questions about Australia.

Pausing on the pavement outside the hostel, she rummaged in her tote bag for her sunglasses and slid them on. She had a mild headache, and her ears still rang from the overloud music in the club last night, but at least she wasn't suffering with a hangover. She'd had one tequila shot with the girls, then stuck with lime and soda water for the rest of the time.

The dancing had been fun, but the clubbing scene wasn't really her thing. She'd only gone because the two Irish girls with whom she was sharing a room had invited her out, and the prospect of a few hours of deafening music and fun-loving company had appealed more than sitting alone feeling sorry for herself.

'Senyorita Walsh?'

She looked up, startled, when she saw a burly man she didn't know in a suit and dark glasses standing in front of her. 'Yes?'

'Senyor de la Vega wishes to speak with you,' he said, and then gestured towards a vehicle sitting at the kerb. 'Please get in, *senyorita*.'

Shifting her stunned gaze from the man to the SUV, Jordan wondered how she hadn't noticed the vehicle sooner, given that it was bigger and shinier than any other in the street. Black paintwork and dark windows gave it a slightly sinister veneer, and she couldn't see who, if anyone, was sitting inside it. Another man of solid build stood by the rear door, which sat open, waiting for her to climb in.

Her heart beginning to pound, she bounced her gaze back and forth between the two men and the tiny hairs on her arms lifted. They were strangers, asking her to get into a car, supposedly sent by a man she barely knew.

She backed away. 'Actually… I—I have somewhere else to be right now… Maybe Mr de la Vega could call—hey!'

Suddenly the man's meaty hand was wrapped around her arm. Her heart tripped with panic and her brain could scarcely compute what was happening before she was tugged forward and bundled unceremoniously into the back of the SUV. She sucked in her breath, ready to scream, but the sound died in her throat as her backside landed, rather inelegantly, on soft leather and her gaze fell on the man sitting farther along the seat.

'Good morning, Ms Walsh.'

Her pulse spiked. Hastily she righted herself, dismayed to find when she looked down that her wraparound skirt had got twisted beneath her and was gaping open, exposing the length of one pale thigh all the way up to her crotch. A fierce blush scalded her cheeks.

Lips tightly pursed, she closed the offending split with an indignant tug. 'I'm not sure it is a good morning, Mr de la Vega.'

The car door closed behind her, shutting her in. Making her acutely aware of the confined space and the potency of the man whose presence seemed to fill every inch of the luxurious interior.

Breathing deeply, she willed her heartbeat to slow and tried not to look as overheated and flustered as she felt. How did he do it? How did he look so cool and refined in his immaculate three-piece suit and tie when the day was stiflingly hot and everyone else was melting?

Not that she could entirely pin the blame for her stampeding pulse and all-over body-flush on the rising mercury or the few seconds of fright his men had given her. But she would *not* think about how ridiculously handsome Xavier de la Vega was. Or how he looked not only cool and urbane in his sleek designer suit but also supremely fit and virile.

One dark brow slanted up. 'Late night?'

Striving for an air of dignified calm, she folded her sunglasses away and pushed back some strands of hair that had slipped from her ponytail and fallen across her face. 'Not particularly,' she said, crossing her fingers at the tiny lie.

Technically it hadn't been a late night but rather an extremely early morning when she'd finally collapsed into her narrow bunk bed in the hostel. As for her roomies—Lord knew what time they'd eventually crept in. They'd both still been fast asleep as of ten minutes ago, one of them lying face-down and fully clothed on top of the bedding. If the girl hadn't been softly snoring, Jordan would have felt compelled to check that she was breathing.

She lifted her chin. 'I was referring to the fact that I hadn't planned on getting manhandled into a car this morning.'

He frowned. 'You were hurt?'

For a second she was tempted to say yes, just to test his reaction, see if he was capable of demonstrating remorse, but she wasn't that good a liar. 'No,' she said, because the man who'd held her had been strong, but not rough, and the only thing truly smarting was her pride. 'But that's beside the point.'

'Which is...?'

She saw a flicker of movement at one corner of his mouth that looked suspiciously like amusement. 'My point,' she said, prising her gaze away from those firm lips, 'is that this is a rather unorthodox way of meeting. You couldn't have called me first?'

'Forgive me,' he said, but his tone and the eloquent shrug of his broad shoulders gave the impression he didn't care one way or the other whether she did or not. 'Given the way you came to my office in person last night, I assumed that you'd prefer face to face.'

*What I'd really prefer is to wipe the superior look off your face.*

The thought rushed into her head from out of nowhere, and the small surge of churlish pleasure she gained from it was quickly overshadowed by shame. She'd never hit another person in her life—had never been so much as tempted to before now. Perversely, the fact that he'd so effortlessly provoked her into thinking about slapping him only made her feel ten times more annoyed.

She considered explaining that she wouldn't have turned up at his offices as she had if Lucia hadn't blocked her calls and denied her an appointment, but she chose not to go there. She hadn't warmed to the leggy brunette, but she had no desire to get the woman into trouble with her boss.

She sighed. 'Look, I know we didn't exactly get off on the right foot—'

'Which I regret,' he cut in, his voice growing deeper, more solemn.

She blinked. 'You do?'

'Yes,' he said evenly, 'and it is something I would like to redress, if you would allow me to.'

And it struck her then—belatedly. She'd been so blindsided, so caught up in her reaction to him, she'd failed to consider the obvious. 'You believe me,' she said, not a question but a statement—because why else would he be here? 'About Camila.'

'Yes,' he said again. 'I believe your late stepmother was my birth mother.'

Emotion more powerful than she'd expected drew her throat tight. She swallowed. 'I… I'm glad,' she said, wanting to say more, so much more, but holding back. His demeanour was calm, imperturbable, but she read the tension in his clean-shaven jaw, saw the slight guardedness in his silver-grey eyes.

And she understood. It was a big thing to process. Eventually he'd be ready. He'd want to know more about Camila, and then Jordan would have the opportunity to share her memories. To talk about the warm, generous woman who'd been her stepmom and best friend for half her life.

'You must allow me to show you some genuine Catalan hospitality,' he said. 'I have a villa on the coast where my housekeeper is preparing a guest room for you as we speak. It is yours for the duration of your stay in Barcelona.'

Jordan stared at him in stunned astonishment. Last night he'd greeted her with open suspicion and barely veiled hostility, and now he was inviting her to his home?

For a moment she wondered if *she* should be suspicious of *him*.

But why?

He'd candidly expressed his regret and now he'd extended an olive branch. Wouldn't she do the same? If she'd behaved poorly, regretted the way she'd treated someone, wouldn't she make an effort to set things right?

She hesitated. Was there any good reason she shouldn't accept his offer?

*You're attracted to him!*

Okay. There *was* that small, undeniable fact. But what of it? There wouldn't be a heterosexual woman on the planet who could meet this man and not feel some level of physical attraction. And that was all it was, she assured herself. A hormone-based reaction to a good-looking man at the height of his prime.

Beyond his looks he wasn't her type, and a man who could have his pick of the world's most beautiful, sophisticated women wouldn't be interested in her anyway. Which meant those surges of heat, the pinpricks of awareness she'd experienced last night and again today, were best ignored for a whole host of reasons—not least of which was the preservation of her pride.

She bit the inside of her lip. None of this changed the fact that he was arrogant and presumptuous—as evidenced by having a guest room prepared for her before she'd even accepted his invitation!

But, no matter how impossible it seemed, this man was Camila's biological son. Did she not owe it to her stepmom to give him another chance?

If she accepted his offer, stayed as a guest in his home, they'd have an opportunity to talk properly—not in his office or the back of a chauffeured car, but somewhere more comfortable and private.

Plus, she still had the letter. *His* letter, by rights. At some point she'd have to relinquish it.

She released her lip and smiled with genuine gratitude. 'Thank you. I'd like that very much.'

The smile she got in return was no more than a brief lift of one side of his mouth, but his grey eyes gleamed with… She wasn't sure what, exactly. Satisfaction?

He gave a crisp nod, then raised his left hand to the window beside his shoulder and rapped the backs of his knuckles twice on the tinted glass.

Seconds later, as if by magic, Jordan's door swung open.

'Juan will help you with your things,' he said. 'I trust it won't take you long to pack?'

She glanced out, saw the long, trouser-clad legs and polished black boots of the man who'd 'escorted' her to the car, then looked back to Xavier. 'We're going *now*?'

His gaze was steady. 'Is that a problem?'

'Er…no,' she said after a slight hesitation. 'I—I guess not…'

She supposed it made sense. The car was already here. And she was travelling light, with a single large backpack, so she wouldn't need more than a few minutes to gather her things.

The big man with the mountainous shoulders—who seemed no less intimidating even now that she knew his name—waited in the reception area while she went to pack. The Irish girls were still out for the count, so she moved about the room quietly and left a farewell note, saying she was checking out due to a change of plans and she wished them well on their travels.

When she emerged, Juan reached for her backpack. 'Let me carry it, Senyorita Walsh.'

Although she was more than capable of carrying her own bag, she gave it up without argument. He was under orders, and she suspected even a burly, tough-looking man like Juan would not wish to invite his boss's displeasure.

'I just need to settle my account,' she told him.

'It is done.'

She frowned. 'But—'

'Please come at once, *senyorita*. Senyor de la Vega does not like to be kept waiting.'

Jordan wasn't happy about it, but she held her tongue. Arguing with the hired muscle was pointless. She would say something to Xavier, though. She couldn't allow him to pay her hostel bill. It didn't matter that she'd prepaid the accommodation and the outstanding charges had just been for a few incidentals. It was the principle that counted. And while she wasn't one to hold a grudge, neither would she forget in a hurry the stinging assumptions he'd made about her motives. The last thing she wanted to do was give him any reason to cast such aspersions on her again.

But when she got to the car, this time thanking the other man who opened the door, she couldn't say as much to Xavier because he had his phone pressed to his ear and was conversing with someone in Spanish or Catalan.

She hesitated, wondering if he'd prefer privacy, but he beckoned her in with a perfunctory wave of his hand. Then he continued his conversation as if she wasn't there.

Which was fine, she told herself as she settled back against the cool leather, carefully arranging her skirt to avoid another incident of indecent exposure. It was Friday, the middle of a working day for him. She could raise the issue of the hostel bill later.

Besides, there was something deliciously indulgent about simply sitting there, listening to that deep, molasses-rich voice of his. His tone was brusque and authoritative, suggesting the call was work-related rather than personal, but still she found his voice utterly mesmerising. And she didn't have to feel uncomfortable about eavesdropping. Besides the odd word she could translate, she didn't understand what he was saying.

'*Un moment*,' she heard him say, and translated that in her head: one moment.

Then she heard, 'Belt up,' and it took her a few seconds to realise he'd spoken in English. Another few to register his silence.

Suddenly her senses prickled. She jerked her gaze from the view outside her window to the man beside her and found his grey eyes fastened on her intently.

A jolt went through her midsection. 'I'm sorry—were you speaking to me?'

His eyebrows snapped down. 'Seatbelt,' he said, and when she didn't immediately move he made an impatient sound in his throat, put his phone down between them and reached across her.

Three seconds. That was how long it took for him to pull the belt across her front and secure the latch, yet still her pulse leapt and her breathing fluctuated wildly as she pressed back against the seat. Somehow he avoided touching her—not even a brush of his long fingers against her clothing—but his face came so close she felt the warm stroke of his breath on her collarbone and caught the subtle scents of sandalwood and something citrusy on his skin.

She swallowed—hard—and he must have heard for his gaze settled on her throat, right where she felt the frantic beat of her pulse. His eyes became hooded and for just a second, no more, his gaze dropped, skimming down the front of her white V-necked T-shirt, then up again.

Their eyes locked and something flashed in his, something hot and furious, almost accusing, that she didn't understand.

Then, abruptly, he pulled back, snapping his gaze away from her as he picked up the phone and resumed his conversation.

Dragging her gaze off his hard profile, Jordan let out a shaky breath. Had she done something wrong? Aside from forgetting to put her seatbelt on?

She glanced down and— *Oh…*

*Oh, no…*

Was that what he'd seen? The clear outline of her hardened nipples thrusting like little beacons of desire against her cotton bra and T-shirt?

Heat suffused her face. Mortified, she folded her arms over her breasts.

For heaven's sake. What was *wrong* with her? With her body? It wasn't as if she'd never met an attractive man before. Her ex, with his square jaw, dark blond hair and deep blue eyes, had always drawn more than his share of female attention and probably still did.

But Josh had always had to touch her—intimately—to induce this sort of powerful, conspicuous reaction.

If Xavier could have this effect without even touching her, what would happen if he actually put his hands on her?

She hugged her arms more tightly over her chest. Spontaneous combustion came to mind.

Which was silly as much as it was unsettling. She didn't even believe in this sort of thing. Not really. Plain old physical attraction she understood, but the much more abstract concept of chemistry…? Not so much.

Whenever she'd heard sex described with words such as *explosive* and *mind-blowing* and *electric*, she'd always dismissed them as exaggeration or pure fiction. Sex with Josh had been enjoyable for the most part, but she didn't remember ever feeling any lightning strikes of sensation or 'explosions' of pleasure. Orgasms for her had been a rather hit and miss affair—secondary to Josh's release—and on the occasions when she had climaxed it had been satisfying, but hardly a 'mind-blowing' event. And, because Josh had seemed to know what he was doing, she'd never imagined there was much more to sex beyond what she'd experienced with him.

Anyway, sexual chemistry was supposed to be a mutual thing, wasn't it? Whatever she'd glimpsed in Xavier's eyes had looked more like anger than arousal—or maybe even disgust. Which was mortifying on a whole other level. Clearly he was not attracted to redheads with modest curves and pale skin covered in too many freckles.

That conclusion was enough to douse any lingering heat—for which she was grateful. Who wanted to feel attracted to someone who very obviously didn't fancy them back?

*No, thanks.* She'd learned at the tender age of six how much rejection hurt. Twenty years later she knew better than to make herself vulnerable to that kind of pain again. She'd made a mistake with Josh, but she'd been smart enough to realise it and *she* had been the one to walk away. And although her heart had felt a bit bruised, and she'd shed a few tears, she hadn't ended up bitter and disillusioned.

She *knew* that good men existed in the world because her dad had been a gentle, loving man. She simply had to make wiser choices when it came to relationships and men.

Mr Right was out there somewhere.

And he most certainly wasn't the man sitting beside her.

Some eight hours later Jordan woke from a nap she hadn't planned on having. Memory crept in slowly, reminding her where she was, so when she opened her eyes she wasn't startled by the unfamiliar surroundings.

She sat up on the bed and noted the shallow angle of the sunlight slanting into the room, suggesting the sun had commenced its evening descent. She checked her watch and *was* startled to find she had slept for well over an hour.

She hadn't meant to sleep at all. She'd only intended to lie down for a minute or so, just long enough to determine if the ornate iron-framed canopy bed, with its diaphanous white curtains and the thick mattress layered in soft snowy linens, was as comfortable as it looked.

It was.

And she had never slept in anything so luxurious. Or so enormous.

It must have been the sheer comfort combined with the fresh air and exercise she'd enjoyed that afternoon that had sent her off to sleep.

She scooted off the bed, walked barefoot over sumptuous pale carpet to the French doors that led to a private balcony and stepped out to appreciate the magnificent view.

From here she could see the path she'd taken on her solitary walk after lunch, zigzagging down no less than six beautifully landscaped terraces to a white strip of sandy beach at the foot of the hill.

Directly beneath her lay the longest section of the wide natural stone terrace that wrapped around three sides of the villa, complete with an inviting infinity pool and the shaded alfresco area where she'd eaten the scrumptious lunch Rosa had prepared for her—which, aside from the housekeeper's brief appearances to check everything was okay and to clear away the dishes, had been another solitary affair.

She hadn't been all that surprised when Xavier had returned to work rather than accompanying her to his villa. Everything she'd read about him painted him as focused and driven, so there were probably very few things that would lure him away from his work responsibilities on a weekday afternoon.

This morning, in the car, he'd only ended his call as they'd pulled up outside the Vega Tower. 'My housekeeper, Rosa, will greet you at the villa and get you settled in,' he'd said, his tone impeccably polite, and then he and Juan had got out, leaving just her and the driver.

Jordan would have tried to chat with the man if not for the dark glass partition between them. Instead she'd focused on the scenery as they'd exited the city, her interest sharpening when, after about thirty minutes, they'd started to climb, weaving up and up through large, sloping groves of olive and citrus trees until finally they'd levelled out at a location that offered glorious views across the glittering blue of the Balearic Sea.

Rosa had appeared on the stone steps at the villa's entrance before they'd even drawn to a stop. The fifty-something housekeeper had a neat salt-and-pepper bob and a broad, welcoming smile, and she hadn't seemed at all fazed by receiving a house guest at short notice.

She'd shown Jordan her room and given her a tour of the main living areas, all of which were light and spacious and luxurious beyond anything she'd ever seen. The grounds were beautiful, too. Outside on one of the upper terraces Rosa had introduced her husband, Alfonso, who worked as the chief groundsman, and their grown-up nephew, Delmar, who was helping his uncle with some landscaping.

The whole place was gorgeous. And tranquil. A home only a billionaire could afford.

Too bad he probably spent more time at work than here, enjoying his amazing home.

Turning away from the stunning view, she went inside and took a shower in the massive en suite bathroom, and afterwards pulled on a pair of navy dress jeans and a short-sleeved white blouse. She hadn't thought to ask Rosa about the dress code for dinner, and she'd never dined with a billionaire in his home before, so 'smart casual' seemed the safest option.

After tying her hair into a loose knot at her nape, she checked the time and decided to make an appearance ten minutes earlier than Rosa had recommended. If her host was a stickler for punctuality she'd rather be early than even a minute late.

The villa was so big she took two wrong turns on her way to the formal dining room before she finally located it. Pausing in the hallway, she touched a hand to her hair, took a deep breath and then walked into the room. Rosa was there and Jordan smiled at her, then shifted her gaze to the long dining table—and the single place-setting at one end.

Before she'd fully processed the implication of that single setting, Rosa said quickly, '*Ho sento, molt*. Senyor de la Vega sends his apologies. He must work late.'

Her heart sank. After all the nervous anticipation, discovering she would be dining alone—again—was a huge let-down.

Seeing Rosa's anxious expression, however, she made an effort to resurrect her smile and said lightly, 'That's okay. Perhaps I'll catch him later, when he gets home.'

Rosa wrung her hands together. 'I am afraid he is not coming home tonight.'

She looked at the housekeeper in surprise. 'He's staying at work all night?' she said, yet even as she spoke she knew it wasn't inconceivable that someone like him would work through the night and into the weekend. He was a workaholic, and workaholics had only one priority.

'He has an apartment above his office,' Rosa said. 'He stays there often. Senyor de la Vega works very hard,' she added, and Jordan couldn't tell from Rosa's tone whether she admired or disapproved of her employer's work ethic.

She regarded the table again. Despite the fine china and the sparkling crystal, the gleaming cutlery and the beautiful vase of crimson calla lilies, the solitary setting looked rather forlorn at the head of the enormous table.

'Rosa, would it be all right if I ate outside on the terrace?'

Out there she'd at least have the birds and the crickets for company. And she could gaze out to sea and watch the sun as it sank below the horizon.

The housekeeper smiled. 'Sí. Of course.'

An hour later Jordan sat on the terrace in the gathering dusk with a full tummy and a glass of white wine, watching the sky turn to lush shades of orange and purple. She could hear laughter and snatches of conversation coming from somewhere nearby. The feminine voice she recognised as Rosa's; the male voices no doubt belonged to Alfonso and Delmar.

She pictured the trio, enjoying their own alfresco meal, and the sounds of their banter sharpened the sense of isolation that had crept over her in the last hour.

She took a gulp of wine. Was this what Xavier had intended all along? To isolate her?

Suddenly his offer of hospitality didn't seem quite so munificent.

But why? Was he somehow testing her? Had he left her up here to see what she would do? What did he *think* she would do? Pocket the silverware? Slip some crystal into her bag? Snatch a priceless painting off the wall and hightail it off the estate before she was found out?

More laughter danced through the still air and she swallowed another mouthful of wine.

She knew this hollow feeling in her chest. It was loneliness. And she refused to let it suck her down into a place of misery. She didn't do self-pity. Self-pity was a waste of time. She'd learnt that as a child in the wake of her mother's departure, when she'd realised that crying under the duvet wasn't going to bring her mother back. She had dried her eyes, got out of bed and focused on the parent she still had. She'd made herself indispensable to her father.

Because if Daddy needed her then he wouldn't go away. Wouldn't leave her like Mummy had.

Jordan shook off the childhood memories. It was history, and dwelling on the past was just another form of self-pity. The best medicine for the blues was to do something, and with that thought in mind she got to her feet, picked up her wine glass and went in search of the laughter.

# CHAPTER THREE

IT WAS CLOSE to one-thirty p.m. on Saturday when Xav arrived home—a couple of hours earlier than he'd anticipated. He grabbed his briefcase, dismissed his driver for the remainder of the weekend and strode into the villa.

He should be dead on his feet. He was operating on little more than two hours' sleep and a gallon of caffeine. But he wasn't exhausted. He was wired. It was how he always felt in the midst of a major business deal. Focused. Determined. *Ruthless.*

It put him in the perfect frame of mind to deal with a certain redhead—a problem he would have tackled sooner, had Peter Reynaud's bloodsucking lawyers not waited until six p.m. last night to return their marked-up version of the one-hundred-and-fifty-page contract. Either they were tearing every damn clause and sub-clause apart to eke out their billable hours, or Reynaud himself was hindering the process.

Furious, Xav had made his commercial and legal teams pull an all-nighter—which meant he'd had no choice but to stay as well. He never demanded anything of his people he wasn't willing to demand of himself.

At least he'd been able to focus one hundred percent on work, secure in the knowledge that his other 'problem' was safely contained for now. Offering up his villa had been a stroke of genius, and she'd played into his hands just as he'd thought she would. Few women could resist the lure of luxury—especially when the luxury was free.

All he needed now was her signature on the paperwork in his briefcase. Once executed, the confidentiality agreement would prohibit her from disclosing any information about the biological relationship between her late stepmother and himself to any third party. In return she would receive a handsome one-off payment—a sum Xav considered a small price to pay for peace of mind. The last thing he wanted was some tabloid journalist digging up the answers to questions he had decided a long time ago he didn't want to ask.

As for that one minor glitch yesterday—that fleeting moment of hot, naked lust that had struck him unawares in the car, when he'd leaned across her to belt her in and her light, feminine scent had curled around him… He'd glanced down, away from those entrancing hazel eyes and soft, full lips—away from *temptation*—only to be transfixed instead by pert breasts and hard, pointed nipples poking shamelessly against the fabric of her T-shirt, just *begging* for his attention.

Lust and fury had collided. Fury at her for tempting him; fury at himself for *being* tempted.

Subsequently, his having to stay overnight in the city had been a blessing in disguise. For a few hours he'd been able to cast her out of his head, shrugging off the incident as nothing more than the base reaction of a neglected libido.

Pausing now in the villa's double-height entry hall, he pulled off his sunglasses and waited, listening for Rosa's approach.

Nothing.

Which was unusual.

His housekeeper of ten years had an uncanny radar for people arriving at the villa—particularly her employer.

He moved deeper into the house and then stopped, canting his head.

He could hear music.

More specifically, the jaunty strains of the *gaita*—the Galician bagpipes that Rosa's husband, Alfonso, had a talent for playing. He heard voices, too. And laughter.

Frowning, he set his briefcase and sunglasses down, followed the sounds through the house and ended up standing outside the kitchen, looking across Rosa's meticulously tended herb and vegetable gardens to the staff cottage where she and her husband lived.

Xav recognised the music now—an old folk song—and it was indeed Alfonso on the *gaita*. He sat in the shade of a massive orange tree at a wooden table littered with the detritus of a group meal, his wiry chest puffing in and out as he breathed life into the old instrument. Rosa sat beside him, smiling and clapping, but it wasn't the housekeeper who held Xav's attention—it was the couple on their feet.

Alfonso's twenty-something nephew, Delmar, who helped his uncle with the odd stint of landscaping on the estate, was performing the steps of a traditional folk dance, while opposite him Jordan Walsh attempted to mirror his moves.

Xav couldn't tear his gaze off her—and it was no wonder, given the clingy tank top and denim cut-offs she wore. The latter left bare the long, slender thighs he'd caught a tantalising glimpse of in the car yesterday, before she'd closed her skirt in that prim display of modesty.

She laughed, the sound surprisingly throaty and appealing, and tossed her head, drawing his gaze to that magnificent mane of copper-red hair with its streaks of glinting gold. She wore it down today, and it flowed over her bare shoulders, thick and wavy, the ends softly curling against the pale upper slopes of her breasts.

Heat punched into his groin, swift and brutal in its intensity, and he gritted his teeth against the unwanted surge. *Dios.* His libido had lain dormant for too many months to count and it was springing to life *now*? In response to *this* woman?

She messed up her steps and laughed that husky laugh again, and then she stumbled and Delmar's big hands wrapped around her waist to stop her falling.

Xav wasn't fully aware that he'd moved—that he'd stalked between the neat borders of the vegetable patches and crossed to the cottage—until suddenly he was standing in the yard, the music had stopped and four startled faces were staring at him.

'*Senyor!*' His housekeeper leapt to her feet with remarkable agility for a woman of her age. 'We were not expecting you so soon.'

'Clearly.' His response came out sharper than he'd intended, but the way they were all staring at him made him feel like an interloper—an outsider in his own home. He didn't like it.

'Can I fix you some lunch?' Rosa offered.

'*Sí.* A sandwich will do. I'll take it in my study.' He turned to Jordan and noted with a stab of satisfaction that Delmar had removed his hands from her body and stepped away. 'Ms Walsh,' he said evenly, and she looked at him with what he thought might be a touch of defiance in her hazel eyes. 'A word in private, please—if you can spare a moment from your dancing lesson.'

Giving her no chance to reply, he turned on his heel and strode back to the villa, detouring to where he'd left his briefcase and collecting it before heading to his study. Assuming she was trailing somewhere not far behind, he didn't slow his pace or glance over his shoulder until he reached the doorway, where he finally paused and looked back— only to see she was nowhere in sight.

His mouth flattened.

*Infernal woman.*

He dumped his briefcase on the desk, returned to the hallway and cast an impatient look down its vast, empty length.

Finally, just as he was beginning to consider the possibility that she'd decided to defy him, she emerged around a corner at the far end of the hallway and, spotting him waiting, hurried towards him on those long, shapely legs. She stopped in front of him, panting a little, each breath moving her firm, high breasts up and down.

He gritted his teeth. *Don't look.*

'Did you get lost?' he said dryly.

'Of course I got lost.'

Her snapped response made him draw back a fraction. 'I was being sarcastic.'

She gave him a droll look. 'Were you? I would never have guessed.'

She jammed her hands on her hips and huffed out a breath, blowing an errant strand of hair out of her face.

'If you actually care to know, I *did* get lost. You stormed off so quickly I couldn't catch up and I took a wrong turn at the kitchen. I didn't know which way you'd gone and this place is…is ridiculously huge.'

Xav took in her flushed cheeks, the cross look on her face and her generally flustered demeanour. A sudden flash of amusement drew the sting out of his temper.

He cocked an eyebrow. 'You think my home is ridiculous?'

Her eyes widened, her expressive features morphing into a look of dismay. 'Of course not!' she blurted, her blush turning a deeper shade of pink. 'I only meant… I meant I wasn't…'

She bit her lip, which had the dual effect of halting her stammered response and drawing his attention to the lushness of her mouth—which in turn fired a pulse of heat into his groin and hampered his ability to concentrate when she took a deep breath and spoke again.

'You have a very beautiful home,' she said, enunciating her words slowly this time, as if selecting each one with care. 'An amazing home, actually. It's just that my sense of direction is hopeless and…well, the villa *is* rather…'

She fluttered her hand in the air, searching, he assumed, for a suitably inoffensive word.

'Big?' he supplied helpfully.

She cleared her throat, her cheeks glowing like hot embers now. 'Yes.'

A crueller man would have let her squirm for a bit longer, but he wasn't quite that merciless. Plus, he had no idea where this urge to tease and provoke had sprung from—or, more dangerously, where it might lead—so he was better off shutting it down. The fact that she'd already had him lurching from arousal to anger to amusement and back to arousal again in the space of mere minutes, when usually he was so adept at governing his emotions, was disturbing enough.

He motioned her into the room, followed her in and then closed the door and crossed to his desk.

'I hope you're not angry with Rosa and Alfonso and Delmar,' she said.

He turned and looked at her. She stood in the middle of the room, her colour still high, her arms folded tightly over her breasts.

'Do I have reason to be?'

She frowned at him. 'I don't know. Why are you asking me? You're the one who marched in looking as if you wanted to throttle someone.'

He *had* wanted to throttle someone. Delmar. An urge for which he could offer no reasonable explanation. All he knew was that he hadn't liked seeing the younger man's hands on her. The familiarity between them. What else besides dancing had they got up to over the last twenty-four hours?

Had she encouraged him?

Pain arced through his jaw and he realised his teeth were clenched. Relaxing his expression, he sat against the edge of his desk and crossed his ankles. Good manners would normally dictate that he offer the lady a chair, but he wasn't feeling especially chivalrous just then.

And he rather liked having her standing there in the centre of his antique Persian rug where he could see her.

*All* of her.

He could tell it made her uncomfortable and he enjoyed that—perhaps a little too much.

Maybe he *was* that cruel.

He folded his arms loosely over his chest. 'I'm not accustomed to finding my house guests fraternising with the staff.'

Her chin came up. 'Perhaps your staff wouldn't have had to entertain your house guest if their employer hadn't been an absentee host. If anything, you should be thanking them. Rosa has been wonderful—and Alfonso. They've very generously shown me some of that Catalan hospitality you promised.'

'And Delmar?' he couldn't resist asking.

*Just how generous had* his *hospitality been?*

Her brow scrunched. 'Of course. Delmar, too. They've all been exceptionally kind. I hope you know how lucky you are to have them,' she added, her tone implying that she considered him entirely unworthy of his employees' services.

*Well, well...* It seemed his little nurse from Down Under was a zealous defender of others.

Xav stilled.

*His* little nurse...?

His jaw tightened again.

Jordan Walsh was not *his* anything.

He unfolded his arms and pushed away from the desk. Time to end this conversation. He'd already derived too much enjoyment from their exchange. There was a reason he wanted her here and it wasn't for fun.

The fact that this brief exchange had not only aroused his libido but stirred a gut-deep feeling within him that Jordan Walsh was a woman of candour, who lacked the guile to harbour any sort of hidden, materialistic agenda, however, was an irony not lost on him.

Which left him...*where*, exactly? Saddled with a house guest he couldn't turn out—not without having to wage a battle against his conscience. He didn't deny he could be ruthless when a situation demanded it, but he never compromised his principles. Never took any action he couldn't justify unreservedly.

*Righteous* was what his younger brother had called him

many times over the years—usually when Xav was taking him to task over some louche, ill-disciplined behaviour.

But Ramon would never understand. How could he? His veins ran with the blood of their parents. The blood of generations of Spanish aristocracy and even royalty. He'd never had to endure those sideways looks. The snide, disrespectful comments.

Admittedly when they were teenagers Ramon *had* beaten the living daylights out of their cousin Diego, after overhearing him call Xav a mongrel, but Ramon had been just as furious at Xav for refusing to engage.

And *that* was what Ramon failed to understand. That Xav couldn't afford to lower himself to his tormentors' level. He had to be better. In every way possible. Maintaining a solid moral compass, ensuring his reputation was unimpeachable—that was what gave him the ability to rise above his detractors and prove to himself as much as to anyone else that he was the better man.

Yesterday he'd used the pretext of regret to coax Jordan Walsh into accepting his offer of hospitality. It had stretched his moral boundaries to do so, but he'd acted without compunction and would do it again. She'd been an unknown quantity, which had made his actions both justifiable and necessary.

And it wasn't as if she could claim mistreatment or hardship. He had done her a favour, surely, plucking her out of that hostel and installing her in the luxury of his home. The only reason she had her pretty nose out of joint now was because she felt neglected.

'It is unfortunate that I could not be here last night,' he said, the words as close to an apology as he was willing to offer. 'I am sure you can appreciate I have a company to run and there are times when work must take priority. You are right,' he added. 'I am fortunate to have good employees. I knew Rosa would make you comfortable in my absence.'

Deciding that now was not the ideal time to present her

with the nondisclosure agreement, he walked to the door and opened it.

'I look forward to seeing you at dinner this evening, Ms Walsh. In the meantime, I have more work to do. So if you'll excuse me…?'

She gave him a long, silent look, and for a few seconds he had the unwelcome sensation of being laid bare. As if those extraordinary hazel eyes could cut to the core of him and see all the flaws and defects that he'd secretly feared existed ever since he was a boy.

Then she blinked, and the strange sensation was gone, and in the next breath so was she, breezing past him and out of the room without a word.

As he closed the door a bitter taste formed on his tongue and his throat caught on a dry swallow.

It had been a long time—ten years, to be exact—since a woman had looked at him in a way that made him feel inadequate. The feeling, he discovered, was no less unpalatable now than it had been then.

That evening Jordan devoted more time and effort to her appearance than she had the night before, showering early so she had plenty of time to wash and blow-dry her hair, then putting on the only dressy outfit she'd brought: gold silk palazzo pants and a black satin halter-neck top. She even applied some make-up, blending her freckles with light foundation, darkening her lashes with mascara and adding a touch of cherry gloss to her mouth.

She didn't do any of it to impress Mr High-and-Mighty. It was all for her: to boost her confidence, give her an extra layer of protection—like armour—so she wouldn't feel as bare and vulnerable as she had today, when he'd made her stand in his office like a naughty schoolgirl hauled in front of the headmaster for a telling-off.

He'd been *so* arrogant. So unbearable. And so infuriatingly, breathtakingly handsome in his pressed trousers and crisp shirt while everyone else had looked hot and ragged, herself included.

His only concession to it being the weekend had been the rolled-up shirtsleeves, the absent tie and the five o'clock shadow—and even *that* had somehow looked immaculate.

Xavier de la Vega might have been born to the daughter of a humble farmer, but he was in every way that mattered besides blood an aristocrat.

*And a jackass.* At least he had been today—having a go at her for *fraternising* with his staff. She refused to believe he was such a snob that he considered the people who worked for him too lowly to socialise with. It didn't fit at all with how Rosa and Alfonso spoke of him. The few times they'd mentioned him in conversation their comments had always reflected an unwavering loyalty and a deep respect for their employer.

No. Something else must have triggered his animus. She just didn't understand what.

Sighing, she slipped her bare feet into a pair of strappy black heels.

Maybe it was just her. Maybe they were destined to rub each other the wrong way.

Which made her heart clench on a pang of regret. She hadn't imagined her relationship with Camila's son would be so…antagonistic.

Or so *incendiary.*

Because, even knowing her pride was at serious risk, she couldn't pretend those little detonations of heat that occurred beneath her skin when she was near him weren't disturbingly real.

It was all very well trying to ignore her body's response to him, but today, as she'd stood in his office and found herself on the receiving end of a very frank, very masculine appraisal, the inevitable flash of heat and awareness had been so overpowering she'd feared he would see some evidence of it.

Even more disturbing had been the trick her imagination had played on her. Or maybe it had been a trick of the light reflecting in those cool grey eyes that had, for a brief moment, made them look blisteringly hot and molten.

Then, to unbalance her completely, there'd been moments when his hostility and surliness had abated and a kind of dry, reluctant amusement had surfaced.

It was all terribly confusing.

And overwhelming.

No wonder her stomach was jumping with nerves as she made her way downstairs.

At least she didn't make any wrong turns on her way to the formal dining room tonight, having finally got the layout of the villa successfully memorised. She paused in the hallway, as she had last night, and touched a nervous hand to her hair, then walked into the room—and pulled up short.

It was empty.

She looked at the long, polished dining table. There were *no* place settings tonight.

'I thought you might like to dine outdoors.'

The deep voice came from behind her and she spun round, a hand splayed over her startled heart.

'Apologies,' Xavier said, one side of his mouth tilting up. 'I didn't mean to frighten you.'

She smiled and shook her head, even though her heart continued to race. In a silk shirt the same shade of steel-grey as his eyes, and dark trousers that hugged narrow hips and long, powerful legs, he looked devastatingly attractive. *Again.* His dark hair was swept off his forehead and he'd shaved since she'd last seen him, leaving his tanned jaw hard and smooth.

'It's fine,' she said, feeling a little breathless. 'And, yes, outdoors sounds great.'

He guided her through a set of French doors at the far end of the dining room and onto the terrace, where a table was beautifully set for two. The summer sun had begun its descent towards the horizon and the warmth of the evening was tempered by a light breeze off the ocean.

He held out a chair for her. 'Rosa mentioned that you'd chosen to eat out here last night, so I thought you might like to do the same this evening.'

She sat down, her awareness of him behind her manifesting itself as a hot, tingling sensation feathering down her spine. As he moved away to take his own seat she caught the same scents of sandalwood and citrus that she'd picked up on yesterday, in the back of the car.

'Thank you,' she murmured, feeling surprised and a little bit wary that he was being so...*nice*. She cleared her throat. 'Did you get all your work done this afternoon?' she asked politely.

'My work is never done.'

She discerned a wry note in his voice, but no hint of resentment or self-pity. He simply sounded matter-of-fact.

He lifted a bottle from a silver ice bucket on the table. 'Wine?'

'Yes, please.' She waited until he'd filled their glasses and returned the bottle before speaking again. 'Is that why you work six days a week?'

'Seven sometimes.'

He grabbed his napkin, snapped it loose and placed it over his lap, performing the simple task with the same precision she imagined he applied to every task he undertook.

He looked at her and paused, one dark eyebrow angling up. 'I take it from your expression you disapprove?'

Hot colour bloomed in her cheeks. Was she so easy to read? 'I don't disapprove of hard work,' she said, sorting out her own napkin and then picking up her knife and fork.

Their starters were already on the table: dainty salads of dark green arugula, with melon, pistachios, crumbled goat's cheese and thin, delicate strips of a cured meat. She speared a cube of melon.

'But...?'

She glanced up, straight into his piercing grey eyes, and felt her pulse kick. 'Focusing on work to the exclusion of all else isn't very healthy,' she ventured. 'Life should ideally be a balance of things—work, leisure, relationships, family…' She paused. 'You must want a family of your own one day?'

She winced inwardly as soon as the question was out. What on earth had made her ask that? It was too personal. She braced herself, waiting for him to suggest she mind her own business.

He surprised her. '*Sí*. And when I have a wife and children it will be my responsibility to provide for them.'

His words immediately conjured an image in her head of a brood of beautiful dark-haired little children, romping through the hallways of this enormous house.

*Camila's grandchildren.*

'Of course,' she said, putting down her fork and reaching for her wine, conscious of a sharp, painful pang in her chest. 'But once you've got kids you won't want to work all the time, will you?'

'I'm CEO of a multinational corporation with a multibillion-dollar turnover,' he said, in that very matter-of-fact tone again. 'I will never have the luxury of a mere forty-hour working week. Which is why I will select a wife who'll be content to focus on my needs and our children's.'

The quintessential corporate wife. *Of course.* Jordan could just picture her, too. She'd be elegant, poised, well-dressed and well-bred—because an impeccable pedigree would be a must—and, of course, stunningly beautiful. Oh, and she'd be the consummate hostess, handing off the children to the nanny while she hosted lavish dinner parties for her husband's friends and associates, naturally at ease in these sumptuous surroundings and never once getting lost in the sprawling maze of marble-tiled corridors and rooms.

Jordan swallowed a large sip of wine. The very thought of the future Mrs Xavier de la Vega made her feel horribly, utterly inferior.

'You might fall in love with a career woman,' she couldn't resist suggesting.

'If my future wife has a career she will need to juggle her priorities and ensure our children come first.' He picked up his own wine and savoured a mouthful before continuing. 'And when I marry it will be for compatibility, not love,' he said, sounding about as passionate as if he were discussing the purchase of a fridge.

The hopeless romantic in Jordan balked. Not marry for love? Love was the *only* thing she would marry for. She knew what a loving, committed relationship looked like. It was what her dad and Camila had had, and she wanted the same for herself. And children, of course. What could be more rewarding, more satisfying, than surrounding yourself with people to love and nurture? People who *needed* you?

As for expecting his future wife to prioritise her children over her career—Jordan would be hard pressed to argue the flipside of that coin. Maybe because she remembered what it was like to be the child of a workaholic parent. Knew the deep, long-lasting hurt and eroded self-worth that resulted from being abandoned by a mother who'd been more interested in climbing the corporate ladder than raising and loving her child.

No…the idea of a woman devoting herself to her children, making them a priority, didn't sound terrible at all.

'You disapprove of this too?'

She put her wine glass down. 'How can you say you won't marry for love?'

He shrugged a broad shoulder. 'Marriage is a union between two parties—not unlike a business partnership—and the success of any partnership relies on common goals and values, not whimsical emotion.'

So cold and clinical. And so wrong! Love wasn't whimsical. Love and true emotional commitment were the only things strong enough to weather the inevitable ups and downs of life.

His attitude to the contrary cast a chill over her skin.

She turned her attention to her salad, as did he. Which was good. *Safe.* Subjects they disagreed upon were best left alone.

Except Jordan just couldn't help herself. 'So…if you're always working…and you're not interested in taking the time to look for a love match…how exactly will you find a wife? Pay someone to do it for you?' she said, half jokingly—and then she saw the flare of dull red across his cheekbones.

*Uh-oh.*

He reached for his wine, took a sip, then set the glass back down, each movement unhurried. Controlled. He would have looked utterly imperturbable if not for the tiny muscle flickering in his jaw.

'Do you find that concept strange, Ms Walsh?' he said at last. 'The idea of hiring a proven professional who can handpick a shortlist of candidates whose needs, goals and desires perfectly align with your own?'

She flushed. 'No, I don't think it's strange. I know there's plenty of matchmaking services out there, and that plenty of people avail themselves of such a service. I'm just not convinced it really works. Or that it's the best way to find your life partner.'

'Is there a better way?' he challenged smoothly. 'Or do you prefer to leave your relationships to chance?'

She felt the flush spread down her neck. Just because that approach hadn't worked out so great for her so far, it didn't mean it never would. 'I prefer to think the right guy is out there somewhere, and that when the time is right I'll meet him.'

'Ah.' His lips gave a cynical twist. 'Destiny?'

'Something like that,' she said, sounding a bit prickly and hating it that she did. 'But I'd prefer *that* to choosing someone based on a clinical checklist of goals and attributes.' She sipped her wine, the crispness of the Sauvignon mingling with the sudden bitterness on her tongue. 'And if you have children?' she asked. 'If you don't love their mother will you love them?'

Xavier went very still all of a sudden. 'What sort of question is that?'

*A perfectly valid one*, she thought defensively, given that he'd declared his idea of a successful marriage was one devoid of love! His children would be her stepmom's grandchildren, and a part of Camila would live on in them. Was it unreasonable for her to want to know if those children would grow up happy and loved?

Just then Rosa appeared, interrupting the awkward moment to deliver a main course of chargrilled peppers and slow-roasted lamb. She cleared their first course plates and set out new ones, giving no indication of whether she sensed the tension between her boss and his guest.

'*Gràcies.*' Jordan managed a smile for the housekeeper. 'That salad was delicious, Rosa.'

She beamed. 'You are welcome, *senyorita*.'

Rosa left and for long minutes they each concentrated on their meal. Twice Jordan opened her mouth to speak, desperate to break the oppressive silence, but both times she lost her nerve at the last second and shovelled a piece of lamb into her mouth instead. Luckily the meat was exceptional—unlike her floundering conversational skills. But how did one backpedal from loveless marriages and children to polite, inconsequential small talk?

'Why did you become a nurse?'

Xavier's deep voice carved through the heavy silence. Jordan lifted her gaze, startled by the fact he'd spoken as much as by the question itself.

'How do you know I'm a nurse?'

'Rosa mentioned it.'

'Oh.'

So he'd had a conversation about her with his housekeeper? Or maybe Rosa had just mentioned it in passing.

Rosa had told her that her and Alfonso's only daughter was a nurse, married and working in Berlin, so Jordan had naturally mentioned that she too was a qualified nurse.

'It's the only job I ever wanted to do. Right from when I was a small child,' she said, smiling because she couldn't *not* smile when she talked about her chosen profession.

Taking care of people wasn't just what she did—it was who she was. Who she had been from the day her mother had walked out and her bewildered father had needed his daughter to step up.

'I can't remember a time I *didn't* want to be a nurse.'

He picked up the wine bottle and refreshed their glasses. 'And why trauma?'

She sat back, lifted a shoulder. 'It's fast-paced, high-pressure… You're helping people—that's the most important thing, of course—but it's also…*exciting.*'

Just thinking about it made her blood pump a bit faster. The only time she didn't love her job were the days when a patient died. Those days were a brutal reminder of the fragility and brevity of life. A reminder that you had to make the most of every moment and appreciate the people you loved, because sometimes they were gone too soon.

Xavier's voice broke across her thoughts. She blinked and swallowed down the little lump that had lodged in her throat. 'Sorry?'

'Do you work in a major hospital?'

'I did for several years. In Sydney, in one of the country's best accident and emergency departments.'

She'd loved that job. Had been so proud to work in that particular trauma centre. She'd beaten over a hundred other applicants for the position.

She hesitated before adding, 'But I resigned a few months ago and returned to Melbourne.'

'So you have a job there?'

She hesitated again. They were venturing into more sensitive territory now, but this was ultimately what she wanted, wasn't it? A chance to talk about Camila...? And yet last night she'd lain awake in that beautiful canopied bed, sleep eluding her, and in a moment of gut-wrenching doubt had wondered if bringing Camila's letter to Xavier had been an act not of kindness but of cruelty.

Because how must he feel? To have learnt of his birth mother's identity and at the same time learnt that she'd passed away and he'd never have an opportunity to meet her?

And yet what had been the alternative? To throw the letter away? Pretend it didn't exist? Jordan couldn't have done that.

She took a deep breath and said quietly, 'No. I moved home so I could nurse Camila through her final months. She had leukaemia,' she explained, a sharp ache hitting the back of her throat.

She glanced down, away from his probing gaze. She hated revealing her grief. She preferred people to see her as strong and resilient—because she *was*.

'You nursed her full-time? Alone?' His voice was quiet now, too.

She looked up and tried to gauge his expression, but couldn't tell what emotion, if any, lurked behind his silvery gaze. 'Yes.'

'That's quite a sacrifice.'

She shook her head. 'I didn't see it like that. Camila was family. There was never any question in my mind that I would nurse her when the time came.' She was silent a moment. 'Camila was so strong and brave. She didn't want me to give up my job, and was upset for a few days when I did. But I don't regret it. The time we had together at the end was special. I'd do it again.'

'A leave of absence wasn't possible?' he queried.

'No. I didn't know how long I'd need. I couldn't expect the hospital to hold my job open indefinitely. And I thought

I might need a break afterwards, anyway. Time to sort out a few practical things.'

Like the family house, which she'd spent a few weeks clearing and tidying but hadn't yet decided whether to sell or keep.

'Before Camila got sick we used to talk about doing a trip to Spain, but we never did. After she died, I decided to come on my own.'

She stopped short of telling him that she'd brought Camila with her. That her stepmom's ashes were upstairs in a small urn and she planned to scatter them into the vast blue of the Mediterranean Sea as soon as she found the perfect spot. Or that—before she had met him—she'd entertained the possibility of inviting him to join her in that act.

She sipped her wine, put the glass down and pushed it slightly away. Too much alcohol would dull her brain. And there was something niggling in her head, floating at the periphery of her thoughts. Something not quite right…

Suddenly icy fingers of realisation gripped her insides. She looked at Xavier. 'How did you know I'm a trauma nurse?'

The widening of his eyes was so slight she almost missed it. Then his expression became inscrutable. He put his cutlery down. Slowly.

A sinking sensation slid through Jordan's stomach. 'I told Rosa I'm a nurse—I didn't mention I specialised in trauma,' she added, the words scraping her throat like coarse sandpaper.

His gaze locked with hers and the look in his grey eyes was unflinching. Unyielding. *Unapologetic.*

'You had me investigated,' she choked out, and he didn't deny it. 'Why?' she demanded—but then she raised her palm in a 'stop' gesture. 'You know what? Scratch that. I already know the answer.'

'Calm down,' he said smoothly. *Condescendingly.*

Which only fanned the flames of her ire.

'Don't tell me to calm down. From the second we met you've questioned my motives. My integrity. Do you honestly expect me *not* to feel offended?' She straightened her shoulders and channelled her indignation into a lofty glare. 'You don't even know me.'

'Precisely, Ms Walsh.' A hint of steel underpinned his voice. 'I do not know you. And I will not apologise for taking precautions to safeguard the interests of myself and my family.'

She let out a humourless huff of a laugh. 'You're unbelievable.' She slapped her napkin onto the table, pushed back her chair and stood.

'Sit down,' he commanded. 'We're not finished.'

She balled her hands into fists. She could feel her anger building now, pushing at the walls of her chest, searing her veins with heat. It strengthened her backbone. Diminished the likelihood of her embarrassing herself with stupid tears.

'We *are* finished, Mr de la Vega. Or at least *I* am.'

She glanced down at her unfinished meal, at the food Rosa had so beautifully prepared and served. With a pang of regret, she turned away and strode into the house.

# CHAPTER FOUR

XAV MANAGED TO restrain himself for a full minute before he flung down his napkin with a muttered oath and went after her.

He scowled at his own idiocy. He rarely made mistakes, but he'd blundered right into that one.

Where the hell had his head been at?

He climbed the stairs, trying to recall which guest suite he'd told Rosa to put her in, and then remembered. The suite at the south end of the villa—as far from his own sleeping quarters as possible.

Finding the door shut, he rapped his knuckles twice on the wood and waited.

Nothing.

'Ms Walsh,' he called out.

He could hear faint sounds of movement from inside the room, but the door remained closed.

*Damn it.*

'Jordan!'

Pinching the bridge of his nose, he raised his fist to knock again.

The door jerked open.

Luminous golden-green eyes glittered angrily at him. 'I'd be grateful if you or Rosa could please call me a taxi.'

'No.'

Her eyes narrowed and then she whirled away and strode towards the bed, where a haphazard pile of toiletries and clothes lay next to her open rucksack. 'Fine,' she muttered. 'I'll ask Rosa myself.'

She was still wearing the outfit she'd worn to dinner, and the swish of gold silk around her long legs and the snug fit of the black top against her high, full breasts stirred the same response of masculine appreciation in him now as when he'd first clapped eyes on her downstairs.

Ruthlessly he quashed his lust and moved into the room. Jordan turned, holding up an envelope, and his gut clenched.

'I'm not convinced you're ready for this,' she said. 'But it's not mine to keep. I hope you'll treat it with the respect it deserves.'

She placed it on the nightstand, then picked up a wallet, pulled out some euros and tossed them onto the end of the bed. 'For the hostel bill.'

She started shoving items of clothing into her bag, her movements jerky and stiff. The only part of her that didn't look rigid was the long silken fall of her magnificent copper hair.

'Stop,' he said.

But his tightly voiced command fell on deaf ears.

She dropped a pair of canvas shoes on the floor, pulled off her high-heeled sandals and jammed them into her rucksack.

He stepped closer. 'Jordan.'

She paused and looked up, and for a second he saw everything in those stunning hazel eyes. Everything she was feeling and struggling to hold in: anger, disappointment, hurt.

It made his gut clench again. *Hard.*

'I think it's best if I go,' she said, her voice quiet, and then she resumed her packing.

Frustration surged and he reached out a hand and grasped her wrist. She froze instantly, her entire body stilling, and he wondered if she'd felt the same jolt of electricity as he.

Gently he turned her to face him, the pulse in the soft underside of her wrist beating erratically against his thumb. 'Stay.'

Her chin rose in challenge. 'Why? So you can keep

an eye on me?' Her tone was a mix of hurt and reproach. 'That's the reason you invited me here, isn't it?'

She tugged her wrist but he held firm, not yet ready to let her go. Enjoying the contact too much.

'I stand by what I said,' he told her, but in a gentler tone than he had used at the table. He had been harsh, more so than was necessary perhaps, but he hadn't enjoyed finding himself in the altogether discomfiting position of having to defend his actions. 'I will not apologise for being cautious.'

She made an indignant sound in her throat and turned her face away.

Lifting his free hand, Xav brought her chin back round with his thumb and forefinger. 'But I have upset you,' he continued, 'and for that I am sorry.'

Her eyes widened, although whether in surprise at the apology or at the dominating touch of his hand, he didn't know.

Whatever the cause, it didn't erase the look of stubborn pride from her face. 'You only want me to stay because you don't trust me.'

He dropped his hand from her chin, before the urge to drag the pad of his thumb across her bottom lip—to see if it felt as lush and soft as it looked—grew too strong to resist.

'That's not true.'

It wasn't a lie.

She was bold and unexpected. From the moment she'd turned up at his offices the other night, spouting the outrageous claim that she was his stepsister, through to today, when he'd come home and discovered her laughing and dancing with his staff, he'd felt as if his carefully controlled world was shifting beneath him.

And tonight… Somehow she'd turned even the act of sharing a meal into an unpredictable affair. How the hell they'd ended up talking about marriage and children and *love,* of all things—that singularly destructive emotion he had vowed to avoid at all costs—he had no idea.

Irritation had made him want to reassert control, turn the focus back onto her.

Earlier in the day, when Rosa had delivered his sandwich, he'd casually elicited her opinion of their guest, and in the midst of her effusive praise of the younger woman she *had* mentioned that Jordan was a nurse. At dinner he'd used that, and then deliberately asked questions that would trip her up if her answers didn't correspond with what he already knew from the investigator's report.

Instead he had tripped himself up, and he hadn't even realised his mistake. He'd been too spellbound. Too captivated by the enthusiasm and passion she exuded when she talked about her work.

And then she'd spoken of her stepmother—*his* birth mother—and her compassion and the sacrifice she'd made to nurse the woman through her final weeks of life had made him feel unexpectedly tight-throated and humbled.

The gut feeling he'd had this afternoon had strengthened into certainty. This woman was no threat.

She tugged her arm again and he realised he was still holding her. Reluctantly he let her go, and as she stepped back, her arms wrapping around her middle, it occurred to him he could let her go altogether. He could let her pack her bag, put her in a taxi as she had asked him to do and send her on her way. He could write all of this off as an unfortunate disruption and get on with his life.

Simple. Practical. Convenient.

So why could he feel his chest tightening and his body tensing in rejection of the idea?

Why did he feel as if he wanted to soothe the look of hurt and vulnerability from her face while at the same time a part of his mind was entertaining dark, carnal thoughts that involved dragging her onto the bed, stripping her naked and doing things with his hands and mouth that would make her forget about leaving and have her begging him instead to let her stay?

*Dios.*

Never before had a woman provoked such a tumult of conflicting urges in him. Not even Natasha, the ice-blonde American heiress who ten years ago had left him deeply embittered, determined never again to make himself vulnerable to that kind of humiliation and pain.

Clenching his jaw, he thrust her cold, heartless, duplicitous image out of his head and focused instead on the hot, stubborn, fiery woman in front of him.

'Then why?' she challenged. 'Why do you want me to stay?'

He pinched the bridge of his nose between his thumb and forefinger, then dropped his hand. 'Because right now you're the only connection I have to the woman who gave birth to me,' he said.

The admission made him feel a little raw inside, even though it was only part of the truth as to why he wanted her to stay—the only part that made enough sense to try to explain. And even that was difficult, because he'd never expected to feel curious about his birth mother. Up until forty-eight hours ago she'd never been anything more to him than a faceless, nameless woman—and then Jordan had walked into his office and shown him a photo. Told him a name. Camila Walsh, nee Sanchez. The woman who'd given birth to him at eighteen and thirty-five years later died of leukaemia. A woman whose stepdaughter had loved her enough to sacrifice her job so she could nurse her through her final days.

He didn't know how he was supposed to feel about all that. He certainly had no hope of articulating it. So he didn't even try.

'I don't think you want to sever that connection just yet any more than I do,' he hazarded instead, and watched a look of telltale uncertainty shift across her face.

Trapping her voluptuous bottom lip between her teeth, she glanced towards her half-packed rucksack, then back to him. 'If I stay,' she said, a slight emphasis on the *if*, 'would you consider coming somewhere with me tomorrow?'

Had he not been distracted by her mouth again, Xav would have registered the distant clang of alarm bells as he responded. 'Where?'

There was a pause. 'I want to visit the village where Camila grew up.'

He jerked his gaze up to connect with hers, the lush perfection of her lips momentarily forgotten.

'It's north of here,' she rushed on, before he could even properly assimilate what she was asking. 'Up the coast and then inland towards the mountains. About a two-hour drive, according to Delmar.'

His gut suddenly tensed. 'He knows—?'

'Of course not,' she interrupted, frowning at him. 'That's your personal business. I would never share that information with anyone else. I just mentioned at lunch that I wanted to visit my stepmom's village and asked for advice on travel times.'

Advice she could have sought from him instead of Delmar.

*If you'd been here.*

He clenched his back teeth together.

'Camila didn't have any living relatives left in Spain,' she went on. 'So you wouldn't have to worry about…you know… Running into someone you're related to…' She trailed off and was silent for a moment. 'Look, I'll understand if you're not interested. But I'm going anyway. I was planning to hire a car, but Delmar has offered to drive me—'

'No.' The word shot from his mouth like a bullet from a gun he hadn't intended to fire.

She blinked. 'Okay…' Her voice was tinged with disappointment. 'I understand…'

He doubted she did, because *he* sure as hell didn't. Admitting curiosity about his birth mother was one thing. Traipsing up the country to visit her birthplace was quite another. But the alternative—Jordan spending the day with Delmar…

'No,' he repeated. 'You misunderstand. I mean Delmar will not be driving you. I will.'

Her eyes went wide. 'Really?'

*'Sí,'* he said, and the smile that broke out on her face then was so radiant his heartbeat lost its rhythm for a moment.

She brought her clasped hands beneath her chin and rose on her toes, and for a second he thought she was going to do something unexpected like lean in and hug him.

Hastily he stepped back, the mere thought of her soft body pressed against his making his blood heat and that huge bed beckon enticingly.

A fine layer of sweat broke out on his skin. 'I'll have Rosa bring a tray with your dessert. Given that we'll be out tomorrow, I'll need to do some work this evening. I will see you in the morning. I'll ask Rosa to serve breakfast at eight,' he said, and pivoted on his heel.

'Xavier.'

Hearing her speak his forename in that soft, husky voice of hers pulled him up short, in spite of his eagerness to retreat.

Reluctantly he turned and she came towards him, that damned envelope in her hand.

'You should take this,' she said.

He hesitated and weighed his options. Reject the letter and risk shattering that soft, hopeful look on her face, or take it and keep the peace?

He took it.

In his study, he dropped the envelope on his desk, went to the sideboard to pour a drink and came back to his desk to sit down. He swallowed a mouthful of brandy and shifted his gaze from the envelope to the manila folder containing the confidentiality agreement he'd left out in readiness on the corner of his desk.

A clear vision filled his head of Jordan ripping the document into pieces and hurling them in his face.

He finished his brandy in one large gulp, then grabbed the folder and shoved it into a drawer, slid the envelope in after it and slammed the drawer closed.

*One day*, he told himself as he opened his laptop and made a start on his emails.

One day he would read the letter his birth mother had written to him.

But not tonight.

The scenery along the stretch of coastline known as the Costa Brava was breathtaking. Jordan had grown up in a small coastal township south of Melbourne, so she was used to ocean and beaches, but the glittering shores of the Mediterranean were in a different class altogether. Each time the sleek convertible powered around another bend, and a new stunning vista opened up before them, she couldn't suppress a little gasp of awe.

Another one caught in her throat now, and Xavier glanced over from the driver's seat.

'Spectacular, *si*?'

*He* was spectacular. As riveting as the scenery in faded jeans and a loose-fitting white shirt with an open collar and rolled-up sleeves. Stubble shaded his jaw and she liked this edgier look on him. He wore dark sunglasses, and his thick black hair was deliciously ruffled thanks to the car's open top.

Every time she looked at him her breath went a little choppy, but it was the moments when he smiled—when his mouth loosened and those deep, attractive grooves appeared in his lean cheeks—that her breath was snatched away completely.

'Stunning,' she agreed, and with an effort peeled her gaze off him and looked out of her side of the car, feeling slightly giddy as she peered down the steep pine-covered cliffs that plunged into the sparkling blue water below.

She'd woken this morning with a tiny glow of optimism in her chest that she was determined to cling to as tightly as she could.

Last night when she'd stormed away from the table she'd been so mad at Xavier, and so determined to leave. She'd felt hurt and exposed, and she'd wanted to stay angry at him, but he'd made it so difficult—or at least that was what she'd told herself as she'd climbed into that gloriously comfortable bed and felt a stab of guilty relief that she wasn't climbing into a narrow bunk in a hostel room shared with strangers.

But the truth was she had been a hopeless push-over, losing the battle from the moment he touched her, when the anger pulsing in her veins had morphed into a very different sort of heat.

And then he'd tipped up her chin and said he was sorry. That the word *sorry* even existed in his vocabulary should have shocked her, but she'd barely noticed the apology. She'd been too distracted. Too busy watching him look at her mouth and too stunned by the knowledge of what she was witnessing in his eyes.

Heat.

*Desire.*

Hot, prickling awareness had washed over her, settling in the pit of her belly and leaving traces of heat long after he'd left the room.

This morning, as she'd made her way down to breakfast, which Rosa had laid out buffet-style on the terrace, her pulse had still pounded unevenly and she'd wondered what she should do with that knowledge.

Ignore it?

Pretend she hadn't noticed?

Try to forget that she'd lain in that big bed last night and dreamt of shocking, inappropriate things that were guaranteed to make her blush furiously when she next saw Xavier?

*Easier said than done.*

And, yes, heat *had* swarmed her face—along with other, less visible parts of her body—when she'd walked onto the terrace and found him already there, sitting at the table with his long legs stretched out in front of him and his dark hair and bronzed olive skin gleaming in the sun.

He'd held an espresso cup in one hand and a palm tablet in the other. As she'd approached he'd looked up and said, *'Buenos días.'* Then he'd enquired how she'd slept and poured her a cup of eye-wateringly strong coffee.

It had all been perfectly polite and pleasant, and that was all. There'd been no heated looks. No lingering gazes. Nothing to suggest that he hadn't walked out of her room last night and either forgotten the moment instantly or dismissed it as being of no significance.

And it was a relief. Really, it was. She hadn't come to Europe looking for a holiday fling, even if her friend Ellie *had* said that it was precisely the kind of liberating, no-strings fun she needed after enduring the toughest few months of her life.

No. She was taking a month to travel, with a list of things to do and see, and then she was going back to Australia to build a new life, since most of her old one was, sadly, now gone.

Anyway… If she were looking for a holiday romance she wouldn't be setting her sights on a man who was as arrogant as he was sexy—and who happened to be her stepmom's son!

The car swept around another bend and she shifted to look at the satnav on the dash.

'Another hour,' Xavier said. 'If you want a drink or a restroom there's a town a few miles ahead.'

'No. I'm fine, thanks. Unless you need a break…?'

'I'm good.'

His eyes were focused on the road, so she let her gaze linger on him for a bit. Just because their relationship would only ever be platonic, at best, it didn't mean she couldn't appreciate that he was a magnificent-looking man.

He looked totally at ease in the driver's seat of the Aston Martin—as competent and self-assured at the wheel of this sleek, powerful machine as he was at the helm of his family's multibillion-dollar business.

Jordan wasn't a car enthusiast by any stretch, but she had to admit that this morning, when Xavier had driven the shiny silver sports car out of its garage into the sunshine, and then lowered the roof, the prospect of riding in the luxurious convertible with the top down had sparked a tiny thrill of excitement.

'What, Jordan?'

His deep voice startled her from her thoughts and at the same time sent a shiver racing across her skin. Before last night she'd wished he would call her by her first name; today she wished he wouldn't. Something about the way his mouth framed the word, combined with the sound of his rich, accented baritone stroking over the syllables, was altogether too…*sensuous.*

'What?' she returned innocently.

'You were looking at me.'

Her face heated. 'You're looking at the road. How can you possibly know what I'm looking at?'

The muscle at the corner of his mouth flickered, hinting at amusement, and her pulse leapt in her veins. They were both making an effort to get along today, and even though the light mood felt a bit forced it was ten times better than the way things had been between them yesterday.

A part of her was still astonished that he'd agreed to come with her. Last night her heart had clenched at hearing him finally admit that knowing who his birth mother had been meant something to him, but a niggle of doubt had made her wonder if he'd just been telling her what he thought she wanted to hear. Asking him to do this trip with her had been a challenge—a test of sorts—to see if his curiosity about Camila was genuine.

'What were you thinking?' he asked now.

'How do you know I was thinking anything?' she countered, feeling a tug at the corners of her own mouth.

Every now and again over the last two hours they'd slipped into a comfortable banter which she was finding dangerously addictive. Xavier in a bad mood was formidable; in a good mood he was downright lethal.

He glanced at her. 'There's always something going on in a woman's mind.'

She pushed her sunglasses up the bridge of her nose. 'That's because we're highly intelligent.' And then, realising she'd just cornered herself with that statement, she added, 'If you must know, I was thinking you look remarkably relaxed today.'

'"Remarkably"?'

She shrugged. 'You know what I mean.'

'No,' he said smoothly. 'Enlighten me.'

She shot him a sidelong glance. 'Well…you're not exactly the most laid-back person in the world.'

A sharp, narrow bend loomed ahead and he slowed and shifted gears. 'Is that your way of sugar-coating what you really want to say?'

They rounded the bend and he accelerated out of it onto a long, straight stretch of road.

'That's my way of being polite.'

'And the less polite version?'

She clamped her lips together.

'Jordan?' He pressed her with a look.

She held out for a few seconds more, then capitulated with a sigh. 'Fine. You're a chronic workaholic. Which means you're *not* relaxed most of the time. You're uptight, probably have a skewed set of priorities, and you would benefit from taking a chill pill once in a while.'

'A "chill pill"?'

'Metaphorically,' she clarified. 'I don't condone recreational drugs.'

She saw the muscle in his cheek flicker again, and it suddenly annoyed her that he seemed to find her amusing when she wasn't trying to be.

'Should I brace myself for another lecture on work/life balance?'

Feeling a touch defensive now, she lifted her chin and pointed out, 'You *did* ask. And, if I recall correctly, you're the CEO of a global corporation with a multibillion-dollar turnover who doesn't have the luxury of a mere forty-hour working week,' she said, quoting his spiel from last night back to him verbatim. 'I suspect any lectures on work/life balance would be completely wasted on you.'

His lips quirked again, and for one pulse-hitching moment she thought he was going to break into one of those lethal smiles that were guaranteed to leave her breathless.

Then he cast her another look and his mouth suddenly flattened. The car decelerated so rapidly her stomach pitched.

She braced her hand on the door as he braked to a stop on the hard shoulder of the road. 'What's wrong?'

He pulled his sunglasses off, his gaze narrowing on her face. 'You said you were wearing sunscreen.' His voice was a low, accusatory growl.

She frowned. 'I am.'

He jabbed a button on the console and the car's roof emerged from its housing.

She made a sound of dismay as it closed over their heads, blocking out the glorious sunshine. 'Why did you do that?'

'Your nose is sunburnt.'

'Oh.' *Was that all?* She shrugged a shoulder. 'That will teach me for buying the cheap stuff—' she touched her forefinger to the end of her nose '—and for having a big nose,' she joked.

His mouth thinned. 'Your nose is perfect.' He pushed his

sunglasses back on and set the car in motion again. 'And you have beautiful skin,' he said gruffly. 'You should protect it.'

A burst of warmth flared in Jordan's chest at the unexpected compliments, despite how tersely they'd been delivered. She willed herself not to blush, but felt the colour rise in her cheeks regardless.

'Look who's lecturing now,' she said lightly, attempting to cover her silly overreaction to a couple of abrupt remarks. 'It's kind of nice, though,' she added, settling back against the seat and casting him a sideways glance, 'you being all…protective. When I was little I used to dream of having a big brother who'd look out for me.'

His jaw tightened. 'Jordan…' he warned in a low, gravelly rasp that should have deterred her but instead sent a hot quiver through her belly.

Catching her tongue between her teeth, she bit down— literally—on the reckless impulse to see how far she could push him in this mood. Chances were his growl was worse than his bite. But she wasn't quite brave enough to find out.

An hour later Xav leaned against the side of his car, ankles crossed, arms folded over his chest, his mind stuck on a single word like a turntable needle stuck on scratched vinyl.

*Protective.*

He clenched his jaw. If what Jordan provoked in him was protectiveness, it sure as hell wasn't of the brotherly variety.

*Dios.*

The sibling reference had been nothing more than a taunt, surely? She couldn't possibly be oblivious to the fact that the subtle, provocative two-way baiting and constant simmering tension between them was sexual chemistry.

When she had strolled onto the terrace this morning, wearing a stretchy yellow-and-white-striped dress that was little more than a thigh-length T-shirt, the hot surge of reaction in his gut had been anything but *brotherly*.

With her flame-coloured hair swept into a high, bouncy

ponytail, her long legs smooth and bare and her feet encased in cute white tennis shoes, she'd looked like a burst of summer sunshine. A sexy, irresistible package of ebullience and warmth.

He'd known in that moment this trip was a bad idea, but he wasn't a man who reneged on his promises. And, while he'd avoided analysing too deeply his feelings about what they were doing today, he wasn't insensitive to the fact that visiting this village where he now stood, in the green forested foothills of the Catalan mountains in the middle of nowhere, meant something to Jordan.

Truth be told, he'd enjoyed their journey up the coast. When was the last time he'd put the top down on his sports car and hit the open road? For that matter, when was the last time he had driven instead of *being* driven? He employed a driver because travelling in a chauffeured vehicle allowed him to work while on the road, but he hadn't realised how much he'd missed getting behind the wheel.

And when had he last consciously appreciated the natural beauty of the Costa Brava, or even his own private slice of the coastline, other than via the window of his jet when he flew in and out of the country on business?

Throw a beautiful woman into the mix—even one who pushed his buttons at every turn—and the result had been a blood-pumping exhilaration that was different from the adrenalin rush he derived from the day-to-day cut and thrust of the business world.

But when they had turned inland his pleasure had begun to evaporate, dwindling with each kilometre that had brought them closer to this dull, isolated backwater.

As he'd parked at the foot of an ancient cobblestoned street, a sobering, unwelcome revelation had struck.

*This* was the place his biological roots could be traced back to. This sleepy, remote village that looked as if it had got permanently stuck in some bygone era.

He suppressed a shudder.

Even as a boy, given to fleeting bouts of curiosity about his biological parents, he'd not once imagined his beginnings to be so…*inauspicious*. As a teenager he'd stopped wondering altogether—any shreds of curiosity ruthlessly crushed, his focus one hundred percent on proving himself worthy of the name he carried to this day with a fierce sense of loyalty and pride.

A feeling of claustrophobia pressed down like a suffocating weight on his chest, and he wanted to climb into his car and floor the accelerator until the village was nothing more than a distant, inconsequential speck in his rear-view mirror.

Except he couldn't. Because Jordan wasn't with him and he didn't know where the hell she'd gone.

He pushed away from the vehicle. He shouldn't have let her wander off alone. By her own admission her sense of direction was non-existent. But when they'd arrived he'd checked his phone and found two missed calls from his brother and a voicemail mentioning Peter Reynaud.

He'd stayed in the car to call Ramon and Jordan had stepped out to give him privacy, stating she was going to stretch her legs.

He'd not seen her since.

He stared up the street. His conversation with Ramon hadn't lightened his mood. His brother had got wind of a competitor sniffing around Reynaud's assets. It renewed Xav's suspicions that Reynaud was intentionally stalling their deal.

Voices caught his attention and he glanced up the street to see a middle-aged couple in hiking gear emerging from a small general store. They disappeared down a lane and then the street was empty again.

Blowing out a frustrated breath, he pushed away from the car and started up the street. He'd taken no more than two steps, however, when Jordan bounded out of the store onto the cobblestones and turned in his direction. He stopped and she hurried towards him, her features animated.

'Xavier!'

The impact of her smile combined with the breathless, eager way she said his name made a pulse throb in his groin.

She halted in front of him. 'You won't believe this.'

He almost snorted. If he'd learned anything about this woman over the last couple of days it was to expect the unexpected. Someone should tattoo a warning across her forehead: *Beware: unpredictable.*

He looked into her upturned face. 'What?'

'The couple who own the store knew Camila,' she announced, her eyes, with those extraordinary striations of amber and green, sparkling up at him. 'Can you believe that? They were childhood friends until Camila went to Australia and they lost touch. They're lovely…'

She sank her teeth into her bottom lip and Xav braced himself for whatever was coming.

'They've invited us to lunch.'

A different sort of tension that had nothing to do with desire gripped his insides.

'Please say yes,' she said in a rush, before he could get out a word. 'They won't know that you're related to Camila. I simply told them I'm with a friend.' She stepped closer, latching those big, beautiful eyes onto his. 'Please, Xavier,' she entreated. 'It'd be rude to refuse. And it would mean so much to me.'

*Dios.* Why did he find it so damned difficult to say no to this woman?

He glanced over his shoulder at the car. For a second he very seriously considered picking her up and throwing her in, locking the doors and driving the hell out of there.

He looked back to Jordan.

Her hands were clasped under her chin now and she looked impossibly cute. Infuriatingly irresistible.

He dragged his palm over his jaw. Expelled a heavy breath. *Damn it.*

'Fine,' he said. 'One hour. No more. And Jordan…?' He

waited for her to stop bouncing on her feet and pay attention. 'They do *not* learn about my relationship to Camila. Understood?'

She gave a vigorous nod. And then, without warning, she stood on tiptoes and pressed a kiss to his cheek. 'Thank you,' she said, her voice low and husky, a touch breathless again.

Xav answered with a grunt and then quickly stepped back, his jaw locked.

'Xavier?'

Somehow he managed to keep his eyes off the lips he now knew were every bit as lush and petal-soft as they looked. *'Sí?'*

'You're scowling.'

He wasn't scowling. He was *concentrating*. Attempting through sheer will to prevent the sudden heat that had lanced his belly from infiltrating other, more visibly reactive parts of his anatomy.

With effort he unclenched his teeth. Ironed out his features. 'Better?'

She tilted her head to the side. 'A bit. Just…smile,' she suggested. 'Try to look friendly.'

She turned and started back up the street, her ponytail swinging like a bright copper pendulum between her shoulder blades, drawing his gaze inexorably downwards to the jaunty swing of her rounded hips and tight buttocks in the short, clingy dress.

His jaw locked again.

*Madre de Dios.*

Give him five minutes alone with her, he thought darkly, and he'd show her *friendly*.

# CHAPTER FIVE

TWO HOURS LATER Jordan sat in the shade of a pergola in Maria and Benito Gonzalez's quaint cottage garden, looking through the pile of photos that Maria had brought to the table with a tray of coffee and sweet treats to finish their meal.

The men had finished their coffee and disappeared fifteen minutes earlier. Benito had asked if he could look at the Aston Martin, having noticed the car through the shop window when they'd first driven into the village.

Xavier had gone one better and offered to take him for a short spin.

Jordan's insides had melted a tiny bit. She'd almost wanted to hug him. For his kindness to the older man. For letting her do this. For keeping the scowl off his face and remembering to smile every now and again.

'You all look so young,' she said, studying an old wedding photo. 'And you and Camila both look so beautiful, Maria.'

Sitting beside her at the table, Maria smiled. 'Mila was beautiful *and* clever. She altered my mother's wedding dress for me and made her own bridesmaid dress.'

Jordan nodded. 'She made my high school graduation gown from a picture I took out of a magazine.'

The memory made her smile. She'd loved that gown. It was the prettiest thing she'd ever worn up until then. Her dad had got all choked up and said she was beautiful, and then she'd cried too, and so had Camila, and they'd all laughed at themselves for being so soppy.

'She made another for my nursing graduation ball.'

Maria reached over suddenly and squeezed Jordan's

hand. '*Ho sento molt*. I am so sorry for your loss, *filla el meu*. And so very sorry that I will not see my friend again.'

Jordan's throat drew tight. '*Gràcies*, Maria. I know that one of Camila's greatest regrets was not having visited her homeland again.'

Maria shook her head. 'No one expected her to come back. I am sad we lost touch, but I was happy for Mila when she left and made a new life for herself. She was never quite the same…after she gave up her child.'

Jordan gave a little start of surprise. Maria had talked about Camila over lunch, sharing light-hearted anecdotes from their childhood, but she'd made no reference to her friend's teenage pregnancy—until now.

Seeing the older woman's gentle expectant expression, Jordan said slowly, 'You knew that I knew?'

'*Sí…*'

Maria reached into her cardigan pocket and withdrew a photo she'd obviously kept back from the rest. She held it out and Jordan took it, and her heart started to thump against her ribs.

The young couple in the snapshot were sitting on a sandy beach. They both wore swimming costumes, had wet hair and wide smiles, and their arms were wrapped around each other.

'Oh, my goodness…' Jordan's throat constricted. 'Camila looks so happy…so…' *In love*. 'And he…'

She trailed off. The handsome, dark-haired young man who was staring with obvious affection at the girl sitting on his lap looked just like— *Oh, God.* She bit her lip.

'He looks like your friend, *sí*?'

The resemblance was striking. It might almost have *been* Xavier in the photo.

Jordan couldn't disguise her stricken expression. 'Oh, Maria…' she breathed. 'Please don't say anything to him.'

Maria gave her hand another firm squeeze, offering reassurance. Understanding. 'I am an old woman who is very good at keeping secrets—and minding her own business,' she added.

Jordan looked at the photo again. Camila had said so little about Xavier's father, and Jordan had sensed the subject stirred great sadness in her stepmom so she hadn't pressed.

'Do you remember his name?'

'*Sí.* Tomás.'

Jordan's own dad's name had been Tom. It was a funny little coincidence that meant nothing, but it made her smile. 'Can you tell me what you know about him?'

Maria nodded. 'Of course...'

Ten minutes later the men returned, Benito wearing a smile on his weathered face that stretched from ear to ear.

Maria offered more coffee, but after a quick glance at Xavier Jordan politely declined. They'd been there for two and a half hours already—an hour and a half longer than he'd wanted to stay.

She helped Maria take the cups and plates back to the kitchen. When they were alone, Maria pressed the photo of Camila with Xavier's biological father into Jordan's hand.

Jordan's eyes widened. 'Oh, no... Maria, I couldn't.'

'*Sí.* Please,' the older woman insisted. 'I want you to have it. You have given me a gift today—to hear about Mila's life in Australia and know that she found happiness.' She smiled, even as her eyes grew bright with moisture. 'I think she was lucky to have such a wonderful daughter—and I think she would have been proud to see what a fine man her son grew into, *sí*?'

Her own eyes stinging, Jordan hugged her. '*Gràcies*, Maria.'

Minutes later she and Xavier were back in the car and the Gonzalezes had reopened their store.

She fastened her seat belt and her chest felt incredibly tight, as if there was so much emotion expanding inside her she would either have to express some of it or burst.

She put her hand on Xavier's arm before he could start the car, then pulled her hand away as soon as she had his attention, the brief contact with warm skin and crisp masculine hairs leaving her fingertips tingling.

'Thank you,' she said, her voice a little husky. 'That really meant a lot to me. I know we stayed longer than you wanted to—'

'It's fine,' he interrupted, turning his attention away from her to start the car.

'I also realise the situation must have felt a little…weird for you—'

'Jordan.' He cut her off again as he revved the engine. 'I said it's fine.'

She sat back, trying not to feel stung as he navigated them out of the narrow streets of the village and onto the long road that would take them back to the coast through a thick swathe of dark green pine forest.

But it was hard to smother her disappointment completely.

Deep down she'd hoped he too might feel as if the experience had been special, in spite of any understandable discomfort. The chance to sit down with people who'd known his birth mother during her early life, to hear stories that would build a picture of her in his mind… Surely it had made him feel something? Something other than *fine*?

They drove in silence, but Jordan's mind was anything but quiet. Her thoughts spun, veering between her conversation with Maria, the photo in her bag and the fact that Xavier's mood was much more brooding than it had been before lunch.

Finally the silence got to be too much. 'Have you ever wondered about your biological father?'

He sent her a look she couldn't read, and then took so long to respond she thought he wasn't going to answer her at all.

'Not since I was a boy.'

Conscious of the sudden nervous patter of her pulse, she ventured, 'If you had the opportunity to find out who he was, would you?'

'No.'

There hadn't been even a split-second of hesitation.

'Really? Why not?'

Another long pause. Then, 'You mean why would I not want to find a man who got a teenage girl pregnant and failed to take responsibility for his actions?' He adjusted his grip on the steering wheel. 'I would think the answer to that is obvious.'

'Maybe he was just a teenager himself,' she suggested.

'Doesn't matter. If a man is old enough to sleep with a woman, he's old enough to take responsibility for the consequences.'

Jordan thought about what Maria had told her. It *was* possible that Xavier's birth father had deserted Camila. It was also possible he'd never known she was pregnant and that his family had conspired to keep the young lovers apart.

'But what if—?'

'Enough, Jordan.' He spoke tersely. 'Leave it alone. This is not your business.'

The rebuke nettled. As did the implication that she was meddling in affairs that didn't concern her. 'Camila was my stepmother,' she said quietly.

'And my birth mother.' He gritted out the admission, as though he found the truth of it distasteful. 'Who was also foolish and irresponsible.'

Jordan gasped. 'That's not fair! You can't judge and condemn people when you don't have all the facts.'

'The facts don't matter.'

His white-knuckled grip on the steering wheel and the hard jut of his jaw told her he was angry now. But so was she.

'Of course they matter. How else will you understand what happened?'

'Understanding what happened won't change the outcome, or the present. The past is irrelevant.'

She looked at him, aghast. 'How can you say that? It's your own history—'

'Exactly,' he bit out. '*History*. Done and dusted. I have no interest in the past.'

Stunned into silence, she studied the severe lines of his profile for a moment, running her gaze from the black slash of his eyebrow to the proud ridge of his nose and down over the lean terrain of cheekbone and jaw—the same hard, exquisitely sculptured jaw she'd impulsively kissed on the street and then wished she hadn't when a blast of heat and longing had sizzled right through to her core.

She swallowed. She didn't want to kiss him now. She wanted to grab those big shoulders of his and shake the arrogance out of him.

She turned her head away, looked out of her window and managed to hold her tongue for the next forty minutes. Only when Xavier's mobile phone rang for a third time in quick succession did the urge to speak get the better of her.

'Maybe you should stop and take that,' she said, continuing to look out of her window. 'No doubt it's a work call.'

She heard him draw a sharp breath.

'*Sí*. We will need to stop.'

She expected him to pull over straight away, on the side of the road, but he drove on for ten minutes towards the coast, to a small, sunny seaside town where a beautiful church and pretty whitewashed buildings huddled around a sandy bay.

As soon as he'd parked up she said, 'I'll stretch my legs,' and stepped out of the car with a sense of *déjà vu*.

She'd done the same thing back in Camila's village, giving him privacy to make a phone call. Heaven forbid the CEO of the Vega Corporation should take a *whole* Sunday off!

'Don't go far,' he called from the driver's seat, and she

slammed the door, saving herself from having to respond to his bossy instruction.

She jammed her sunglasses on and looked around. Whether by chance or design, he'd chosen a spot that gave her a choice of shops and cafés in one direction and a beach in the other.

The beach beckoned, and the instant she took off her shoes and sank her toes into the silky-soft sand her spirits lifted. It was a gorgeous spot, and not overcrowded, with sunbathers and swimmers enjoying themselves without having to compete for their own piece of sea or sand.

She walked a short distance and was tempted to sit down and linger, but the sun was fierce and she didn't have her sunhat. She'd be better off sitting in the shade of a café awning.

She retraced her steps and then bent down to brush off her feet and slip her sneakers back on. She had just finished tying her laces when a football hurtled up the beach towards her, a tall, shirtless young man in hot pursuit. Automatically she stuck her foot out to stop the ball and its pursuer skidded to a halt in front of her.

'*Gràcies.*'

He stooped to retrieve the ball, and as he straightened his gaze travelled up her body, taking her in with unabashed interest from her ankles to her face. He grinned at her and she couldn't help but grin back. He had the ripped physique of a man but she guessed he was in his late teens, and he was hardly threatening.

'*No hay problema,*' she said, borrowing a phrase she'd heard Rosa use.

Her young admirer cocked his head, long dark hair flopping in his eyes. 'You are English?'

'Australian.'

'Ah. Home of koalas and kangaroos, *sí*?'

She laughed. 'Yes.'

His grin broadened. 'And beautiful women.'

She laughed again, shaking her head at his cockiness.

He glanced over his shoulder to where his friends—a group of fit-looking young men and bikini-clad girls—stood waiting for him to bring back the ball. 'You would like to come and play, *bonic*?'

Amused, she opened her mouth to decline, but just then a shadow fell across the sand and her nape prickled with awareness.

'Jordan.'

She stilled at the sound of Xavier's deep voice behind her. How had she known it was him before he'd even spoken?

He came and stood close beside her and the prickling awareness migrated to other parts of her body.

'Is everything all right?'

She glanced at him, registered the dark scowl on his face and felt annoyed with him all over again for dampening her day with his bad attitude.

'Perfectly,' she said breezily.

'Then let's go.'

The command—and his obvious expectation that she'd obey—only stirred her anger. A reckless urge gripped her to push back and get under his skin somehow.

She looked at the younger man and shrugged. 'My brother,' she said, on a heavy sigh. 'He can be a little—' she rolled her eyes '—*overprotective.*'

He glanced from her to Xavier, looking confused, no doubt due to the lack of physical resemblance. He took in Xavier's powerful form, the aggressive stance, then backed away, firing a rueful shrug at Jordan. 'Another time, *preciosa.*'

Jordan waved her fingers at him and then, her bit of mischief complete, strode past Xavier and back along the footpath to the car, ignoring him as much as it was possible to ignore the presence of a thundercloud at one's back.

She reached for the door handle, but her fingers had barely brushed the metal before her wrist was seized and she was spun around unceremoniously and backed against the car.

She gave a startled cry, then an outraged gasp as Xavier whipped off her sunglasses and tossed them onto the roof.

'Hey!' she protested, even as she instinctively knew the welfare of her sunglasses was the least of her worries just then.

He discarded his own, then palmed the back of her skull while his other hand released her wrist and claimed her hip in a hold that was blatantly possessive and intimate.

She stared at him. 'Xavier?' Her voice emerged as a breathless whisper. 'Wh-what are you doing?'

'Making a point,' he rasped.

And then his mouth came down on hers and Jordan felt as if she'd slammed into a wall of electricity, shock and heat consuming her so completely she could do nothing more than tremble and burn under the savagery of his kiss.

And it *was* savage. Like no other kiss she'd ever experienced before. A kiss of anger and dominance and control. It should have horrified her, incensed her, but there was something sinfully sensual, darkly exhilarating, about the way his firm lips moved with such brutal purpose over hers.

She made a sound she told herself was protest but feared was actually acquiescence. Heat stung her body in places he wasn't even touching. And where he did touch… She felt branded. *Claimed.* By his hands. His mouth. Even the scrape of his thick stubble on her skin seemed like a deliberate attempt to mark and punish.

Never in her life had she been kissed with such utter, breathtaking mastery.

Her mouth yielded under the relentless pressure of his and he went deeper, angling his head and prising her lips apart, stroking his tongue boldly against hers so the combined tastes of coffee and almonds and virile male burst in her mouth like an intoxicant, dangerous and shocking and yet oh-so-delicious.

A deep, responsive shiver rippled through her muscles, and she thought she felt a similar shudder go through him. But then, abruptly, he tore his mouth off hers, throwing her into a state of dazed confusion.

'I am not your brother.'

It took a moment for her shellshocked brain to comprehend what he'd said. Still holding her trapped between the car and his body, he shifted his weight until suddenly the hard, unmistakable ridge of his full male arousal pressed against her belly.

'Do not test me,' he said, his voice a low rumble of warning, 'and expect me to behave as if I am.'

Clamping her upper arms, he moved her sideways, then released her to open her door.

Heart pounding, hands trembling, she retrieved her sunglasses from the roof and pushed them onto her face. She should say something, she thought weakly, balling her hands at her sides. Something assertive, something to express the anger and indignation she should be feeling—*was* feeling, she corrected herself. But in that moment, with her mind still reeling and her body feeling strangely deprived now that he'd moved away, all she could focus on was getting herself into the car before her knees gave out.

The drive back to the villa took an age. A wall of silence had descended, thick and unscaleable, and Jordan could think of nothing to say to breach it.

Nothing that wouldn't betray how deeply shaken she felt.

Xavier had *kissed* her.

More, he'd revealed his arousal in a manner so blunt and brazen she should have been scandalised. But instead she'd been turned on. And she couldn't stop thinking about it. Couldn't stop remembering how his mouth had felt on hers. Couldn't forget his taste. Couldn't stop replaying that kiss, in all its brutal, breath-stealing glory, over and over in her head.

But the most disturbing thing of all was the hot blaze of yearning in her belly.

*Xavier had kissed her.*

And she wanted him to do it again.

He shouldn't have done it.

Xav pinched the bridge of his nose and cursed himself for the hundredth time since they'd got back to the villa. He shouldn't have kissed Jordan the way he had, with anger and arrogance and a dark compulsion to punish.

And yet he'd be lying if he said he hadn't enjoyed every damned second of plundering those soft, honeyed lips.

She'd enjoyed it, too. He was sure of it. She'd made a sexy little moaning sound in her throat and softened her mouth under his, granting him access to go deep, to stroke his tongue in and taste her…which had been his undoing.

Because now that he knew how sweet she was, his taste-buds cried out for more.

And his body ached. *Wanted.* Wanted what he shouldn't have.

Biting back another curse, he shut his laptop and stood up from his desk. He'd stared at the same columns and rows of figures for over an hour. Clearly work wasn't going to provide the distraction he'd hoped for.

He moved through the open French doors of his study and stood on the terrace, hands shoved in his jeans pockets, his gaze drifting out across the ocean to where the sun's glow was no more than a dying ember on the horizon.

It wasn't only the kiss that had played endlessly on his mind these last few hours. It was everything that had happened today. The village. The Gonzalezes. The stories about Camila Sanchez that he'd listened to over lunch…

The harsh things he'd said to Jordan in the car afterwards, which he now regretted.

Returning here, to the unapologetically plush surroundings of his home, had evoked in him a raft of strange emotions. He wasn't an idle man—he worked hard and always would—but there was no disputing the fact that his life had been one of privilege and opportunity. A life he'd have been denied had his birth mother chosen to keep him.

He lived the life of an aristocrat. He bore the de la Vega name. He sat on the Vega Corporation's board, owned a slice of the empire and held the position of Chief Executive—a role coveted by certain members of the extended de la Vega clan who believed it wasn't his birthright.

And they weren't wrong.

*Dios.* Wouldn't his father's cousin Hector and his son Diego just love to know that Xav had been born the illegitimate son of a farmer's daughter?

The sound of splashing water filtered into his thoughts and he found himself sauntering along the stone terrace and around the corner of the villa to where the swimming pool was located. He neared the water, saw a flash of long, pale limbs and froze, realising too late his mistake.

There was only one person—one *woman*—who'd be swimming in his pool.

He turned to leave.

'Xavier!'

Her soft voice curled through his insides like the silky song of a siren, sweet and seductive and impossible to resist.

'Would you hand me my towel, please?'

*Damn it.*

He turned back, saw the fluffy white towel on the lounger next to him and grabbed it just as she hoisted herself out of the water. Extending his arm so he didn't have to get too close, he held the towel out. But she didn't take it straight away, instead lifting her arms to wring out her hair.

Jaw clenched, he tried looking anywhere but at her. *Impossible.* Especially once he'd caught an eyeful of pert breasts and budded nipples under the wet, clingy Lycra of her crimson bikini top.

'For God's sake, Jordan,' he gritted out, before his self-control caved in and he let his gaze sweep the rest of her. 'Take the damn towel.'

Her eyes widened, and then her mouth pursed and she snatched the towel from him, wrapping it sarong-style around herself.

'You've had four hours to cool off,' she muttered. 'Don't tell me you're *still* angry.'

Angry? He almost laughed. Try deeply sexually frustrated. Or how about conflicted?

Because it was an unfamiliar kind of hell he found himself in—desiring a woman he shouldn't have. A woman who wasn't remotely suitable for him.

Over the past decade he'd been judicious in his choice of lovers. Not only because he'd felt the need to counterbalance his brother's playboy antics but because as Chief Executive he held himself to a higher standard. To command respect his behaviour had to be beyond reproach—not only in his professional life but his personal life as well.

Always there'd be those like Hector and Diego, hovering in the wings, watching and waiting for him to screw up, to prove himself unfit for the role.

As a rule he kept his relationships low-key and avoided one-night stands. He chose lovers who were emotionally mature and discreet about their personal lives, and he demanded exclusivity for the duration of their relationship, whether that be for two months or two years.

And he never, *never*, made himself vulnerable the way he had with Natasha.

When he'd hit thirty and succeeded his father as CEO he'd felt more keenly than ever the external pressure to 'settle down'. Many of his peers had taken wives, started producing the requisite heirs to their personal fortunes and empires. Conservative board members and shareholders preferred a leader who represented stability and family values. Hell, even his own brother had traded in his hedonistic lifestyle for the domestic idyll of marriage and fatherhood, giving their delighted parents their first grandchild—a baby girl—a few months ago.

Consequently Xav had become even more circumspect in his choice of lovers, narrowing his criteria to exclude women who didn't have the qualities of a desirable marriage partner.

The problem was that most women clung to the flawed romantic ideal of marrying for love, and he was too brutally honest to let a woman believe he would ever love her.

Respect, physical gratification, even affection…he could do all of these things. But love? With all its pressure and expectation and potential for pain? No.

Unfortunately that made finding the perfect woman damn near impossible. Which was why he had recently engaged the services of an exclusive high-end matchmaker— the very idea of which had drawn the patent disapproval of the woman standing before him now. A woman who'd also appeared scandalised at the idea of marrying for compatibility and not love.

And right there was all the deterrent he should need— without even going near the mind-bending fact that she was his birth mother's stepdaughter—and yet here he stood, mesmerised by a pair of golden-green eyes, a supple body and a lush mouth that made his own water hungrily at the recollection of driving her soft lips apart and delving into the honeyed depths—

'Xavier?'

His name was no more than a husky whisper across those beautiful lips, but it snapped him back to full consciousness. His palms felt cool and damp, and he saw with a jolt that his hands were curled over Jordan's wet shoulders. And he was close. So close their thighs and torsos almost touched. Her head tipped back on her slender neck to look up at him. Her eyes were big and round, lips parted.

*Dios.*

He didn't even remember moving. He jerked his hands

off her body, stepped back, but she came with him and he realised one of her slim hands gripped the front of his polo shirt.

'Xavier, please… You've barely said a word to me since…'

She trailed off and he read frustration and confusion in her flushed face, but also desire. It was there in her widened pupils and her softly parted lips. In the way the hectic colour spilled down her throat and décolletage and stained the pale upper slopes of her breasts.

If he chose to do so right now he could carry her up to his room, peel away the wet bikini and satisfy his desire to taste her until she came against his tongue, and she wouldn't stop him.

The deeply erotic thought had him hardening and lengthening in his jeans until the tight fit of the denim was almost unbearable.

Never before had his self-control been so sorely tested…

'Jordan—'

'Don't.' A fierce look crossed her face. 'Don't say sorry. Or tell me you regret it. Because I don't.'

He heard the pride and defiance in her voice, and if he'd had any capacity whatsoever for gentleness just then he would have tried to spare her feelings. But the only way to keep a tight rein on his lust and prevent himself weakening was to be hard. Adamant.

'I do regret it,' he said, grasping her wrist and disentangling her fingers from his shirt. 'The kiss was a mistake.'

Hurt flashed in those big hazel eyes but her chin stayed boldly elevated. 'It didn't feel like a mistake to me. It felt pretty…amazing.'

He didn't like the way his pulse kicked then, as if his body agreed with her assessment.

'It *was* a mistake,' he repeated. 'And it won't happen again.' He released her wrist and stepped back. 'Goodnight, Jordan.' And he stalked back to his study.

# CHAPTER SIX

JORDAN WOKE IN the morning feeling as mortified as she had when she'd crawled into bed last night.

She stared at the canopy above her head and pressed her palms to her cheeks. Just thinking about what had happened by the pool—or rather what *hadn't* happened—made her face burn and her stomach shrink all over again.

After hours of feeling as if her body was in the grip of a prolonged flush, she'd put her bikini on and slipped quietly out onto the terrace for an evening dip. She hadn't seen Xavier in hours. He had distanced himself as soon as they'd arrived at the villa, stalking off to his study and then letting her know via Rosa that he was working and wouldn't be joining her for a meal.

Jordan had filled the intervening hours with a bout of determined activity, taking a long walk down the tiered terraces to the private beach at the bottom of the property, then back up through the citrus orchards on the gentle slopes behind the villa.

On her return she'd followed her nose to the enormous kitchen, where the divine smells of fresh baking had wafted in the air. Rosa had fixed her a snack and then sat down and shared a pot of tea with her.

But nothing had distracted her completely from thoughts of *that* kiss.

Or, more disturbingly, from thoughts of what that kiss might have led to had they not been standing on a public street but somewhere more private.

As for what had possessed her to ask him to hand her the towel when she'd been perfectly able to fetch it herself... She only knew that her heart had leapt into her throat when she'd surfaced from under the water and spied him walking away. She'd called out his name on impulse, then quickly had to think of something to say.

He'd looked so attractive. Still in jeans, but with the white button-down shirt replaced by a black polo shirt that showed off his tanned, muscular arms and fitted snugly across his powerful shoulders and chest. His physique looked more like that of a professional athlete than a desk-bound executive. She'd wondered how a man who spent so much time in boardrooms and offices kept himself so lean and fit.

And then her ability to think anything at all had fled. His hands had come down on her shoulders and his expression had changed from annoyed to something much more intense.

He'd been going to kiss her again—she was sure of it—and her heart had raced, pumping a dizzying mix of desire and adrenaline into her bloodstream.

Without realising it she'd gripped the front of his shirt and tipped her face up. *Wanting* to be kissed. Wanting to experience the same heady rush of excitement and endorphins as when he had trapped her against the car with his hard body and claimed her mouth with deliciously brutal force.

But then he'd abruptly backed off and she'd made an utter fool of herself, clinging to his shirt. Telling him she thought their kiss had been amazing.

Oh, *God*. Had she really said that?

She squeezed her eyes shut. Why, oh, why had she set herself up for such a humiliating rejection?

And yet… He hadn't been unaffected by their kiss, had he? As evidenced by his erection!

An erection he had shamelessly and shockingly made her aware of.

She groaned. She was mortified *and* confused.

She got up and opened the blinds and the French doors, breathing deeply as fresh air and bright sunlight flooded the room. The exquisite view from the balcony never failed to amaze her. For a moment she stood and drank in the vista, imprinting the vivid colours of the landscape and the bright blue sea into her memory.

She couldn't stay. Xavier's withdrawal had sent a clear message. If she remained she'd outstay her welcome, and she couldn't bear the thought of lingering where she wasn't wanted. Besides, she had planned to spend only six days tops in Barcelona. Time enough to sightsee, do the day trip to Camila's village and give the letter to Xavier.

Check, check and check.

She headed for the shower. It was almost nine o'clock. A very late time to get up for her, but she supposed that was what happened when you lay awake half the night with an erotic slideshow of illicit imaginings running through your head.

On the upside, Xavier had most probably left for work by now, and the idea of not having to face him brought a surge of cowardly relief. This way was best. She'd spare him the inevitable awkwardness and herself any further embarrassment. She'd leave him a nice thank-you note, plus the money he hadn't taken the other night for the hostel bill, and go on her way with a clear conscience.

When she went downstairs with her backpack Rosa looked startled, and then dismayed when she explained she was leaving. The housekeeper insisted she at least stay for a cooked breakfast and she gratefully accepted.

Sitting on a stool at the enormous granite-topped island while Rosa bustled around the kitchen, she took out her palm tablet and booked a ticket for the next sailing to Mallorca.

Rosa slid a fluffy, delicious-looking omelette in front of her, disappeared for a few minutes while she ate, and returned with the envelope she'd asked for earlier.

When her taxi arrived she pressed the envelope with her note and the money inside it into Rosa's hand. 'Please give this to Xavier.' She leaned in and hugged the older woman.

'Thank you so much for your hospitality, Rosa. I'm sorry I've missed Delmar and Alfonso. Please say goodbye to them for me.'

Only when she was in the taxi and nearing Barcelona's busy port did she acknowledge the hollow feeling in her chest. It was so similar to the feeling she'd had in the days after her dad died, and again after Camila passed, that she couldn't understand why it should accost her now—and so intensely.

On impulse she opened her tote bag and found the photo Maria had given her. Xavier and his biological father were so alike, with those lean, dark good looks, it made her heart clutch to see it.

It wasn't difficult to imagine how a young Camila might have fallen head over heels.

An ache pressed against her breastbone. She felt as if she was stealing something precious from Xavier by not showing him the photo. Not sharing what she knew of his birth father.

But she'd tried.

And he had made it clear—*very* clear—he wasn't interested.

Maybe down the track she would write to him from Australia. Explain what Maria had told her. Then he could decide whether to use the information or discard it.

The taxi pulled up outside the ferry terminal and Jordan put the photo away. The driver helped her retrieve her backpack, and then it took her a moment to sort out the right bills and coins to pay him.

Once he was happy she hoisted her pack onto her shoulder, turned towards the terminal—and slammed into a wall of solid muscle.

The impact combined with the weight of her pack threw her off-balance, and she stumbled backwards with a startled cry.

Strong hands caught her by the upper arms, stopping her from falling.

She looked up and her mouth dried.

'Xavier!'

'Running away, Jordan?'

She tried to focus on what he'd said instead of the heat of his hands, which felt like branding irons on her bare arms. 'Wh-what?'

In her peripheral vision a big, dark-suited man emerged from inside the terminal and strode towards them.

Juan.

He lifted his hand in the air and signalled to someone she couldn't see.

She turned her attention back to Xavier. His expression was inscrutable, but the hard glint in his gunmetal gaze told her he wasn't happy.

Her mind spun.

*Rosa.* Rosa must have called him. How else had he known she'd left? Where she'd gone?

Her voice was a croak of confusion. 'What are you doing here?'

'You left without saying goodbye.' His tone was mild, as though he'd dished out nothing more than a gentle rebuke, but she sensed the pull of a dangerous undercurrent in the air.

She sucked in her breath, ignored the stab in her belly that felt a bit like guilt. Did he really think she'd buy into the idea that *he* was the wounded party? If anyone had reason to feel slighted it was her. He'd invited her to his home under false pretences. He hadn't trusted her. He'd had her *investigated*. And then he'd messed with her in the cruellest way possible. He'd kissed her and left her wanting more, then rejected her and left her feeling like a fool. Humiliated.

She hiked up her chin. 'I left you a note.'

A muscle flickered in his cheek, and this time his voice

was not so smooth. 'Do you think a *note* is the best way to finish things between us?'

Her heart thumped against her ribs. Finish things? What things? There wasn't anything *to* finish.

Was there…?

'Xavier—'

'Not here.' He dropped one hand, but kept the other on her arm, turning her away from the busy terminal.

A big black SUV pulled up to the kerb and she eyed it with a growing sense of *déjà vu*. Too fast for her to stop him, Juan took her tote bag from her hand and slipped the backpack off her shoulder.

Her heart lurched into her throat. 'Wait—stop.'

Both men ignored her. Xavier opened the rear door and she braced her palm against the top of the frame. Her initial shock was receding. In its place came agitation—and anger.

A shrill note entered her voice. 'I said *stop.*'

Xavier stilled. Then he released her arm, slid his hand around her waist and tugged her in close.

Anyone watching would have seen an intimate embrace, would have been unaware of the tension in the taut lines of his body beneath the tailored suit, or the tacit warning in the strong press of his fingers at her waist.

'I would prefer you didn't make a scene,' he murmured, and his mouth was so close to her ear she felt the warmth of his breath feather over her skin and caught his citrus and sandalwood scent.

Her senses reeled. It took all her strength to keep her knees locked so she didn't give in to temptation and lean into all that male hardness and heat.

She controlled her voice. 'I can't go with you.'

'Can't or won't?'

She glared. 'I need to check in for the ferry. I've already bought a ticket for the next sailing.'

'I'll buy you another one.'

She opened her mouth, but then a taxi driver honked his

horn and gesticulated out of his window at the SUV, which idled in a drop-off only zone.

Juan yelled at the driver and the driver bellowed back.

People started to look.

'Jordan,' Xavier urged, his mouth tightening, the fingers at her waist sinking deeper.

She flung her hands up. 'Fine! I'm getting in.'

And then she was going to tell him exactly what she thought of his arrogant, domineering behaviour.

Or at least she *would* have done, she assured herself ten seconds later, if he hadn't climbed in from the other side and at the same time pulled his ringing phone from his jacket and answered it.

She wanted to snatch the phone and throw the damned thing out the window.

Instead she bit her tongue while he conducted a conversation with someone else. Someone far more important than her, obviously. She folded her arms and focused on her anger as the car pulled away from the port.

She needed to stay mad.

If she stayed mad then maybe she could ignore this fluttery, breathless sensation in her chest that felt an awful lot like excitement.

*Excitement?*

Honestly. What was wrong with her? He'd virtually abducted her off the street. Again. The only thing she should be feeling was outrage.

He didn't end his call until they were descending into the basement of the Vega Tower, by which time her anger was a low simmer that rapidly changed to dismay and a faint sense of panic.

As soon as he'd slipped his phone back into his jacket she blurted, 'I can't go into your offices dressed like this!'

She could just picture the beautiful, flawless Lucia, looking at her in her denim cut-offs and tank top with barely concealed horror.

His gaze slid over her, settling briefly on her bare thighs before lifting back to her face. For a second, as their gazes meshed and her breath snagged, she thought she saw a flash of heat in those metallic grey eyes before his features grew shuttered again.

'We're not going to my office.'

They went instead to the very top of the tower, via a dedicated lift that ran from the underground car park and gave access to two other levels: the forty-fourth floor, where the executive offices were located, and the floor above, which housed the corporate apartment that Rosa had mentioned as being where he sometimes stayed when he worked long hours.

The lift was one of those super-fast types that made her feel as if her stomach had relocated to her knees, and yet every second of the brief ride felt more like a minute, and every one of those was excruciating.

Because Xavier couldn't behave like an ordinary person and face the doors. No. He had to stand with his back to one of the side walls, so that no matter where Jordan stood she couldn't escape his incisive gaze.

As if she was going to perform some kind of Houdini act and disappear from under his nose while the lift was moving!

He stood tall and silent, his hands in his trouser pockets, her bags sitting on the floor beside him.

And he watched her.

She knew it—could feel his gaze like the stroke of a warm hand across bare skin even as she concentrated hard on the toes of her tennis shoes.

*Coward. Look at him. Show him you're just as mad at him as he is at you.*

And he *was* angry. She didn't need to sneak a look at the tight clench of his clean-shaven jaw to know it. When irritated or frustrated he pinched the bridge of his nose, but when he was angry—truly angry—he simply went very, very still.

Like he was now.

It gave her a small shock to realise she knew all this about him. She'd known him for—what? Five days? Somehow it seemed longer.

*So what? Stay mad*, she reminded herself—an instruction she promptly forgot as she stepped from the lift straight into the expansive glass-walled living area of Xavier's penthouse apartment.

*Wow.*

It was nothing like the beautiful stone villa on the coast, but just as spectacular with its panoramic bird's-eye view of the sprawling city and the wide blue of the ocean beyond.

Automatically she moved to one of the floor-to-ceiling windows for a better look. From up here she could see the port in the distance and a number of berthed ships, one of which was probably the ferry that would have taken her away from here.

Away from him.

Away from this overwhelming attraction she didn't know how to handle and away from the danger of humiliating herself again.

She glanced at her watch. There was still over an hour until the ferry was scheduled to leave.

'Forget it, Jordan.'

She turned and frowned. 'Forget what?'

'You're not taking that ferry.'

It annoyed her immensely that he could read her thoughts as easily as she could read the idiosyncrasies of his body language.

She felt equally annoyed at how devastatingly gorgeous he looked, standing there in the middle of his living room in his dark grey suit, every bit as sleek and expensive-looking as the designer decor and stunning pieces of artwork that lined the interior walls.

She licked her lips, but there wasn't enough moisture in her mouth to alleviate their dryness.

'Why am I here?' she challenged, choosing to skip the more obvious *Why are you angry?*

She didn't need a psychology degree to work that out. Anyone who spent time with this man would see he had a penchant for control—and people who liked being in control didn't like surprises…unless *they* were doing the surprising.

She guessed her upping and leaving without saying goodbye in person had surprised him.

Throw a hefty dose of male ego and dented pride into the mix and you had all the ingredients for a grown man's temper tantrum.

So, yes. She wanted to know what he planned to do now.

Vent his anger?

Yell a bit?

Yell a *lot*?

She shook off any lingering cowardice and raised her chin, giving him a bold, defiant look.

*Do your worst.*

Because, really, how frightening could his worst be? She was a trauma nurse who'd worked the weekend night shift in Accident & Emergency. She had placated belligerent drug addicts. Fended off breast-and-butt-grabbing drunks. Had the unmentionable contents of a bedpan thrown at her…

A billionaire in a bad mood? *Pfft.* Child's play.

His eyes narrowed. And then *he* did something surprising and removed his suit jacket, shrugging his broad shoulders out of the expensive fabric and dropping the jacket onto the end of the long, coffee-coloured sofa behind him.

Jordan's eyes widened, but he didn't stop there. He upped the surprise factor another notch by lifting his hands to his throat, working his tie loose and sliding it out from under his collar.

Her breath shortened, and for one slightly hysterical moment she wondered if they were playing some kind of bizarre game of one-upmanship. Because when she thought about it they'd been surprising the hell out of each other from the moment she'd walked into his office last week and told him her late stepmom was his biological mother.

If she were keeping score she would have said before yesterday that they were level pegging. But then Xavier had stormed into the lead with that blistering, spine-loosening kiss she was trying very hard *not* to think about right now.

He threw the tie onto the sofa, then undid the button of his collar one-handed. His gaze stayed on hers, direct and unsettling, and she couldn't for the life of her look away.

'We have unfinished business.'

She swallowed, but her throat was dry and her voice came out husky. 'What business?'

He stalked across the plush carpet towards her and she stood like a deer in headlights, trapped by the silver snare of his gaze. On some deep, instinctive level she understood what was happening. Understood that beneath the ruthless self-control there wasn't only anger and ego railing against their restraints but something much more primal and volatile. Something that, if he chose to unleash it, neither of them would escape from unscathed.

And yet her conscious mind couldn't process it. Couldn't reconcile the hot, glittering intent in his eyes with the cold slap of his words from last night.

*'It was a mistake—and it won't happen again.'*

He stopped in front of her and she felt her pulse spike and her entire body tremble. But, even knowing what he intended, she couldn't make herself move. She felt as if she were in the grip of some sort of delirium—like a storm chaser standing in the path of a destructive tornado, torn between excitement and terror.

His hands came up and bracketed her head, his long fingers splaying into her hair. 'This business,' he said, his voice rough and deep. And Jordan had scarcely a second to snatch in her breath before his mouth rocked savagely over hers.

She didn't feign shock. Didn't make any token attempts to resist. The simple, irrefutable truth was that she'd yearned for him to do this, ached for him to touch her again, and denying it was like trying to hold back a storm.

Impossible.

She wanted to run *into* the storm. Wanted it to sweep her up and consume her in its chaos. Drown out the voice of sanity that would tell her all the reasons why they shouldn't do this.

His kiss wasn't gentle and she didn't want it to be. It was searing and fierce. Dominating and deep. He cradled her skull and prised her lips apart, driving heat and sensation into her mouth, demanding a response that she gave with a bold flick of her tongue against his.

She felt his tiny jerk of surprise, heard a small growl of what she hoped was approval in his throat, and then she was kissing him back, and it was wild and passionate. An urgent, breathless clash of lips and tongues unlike anything she'd experienced before.

Driven by instinct, and a feverish need for greater contact, she clung to his shoulders and arched against him, revelling in the delicious rub of hard male muscle against her softer curves.

When his strong hands curled under her buttocks and lifted her it seemed like the most natural thing in the world for her to wrap her legs around him and continue kissing him as he carried her effortlessly across the room.

He stopped at the sofa and she unhooked her ankles as he lowered himself to a seated position on the cushions, bringing her with him so that she sat astride him, her bare legs straddling his muscular thighs. The slightly rough landing bumped their mouths apart and she sat back, hands braced on his wide shoulders to steady herself, and looked at him.

His eyes glittered under heavy lids and dark colour slashed his cheekbones. Like her, he was breathing hard.

'*Dios,*' he said, his voice little more than a harsh whisper. 'What spell have you cast over me, woman?'

His ragged words and the heat in his eyes sent a ripple of heady pleasure through her. To know that he felt as helplessly compelled by their attraction as she, that his desire for her pushed him to the limits of his control, made her feel sexually powerful and confident in a way she'd never felt before.

She licked her lips and leaned forward, eager to have his hot mouth on hers again. But he stopped her, putting his hands on her rib cage, tantalisingly close to her breasts.

He eased her back and said, 'I want to look at you,' and her flushed cheeks grew even hotter.

Reaching up a hand, he stroked the tip of his forefinger over her bottom lip, then trailed his fingers along her jaw, igniting a shower of sparks beneath her skin. Light as a feather, his touch continued down her throat, over the ridge of her collarbone and lower, eliciting a shiver of delight she couldn't suppress.

'Like silk,' he murmured, and then closed his hand over her left breast and squeezed in a way that was brazen and possessive and made her a gasp aloud. 'Take your hair down,' he commanded, and it didn't even occur to her to take exception to his tone. She was too far gone, too aroused, and for some reason the arrogant air of authority that normally rubbed her the wrong way only turned her on.

His hands had already played havoc with her ponytail, leaving it slightly askew, with long strands hanging loose about her face. She pulled the elastic band off and freed the rest, shaking her head until the wavy tresses tumbled over her shoulders and down her back.

Xavier lifted his hands and smoothed the hair back from her face, then drifted his long fingers through the silky ends and murmured something in Spanish. Voice husky, he reverted to English and said, 'Take off your top, Jordan.'

There was something deliciously risqué about his ordering her to strip for him. Before her confidence could waver, she pulled her tank top up and over her head and let it fall from her fingers, watching his eyes darken as they focused on her breasts, encased still in the cups of her cotton bra. She saw his jaw lock tight, as if he waged some fierce internal battle, and again she became aware of the power *she* wielded, even though he was the one issuing commands.

Emboldened by the knowledge that she could so easily drive him to the brink of his control, she removed her bra and at the same time rocked her hips forward so she rubbed intimately against the hard ridge of flesh inside his trousers.

He sucked in his breath, then hooked his arm around her waist and flipped her on her back on the sofa. 'Temptress,' he growled, looming above her, his eyes shimmering with hunger and the promise of retribution as he palmed one of her breasts and dragged his thumb over the extended nipple.

Sensation arrowed from her breast down to the place between her legs where she ached with need. She gasped and arched her back in a wordless plea for more—more than just that fleeting, teasing caress of his thumb—and a smile of sensual satisfaction curved his mouth.

It was an utterly masculine smile that said he knew exactly what she wanted from him, exactly what her straining body craved and needed, and the dark glitter in his eyes promised to deliver.

He leaned down, finally took possession of her mouth again, and his kiss was deep and scorching, dragging the air from her lungs and making that needy ache in her pelvis burn exquisitely hot and bright. She could have kissed like that for ever, lost in the midst of hunger and passion, all rational thought conveniently suspended.

When his mouth left hers she almost moaned in protest, until she realised his lips weren't going far—just to the edge of her jaw, then along to the soft skin beneath her earlobe and down the curve of her throat, pressing searing kisses to flushed, sensitive flesh that quivered in anticipation of each new touch, all the way to the tip of her breast.

Jordan caught her breath, knowing instinctively what he would do next, and yet still she wasn't fully prepared for the lightning-hot sensation of him capturing her nipple between his lips and sucking her deep into his mouth. Her body arched and she tunnelled her fingers into the soft, thick hair at the back of his head, crying out at the unbearable pleasure he inflicted, afraid this sweet torture on its own would make her come.

He lavished the same attention on her other breast before blazing a trail of fire with his mouth down to her navel, where his tongue circled and dipped in an erotic fashion before travelling lower.

The ache between Jordan's thighs became so intense, so consuming, that when she heard him say, 'Raise your hips,' she obeyed automatically, realising only once her shorts and knickers had hit the floor that he'd stripped her completely naked.

His big hands stroked up her inner thighs and then pushed them apart, opening her up to his unabashed scrutiny.

'Xavier...' His name fell from her lips on a breathless whisper, and she didn't know if it was plea or protest.

'Perfección,' he murmured, and her cheeks burned at being so explicitly exposed and studied.

Slowly he ran a fingertip down through her bright red curls and then delved deeper, finding the place where she was hot and wet and thrumming with need. He looked up, caught her gaze and held it captive as he pushed his finger inside her.

Instantly she felt her inner muscles tighten, responding needily to the deep, intimate caress. He slid a second finger in, stretching her a little wider, increasing the pleasure as he stroked into her, sliding deeper and finding just the right spot...

*Oh, God.*

Her body tremored, rushing towards climax even before he lowered his head and used the hot, velvet slide of his tongue to hurtle her over the edge.

It was the hottest, most intense orgasm she'd ever had, exhilarating and yet embarrassing at the same time, because she came so fast and hard she couldn't control herself. Couldn't hold back the loud moan that climbed her throat or stop the almost violent contortion of her body as the spasms of pleasure hurtled through her.

Mortified, she turned her flaming face into a pillow as Xavier rose from between her legs. How had she fooled herself into thinking even for a second that he wouldn't be in total control of this encounter? Of *her.*

He slid his hand under her cheek and turned her face towards him. She kept her eyes closed and he laughed softly.

'It's a little late for shyness, *amante.*'

She forced herself to look at him. 'You've still got all your clothes on,' she croaked, 'and I've already—' She threw her forearm over her eyes, unable to finish.

He eased her arm away and made her look at him again. 'The first of many,' he said, his voice a deep purr of promise that sent a delicious shiver down her spine.

His head lowered and her embarrassment receded beneath a surge of anticipation as those sensual lips descended towards hers.

And then a loud chirruping sound came from the other end of the sofa and he tensed above her.

It took her a moment to realise it was his phone ringing.

He swore and started to draw away, and for a second she wanted to wrap her arms around his neck, pull him down to her and demand he not answer it.

He did answer it. Of course. And she saw his expression change as he listened, saw how after a minute he frowned down at her, naked and spreadeagled on the cushions, as if he were only just then noticing her and wondering why a naked woman was lying on his sofa.

Mortification flooded back. Along with a cold dose of sanity. Swiftly she sat up, covering her breasts with her arm while reaching with her other hand for her discarded clothing.

Xavier turned away, sparing her the indignity of having to dress in front of him. He was speaking now, in a rapid stream of Spanish, and his voice grew muted as he walked into another room.

Jordan dressed quickly—and then didn't know what to do with herself. Or what to *think* of herself, for that matter, after what had just happened.

She walked over to the window and took a couple of deep breaths.

Madness.

That was what it had felt like. Crazy and breathless and desperate, and well beyond anything she'd experienced.

Not that she had a ton of experience with men. Josh had been her one and only lover. They'd worked at the same hospital in Sydney, so she'd known him for several months before they dated and slept together. After several more months he'd suggested she move in with him and she had, believing for a time that he was *the one*.

Foolish her. Josh was already married—to his career. He didn't need a wife—just a woman who would stroke his ego and happily take a back seat to his ambition to become the best and most lauded cardiothoracic surgeon in the world.

Ellie, bless her, had helped her move her things out of his place, given her a great big sympathy hug and then told her she'd done the right thing 'dumping that arrogant jerk'.

Jordan blew out a heavy breath. Xavier had Josh beaten hands down in the arrogance department.

She closed her eyes and leaned her forehead against the glass.

*Heaven help her.*

# CHAPTER SEVEN

Xav DROPPED HIS phone onto the dresser in the master suite and went through to the bathroom. He leaned over the basin on the marble vanity and sluiced his face in cold water, then grabbed a towel and scrubbed his skin dry.

What he desperately needed to do was douse his entire body in ice-cold water, but he didn't have time for a shower.

His brother was downstairs in his office. It had been Ramon on the phone.

Xav cursed. Ramon had told him days ago—*and* reminded him during their phone call yesterday—that he was bringing his wife, Emily, and their baby daughter, Katie, to Barcelona for a week. They'd agreed to have lunch today to discuss the Reynaud deal, among other things.

How the hell had he forgotten?

He braced his palms on the edge of the vanity unit and pulled in a shuddering breath.

His mind had been elsewhere—that was how he'd forgotten. Arriving at the office at seven a.m. after a restless night, he'd tried to focus on work and instead found his mind returning repeatedly to the events of yesterday. In particular his abrupt treatment of Jordan by the pool.

He'd seen the hurt in her eyes before he'd walked away. Hurt she hadn't deserved. He'd rejected her for the right reasons, but the way he'd gone about it had been harsh. Wrong.

And walking away from her, shutting himself in his study for the rest of the evening, hadn't stopped the incessant *wanting*.

He had only himself to blame. Yes, she had provoked him, flirting with that guy on the beach, shoving the brother thing in his face, knowing it would push his buttons, but he'd spent a lifetime training himself not to react impulsively to provocation.

But this time he had reacted.

He'd kissed her out of anger and an inability to subdue his desire. Then he'd punished *her* for it, shutting her out, speaking barely a word to her afterwards.

By mid-morning a tight knot of guilt had settled in his gut.

He prided himself on being a man of principle and strong moral character—better than those who would undermine him—and yet he couldn't view his behaviour yesterday with any sense of pride.

As for his behaviour today…

He clenched his jaw and stared down at his white-knuckled hands, reluctant to look at his reflection in the mirror for fear he would see not himself but some half-crazed Neanderthal he hardly recognised.

How the hell had he ended up doing what he'd just done out there on the sofa?

It had been the furthest thing from his mind when he'd picked up the phone and called Rosa.

His plan had been simple. As simple as he and Jordan sharing a polite, civilised meal that would allow him to claw back some self-respect and prove he wasn't the bastard she had every reason to believe him to be.

Above all he'd resolved to keep a lid on his lust and, if necessary, rebuff any of her advances.

*Gently.*

Except when he'd called his housekeeper to tell her he'd be home to dine with his guest this evening Rosa had promptly told him his guest was gone.

At first he'd thought she meant that Jordan had ventured out for the day, and for a second he'd regretted not having had the forethought to put a car and driver at her disposal.

But, no. Rosa had meant *gone* gone.

*Not coming back* gone.

*For ever* gone.

Shock had mingled with disbelief, making his stomach harden, his chest tighten.

And then the anger had come—swift and hot and all-encompassing.

*She'd left.*

Of course he'd known her time in Barcelona would be limited. But to leave without a word? Without so much as a goodbye?

He didn't think his heart had ever thundered with such ferocity in his chest.

During the trip to the ferry terminal his blood had pounded with increasing agitation.

He knew there was only one daytime sailing to Mallorca, the other being late in the evening, so his chance of intercepting her was good.

But what if Rosa had been wrong about Jordan's plans?

Fortunately Rosa had been right.

And when Jordan had climbed out of the taxi, just metres away from where he stood, the mix of triumph and relief he'd felt was like a shot of adrenaline straight to his heart.

Only then had he fully appreciated that he'd acted—yet again, where Jordan was concerned—entirely on impulse, and hadn't thought ahead to what he would do after he stopped her.

He pushed away from the vanity now, returned to the bedroom and looked for a fresh shirt and matching tie in the walk-in wardrobe.

The smart thing for him to have done after his call with Rosa would have been to shrug his shoulders. Let Jordan go. But something about that woman fused his brain. Impelled him to make rash decisions. And, just like on Saturday, every instinct in him had railed against her leaving.

He unbuttoned his shirt and yanked it off, caught the scent of jasmine on the fabric and something earthier, muskier. He swallowed hard.

Truthfully he'd not had sex on his mind when he'd brought her up here, but he *had* struggled to harness his anger, even as a voice in his head had urged him to consider that his behaviour yesterday had given Jordan a perfectly valid reason to flee.

Perversely, that thinking had only made his mood deteriorate and his temper spike—because then he'd been angry not only at her but at himself.

Wrap all that in an atmosphere charged with sexual tension and sparks had been inevitable.

He buttoned up the fresh shirt, pinned gold cufflinks at his wrists, then grabbed the tie.

Jordan had lit the fuse. Hoisting her chin like she had, pursing her lush lips in a tight moue and throwing him that look of defiance...of pure, unadulterated challenge...

A man of principle he might be, but he was only mortal. And mortal men had limits.

*Desires.*

He scowled at his reflection in the mirror as he checked the knot of his tie was straight.

He'd never had a problem controlling his physical urges. His baser instincts. But he'd lost himself out there. Utterly. Completely.

Lost himself in *her.*

He smoothed his hair, where Jordan's hands had messed it up, then turned from his reflection with a sneer of self-disgust.

He'd been rough at first, kissing her like a lusting barbarian with no self-control and no knowledge of how a man should treat a woman.

She should have slapped him. Instead she'd arched those beautiful supple curves against him and kissed him back with an equal fire and, he'd sensed, a little anger of her own.

But he'd also sensed an honesty in her response. A refusal to play coy. There might have been an edge of savagery to their kiss, but it had also been raw and real, unlike anything he'd experienced before.

He had no doubt that if Ramon hadn't called he'd be buried deep inside her right now, oblivious to the fact that it was the middle of a work day and his secretary had no clue where he was. And to think he'd almost ignored his phone. Thank God he hadn't. His brother was one of the few people who knew the code to his apartment. Ramon could have walked in at any moment.

It was only that knowledge that had forced Xav to turn his back on Jordan and walk away. Because one glance at her lying naked on his sofa, hair tousled, lips swollen from his kisses and her skin still flushed from her stunningly sensual climax, and he'd wanted to throw down the phone and resume where they'd left off, regardless of the risk.

He slid his phone into his pocket. He had told Ramon to wait for him in his office and he needed to get down there. Before his brother—and his secretary—grew suspicious about his whereabouts.

As for Jordan… The idea he'd entertained of playing the perfect gentleman over a polite, civilised dinner now sounded more like an evening of agonising torture.

The truth was they'd gone beyond polite—way beyond—and there was no going back.

What he *did* need to get back was his focus and his concentration on work—something that had been woefully lacking in recent days.

With his body still in a state of semi-hardened arousal and his thoughts consumed by a certain redhead, however, he knew there was only one way to make that happen. And that was to finish what he'd started on his sofa.

Jordan heard movement behind her and turned from the window.

Xavier was off the phone. He wore a fresh shirt and matching tie, and she noticed he'd smoothed his hair.

It looked so perfect her fingers itched with a crazy urge to muss it up again.

He grabbed his suit jacket and put it on, and disappointment flared even though she'd already assumed they wouldn't pick up where they'd left off.

He came towards her and her treacherous body prickled with heat. He looked suave and imperturbable again—as if ten short minutes ago he hadn't had his face buried between her legs.

Her face flamed and she cursed mentally. She needed to control her thoughts. As Xavier seemed able to do. He'd obviously had no trouble diverting his mind from sex. Why did men compartmentalise so much better than women?

He kept coming and her pulse stumbled. Had there not been a wall of glass behind her she would have stepped backwards. She crossed her arms instead.

He slipped one hand around her waist.

Her eyes widened.

Then he raised her chin with his fingers and she blinked up at him—right before he planted a soft, lingering kiss on her mouth.

Her breath was bottled in her throat. Who would have thought the lips that before had scorched and devoured and subjugated could be so...*gentle*?

By the time his head lifted her knees had developed a serious wobble.

His gaze held hers. 'Forgive me, but I must return to the office.'

Afraid her hands might roam where they shouldn't if she freed them, she kept her arms folded, which provided the added benefit of a safety barrier between his chest and her breasts.

Blast him, she thought churlishly. Why couldn't he have said something arrogant and infuriating? Arrogant and infuriating she could deal with. But tender and apologetic...?

*Not fair.*

She turned her head to stare out of the window, because looking at the chiselled perfection of his face was not helping her to think straight. 'Am I supposed to sit here and wait for you? Because if we're done here I could still make that ferry sailing.'

He brought her chin back around, forcing her to look at him. '"Done"?' His grey eyes gleamed. 'I think we're a long way from done—' the hand on her back tugged her closer and she gasped at the feel of his erection through their clothing '—don't you?'

Heat singed her cheeks. And other parts of her anatomy. She scowled. 'You said it was a mistake…kissing me,' she reminded him. 'You said it wouldn't happen again.'

He looked unconcerned. 'I was wrong. It happens once in a while,' he added, so deadpan she thought he was serious—until she saw the infinitesimal twitch at the corner of his mouth.

Her heart knocked against her ribs at this unexpected glimpse of teasing humour. It wasn't the first evidence she'd seen of a lighter side to Xavier, but coming now, on the heels of their intense sexual encounter, it threw her.

Was that his intent? To keep her off-balance? As a way to maintain the upper hand? Or was she being oversensitive now?

Drawing in a deep breath, she changed tack. 'Am I a prisoner here?'

His eyes narrowed at that. His hand slid off her waist and she told herself she didn't regret the loss of physical contact.

He pulled his phone from his pocket. 'I'm texting you the code for the elevator,' he said, doing it as he spoke, 'so you can come and go via the car park with privacy. If you prefer to stay in, you can relax here and no one will disturb you. There's an outdoor terrace and a lap pool, and you'll find the kitchen is stocked with essentials.' He slid the phone back into his pocket and settled his gaze on her. 'The answer to your question is no, Jordan. You are not a prisoner.'

She bit her lip. Her head spun as her brain desperately tried to make sense of what was happening here. What it *meant*. He'd not said it in so many words, but by providing her with unfettered access to and from the apartment he'd also given her the freedom to walk out and not return—yet he'd made it clear he didn't want her to leave.

Why? So they could finish their *'unfinished business'*? Was this about sex? *Just* sex? And, if so, why was she not scandalised by the idea?

*Because you want him.*

She felt her face flush again. Frustrated, and more than a little confused, she tore her gaze from his and turned back to the window. She didn't do casual sex. And that was what sex with Xavier would be. How could it be anything else? They lived on different sides of the world. She was just a tourist in his country. And, geography aside, he wasn't someone she'd ever set her long-term sights on anyway. They'd already clashed over their differing views on love and marriage. Theirs would be a short, steamy affair—nothing more.

*Perfect!* That was what Ellie would have said if she was there. Oh, Jordan could just see her friend's startling blue eyes glittering with glee. *Do it*, she'd say. *Live a little. Life is short and unpredictable.*

As trauma nurses, they both knew just how unpredictable life could be. How quickly and unexpectedly a life could end or change irreversibly. Jordan had lost her dad and her stepmom within four years of each other, and they'd both gone before their time. They'd had twelve wonderful years together, but they should have had longer.

What would Camila have thought about the attraction between her stepdaughter and Xavier?

He was her *son*.

Jordan imagined Ellie would have a ready answer for that too: *So what? He's not your brother!*

And hadn't Xavier made that same point with devastating effect yesterday?

She rubbed her fingers over her forehead. A week ago she hadn't thought sexual chemistry was really a thing. Now she knew better. But why couldn't she have made the discovery with a different man?

Why *this* man?

Her temples started to throb.

Was this powerful, overwhelming attraction a purely physical thing? Was it only Xavier's sublime good looks and potent masculinity that drew her? Or was it something else? Was a part of her subconsciously looking for a deeper connection with him because he was a living, breathing link to Camila, whom she missed desperately?

Good grief. Now she was really overthinking things!

She groaned inwardly.

Or maybe she groaned aloud, because in her peripheral vision she saw Xavier move, then felt his hands curl gently over her shoulders from behind.

His touch set her pulse racing, as always, and yet there was something oddly grounding in the warmth and strength of those big, capable hands and the sense of his solid body behind her.

She felt his breath stir her hair as he spoke.

'I'd like to spend more time with you, Jordan.'

She swallowed. Was that code for *I want us to have sex*? She didn't know. She'd never been in this sort of situation before. Was there an etiquette? If there was, Xavier would know. Didn't wealthy men change their women as frequently as they changed their suits?

There was a silence, and then she heard him sigh. His hands tightened a little on her shoulders, and his voice lowered to a deep husk.

'I want you, Jordan. I can't deny that—not after what just happened on that sofa. We have a powerful chemistry, and I don't believe you want to walk away from it any more than I do right now.'

His candour shocked her, and yet his willingness to offer up such blunt honesty spoke to something inside her. Lent her the courage to offer some plain-spoken words of her own.

She turned, dislodging his hands from her shoulders in the process, and looked up at him. 'You accused me of running away today, and I suppose I was, in a way. After last night, by the pool...' She hitched a shoulder. 'I was embarrassed—and confused. You kissed me, Xavier, and then you rejected me. How was I supposed to feel? I thought I was doing us both a favour by leaving. I didn't mean to offend you or to seem ungrateful.'

She took a breath. Even her neck and the tips of her ears burned now, so she knew her blush was scarlet. But she forced herself to continue.

'Last night you said kissing me had been a mistake and now you're saying you were wrong... So I think maybe... even though you didn't do it in the nicest way...you were trying to do the right thing last night and be honourable, because you thought doing anything else would be taking advantage of me...'

*Oh, God.* Was she making any sense? Or just making a fool of herself?

She gulped in another lungful of air. Her heart pounded so hard she could hear the blood rushing in her ears. 'But now that we've...'

She flapped her hand in the general direction of the sofa, and Xavier lifted an eyebrow.

'Been intimate?'

More precisely she'd been thinking he'd given her the most amazing orgasm of her life. She decided to keep that to herself. 'Yes, now that we've done that...' And now she really had to screw up her courage, because she'd never had a conversation quite like this in her life, and the enigmatic look on Xavier's face gave her no clue what he was thinking. 'You're right. I don't think I want to walk away just yet.'

Because she was pretty sure that what she'd be walking away from was wild, passionate sex the likes of which she'd never experienced before and might never experience again.

Ellie was right. Life was unpredictable. Short. And too often filled with suffering and pain. She'd seen people lose loved ones and her empathy was strong, because she herself was intimately acquainted with that kind of loss. Her dad had died unexpectedly. And then had come Camila's illness and eventual passing… Towards the end there'd been days with Camila that had been harrowing and heartbreaking. Even now there were days when she woke and her stomach felt knotted, her chest tight.

But the woman who had sat on Xavier's lap a short while ago, who'd loosened her hair and daringly removed her bra—that woman hadn't felt pain, or grief, or loneliness. She'd felt only pleasure and excitement and the heady, delicious thrill of anticipation.

For just a few short days Jordan wanted to feel that—and more.

Boldly, she held his gaze. 'I want you, too.'

*'I want you, too.'*

'Are you listening, *hermano*?'

Xav jerked his head up. 'What?'

Ramon eyed him across the meeting table in his office. 'Where is your head today?'

Xav sat forward, pushed aside the plate at his elbow and grabbed his pen. He and Ramon had decided on a working lunch in the office rather than in a restaurant, where discussing sensitive matters might be difficult.

Ramon lounged in a chair on the other side of the table. He'd rolled up his shirtsleeves, removed his tie and loosened his collar. Xav supposed he should be grateful his brother hadn't yet removed his shoes and propped his feet on the table.

'First you forget our lunch,' Ramon needled, 'and now you seem incapable of concentrating for more than five minutes at a time.'

Xav scowled. 'My concentration is fine.' *Liar.* 'What else have you heard about Lloyd Anders?'

'Nothing more than what I told you yesterday. He and Reynaud were spotted having lunch together last week in New York. And then Anders wined and dined Reynaud and his wife on Friday night.'

'At *our* Manhattan club?'

'*Sí.*'

Xav gritted his teeth. He and Lloyd Anders had been business rivals for years, with their respective companies often competing for the same acquisition. He should have known a prize like Reynaud Industries was too tempting for Anders to ignore. But to make his move at the eleventh hour, when Xav was so close to finalising a deal with Reynaud, and then to have the balls to entertain Peter Reynaud and his wife in one of the Vega Corporation's own clubs...

Xav put his pen down before he snapped it.

'Frankly, I'm surprised Reynaud would consider Anders as a potential suitor for the business,' Ramon said. 'Reynaud is conservative. Old school. He has a paternalistic leadership style. If his son hadn't gone into medicine and his daughter hadn't died of leukaemia he'd be passing the company on to his children, not selling.'

Xav paused in the act of pouring himself another coffee. 'Leukaemia?'

'*Sí.* Died in her late teens.' Ramon pushed his cup across the table for a refill, a frown settling between his brows. 'Must've been devastating.'

It wasn't the sort of observation Xav would have expected his brother to make. But, he conceded, Ramon had undergone a remarkable transformation in the past year.

From careless playboy to husband and father. Of course he'd have some idea of how traumatic it must be to lose a child. At eighteen he'd got a girl pregnant and she'd miscarried the baby. Now he had a daughter he cherished and, Xav suspected, would protect with his life.

He set the coffee pot down, recognising the sharp tug in his gut for what it was.

*Envy.*

Growing up, Ramon had been impulsive and reckless while Xav had done everything right. He'd played by the rules, put work before pleasure, strived every day to be the perfect son and make their parents proud.

He'd thought he would be the first to marry and give their parents grandchildren.

Not that he begrudged his brother and sister-in-law their happiness. Nor did he resent the existence of baby Katie. She was a beautiful child who carried the de la Vega genes—something his own offspring would not, regrettably, be blessed with.

The thought gave him pause.

He had chosen ignorance when it came to his genetic heritage, but what if he had children who one day wanted to know from whom they were descended? Was it his right to deny his offspring that knowledge?

A chill brushed his neck.

Could he unwittingly pass on genetic disorders to his children?

*Was leukaemia hereditary?*

'Anders hardly represents the kind of traditional values Reynaud holds in high regard,' Ramon said. 'The guy's in his midforties and already has two ex-wives. His last mistress looked as if she was barely out of college.' Ramon smirked. 'And didn't a story surface during his second marriage of a *ménage à trois* with the maid?'

Xav shook his head. He had no interest in the sordid details of Anders's personal life. Xav took pains to avoid the tabloids—both reading them and being *in* them.

How did Reynaud view *him*? He kept his nose clean, but the fact remained he was thirty-five and unmarried. Most people assumed that wealthy bachelors led a lifestyle of indulgence and excess whether they actually did or not.

He did not.

*And the redhead upstairs...?*

Xav ignored the snide inner voice. Jordan was not an indulgence. She was a sudden distracting itch he needed to scratch so he could move on and re-establish some normality.

He checked the time on his phone and stood. 'I have another meeting. Are you staying here this afternoon?'

Ramon drained his coffee. 'For a couple more hours. Lucia has set me up in the spare office down the hall. I'll come in for a few hours each day this week.'

'Fine.' Xav gathered up his papers. 'You're staying at Mamá and Papá's?'

'Of course. They insisted. Emily's barely been able to prise Katie from Mamá's arms.'

Ramon got up and collected his own things.

'Don't forget the family lunch on Saturday. Mamá will be upset if you don't show.'

Xav cursed under his breath. Five days from now... Would he and Jordan have had their fill of each other by then?

'The apartment's undergoing some renovation work,' he said, the lie sliding off his tongue with almost disturbing ease. 'Stay clear of it.'

The last thing he needed was Ramon stumbling across Jordan. How would that conversation go?

*Brother—meet my late birth mother's stepdaughter. Yes, I'm sleeping with her.*

Or at least he would be soon.

It was a thought that tested his concentration as he sat down with the heads of his commercial and legal teams.

That meeting went on for an hour. The next one forty-five minutes—thirty of which he spent in his head, replaying the little speech Jordan had delivered upstairs.

How many people did he know who were as straightforward and honest? Willing to speak their minds even when it discomfited them to do so?

She'd berated him for his behaviour, interpreted his actions with unsettling accuracy, and then baldly stated that she wanted him—all while blushing like an ingénue.

He'd never been so turned on listening to a woman talk.

And he'd never wanted a woman as desperately as he wanted Jordan Walsh.

# CHAPTER EIGHT

HE'D TOLD HER he'd be back no later than six.

When he stepped into the elevator it was almost seven. He punched in the security code and felt his heart pound as if he'd taken the stairs instead—all the way from the basement.

Anticipation, he told himself.

Yet he'd be lying if he didn't acknowledge that his pumping blood also fed a small vein of disquietude.

When Lucia had put a call through from one of the directors right on six o'clock he'd sent a brief text to Jordan advising her that he'd been waylaid.

He'd received no response.

What if, even after her blushing confession about wanting him, she'd changed her mind and fled?

The very thought sent a vicious twist of reaction through his stomach. He'd want to go after her, but he wouldn't. He'd barely been able to rationalise his actions the first time. If he chased her down again he'd look like a madman.

He stepped out of the elevator and scanned the large open-plan living space.

Her bags were gone.

His hands curled into fists.

No. *No.*

'Jordan?'

He checked the kitchen, found it empty, and was about to turn and stride out when his gaze caught on a bowl filled with a bright assortment of fruit on one of the black granite surfaces.

The tension in his muscles eased a bit. The bowl hadn't

been there earlier. How likely was it that Jordan had decided to leave him a parting gift of fruit?

Quickening his pace, he headed towards the bedrooms, and there, in the smallest of the rooms, were her rucksack and handbag.

Mildly amused, he grabbed the bags and took them to the master bedroom. Did she think he would let her sleep in a separate room? He wasn't the kind of man who took his pleasure with a woman and then slept alone. When he took a lover to his bed he expected to find her next to him in the morning, preferably with a smile on her face and a body that was soft and willing.

He returned to the living room and spotted what he'd missed earlier—the large sliding door to the terrace sitting slightly ajar. He still couldn't see her, though—not until he went outside and saw she'd dragged one of the loungers into a shaded back corner of the terrace to escape the sun.

Was she sleeping?

He approached quietly. She lay on her side, her long legs curled up, her cheek resting on the back of one hand. Her hair flowed loose and he marvelled at the melding shades of red and copper and gold that never failed to fascinate him.

A paperback lay on the ground, a cardboard bookmark next to it. The haphazard placement of each suggested the book might have slipped from her grasp when she'd nodded off.

Would she be annoyed when she woke to find she'd lost her place?

He found his mouth curving as he pictured that little scowl she developed when she was unhappy about something—the one that made her look about as fearsome as a grumpy kitten with its hackles up.

He'd seen that expression a number of times in the last five days—usually when she was making her dissatisction with his behaviour known.

It occurred to him there was no one in his life who dared

to call him out on his arrogance the way she did—except maybe for his mother, who did so only occasionally and was wise enough to know when to give his temper a wide berth.

He crouched beside the lounger, unable to resist tucking a stray copper curl behind her ear. Her nose was still pink from yesterday, and he was pleased she'd sought the shade to protect her skin.

She stirred, her soft lips parting, but her eyes stayed closed. She whispered something and he leaned in to catch the words.

'Is she coming back?'

He realised she was still asleep, or maybe hovering in that place between sleep and wakefulness where dreams and reality sometimes blurred.

Had she meant Camila?

His heartbeat slowed as he thought back to that first meeting in his office.

Six weeks. Wasn't that how long she'd said it had been since her stepmother had died?

It wasn't long.

A sudden surge of tenderness took the edge off the potent, ever-present desire that hummed inside him like an electric current when he was around her.

Jordan projected such natural buoyancy and strength it was easy to forget she must still be grieving. Hurting.

His chest tightened and for a moment he had a strange sense that he shared in her loss. That somehow Camila's passing had forged a bond between himself and Jordan—a connection that ran deeper than sexual attraction.

As swiftly as the feeling overtook him, however, he shook it off. How could he grieve for a woman he'd never known?

He leaned in again and spoke softly. 'No, *querida*. She's gone. But I'm here.'

He scooped her into his arms and stood, and she murmured some unintelligible words and burrowed her face into his neck.

In the master suite he lowered her onto the bed, his brain waging a fierce battle with his body. One urged him to tuck a blanket around her and walk away. The other wanted to undress her and explore every inch of her luscious body.

He started to straighten, but her arms tightened around his neck.

'Xavier?'

He looked down, straight into those extraordinary golden-green eyes, wide open now, staring up at him, searching his.

'Where are you going?' Her voice was deliciously husky. 'I've been waiting for you.'

It was all the invitation he needed. Planting his hands either side of her head, he lowered himself to the bed and settled his mouth over hers.

She opened to him immediately, and he almost groaned at the feel of her plump lips softening and parting under his.

For seven hours he'd thought about doing this. Seven hours of struggling to concentrate through meetings and phone calls and the usual endless influx of emails and papers crossing his desk, all demanding his time and attention.

He cupped her jaw in one hand, holding her still so he could explore the contours of her mouth with his lips and tongue, forcing himself to take a gentler, more leisurely approach than he had previously.

He intended to have her as many times as he desired—as many times as was necessary for his lust to burn itself out—but he didn't want their first time to be a rushed, frantic coupling. He wanted to savour her, inch by exquisite inch, to prolong the experience and wring every drop of pleasure from it—for him and for her.

The problem was, while frustration and anger weren't driving him now, his hunger for her felt no less urgent and raw. Thirty seconds of kissing and already he was having to restrain himself.

He angled his head and took the kiss deeper, dipping

his tongue in, enjoying the way hers came out to duel and dance with his, her strokes and thrusts growing bolder by the second.

He felt her hands slide to the back of his head, her fingers clutching at his hair, and then she sucked his bottom lip into her mouth, the mischievous nip of her teeth shooting a dart of heat straight to the base of his groin.

Now he did groan—a deep, masculine sound of appreciation that rumbled up his throat.

She was honey and temptation—sugar and sin—mixed together in one soft, seductive package.

He felt sweat film his brow just as Jordan tugged on his tie and whispered against his lips.

'You're overdressed.'

Yes—and hot as hell. But to undress he would have to stop kissing her.

Instead he yanked his tie loose, managed to shrug one shoulder out of his jacket, but finally frustration—and the desire to feel nothing but heat and sweat between their bodies—forced him to raise his head.

'Don't move,' he growled.

He shed his clothes, snapping a few buttons off his shirt and losing his cufflinks on the floor in his haste. Jordan was up on her elbows, watching, her eyes growing wider with each item of clothing he removed.

When he pushed his boxers down and kicked them off, freeing the long, heavy shaft of his erection, her teeth sank into her bottom lip and her thick copper lashes swept down and shielded her eyes from view.

He crossed back to the bed, leaned down and took her face in his hands, and kissed her, long and slow, before easing back.

'Lift your arms,' he ordered, desire roughening his voice, and she did so, allowing him to pull her top up and over her head.

With deft hands he stripped away the rest of her clothing

until she lay completely naked on the bed, and for a moment his breathing stopped as he feasted his hungry gaze on the long, graceful lines and lush curves of her body.

A pink blush spilled down her neck, belated shyness making her move to cover herself.

'No.' He caught her wrists and pulled her arms above her head. 'You're beautiful.'

And then he came down onto the bed and lost himself in a thorough, sensual exploration of her body. Her pleasure, he quickly discovered, intensified his, and he let her responses guide him, paying close attention to her soft gasps and delightful moans, to the little telltale shivers that rippled through her body.

One by one he found her pleasure spots. By the time he trailed kisses along her smooth inner thighs he knew she was close to the edge.

Remembering how he'd made her climax on the sofa, he used his hands and mouth in the same way now, and within seconds her spine arched and she cried out and came in a beautiful, shuddering rush.

Heat ripped through his body, and in that moment he knew that watching Jordan in the contorted throes of orgasm was the single most erotic experience of his life.

He sheathed himself with a condom and noticed that his hands shook.

'Xavier…' Her voice was husky, plaintive, and he moved over her, covering her body with his.

'I'm here, *amante*.'

Her hands stroked over the muscles of his shoulders and back and down to his buttocks, drawing him to her as he positioned himself between her spread legs. Their gazes meshed for a moment, then he drove his hips forward and they both gasped as he thrust himself deep inside her.

His breath shuddered out of him, and then Jordan raised her knees and tilted her pelvis, causing friction, and he hurriedly sank his fingers into her hip.

'Wait,' he rasped, teeth gritted, needing a moment to rein himself in.

He closed his eyes. She was so hot. So tight. He felt her flesh stretch to accommodate his considerable width, then contract again, gripping him along every sensitised inch of his shaft.

'Xavier?'

He opened his eyes, saw uncertainty and concern on her beautiful, flushed face.

She reached up and lightly touched his clenched jaw. 'Is...is everything all right?'

He relaxed his expression. *'Sí, querida,'* he said, his voice hoarse. 'Everything is perfect.' He smoothed her hair back from her forehead and kissed her on the mouth. 'You're perfect.'

He moved and felt the tight, greedy clench of her internal muscles as he slowly drew out and then, at the last possible moment, plunged back in. The sensations were exquisite, torturous.

The slow, steady rhythm he'd intended to set to coax her towards climax again lasted all of five seconds.

He couldn't hold back. His body screamed for release. Demanded that he *take*. With a low groan of surrender he gave himself over to the dark, animalistic urges inside him and let go, each thrust harder, deeper than the last.

Jordan wound her arms around his neck, raised her mouth to his ear and whispered something shockingly dirty that drove him over the edge.

And then there was nothing but a streak of white-hot sensation and the rough, savage sound that ripped from his throat.

It took Jordan a long while to float back to earth. For a time she wondered how all the tiny scattered pieces of her could possibly reassemble themselves so that she looked and felt the same as before—and then she decided they wouldn't.

It wasn't possible.

After that mind-blowing, body-shattering experience she would never be the same again.

She would certainly never look at sex in the same light. Because now she knew. Knew that what she'd experienced with Josh had been a pale imitation of what true unbridled passion looked like. That sex with a man who elevated her pleasure above his, who knew where to find every erogenous zone on her body and how to make her feel worshipped and desired, was a thrilling experience every heterosexual woman should have at least once in her life.

Not that Jordan could imagine once being enough.

Not even close.

'What are you thinking?'

The deep rumble of Xavier's voice penetrated her thoughts. Without lifting her cheek off his shoulder she tilted her face to his. She lay in the circle of his arms, tucked against his side, her forearm draped over washboard abs so impressive she'd already promised herself she'd eat less chocolate and do sit-ups every morning.

Or maybe just sit-ups, she amended. Life was too short to deny herself chocolate.

*Or wild, exhilarating sex...*

'Jordan?' His arms tightened around her and his large hand stroked up and down her arm.

She felt her heart thud unevenly. She reminded herself she mustn't enjoy this part too much. They'd had amazing sex, but she would not build it into something it wasn't in her head. Her rose-tinted glasses would remain firmly under lock and key.

But a little post-coital euphoria wouldn't do her any harm. Besides, how could she pretend that being cocooned in these big, strong arms was anything less than bliss? Not to mention a surprise. Who would have pegged the formidable Xavier de la Vega as a cuddler?

Smiling to herself, she tucked her chin back down and

let her gaze drift across his hair-roughened chest. 'What was the question again?'

'What are you thinking about?'

She was thinking he had ruined her future sex-life, because no other man would ever compare. 'I reserve the right not to answer that question.'

'On what grounds?'

'On the grounds that my answer may go to your head.'

'Which head?'

She was slow to register his meaning. Then a snigger escaped her. 'I can't believe you said that.'

'Says the woman who asked me to f—'

She jerked up and slapped her fingers over his mouth. 'That's different,' she defended, colour singeing her cheeks. 'That was in the heat of the moment.'

And the heat in that particular moment had been blistering—so intense Jordan had half expected the sheets to ignite and engulf them both in flames.

She'd sensed the change in Xavier, known the exact moment his prized control slipped from his grasp. Had he been another man, his sheer size and the power of his body as he surged between her legs might have made her feel vulnerable, but she trusted Xavier, and instead of fear she'd felt a thrill of wild excitement. His control had been in tatters because of *her*, and that intoxicating knowledge had made her brazen. Daring.

He grabbed her wrist and tugged so she ended up sprawled over his chest. Her pulse quickened. The light abrasion of chest hair against her sensitive breasts was far too tantalising.

His grey eyes gleamed. 'I never would have picked you for a dirty talker, Ms Walsh.'

Neither would she. But then she wouldn't have picked herself for a one-night stand kind of girl, either.

The thought was unwelcome and sobering. A reminder that this—whatever 'this' was, exactly—was temporary.

Just how temporary she hadn't yet worked out. For all she knew Xavier could be intending on taking her back to the ferry terminal tomorrow. Maybe for him once was enough.

A tiny sliver of ice pierced her euphoria.

Quickly she rolled away, managing to reach the side of the bed before a strong arm looped around her waist and hauled her back against a hot, muscular body.

Xavier growled in her ear. 'Where do you think you're going?'

Treacherous heat poured through her. 'I—I put my things in one of the other bedrooms.'

She hadn't wanted to make any assumptions about where she'd sleep—and she was glad now that she hadn't. It gave her an excuse to vacate his bed without suffering the humiliation of being asked to leave. The cuddling had been nice, but just because he held her in the immediate aftermath of lovemaking it didn't mean he wanted her in his bed all night.

'I moved your things. They're here…in the dressing room.'

'Oh.' And now she felt foolish.

'Do you have a problem with sleeping in my bed, Jordan?' His voice was dark and velvety, with the tiniest hint of menace.

'No. I just…' She tried for a careless shrug. 'I don't know what the rules are, that's all…' Her face burned. 'I don't usually do this sort of thing.'

With a manoeuvre that left her startled and breathless, he flipped her on her back and loomed above her. '"This sort of thing"?'

She swallowed. 'Casual sex.'

He made a low, rough sound. 'I'm pleased to hear it.'

*Pleased to hear what?* That she was nowhere near as experienced as him? She wished she'd said something different. Something that would have portrayed her as a woman of the world. The type of woman who could blithely indulge in a sexual fling and walk away without a backward glance.

He circled her left nipple with his fingertip. 'There's only one rule you need to know, *amante*.'

She tried to ignore the little ring of fire his finger created. 'What does that mean?'

'What?'

*'Amante?'*

His lips curved in a smile that was altogether too sexy. A smile that made her body heat and her insides melt. The heat was welcome, but not the melting. The melting of organs—especially the one in her chest—was strictly forbidden.

'Lover,' he said, and then dipped his head and drew her nipple into his mouth.

*Oh, God.*

She fought to concentrate. 'And—' She gasped as he sucked harder. 'Wh-what's the rule?'

After several more seconds of inflicting sweet torture on her he lifted his head and locked his glittering gaze onto hers. 'You don't walk away from this—from *me*—until we've burned it out.'

Which meant he believed their attraction had a shelf life. Was that how it was with this kind of crazy, intense chemistry? Did the passion flare hot and bright for a brief time and then naturally extinguish itself?

She didn't know if she found the idea reassuring or depressing.

His hand trailed over her stomach and she lost her train of thought. Tiny tremors of anticipation quaked through her. His mouth descended towards hers.

And then a grumbling noise, horribly loud and endlessly long, filled the air.

Jordan froze.

Xavier lifted his head and looked at her. 'Was that your stomach?'

Wishing she could disappear, she covered her face with her hands. 'Yes!' She glared at him through her fingers. 'Are you laughing at me?'

He was. Which meant she had not only his sexy smile to contend with, but the rich, delicious sound of his low laughter.

He straightened, took her hands and pulled her into a sitting position.

She gave him a look of dismay. 'What are you doing?'

'*We* are getting up,' he said. 'And then I'm ordering some food.'

She dropped her gaze to the very impressive semi-erect appendage between his legs. She raised an eyebrow. 'Wouldn't you rather do something else?' *She* would.

'*Sí.* But you need to eat.'

'I'm not hungry.'

He tipped up her chin. 'That's a lie. We both need to eat. And believe me, *amante*—' his sudden smile was wolfish '—you'll need the energy for the night ahead.'

If watching Jordan climax was at the top of his list of most erotic experiences, then watching her devour half a dozen raw oysters came a close second.

She picked up another shell. 'These are *so* good. Aren't you having any?'

She angled the shell, swallowed the oyster down and closed her eyes, savouring the taste on her tongue for a moment before tipping her head back and letting the fish slide down her delicate throat.

Xav shifted on his chair, grateful they were seated at his dining table in the open-plan living area. The tabletop hid what his sweatpants most definitely did not.

'I can take or leave shellfish.'

'You don't mind if I have the last one?'

He flourished a hand. 'Be my guest.'

She made short work of the last oyster, wiped her mouth on a napkin and took a sip of her white wine. Her gaze moved over the selection of tapas dishes spread across the table. 'This is fancy for takeout.'

'It's from a local restaurant.'

'And they deliver?'

'They do for me.'

She pulled one of the plates closer, eyeing the deep-fried balls of potato and minced meat drizzled with aioli and spicy sauce. 'I think I know these—they're *bombas*, aren't they?'

'*Sí*. You've had them before?'

She nodded. 'My first night here. I went for a wander through the city and ended up eating at a small tapas bar.' She picked up her fork. 'I remember these were delicious.'

He frowned. 'Alone?'

She finished her mouthful. 'Yum! Even better than the ones I had before. Yes.' She glanced up at him. 'Alone.'

The thought of her walking the city streets at night unaccompanied sent an icy trickle down his spine. 'Why do this trip on your own?' he asked abruptly. 'Don't you have someone who would have travelled with you?'

She shrugged. 'My friends are working. And if one of them had taken some leave to come with me it would have meant a more disciplined timeframe and itinerary. I don't have a job waiting for me, and travelling by myself gives me flexibility. If I want to spend a few extra nights somewhere, or change the order of places I visit, I can.'

He couched his next question in a more casual tone. 'How much time did you plan to spend in Spain?'

She pushed her hair out of her face. 'About three and a half weeks. I plan to travel for about a month altogether, but I want to do a few days in London on my way back.'

'Why London?'

Another shrug. 'It's on my list. I've always wanted to see *Les Misérables* in the West End.'

'You have a list?'

She broke off another chunk of *bomba*. 'I have two lists. A "must" list and an "if there's time" list. Both include places to see and things to do.'

He sipped his wine. 'What else is on your "must" list?'

She swallowed her food. 'Mallorca,' she said with a pointed glance. No doubt to emphasise that Mallorca was where she'd be now, if not for him.

Xav sent back a smouldering look to remind her she hadn't complained about that an hour ago, when she'd been naked and underneath him.

Her face turned pink and she cleared her throat. 'Madrid and…um… A few other places.'

An idea flashed into his head. One that, as he turned it over a few times and examined it more closely for potential flaws, seemed remarkably brilliant and foolproof.

'Come with me to Madrid for a few days.'

She blinked at him. 'What?'

'I have some meetings to attend in our office there.' Meetings that were currently scheduled for next week, but he would have Lucia bring them forward. 'I have an apartment in a separate building from the offices—near the Museo de Prado.'

She put her fork down. 'You'll be working during the day?'

'Of course. And you'll be busy sightseeing. I'll put a dedicated car and driver at your disposal. And then the evenings and the nights…' he pushed his chair back, reached for her hand and pulled her into his lap '…will be ours.'

It was perfect. Jordan wanted to see Madrid, and he wanted more of Jordan. One night together was not going to be enough. And taking her out of Barcelona was ideal. It eliminated any risk of her encountering his brother or anyone else from the family.

She bit her lip. 'I don't know…'

He rose with her in his arms and saw that adorable scowl forming on her features. But he also saw her pupils widen, heard her breathing grow shallow. She wanted him again already, and given how she'd come apart in his arms earlier he didn't imagine one night would be enough for her either.

'Hey!' She wriggled her luscious body against his. 'What are you doing? I'm not finished eating.'

His body hardening rapidly with need, he headed for the bedroom. 'It seems you may need some persuading.'

She opened her mouth and closed it again.

He lifted an eyebrow. 'Objections?'

Her scowl receded. 'No. But I warn you now—' she looped her arms around his neck '—I may need an *awful* lot of convincing.'

# CHAPTER NINE

'OH, MY GOODNESS…' Jordan stepped off the bottom tread of the long staircase that had brought them deep underground and looked around her. 'This is amazing.'

She glanced up at Xavier and his easy smile, combined with the warm press of his palm against the small of her back, had a dangerous effect on her equilibrium.

He turned her towards an approaching maître d'. 'Four hundred years ago this was a network of winery cellars run by monks,' he said. 'Now it's one of Madrid's finest restaurants.'

The windowless space might have felt stuffy and oppressive, but it had been so beautifully restored that instead it felt welcoming and intimate.

Following the maître d', they walked beneath centuries-old arches of brick and stone, through an enchanting labyrinth of narrow passageways that linked a series of dining alcoves and galleries of varying shapes and sizes.

Isolated from the noisy, bustling city above, and with soft music piped through invisible speakers and subtle, atmospheric lighting enhancing the sense of tranquillity and seclusion, it was the perfect place for a couple to enjoy a romantic night out.

Ignoring the pang behind her ribs that warned her against yearning for things she shouldn't, Jordan smiled and thanked the man who'd shown them to their table, set in its own alcove, and held out her chair.

This was *not* a romantic date. She and Xavier were simply marking their third and final night in Madrid by doing something different. Something other than spending the whole evening at the apartment and ordering in.

Not that she'd minded that, of course. She'd packed her days with sightseeing, and by the time the evenings had rolled around all she'd wanted to do was see Xavier. She hadn't cared what they did, so long as they were together. But when he'd suggested they dine at a restaurant tonight she'd thrilled to the idea of going out with him.

A waiter brought the wine Xavier had ordered, noted their food selections and disappeared.

'What did you do today, *querida*?'

She smiled. When he'd asked that question last night, and the night before that, she'd been naked and sated, lying in his arms with her head resting on his chest. The first time she'd assumed he was just being polite, making conversation because that was what men thought women wanted. She'd expected him to listen with only half an ear, but his murmured comments and further questions had proved he was listening attentively and she'd realised his interest was genuine.

She sat forward and gave him a brief rundown of her day's sightseeing, which included, among other things, a visit to an impressive art museum housed in a neo-classical palace, a walk to one of the city's oldest squares, and a wander around the boat lake in Madrid's beautiful Retiro Park.

He frowned. 'You could have saved your feet a lot of walking if you'd accepted my offer of a driver.'

She shook her head. 'I told you. I like walking. And you see so much more than you do from the window of a car.'

He sipped his wine. He looked ultra-gorgeous tonight, his jaw dark with five o'clock shadow and his bronzed skin set off by a black open-collared shirt. 'Did you reach your friend?'

She pulled her gaze off the triangle of dusky skin at the base of his throat. 'Yes.'

'And everything is fine?'

She hesitated. 'Yes. A friend of hers is housesitting for me in Melbourne. She wanted to let me know that a local real estate agent had been in touch to say he has an interested buyer.'

She'd woken this morning to a text message from Ellie.

We need to talk!

Xavier, on his way out to the office, had seen her frown, asked her what was wrong, then told her to use the apartment's landline to call Australia.

Jordan wasn't lying about the estate agent. But that hadn't been Ellie's main bit of news. A nursing position was coming available in the emergency department at the Sydney hospital where Jordan had worked and where Ellie still did. Jordan had been well regarded during her time there, and the nurse manager had asked Ellie about Jordan's availability.

She would still have to go through the formal application channels, which meant cutting her trip short by a week and flying to Sydney for an interview, but the odds of her landing the position were good.

Ellie had almost squealed with excitement. And it *was* incredible news. To go home and practically walk back into her old job would be a solid first step towards getting her life back on track.

So why didn't she feel more excited? And why was she reluctant to tell Xavier about it?

Perhaps she simply wasn't ready for 'real life' to intrude just yet. For this fairytale bubble she felt as if she were floating in to burst.

'You own a house?'

'I inherited it. It's the home my father and Camila owned.'

'And you wish to sell it?'

A weight dragged at her chest for a moment. She'd had some happy times in that house, but the people she'd shared those times with were both gone.

'I haven't made up my mind, but I suspect that's what

I'll end up doing. Even if I stay in Melbourne the house is too big for me. It was too big for Dad and Camila, really, but it's right by the ocean and Camila adored the sea—' She caught herself. 'Sorry,' she muttered, dropping her gaze to her wine glass. 'I know you're not interested—'

'Don't.' Xavier reached across the table and covered her hand with his. His mouth firmed, but his voice was soft. 'If anyone should apologise it is me.'

Her skin tingled under the warm pressure of his fingers. Heart beating a little faster, she looked up. 'What for?'

His thumb stroked over her knuckles. 'For what I said in the car on Sunday. It was disrespectful. It is not my place to judge Camila or to make assumptions about the situation she found herself in. The fact is she made a choice thirty-five years ago that was ultimately for my benefit, and for that I am grateful to her.'

Jordan's throat stung, and for a moment she had to look away. She swallowed, then let her gaze connect again with his. 'Thank you. That means a lot to me—and it would have meant a lot to Camila.'

He caressed her knuckles once more and then withdrew his hand. As he did so Jordan noticed a man watching them from a table in another alcove, just visible beyond Xavier's left shoulder. She didn't recognise him, or his beautiful female companion, but he held her gaze for a moment before looking away.

Xavier brought her attention back to him. 'When did you lose your father?'

'Four years ago,' she said quietly. 'It was a stroke. Sudden and unexpected.'

'I'm sorry.'

She smiled sadly. 'Me, too. He was a wonderful man. Very gentle and kind.'

He was silent for a moment. 'And your mother?'

She shook her head. 'She left when I was six. I don't have a relationship with her.'

She rarely spoke of her mother. It had been twenty years since Jacqueline Walsh had left the house to go to her precious job and not bothered coming home to her husband and daughter. Jordan had buried that hurt a long time ago, somewhere very deep.

'Dad met Camila when I was ten and they married a year later. From then on she was who I thought of as my mom.' She pushed a smile onto her face. 'They were lovely together. Truly happy. The perfect couple.' Emotion knotted her throat again, and she quickly moved on. 'Speaking of happy couples—did you know that Rosa and Alfonso are about to have their thirtieth wedding anniversary?'

'I did.'

Jordan pulled her chin back and blinked. 'Really?'

Her patent disbelief earned her a look of wounded affront.

'You think I'm a cold, heartless boss who knows nothing about his employees?'

When she hesitated a second too long his eyes narrowed and his voice turned low and silky.

'I see I shall have to disabuse you of some of your erroneous notions later tonight.'

Laughter rose in her throat then, and her pulse skipped in her veins. This lighter, teasing side of Xavier never failed to surprise and delight her.

The fact that neither of them had yet broached the question of what would happen when they returned to Barcelona tomorrow was something she chose not to think about just now.

'So naturally you've given them both some time off so they can celebrate?' she challenged.

'*Sí.* Along with first-class air tickets to Berlin to see their daughter and son-in-law.'

Suddenly her insides went a little mushy. 'Rosa didn't mention you were doing that.'

'She doesn't know. Alfonso is surprising her. He came

to me a few months ago, without Rosa's knowledge, to discuss the two of them having some time off. They haven't seen their daughter in a long time and he wanted to take Rosa to Germany for their anniversary. I agreed to the time off on the proviso that he allow me to pay their airfares.'

Ridiculously, her eyes welled. 'Oh, Xavier. That…that's such a lovely thing to do.'

He shrugged. 'They've given me ten years of loyal service. It is something small I can do to show my appreciation.'

Only a billionaire would dismiss such a gesture as 'small'. She swallowed down the silly lump in her throat. It was difficult to reconcile the man in front of her—a man who clearly had a generous heart buried inside that impressive chest of his—with the one who'd expressed such cold, clinical views about love and marriage.

What could possibly have happened to him to make him so cynical?

Quelling her curiosity, she asked, 'When are they going?'

'Tomorrow. For ten days.'

'Ten days without Rosa's cooking? That's a lot of take-out,' she teased.

He twisted the stem of his wine glass between his thumb and forefinger. 'Stay,' he said suddenly, fixing his gaze on hers.

Her heart stalled for a moment, then took off at a frantic pace.

'While Rosa and Alfonso are away?'

'*Sí.*'

She willed her pulse-rate to calm. For a split second she'd thought—

'I'll take you to Mallorca over the weekend,' he said. 'And London the following weekend.'

Her heart sank a tiny bit. She thought of the private jet they'd flown in, of his luxury homes in Barcelona and Madrid, then tried to imagine the sort of opulent place they would stay in Mallorca or London. Was this the kind of incentive he thought would keep her in his bed for another week? The promise of free luxury travel and swanky accommodation?

He didn't know her at all. If he did he'd know she would settle for the promise of something far simpler and less expensive—like a whole uninterrupted day with him. A whole twenty-four hours with no work, no phone calls, no emails... Nothing but him and her, talking, teasing, getting to know one another...making love.

She looked down, twirling her glass between her hands. Maybe the high life was what wealthy men expected their mistresses to demand.

*Mistresses.*

*Ugh.* Was that what this fling, or affair, or whatever you called it, made her? A rich man's mistress?

'I'm not sure,' she said, lifting her gaze and accidentally catching the eye of the man she'd noticed earlier. She quickly looked away and focused on Xavier. 'Let me think about it.'

His eyes held hers again, and suddenly the air shimmered with a potent mix of heat and sensuality. 'Do I need to remind you how persuasive I can be, *amante*?'

Desire tugged in her belly, so intense it almost took her breath away, and she wondered if he was right about a passion like theirs having an expiry date. If he was, would she be foolish to walk away from it prematurely? To deny herself the enjoyment of something she might never experience again?

The waiter reappeared then, with their starters, and they ate and moved on to an easier, less sexually charged conversation.

She was fascinated by the multiple facets of his family's business—or perhaps it was his obvious commitment and passion for his work that captivated her as he patiently answered her questions.

And saddened her.

How would his future wife and children ever compete for his attention when his work consumed him so completely?

Her heart ached at the thought of his children—Camila's grandchildren—feeling the way her mother had made her feel.

Unloved. Unimportant. *Unwanted.*

And yet... Xavier had made it clear he wanted a family, hadn't he? Moreover, when she'd questioned whether he would love his children he'd reacted almost angrily. Which had to mean...what? That he believed in parental love but not in love between a man and a woman?

Why not the latter? He was capable of tenderness. Affection. She experienced that side of him every time he held her in the aftermath of their lovemaking. Every time his strong arms cocooned her and held her to his side, or her back snuggled against his front. He made her feel protected and cherished. Made her long for something deeper, stronger, more permanent than just sexual gratification.

Was that how his future wife was destined to feel? Would she forever yearn for something her husband wasn't willing to give? Or would her patience be rewarded? Because surely it wasn't a leap too far to think that tenderness and affection could eventually turn into love...

Jordan reached for her wine, her hand a little unsteady as she took a sip. She was letting her thoughts drift along a dangerous path. Maybe even subconsciously casting herself in the role of his future wife.

Which was crazy. Xavier desired her—she didn't doubt that—but she would never fit the mould of perfect corporate wife.

Annoyed with herself, she put down her glass, picked up the dessert menu and concentrated on reading it. Everything looked divine, but she'd eaten so much already.

'The cheesecake sounds good,' she mused. 'But I'm not sure I have the room.'

'We could share one,' Xavier suggested.

And in the end they did—and Jordan told herself that it wasn't the *slightest* bit romantic.

They finished off with *digestifs* of brandy—and that was when the male diner whose eye she'd been studiously avoiding stood up and approached their table. She opened her mouth to warn Xavier but she was too late. The man was already beside him, clapping a hand over his shoulder.

*'Buenas noches, querido primo.'*

Xavier's entire body tensed, and before he even looked up and acknowledged the other man the atmosphere grew frigid.

Jaw locked tight, he sat back in an abrupt way that forced the man's hand off his shoulder. 'Diego.'

Gone were the relaxed lines of his face and the smoky warmth in his silver-grey eyes. His expression was fixed and unreadable. The men exchanged a few sentences in Spanish, and Jordan didn't need to understand the language to know these two weren't friends. Their tones weren't aggressive, but Xavier's words were clipped, his body language closed-off, and although the other man smiled there was an antagonistic quality to his manner.

More than once his gaze strayed to her, but Xavier made no effort to introduce her and she grew increasingly uncomfortable.

Then, abruptly, the man turned to her and stuck out his hand. *'Hola, soy Diego de la Vega. Mucho gusto.'*

Jordan froze. De la Vega? These two were *family*?

Not wanting to appear rude, she put her hand in his and said simply, 'Jordan Walsh.'

Instantly she regretted offering her hand. The way he gripped her fingers and sent his gaze travelling down her body, as if he didn't already have a beautiful woman waiting back at his table, made her skin crawl.

'Ah, you are English?'

She reclaimed her hand. 'Australian,' she said automatically, then wished she hadn't when she flicked her gaze to Xavier and saw his face darken.

He stood so quickly his chair scraped on the stone floor, and the physical dissimilarity between the two men was immediately apparent. Diego de la Vega was good-looking, but he didn't have Xavier's height or the same powerful build, and he didn't possess one iota of the raw masculinity and charisma Xavier exuded.

He looked at her. 'Let's go,' he said evenly, and she didn't need further prompting.

Whoever he was, Diego de la Vega made her uneasy; she was more than happy to leave.

Fortunately Xavier had already paid the bill. He said a curt *'Buenas noches'* to his relative, and then they made a quick exit—though not before Jordan had fielded a look from Diego that not only glinted with ill-concealed curiosity but also, she thought, a hint of malevolence.

Suppressing a shudder, she emerged onto the street and turned to Xavier. His jaw was still tight, his mouth compressed. 'Who *was* that?'

'My cousin.'

Hand on her elbow, he guided her into the back of the chauffeured vehicle that waited at the kerb for them. He joined her from the other side and then stayed frustratingly silent.

After two minutes of his brooding, she could no longer hold her tongue. 'Why is there so much animosity between you two?'

He continued to look out of his window. 'We don't get along.'

She stared at his profile, so strong and proud. So achingly handsome. 'I could see that,' she said patiently. 'I'm asking you why.'

He paused for so long she thought he wasn't going to answer. 'We fell out over a woman.'

Jordan was silent as she absorbed that. So he had once felt strongly enough about a woman to feel territorial over her?

'Recently?' she asked, conscious of a hot, unaccountable twinge of jealousy.

'Ten years ago.'

Foolishly, she felt relieved. 'Is that why you didn't introduce me?'

He turned his head to look at her, and she cringed inwardly, knowing that he must have heard the hint of hurt in her voice.

The truth was she *did* feel hurt. Regardless of this spat the two men had had a decade ago, Diego was Xavier's family—and yet he hadn't thought her important enough to introduce her. Perhaps he'd thought he was protecting her—and admittedly Diego *had* unnerved her—but at the same time Xavier had made her feel small. Insignificant.

'He's not a nice man, *querida*.'

His voice was gentler now, but Jordan sensed he was holding something back. Something more serious than a fight over a woman.

'What else?'

He frowned. 'What do you mean?'

'There's something else,' she pressed, running with her instincts. 'Besides the woman. Some other reason you and Diego don't get along.'

He looked out of his window again, silent for another long moment. '*Sí,*' he said at last. 'But it's…complicated.'

'You don't think I can understand "complicated"?'

'I don't think it's anything you really want to hear about.'

'If I wasn't interested,' she said gently, 'I wouldn't have asked.'

He pulled in a breath and released it slowly. Then he turned back to her. 'There are certain members of the extended de la Vega family—including Diego and his father, Hector, who is my father's first cousin—who have never accepted me as one of them.'

It was Jordan's turn to frown. 'One of "them"?'

'A de la Vega.'

She was silent for a moment, trying to make sense of what he was telling her. She thought she understood, and yet it seemed ludicrous. Unbelievable.

'Because you're adopted?'

'*Sí.*' His voice was tight. 'Because my veins do not run with true blue de la Vega blood.'

She felt a spurt of outrage. 'But…that's ridiculous!'

His smile was grim. 'That is the way of it.'

'So they…what? Ignore you at family gatherings? Leave you off the invitation list?'

He gave a humourless laugh. 'If only it were that simple.'

'What, then?'

He shook his head. 'You don't want to know about these things, *querida.*'

'I do,' she insisted, turning sideways in her seat—as much as her seatbelt would allow—to see him better. 'Tell me.'

He blew out another breath. 'For more than sixty years the position of CEO of the Vega Corporation has been handed down from father to son. My grandfather and Diego's grandfather were brothers. They both wanted the position. But my grandfather, as the eldest, was given the role. The rivalry between the brothers continued to the next generation, to their sons—'

'Your father and Diego's father?'

'*Sí.* My grandfather handed the position to my father, Vittorio, and he, in turn, handed the reins to me five years ago.'

'And Diego's father didn't like that?' she surmised.

'Hector's stance has always been that I have no birth right to any part of the family business. As a board member he officially objected when the CEO role was offered to me, but he couldn't garner enough support from the rest of the board to veto my appointment.'

She shook her head, appalled. 'That's snobbery and prejudice.'

'It's more than that. Hector is power-hungry. He wants me out and Diego in.'

'Diego as CEO?' After one brief encounter she barely knew the man, but her gut told her his leadership qualities would pale next to Xavier's. 'But what about your adoptive brother?'

'Ramon has never had any interest in the top job.' Another mirthless smile curved Xavier's lips. 'He says he's allergic to board meetings.'

'And your father?'

Surely Vittorio de la Vega didn't idly stand by while his adopted son was vilified by his own family.

'He stood down as Chairman last year after a health scare—problems with his heart. He remains on the board but he's taken a step back from the politicking. I prefer it that way. I don't want him stressed. He's given his pound of flesh to the business over the years—and he trusts that I can handle whatever Hector throws at me.'

Jordan heard both concern and respect in Xavier's voice. 'You care for him very much?'

'Of course.' He spoke without hesitation. 'For both of my parents. They're good people. The attitude of certain family members towards me has been…difficult for them. Upsetting.'

'And for you?' she queried gently.

He shrugged. 'It has simply made me work harder—to prove I can be better than the likes of Diego and Hector.'

Jordan felt her heart squeeze. Looking at him now, armed with this new knowledge, she saw so much more than a proud, driven, ambitious workaholic. She saw a man who'd had to work hard to prove himself over and over again. Who'd had to fight for acceptance and no doubt watch his back every step of the way.

It was no wonder he came across as arrogant and formidable at times. A man who had enemies constantly attempting to undermine him couldn't afford to show weakness.

Her chest burned with outrage. 'Were they cruel to you when you were a child?'

Another dismissive shrug. 'Diego and a few other cousins on his side of the family resorted to taunts and name-calling when the adults were out of earshot. It was nothing I couldn't handle.'

'What sort of names?'

'Nothing suitable for your delicate ears.'

She scowled. 'I wish I'd known all this when I met Diego at the restaurant. I would have punched that slimeball in the nose!'

Xavier looked at her, shocked, and then he threw his head back and laughed, the sound deliciously deep and full-bodied as it reverberated around the car's interior.

His voice was rich with amusement when he spoke. 'That is very sweet, *querida*, but I'm willing to bet you've never hit anyone in your life.'

'There's a first time for everything,' she muttered, and then sucked in her breath to say more.

But he moved suddenly, and before she could guess what he intended he'd removed her seatbelt and dragged her onto his lap.

'Enough talking,' he growled. 'I can think of better things to do with my mouth.'

Shock—and a surge of anticipation—made her voice breathy. 'What happened to being safety-conscious?'

His silver eyes glittered. 'You're safe in my arms, *amante*.'

She wasn't so sure about that, given the look of carnal intent on his face.

Then he stroked his hand over her breast and pressed an open-mouthed kiss to the base of her throat, and suddenly the last thing on Jordan's mind was being careful—or safe...

At six-forty-five a.m. on Friday they boarded his jet on the tarmac in Madrid for their return to Barcelona.

Jordan hadn't complained about their early rising, but

she had looked deliciously flushed and dishevelled as she'd raced around the apartment gathering up her things before the car arrived.

Her last-minute rush to pack had been his fault. He'd joined her in the shower, pressed her back against the tiles and done things to her under the steaming water that had consequently made them both run late—but she hadn't complained about that either.

In the final minutes before they'd left the apartment she'd flown back into the bedroom, looking for something, and Xav had spied her journal on a side table in the living room. It had lain open at a page on which she'd written her list of things to see and do in Spain, and although he hadn't intended to look one item had caught his eye before he'd closed the journal and called out to her that he'd found it.

The flight crew readied the aircraft for take-off and for the next hour Jordan dozed. Curled up on the seat next to him, head resting on his shoulder, she teased his senses with her subtle floral scent and soft, feminine warmth.

Time and again he found his gaze resting on her instead of on the document he'd opened on his tablet. Even in sleep she glowed with that irrepressible vitality that belied the pain she'd suffered. She wasn't yet thirty, yet already she'd lost two parents—three if you included her biological mother.

He felt a touch of anger when he thought of Jordan being abandoned by her mother. She'd skimmed over the fact as if it barely mattered to her, but no one, especially a child, could weather that sort of rejection without sustaining a few psychological scars.

Had his own biological mother played an instrumental role in healing Jordan's wounds?

He tucked a stray curl behind her ear and for the first time felt a deep sadness in his chest at the thought that he would never meet his birth mother. Jordan had loved and respected her stepmother; that fact alone told him Camila Walsh had been a good woman.

His mind turned to the letter she'd written to him—the letter he'd not yet read—and it struck him then, with a force that made the breath jam in his throat, what a gift it was. A gift he held in his possession only because Jordan had come halfway around the world to deliver it to him.

On impulse he pressed a kiss to the top of her head and she stirred, tipping up her chin and blinking sleepily at him.

'Are we there?'

Her lips were soft and pink, and he studied the plump contours with a mix of lust and tenderness. Last night, after leaving the restaurant, he'd told her things he'd never revealed to another woman, opening up in a way he ordinarily would have found discomfiting. Instead it had deepened the sense of intimacy between them, so that later, when he had taken her to bed, when he'd joined his body with hers in the most intimate way possible, their physical connection had felt much more unique and powerful.

Had Jordan felt it, too? Was that why she'd finally agreed to stay for another week?

He brushed his fingers over the satin slope of her cheek and for a moment felt intensely envious of the man who would one day fulfil her romantic dream of love and happily-ever-after. He couldn't be that man—he would never lay himself bare to that kind of risk and expectation—but for now she was his, and he would give and take as much pleasure as their time together allowed.

He stroked the pad of his thumb over her bottom lip and smiled. 'Not yet, *querida*,' he murmured. 'Go back to sleep.'

At a little after two-thirty Xav stood at the window of his office, staring out across the city, his mind adrift until the sound of Ramon's dry, half-amused voice dragged him out of his head.

'Daydreaming, *hermano*?'

He turned, shot a deliberate look at his watch and raised an eyebrow. 'Did you forget to set your alarm?' He eyed his brother as he sauntered in and sat down in front of his desk. 'I came to the office from Madrid and managed to get here five hours earlier than you.'

Ramon shrugged, unconcerned. 'Katie had a bad night, which means Emily had a bad night. I stayed at the villa this morning to look after Katie so Em could rest.'

That didn't sound like his sister-in-law. Emily might look delicate, but he knew she was a strong, capable woman. Not the type to be fazed by a sleepless night. 'She's unwell?'

'She's fine, but she had a virus a couple of weeks ago. She tires easily.'

He sat down behind his desk. 'Mamá couldn't have helped?'

'She offered, but she had some errands to run, and then one of her luncheons in the city, so I told her to go.' He stretched out his legs. 'How was Madrid?'

'Fine. Mostly meetings. No dramas.'

If he didn't count running into their cousin Diego. Unease ran through him like a trickle of icy water, but he shook off the sense of foreboding. Diego had witnessed nothing last night that he could wield as a weapon. He'd seen his cousin dining out with a beautiful woman—that was all. It was unfortunate that Jordan had revealed her full name, but Diego would have to dig deep and connect a lot of obscure dots before he unearthed anything significant.

Xav leaned back in his chair and took a breath. 'I can't make it tomorrow,' he said, and saw surprise flash across his brother's face.

'Why not?'

'I have another commitment.'

One with red hair, soft curves and a ripe mouth he seemed to have developed a permanent craving for.

Ramon frowned. 'You haven't seen Emily or Katie yet.

Em will be disappointed. We're returning to London on Sunday.'

'I'm sorry.'

Ruthlessly he quashed the flare of guilt. His time with Jordan was limited, whereas his family would always be relatively close and accessible. His parents' home was a thirty-minute drive from his. Ramon and his family, in London, were only two hours away by plane. He could see any of them any time—just not this weekend.

Ramon held his palms up. 'Fine. I assume you've told Mamá?'

'I'll call her.'

Although it wasn't a conversation he looked forward to. Very rarely did he disappoint his mother. For years that had been Ramon's speciality, and Xav had lost count of the times he'd taken his brother to task for his selfish behaviour.

Things were different now, of course. Ramon was different. He'd settled down, returned to the family fold.

Another trickle of unease went down Xav's spine. Now *he* was the one about to upset their mother. Was that what his lust for Jordan had reduced him to? Was she his drug of choice and he little better than a junkie who would do anything—even lie to and disappoint his family—to guarantee his next fix?

'You can tell her in person.'

He looked at his brother. 'Excuse me?'

'Mamá. She's coming here after lunch.' Ramon glanced at his watch and frowned. 'If you haven't seen her, then she's late. She said she'd be here around two. Unless…'

A sudden ripple of tension went through Xav's shoulders. 'Unless what?'

Ramon grimaced. 'She might have gone to the apartment first. I let slip about the renovation, and you know how she likes to put her two cents in when it comes to decorating. Sorry, *hermano*. She's probably up there right now changing the entire colour scheme.'

'*She* is right here, *mis queridos hijos*, so be careful what you say.'

Both men straightened in their chairs and swung their gazes towards the doorway.

Elena de la Vega smiled at her sons. Then she walked into the office and placed an elegant hand on Ramon's shoulder.

'*Querido*, would you give me a moment alone with your brother, please?' She waited for the door to close behind him, then sat in the chair he'd vacated, fixed her caramel-brown eyes on her eldest son and said, 'I've just had an interesting conversation with the very beautiful and utterly charming young woman in your apartment.'

# CHAPTER TEN

JORDAN PACED THE full length of the living area at least a dozen times before she paused, took a deep breath and told herself to calm down.

But she couldn't.

How could she be calm when she knew Xavier was going to be furious? *Livid.*

If only she'd stayed out a bit longer. Explored a few more of the quaint streets in the city's medieval Gothic Quarter. But three days of full-on sightseeing in Madrid and four nights of vigorous lovemaking had finally taken their toll. The idea of whiling away the afternoon with a book, stretched out on one of the loungers by the apartment's pool, had been too tempting to resist.

And then Xavier's mother had walked into the apartment.

His *mother.*

Her stomach tied in knots, she began to pace again, her bare feet taking her on another circuit of the living area and then out onto the sun-warmed terrace. But the fresh air didn't help; her mind continued to spin in ever-decreasing circles, tighter and tighter, until her thoughts narrowed down to a single, soul-crushing certainty.

*He would end it now.*

He would be so angry about what she'd told his mother he'd change his mind about her staying and ask her to leave.

And this time his rejection wouldn't just sting, like it had the night he'd spurned her by the pool. It would burn. Painfully. Horribly.

Because she cared now. More than she had before.

How could she not? They'd been intimate together. They'd shared things. Oh, she wasn't fooling herself with romantic delusions. She understood this was an affair, not a proper relationship. But she'd have to be carved from stone to feel absolutely nothing.

And she knew him better now. He was proud and honourable and generous and hardworking. She didn't only desire him, she liked him. Respected him.

*Oh, come on. It's more than that.*

Desperately she shut out the voice in her head. Feelings of love—true love—took time to develop. You couldn't fall head over heels for someone in less than two weeks...

With a groan of despair—because she feared that was precisely what she'd done—she stopped again and covered her face with her hands.

For a moment—just a moment—she thought about how easy it would be to flee. Not to have to face Xavier. To avoid his anger, the inevitable rejection—

'Jordan?'

She froze. *No.* She wasn't ready for him. Not yet. She needed more time. More time to shore up her emotional defences. More time to slip into whatever kind of cool demeanour mistresses adopted when they were about to be unceremoniously dumped.

'What are you doing?'

Did he sound angry? She couldn't tell.

She pulled in a deep breath, dropped her hands and faced him. He moved towards her, as darkly handsome as ever in his tailored suit, his short hair glossy black in the sunlight. His expression was serious but not, she registered with a rush of surprised relief, angry.

Perhaps it was that which gave her the courage to answer candidly. 'I don't know... Panicking, I think.'

She huffed out a small, self-deprecating laugh, but Xavier's expression remained serious.

'Why?'

She eyed him warily. 'Has your mother spoken with you?'

He came closer. *'Sí.'*

Her shoulders slumped under the weight of guilt. 'I'm so sorry,' she said in a rush. 'I got such a shock when she walked in—I'm sure she did, too. And then she introduced herself and I realised she was your mother and... She was so lovely... I was just—I couldn't lie to her about who I was. It felt wrong—'

She broke off and looked at him, feeling utterly wretched, conscious she was babbling. She felt as discomposed as she had the day he'd summoned her to his study at the villa. Why did he have this effect on her? No one else had ever done this to her. Turned her into a flustered, scatterbrained wreck.

She tipped her head back to look at him, said hesitantly, 'Aren't you angry?'

He lifted his hands and curled them over her shoulders, his thumbs brushing the sides of her neck. 'That you respected my mother by not lying to her?' He shook his head. 'No, *querida*. I'm not angry.'

Another surge of relief, this one even more powerful, made her legs feel weak. Or maybe that was simply the impact of Xavier standing so close. She'd lost count of how many times they'd made love, yet still her body ached for his touch so intensely it frightened her.

'I still feel awful,' she confessed, letting her hands slide up between them, flattening her palms on his chest. She couldn't stand this close and not touch him. 'Talking with your parents about Camila was something you were entitled to do in your own time, whenever it felt right. Now, because of me, it's been forced on you...' She bit her lip. 'Was she upset?'

The sides of his thumbs idly stroked up and down her neck, sending tiny shivers of sensation across her skin.

'Only a little. My mother has a very understanding nature.'

'Do you think she guessed that we're...?' She felt her face flame. 'You know...'

He gave a glimmer of a smile. 'Having a relationship?'

Her heart missed a beat. *Relationship?* Was that how he thought of their affair? She nodded, telling herself not to read anything into it.

*It's just a word.*

'She didn't ask me outright,' he said. 'But I suspect she's guessed.'

Jordan let out a little groan of embarrassment, her gaze darting down to her T-shirt and shorts. Elena de la Vega had been pleasant and friendly, but what must she have been secretly thinking? That her son's standards had dropped considerably from the sophisticated women he usually saw, no doubt.

Xavier, as though he'd read her mind, tilted her chin up and said, 'She thought you were very charming. And very beautiful.'

Her eyes widened. 'She did?'

'*Sí.*' He paused, his gaze moving thoughtfully over her face for a long moment. 'In fact you've made such an impression she's asked me to invite you to a luncheon at my parents' house tomorrow.'

She blinked. 'Really? Gosh, I…' Her heart beat a little faster. *Lunch with his parents?* 'How do you feel about that?' she asked carefully.

'I think if I fail to persuade you to accept my mother will be extremely disappointed and I may never hear the end of it.'

An evasive answer, revealing nothing of his true thoughts.

Jordan pressed her lips together, silencing the urge to push, to dig for some declaration of feeling that would probably never exist outside her fantasies.

Anyhow, perhaps it didn't matter what Xavier thought or felt. The invitation was from Elena de la Vega, not her son. Jordan had liked her immensely—had felt a bond of sorts as soon as they'd started talking about Camila.

Elena's eyes had clouded with sadness and compassion on learning of Camila's passing, and then with tears when Jordan had explained that she'd met Xavier because she'd brought a letter to him that her stepmom had written.

She'd hoped Elena might assume that she was simply staying as a house guest at the apartment, but if the older woman had already guessed something more was going on… Well, there wasn't anything to hide, then, was there?

Her mind made up, she smiled. 'It's kind of your mother to invite me, and I wouldn't want to disappoint her—or offend her. So…yes. I accept.'

'Good,' he said, although she couldn't tell whether he truly meant it.

He dropped a swift, perfunctory kiss on her mouth that was barely satisfying, then took his hands off her shoulders. Immediately her body craved their weight and warmth again. She let her own hands fall from his chest before the desire to grab his shirt and pull him back for a proper kiss overpowered her.

He glanced at his watch. 'I won't be later than six. We'll stay at the villa tonight, *sí*?'

She nodded, pasting on a bright smile that slid off her mouth as soon as he was gone.

Xavier mightn't have been angry, but he hadn't looked particularly happy, either.

Jordan dressed for lunch in a simple sleeveless pale lemon sundress she'd bought on impulse from a boutique sale in Madrid, and paired it with open-toed shoes. She carefully applied a bit of make-up, attached plain gold hoops to her ears, and was attempting to scrape her hair into some kind of sophisticated up-do when Xavier came up behind her, gently pulled her wrists down and removed the few pins she'd already inserted.

'I prefer it down,' he said, holding her gaze in the mirror until heat began to surge and eddy around them.

He was clean from the shower and wore nothing but a white towel loosely around his hips, and the mere sight of all that hard, masculine flesh sent tingles racing over her skin.

'Xavier…' she whispered, her tone a mix of plea and admonishment. 'We don't have time.'

He grinned, which made her pulse skip, then kissed her shoulder and moved away, leaving her to deal with suppressed desire on top of a belly full of nerves.

Nerves that had doubled in intensity ever since he'd mentioned that she would meet not only his parents at lunch, but his brother, Ramon, and his wife and their four-month-old baby daughter, who were visiting from London.

They drove to his parents' villa in the Aston Martin. It made a nice change from sitting in the back of chauffeured vehicles, and she sensed that Xavier enjoyed being behind the wheel.

His mood was lighter this morning, making her wonder if yesterday's quieter, more pensive mood had resulted from work issues rather than his mother's unexpected visit.

Whatever had set him brooding, it hadn't affected his sex drive, though. Last night's lovemaking had been intense and mind-blowing, his demands on her body exquisitely relentless. When she'd clung to him weakly and whimpered that she couldn't possibly climax again he had seemed to take it as a personal challenge, and had set about driving her to yet another shattering peak with ruthless, breathtaking mastery.

They'd even made love in the pool, where the cool, satiny feel of the water against hot, naked skin had intensified every sensation.

Jordan felt deeply grateful and relieved that Rosa and Alfonso were in Berlin, for they surely would have heard her wild screams of release from the staff cottage.

She took a deep breath now, as Xavier braked to a stop in front of Elena and Vittorio de la Vega's beautiful traditional white villa.

Perhaps sensing she was nervous, he lifted her hand and

kissed her knuckles. 'You look beautiful,' he murmured, and her heart swelled with an emotion she tried very hard to suppress.

And then, before they'd even emerged from the car, Elena was there, the warmth of her smile and her effusive greeting like an instant balm to Jordan's nerves. She watched Xavier put an arm around his mother and kiss her cheek and it touched her deeply—maybe even made her feel a little bit hopeful—to see the obvious love and respect between mother and son.

Whatever beliefs Xavier held about himself, he *was* capable of love.

They walked with Elena through the villa, and just before they stepped out onto the shaded terrace where the others were gathered Xavier linked his hand with hers, entwining their fingers, tugging her to his side.

The gesture felt both intimate and proprietorial and, knowing it would send a message to his family about their relationship, she sent him a quizzical look. But his expression was enigmatic, giving her no steer on exactly what message he wanted to send, so she simply went with it, telling herself to enjoy it without overanalysing.

And enjoy herself she did. So much so that after three pleasurable hours it felt strangely wrenching to say goodbye to these people she'd only just met and barely knew.

Ramon's wife, Emily, hugged her and slipped her a business card with her personal mobile number jotted on the back. 'Call me if you make it to London. I'd love to catch up. And if you're in the market for babysitting, definitely call me.' She grinned. 'I've never seen Katie sit so happily in a stranger's lap before. She adores you!'

On the drive home she felt an oddly melancholy mood slip over her, and she sat quietly in the front passenger seat, content to watch the scenery until Xavier's voice gently penetrated her thoughts.

*'Querida?'*

She turned her head to look at him. 'Sorry? What was that?'

'Is everything all right?'

She offered up a smile. 'Yes, of course.'

There was a pause. 'You didn't enjoy yourself this afternoon?'

'I had a wonderful time,' she quickly assured him.

'But something has upset you?'

She shook her head. 'Nothing's upset me.' She really *had* had a lovely time. 'I just…'

He took his eyes off the road for a second to glance at her. 'What?'

She was silent for a long moment. She didn't know how to articulate what she was feeling. Not without sounding envious and self-pitying.

Finally she just said, 'You have an amazing family, Xavier. Don't ever take them for granted.'

*Because one day they'll be gone, by choice or by fate, and you'll realise the people you love, and the ones who love you back, are rare gifts indeed.*

Xav walked into the cool of the villa, set his keys down and drew Jordan into the circle of his arms.

She came to him without resistance, shaving the edge off his unease, quelling his concern at her strange turn of mood.

She'd been superb with his family, charming them all as he'd known she would. It was ironic that what he had at first viewed as a potential disaster yesterday had, in fact, been a catalyst for shifting his mind, and his intentions, in a direction he suspected they would have eventually gone anyway—just a little more slowly.

Of course he'd have preferred it if things had panned out in a different, more controlled way, but he appreciated how Jordan had handled her unexpected encounter with his mother. When he'd gone up to see her she'd been flustered, understandably, and given his own preoccupation with the unanticipated turn of events he perhaps had not consoled her as well as he could have.

But she seemed to have taken it all in her stride—another quality to add to her list of attributes.

He stroked her spine through the fabric of her pretty yellow dress. She looked good in anything she wore—and he rather liked those little denim shorts that showed off her legs—but it was nice to see her in something more feminine. It made him want to drape her in jewels—yellow sapphires and emeralds to match her eyes—and commission a dozen bespoke evening gowns that would showcase her luscious curves to perfection. She would, he knew, turn heads wherever they went.

'What do you want to do this afternoon, *querida*?'

She eyed him. 'Don't you have work to do?'

He did. Fifty-odd unopened emails, a bid for a multimillion-dollar construction project in Dubai awaiting sign-off, and the latest time-wasting communication from Reynaud's lawyers to read.

None of which, at this very second, mattered more than putting the smile back on Jordan's lips.

His mother's words, spoken today out of earshot of anyone else, came back to him.

*'Go gently with her, Xavier. She is vulnerable. I like her and would not wish to see her hurt.'*

He'd looked at his *mamá* and wondered if they were talking about the same woman. 'She's strong,' he'd countered. It was another of her qualities he admired.

'Yes,' Elena had agreed. 'But she is grieving—and strong people hurt, too. They are just better at making the world think they don't.' Then she'd reached up and patted his cheek. 'Rather like someone else I know.'

Of course his mother was not only perceptive and wise, she was right. Jordan was still grieving Camila's loss. Spending time with his family had reminded her of the loved ones she'd lost and precipitated this sudden bout of sadness.

He didn't like it. Didn't like the shadows in her eyes, the downturn of her lovely mouth.

'No work today,' he declared. 'Tell me what you want to do. Your wish is my command.'

She pressed a cool palm to his forehead and frowned. 'Are you feeling unwell, Senyor de la Vega? You don't seem yourself.'

He moulded her soft body to his, snugly enough for her to feel his arousal. 'Come to think of it…' he murmured. 'I do have an ache that may need some attention. What would you recommend?'

She pursed her lips, contemplating. 'I would suggest you go straight to bed.'

His lips quirked. 'Is that your professional opinion, Nurse Walsh?'

'It is,' she said solemnly.

'In that case—' he scooped her up and she laughed, and he thought it might be the sweetest sound he'd ever heard '—who am I to argue?'

# CHAPTER ELEVEN

JORDAN FELT THE subtle shift in their relationship—and, yes, she was allowing herself to use that word loosely in her head—over the course of the weekend.

Some things were obvious. Xavier barely set foot inside his study, for instance, and there were several occasions when his phone was conspicuous by its absence—like when she'd made him take her on a hike to the highest point on the estate, a spot he admitted with some chagrin he'd never walked to before, and when they'd meandered down to his private beach for a naked moonlit dip in the ocean.

Other things were less obvious. Like the times she would look up from her book or a task and find his gaze resting on her, his expression pensive, enigmatic. Once or twice she felt as though she were being quietly assessed—though for what purpose she couldn't have said. The idea that he might be comparing her with former mistresses was, she discovered, an unpleasant thought that served only to send a hot streak of jealousy and insecurity through her.

'What are you thinking, *amante*?'

She lifted her head off the lounger. Sprawled in the one alongside her, he was a mouthwatering sight in nothing but a pair of black swimming trunks. He'd just swum fifty lengths of the pool and droplets of water glistened in his chest hair and snaked in rivulets over his taut, well-defined musculature.

She adjusted her sunglasses and tried not to ogle him. 'I'm not thinking about anything. I'm reading my book.'

'You've stared at the same page for the last ten minutes.'

She dropped the book into her lap. 'Men are not supposed

to be that observant,' she grumbled, then smiled when he chuckled. She couldn't resist him in this mood.

'So what's on your mind?' he pressed.

Jordan put her book aside, pulled her knees up to her chest. 'Honestly?'

He looked at her, silent for a moment, as though sensing the tone of their conversation was about to change.

'*Sí,*' he invited. 'Honestly.'

She pushed her sunglasses onto her head, even though it would have been easier to hide behind them. But she couldn't always protect herself, could she? Lord knew she'd tried, ever since she was a child—making herself indispensable, ensuring she was needed, even choosing a profession that made her feel useful. Valued. But still she had lost the people she loved the most…her dad, Camila.

A week ago Xavier had accused her of running away, and he'd been right. Running away was easier than facing rejection. Hadn't she even tried to leave his bed after the first time they'd made love? Fearing that if she didn't he would throw her out of it? He hadn't. Just as he hadn't demanded she leave on Friday, after his mother had visited, even though—to her shame—one of her first thoughts had been to flee.

And now… Now she wanted to be brave. For herself. For Xavier. Because maybe this was more than just chemistry with an expiry date…

She took a deep breath. 'I want to apologise. For something I said to you on our first evening together.'

He'd gone still, but she sensed it wasn't an angry stillness.

'Go on,' he prompted.

She hugged her knees, swivelled round to face him. 'I asked you if you would love your children as—as if there was a possibility you wouldn't,' she said quietly. 'It was a terrible thing to imply, and I'm sorry. Yesterday, seeing you with your parents… Well, I could see how much you love and respect them, so family is obviously important to you. I imagine that when you have children you will love them very much.'

He was silent again. Jordan could hear her heartbeat in her ears.

Then he reached his hand across and circled her ankle, gently stroking his thumb over the top of her foot. 'Thank you, *querida*. But your apology is not necessary. In those first days of our acquaintance I didn't present myself in the best light. You weren't unjustified in thinking the worst of me.'

Jordan breathed deeply again. That hadn't been so hard… but this next bit might be.

'Your parents are lovely, Xavier,' she said with a soft smile. 'And they so obviously adore each other after many years of marriage.' She paused. 'I wondered why, when you have such a beautiful example of a loving marriage, you would dismiss that for yourself.'

She felt his fingers tense on her ankle, the grip almost painful, but forced herself to finish.

'Does it have anything to do with the woman you and Diego fought over?'

Xav saw her slight wince and withdrew his hand. He didn't desire to have this conversation. He had told her before he wasn't interested in the past and he meant it. But he recognised that she was looking for something from him. Something he feared he couldn't give her.

Yet he could give her other things. More important things. More valuable things.

This, perhaps, was the opening he needed. One brief, uncomfortable conversation was an acceptable sacrifice to get what he wanted. And in the past forty-eight hours it had become crystal-clear in his mind that what he wanted was Jordan.

He shifted on the lounger, creating space and holding out his arm. 'Come, *querida*.'

She hesitated, but then came to him, curling into his arms, her body soft and warm through her thin sarong.

He removed her sunglasses, resting his jaw on top of her head. 'Ten years ago I met a woman I came to believe I wanted to marry.'

Jordan was silent a long moment. When she spoke he felt the warmth of her breath on his chest.

'Because you thought you loved her?'

He drew air through his nose, exhaled it slowly from his mouth. '*Sí.* I believed she was…special.'

So 'special' he had introduced her to his family. Told his mother she was The One. Bought an expensive ring.

'Who was she?'

'A young American heiress. We met through social circles.'

'And what happened?'

'I proposed and she turned me down.'

'She didn't love you?' she asked gently.

'No.'

Jordan rose up on her elbow. 'I'm so sorry, Xavier.' Her eyes were soft with compassion. 'That must have been incredibly difficult—and painful.' She paused, biting her lip. 'But…would you deny yourself the chance to love again just because of one bad experience?'

His gut knotted with tension—and a touch of anger. A *bad* experience? It'd been the single most humiliating, soul-destroying experience of his life.

But she wouldn't understand that unless he told the whole story.

'There's more.'

He eased her head down to his shoulder again. He didn't want her watching him. Already he felt too exposed.

'She told me she would've married me in a heartbeat if I was my parents' biological son. She said there was no point marrying into aristocracy if her children wouldn't inherit the bloodline.'

Memory churned in him like acid. Natasha had dismissed their relationship as just a bit of fun. She'd even admitted that she'd allowed him to introduce her to his family in the hopes of snaring his brother.

He made a rough noise in his throat. 'She said she couldn't possibly marry someone of "unknown origin" for fear of what her children would inherit.'

*'What?'*

Jordan popped up again. This time she wouldn't be encouraged back down. Angry colour bloomed on her cheekbones.

She shook her head, curled her hand into a fist on his thigh. 'And where does that scumbag Diego fit in?

He tucked a flying curl behind her ear. Her furious indignation on his behalf was almost adorable. Incredibly he felt his chest lighten—enough for him to be able to admit, 'He slept with her within days of our break-up. And ensured the reason why she'd rejected me became gossip fodder in our social circles.'

'Oh, Xavier.' She touched his jaw. 'I'm so sorry.'

'It is in the past.'

'Yet it affects your life to this day.'

He shook his head. 'It doesn't.'

'How can you say that?' she persisted. 'When you won't let yourself love?'

'It is not a matter of allowing myself. I simply have no interest in it. A few people, like my parents, find it—or a version of it, at least—but others waste their lives looking for it. Or waiting for it.'

She dropped her hand. 'You think love is a waste of time?'

He shrugged. 'I don't believe love is the magic bullet many people think it is. It comes with pressure, expectation. Those things can break a relationship.'

She frowned, pulled back. Xav reined in his frustration. This wasn't the reaction he wanted.

He kept an arm around her waist. 'There are many things besides love—*good* things,' he emphasised, 'that can contribute to a successful relationship.'

'Like what?' she said, her voice croaky.

Sensing her on the edge of flight, he tightened his hold. 'Respect, friendship, affection, security…' He traced his fingertip over the swells of her breasts above the sarong and her skin flushed with goosebumps. His voice roughened. 'Desire.'

He saw her eyes flare. Saw the moment she understood. 'What are you saying?'

'You know, *querida*. We're good together. We can *have* something good together. Something lasting.'

All she had to do was see sense and give up on her silly notion of love.

Her breathing was uneven. 'You said we'd burn out… it's just chemistry—'

'I was wrong. I do not say this to be boastful, but I've had many lovers. This attraction we have…it's powerful, different… It won't burn out.'

'Xavier…' She braced her hand on his chest. 'I've received a job offer—in Sydney. I need to attend an interview in a couple of weeks—'

'It's not confirmed?'

'No, but—'

He laid a finger against her lips. 'Then you have time. Let us enjoy this next week, *sí*? No pressure.'

The uncertainty on her face only intensified his resolve. There were two options here. She would either stay or walk away. The latter he couldn't countenance. This woman had affected him like no other. Hell, sitting in his desk drawer right now were résumés from the exclusive matchmaker for three beautiful, eligible women, and not one of them stirred his blood like Jordan did.

He needed to start his campaign of persuasion with a

win. Demonstrate he was the kind of man she wanted to be with.

He smoothed her hair back from her face. 'Since we are having an honest conversation, I have a confession. In Madrid, when I found your journal, it was open—and I saw something.' He paused. 'You have brought Camila's ashes to Spain, *sí*?'

She blinked, and a look of such naked vulnerability came over her face he wanted to hold her against his chest and never let go.

'Would you like me to be with you when you scatter them, *querida*?'

Her mouth trembled and tears welled in her eyes. Big, fat tears that rolled down her cheeks and made his chest ache.

He brushed them away with his thumbs. 'Is that a yes?'

She curled her hands over his wrists and whispered, 'Yes.'


Jordan went into the week in a state of shellshock—and Xavier gave her no chance to recover.

On Monday he surprised her with a visit to an exclusive day spa where, for several hours, a team of beautiful therapists scrubbed and plucked and buffed her until every inch of her glowed.

On Tuesday morning they flew to London and went to the penthouse suite at one of Ramon's private clubs. In the afternoon Xavier disappeared to a meeting, leaving her in the suite with a personal stylist who arrived with a vast collection of evening gowns, a bottle of champagne and a case full of make-up and hair products. In the evening he took her to see *Les Misérables*. They had the best seats in the theatre, of course, and afterwards ate a late supper at a Michelin-starred restaurant.

But as the week progressed it wasn't the pampering, or the posh restaurants and luxury suites, or the beautiful evening gown she wore in London—or even their incredible, intense lovemaking—that made her wonder whether she could compromise. Whether she could settle for what he offered and live without ever hearing those three little words.

Rather, it was the little things that cost nothing that burrowed under her defences.

It was the look of stupefied awe on his face when he first saw her in the evening gown.

It was the almost imperceptible tremor in his hands as he helped her put on a stunning choker of diamonds and yellow sapphires and his anxious expression when he asked her if she liked it.

It was the hour they spent with Emily and Ramon at their beautiful Chelsea home before returning to Barcelona. She'd blown raspberry kisses on Katie's tummy and looked up to find Xavier watching, a smile playing about his mouth. That night, after making love, he gently kissed her stomach and said how sexy she would look when she was round with child, and what a wonderful mother she would be.

It was every shared smile, every lingering look, every moment of heart-rending tenderness.

Early in the week she attempted to broach the subject of his birth father. Now she knew about the brutal rejection he'd suffered, his reluctance to learn about his biological origins made more sense. It was fear. That awful woman had put the idea in his head that he might somehow be defective.

But he shut her down. Gently but nevertheless firmly.

On Wednesday she contacted Maria Gonzalez anyway. Asked the older woman if she'd assist her to make some discreet enquiries.

Maria was delighted to help, but she was also concerned. 'There was a man here last weekend. Asking about Camila. He said he was tracing family history, but something did not feel right. I did not know if it was important enough to call you.'

Jordan's nape prickled. 'Did you tell him anything?'

'No. Benito sent him away. Told him we did not remember her. But he spoke to other people. People who may have known Camila.'

When Xavier came home he looked unusually tired. He said he was fine but, seeing the lines of strain around his mouth, she decided it wasn't the time to mention Maria's concerns.

On Thursday night, before the sun set, they walked down to the beach and scattered Camila's ashes into the ocean. Afterwards they spread a blanket on the sand, opened a bottle of brandy—Camila's favourite tipple—and saluted her.

Xavier pulled her back against him, his arms strong, his body warm and comforting. 'Tell me about her,' he invited, and she did.

By the time they went to bed that night she'd accepted that she was hopelessly, desperately in love with this man.

And then finally, on Friday morning, it all came to a terrible, terrible end.

# CHAPTER TWELVE

SHE WOKE WITH a start and a single word comprised her first thought.

*Friday.*

The day she had promised herself she would make her decision. The hospital in Sydney had confirmed an interview for next Thursday. She needed either to withdraw her application or change her return flight to depart Spain on Sunday.

*She loved him.*

The thought made her heart leap, and at the same time filled her with a bone-deep ache of desperation and despair.

He had made his position clear. Love was not on the table. Not part of what he was offering. And yet she still hoped. Still held her breath for those three tiny yet monumental words.

There was still today, she thought with an optimism she had to force with every ounce of will she possessed. She could wait and make her decision tonight.

She got up and slipped on a robe. Morning sunlight slanted through the bedroom's shutters, casting pale yellow stripes across the navy satin sheets.

Xavier had decided to work from home today. She didn't know whether that was significant. Perhaps he, too, had mentally marked Friday as D-day. Given the sheets on his side were cold, he must have risen early, decided to let her sleep and gone to his study.

The door was ajar. She listened for a moment to ensure she wouldn't intrude on a phone call, then went in.

Xavier wasn't at his desk. He stood at the French doors

to the terrace, staring out, and the instant Jordan's gaze fell on him a cold wave of anxiety washed over her.

His hands were fisted and the taut, rigid lines of his body screamed tension. Even from behind, without his expression visible, he looked like a man poised on the edge of violence.

'Xavier?'

He turned, and she gasped at what his hard-set features revealed. There was anger, even rage, but she saw bleakness, too. He stalked across the office, took her briefly in his arms, kissed her forehead, then drew her to a chair.

She stared at him, her heart racing, her mouth dry. 'Xavier, what's happened? You're frightening me.'

He picked up a computer tablet from his desk. 'Sit. I need to show you something. And it's not pleasant.'

'Okay,' she said slowly, and lowered herself into the chair, legs trembling. 'Just…just give it to me, then.'

Mouth grim, he handed over the tablet—and Jordan's horror was instantaneous.

On its own, the salacious tabloid headline was shocking—*Vega Corporation CEO Cavorts with Stepsister!*—but it was the photograph that sent mortified heat sweeping over her skin, followed by a wave of cold, prickling sweat.

Reluctantly she scrolled and—*Oh, God*—there were more photos, all taken with a powerful telephoto lens.

'This was last Friday,' she whispered.

The night they'd fooled around in the pool.

She covered her mouth with a trembling hand. She felt sick. Violated. Every photo was hideously explicit. It wasn't so bad for Xavier. A bare male torso was hardly risqué, although one shot had captured half a toned buttock. But for Jordan…

She burned with humiliation and shame. She couldn't even look up and meet Xavier's eye.

She scrolled down and read the text, but could barely absorb the words. Her mind was too shaken. Some things penetrated or jumped out. Names, for instance. Xavier's. Hers. Camila's.

Then her eye caught on another name.

Tomás Garcia.

*Xavier's birth father.*

Jordan doubled her efforts to focus and her grip on the tablet grew tighter, and tighter. Horror turned to outrage. 'These are lies!'

Xavier gave a grim smile. 'Regrettably, I think the photos speak for themselves, *querida*.'

'No.' She put the tablet down. Just holding it made her feel dirty. 'I mean about your father.'

His gaze hardened. 'Vittorio de la Vega is my father.'

'You know what I mean,' she said, but gently, because he had to be hurting. 'This can't be true.'

'Yet there it is in black and white,' he said flatly.

'In a *tabloid*.' She spoke more forcefully now. 'They print rubbish. Half-truths. Lies.' She stood. 'Tomás Garcia was *not* a criminal.'

His jaw flexed. 'And you know this how?'

'Because I knew Camila. I think she had strong feelings for Tomás. I don't believe she would have fallen in love with a bad man.'

His expression grew shuttered. 'Well, we'll never know now, will we? Because they're both dead.' He moved behind his desk. 'In any case, it is irrelevant.'

His coldly dismissive tone made her flinch. 'How can you say that?'

'Because my only priority right now is damage control.' He waved to where the tablet sat. 'This harms not only me but the company. We have shareholders, clients, investors, joint venture partners who will all be concerned about the negative impact of a deliberate attack on my reputation and the company's image.'

Belatedly she registered that he wore business attire. 'Who do you think is responsible?'

A vein pulsed in his temple. 'Diego and Hector.'

Jordan sat back down with a thump. 'Oh, no. I've just remembered. I was speaking with Maria Gonzalez on Wednesday. She said a stranger was in the village last weekend, asking questions about Camila.'

Xavier stilled in the act of gathering papers. 'Why were you speaking with Maria Gonzalez?'

She couldn't lie. 'I—I asked her if she would help me trace your birth father,' she confessed.

An awful stillness—the kind that said he was utterly furious—pervaded his whole body.

A terrible quietness came to his voice. 'Why, Jordan? When I specifically stated I wasn't interested?'

She swallowed. 'Because I thought it would help you.'

'Do I strike you as a man who needs your help?'

Something in his tone, in the way he said *your* help, raked painfully over her flesh.

She notched up her chin. 'No. You strike me as a man who's too proud to ask for *anyone's* help. Too proud to admit that you might not have everything perfectly under control.'

His jaw hardened. '*Gracias.* That was a most insightful assessment. Anything else you'd like to add, since you're clearly quite the expert on me?'

She blinked back the hot sting of tears. 'Yes,' she said—because why not go for broke? Her heart was already bleeding.

She pulled the edges of her robe together and stood up for added courage.

'I think you're a strong, principled, incredible man, Xavier de la Vega, but I also think you're afraid. I think you've pushed yourself towards perfection your whole life to prove you're worthy, but deep down you fear you're not. I think love scares you, but only because you're afraid to *be* loved—because you think it means constantly living up to someone's expectations. Constantly proving yourself. But guess what?' She took a breath. '*You're* the only one who puts impossible expectations on yourself. The people who love you accept you as you are.' She flicked away a tear before it fell. 'You might be able to control everything else in your life, but you can't control who loves you. And I'm sorry to say I do.'

Before he cut her down with another pithy response, she strode from the room.

Xav drove to work in the Aston Martin, barely keeping within the speed limit.

His gut churned and his blood pumped so hard he feared for his arteries.

This morning, right on cue, Hector had called an impromptu board meeting.

*The bastard.*

Xav wanted to wring his neck—and Diego's. Not for a second did he doubt their culpability.

He stalked into the office, barking out orders and summonses. Lucia was flustered. Whether from stress or because she now knew what her boss's butt looked like naked, he didn't care to guess.

He slammed his door shut. He had to focus. Prepare. But damn if he could get Jordan's impassioned speech out of his head. He still felt the impact of every word. It was as if she'd taken a scalpel to his chest, slicing away layers of skin and muscle and bone until only his heart remained, unprotected and defenceless.

He wanted to punish her for defying his wishes, shake her for saying things no one else dared say to him and demand she take back her declaration of love.

He also wanted to gouge out the eyes of every man on the planet who'd ogled the photos of her lush breasts in the last twelve hours.

Those breasts belonged to him.

Every damn part of her belonged to him.

He breathed deeply. He also wished he could un-see those

words he'd buried in a recess of his brain, because he had no emotional capacity to deal with them right now: Tomás Garcia—his birth father—had been shot and killed thirty-three years ago while holding up a convenience store.

Within the next half-hour his brother and his parents arrived. Xav faced them with a throat thickened by a mix of humiliation, gratitude and exasperation. 'I told you, you didn't need to come.'

'And miss the fireworks?' Ramon, sharp in a three-piece suit, slapped him on the shoulder. '*Hermano*, I've waited many years to see you in the hot seat for once, instead of me.'

Xav turned to his parents, searched their faces for disappointment or disapproval and found neither.

His father, also smart in a bespoke suit, stood between his sons and gripped their shoulders, the gleam in his eye almost anticipatory. 'It's been too long since I went a few rounds with Hector. That old scoundrel doesn't know what he's in for.'

Xav felt his chest expand. He'd thought he could handle this alone, but now his family were here he was overwhelmed by the strength of his gratitude. By the strength of their unconditional love.

His mother took him aside. 'How is Jordan?'

'She's all right.'

His conscience pricked. He had no idea if that was true. He hadn't had time to chase her after she'd stalked from his study. He'd had to get himself here.

A sudden cold sweat hit between his shoulder blades. Was she at this very minute packing her bag? Preparing to run?

He fisted his hands, a silent, primal scream rising inside him. He could not lose her.

*Damn this board meeting.*
*Damn Hector and Diego.*

Lucia popped her head in. 'Everyone's here and waiting in the boardroom.'

His mother sat down. 'Good luck, *mis queridos*. I shall wait here.'

The meeting was hellish, worsened by the unexpected presence of a smirking Diego.

'He's a shareholder—and family,' Hector blustered when Ramon challenged Diego's attendance.

When the PR Director started outlining a multi-faceted strategy for mitigating the reputational risk Xav tuned out. He wanted out of there. *Needed* to be out of there. Jordan could be running right now. To an airport, a train station, a ferry terminal, a bus depot. Did he have enough people to cover every possible departure point?

Afterwards the PR guy asked Xav to hang back for a quick word. He gritted his teeth and checked his watch. 'You have one minute.'

Ramon waited in the anteroom, one shoulder propped against the wall. Across the space Diego lingered, looking at his phone.

Xav walked past without acknowledging him, then stopped abruptly and swung back. '*What* did you say?'

Diego was smug. 'I said are you rushing home to slutty sis?'

In a move thirty years overdue Xav swung his fist, his knuckles connecting with Diego's nose with a painful but savagely satisfying crunch. Diego went down on one knee, clutching his bloodied nose, his watering eyes agog.

Xav leaned down. 'You're talking about my future wife and the woman I love,' he snarled. 'So watch your mouth, *cousin.*'

On his way to the car he called Lucia. 'I'm not coming back to the office.'

'Peter Reynaud has just called. He wants to video conference this afternoon.'

'Tell him I'm not available.'

If the deal went belly-up, so be it.

* * *

Xav's heart thundered as he navigated the final stretch of winding road up to the villa.

Despair outweighed hope. Thirteen times he'd called her mobile. Thirteen times he'd got her voicemail.

He had only himself to blame. What reasons had he given her to stay? Plenty, he'd thought until today—but they were the wrong reasons. He'd tried to seduce her with a taste of the lifestyle he could provide, but Jordan couldn't be bought.

Only one thing mattered to her, and it was the one thing he'd refused to give. He'd wanted Jordan in his life, but on *his* terms. And, frankly, his terms had sucked.

He slammed to a stop in front of the villa, frowning at the blue Mercedes sedan in the courtyard.

Hope grabbed a foothold.

He strode inside and scaled the stairs two at a time. If her things were still here—

'Xavier.'

His heart stopped. He turned and she stared up at him from the bottom of the stairs. Relief surged—so powerful he gripped the iron balustrade to keep himself from swaying.

He flew back down, ready to gather her into his arms, to tell her what he needed to tell her, but she stopped him with a palm on his chest.

'There's someone here,' she said. 'Someone I've brought to meet you.'

Before he could speak she walked into the living room, leaving him no choice but to follow. Her hair was caught in a ponytail and she wore the wraparound skirt she'd worn that day he'd practically kidnapped her outside her hostel. He wanted to loosen her hair, pull the ties on her skirt—

'Xavier—' She cleared her throat. 'This is Luis Garcia. Luis is your uncle…' She paused, and her smile wobbled a bit. 'Your biological uncle.'

His gaze snapped to the man rising to his feet and a sensation he'd never experienced before punched through his chest. Luis Garcia was tall, broad-shouldered, and distinguished-looking in a suit, and as he came forward with his hand outstretched Xav, for the first time in his life, looked into the face of someone whose features were strikingly like his own.

'I'll leave you two to talk,' Jordan murmured, and retreated from the room.

Her trembling legs carried her all the way to Xavier's bedroom, where she sank onto the end of the bed. She pressed her hand to the base of her throat.

Had she done the right thing?

Only time would tell.

Tears of bittersweet joy stung her eyes. After their awful parting this morning, the look on Xavier's face when he'd seen her just now and his unmistakable eagerness to take her in his arms had sent her heart soaring. But she'd had to remind herself that his desire to make peace didn't mean anything had changed.

She drifted onto the balcony and stayed there for a long time, until eventually she saw Xavier and Luis emerge into the sunlight below.

They shook hands, and there seemed to be some kind of camaraderie between them, and then Luis drove away.

Xavier must have sensed her gaze. He turned and looked up and their eyes locked, but she couldn't tell anything from his expression. Then he came inside and she waited for him in the bedroom, knowing he would come to her.

As soon as he walked in he folded her in his arms, and she almost sobbed it felt so good.

He spoke against her hair. 'Thank you.'

She could have stayed there for ever, tucked against his warm, strong body, but she eased away. 'He told you everything?'

He nodded, compressing his lips for a moment, as though

he didn't trust himself to speak, and her heart swelled to see him so moved.

Tomás Garcia had not been a criminal. An innocent bystander, caught up in a vicious armed robbery, he'd stepped into harm's way to protect a female store worker. He had died a hero.

'He never knew Camila was pregnant,' she said. 'His parents kept them apart.'

'*Sí.*'

Their gazes fused, and she felt as if her insides were filling with molten silver.

'Stay, Jordan.'

The quiet plea catapulted her back to that first night when she'd tried to leave and he'd implored her to stay. How could so much have changed in two weeks? How could *she* have changed so much?

She opened her mouth but he surged forward, and suddenly his mouth was on hers.

For a second she stiffened, expecting his kiss to be searing and fierce, an explicit, forceful reminder of their explosive chemistry. But it was something else. Something deeply intimate and tender. Something that melted her from the inside out and made her tummy flutter with hope.

His hands framed her face, anchoring her as he raised his head.

'Xavier—'

'I love you.'

Her breath caught. 'What?'

'I love you, *querida*,' he said. 'And everything you said this morning, as difficult as it was to hear, was right. In that board meeting I was under attack—but I had people beside me who love me, who had my back and will always have my back. I could have done it without them, but I didn't need to. Because they were there, without judgment, without criticism. And through most of that meeting all I could think about was getting back here. Those photos—' His jaw clenched for a second. 'I want to be the man who protects you, the man who has your back, the man who stands by your side and accepts that he's human and imperfect.'

Tears clung to her lashes. 'I love you, too,' she whispered.

'Marry me,' he said.

She laughed. 'Is that an order?'

'*Sí.*' He lifted her left hand and stroked her fingers. 'I will buy you a magnificent ring.'

She started to say that she didn't need a big diamond, just something small, given with love, but then she gasped. 'Xavier! What happened to your knuckles?'

'I punched Diego—defending your honour.'

Her eyes widened, then she grinned. 'Did it feel good?'

'Very.' Xavier flexed his hand and grinned back. Then he tugged her towards the bed. 'But I know something that will feel even better.'

At midnight, unable to sleep, Xavier gently disentangled himself from Jordan's soft, sleep-heavy limbs, pulled on a pair of drawstring pants and went to his study.

He poured a brandy, sat at his desk and read the letter his birth mother had written to him in the weeks before she died.

When he got to the end he wiped his cheeks, put the letter away and raised his glass to Camila Walsh—the woman who had not only given him life, but given him the love of his life.

Jordan.

\* \* \* \* \*

# CARRYING HIS
# SCANDALOUS HEIR

**JULIA JAMES**

For Kathryn – thank you for all your hard work!

# CHAPTER ONE

CARLA LOOKED AT her watch for the umpteenth time, glancing out across the crowded restaurant towards the entrance. Where *was* he? Anxiety bit at her, and an emotion more powerful than that—one she had never felt before. Had never thought to feel about the man she was waiting for.

She had thought only to feel what she had felt the first time she had set eyes on him. And she so desperately wanted to set eyes on him again now—walking in, striding with his effortlessly assured gait, tall and commanding, with that inbuilt assumption that he could go wherever he liked, that there would always be a place for him, that people would move aside to let him through, that no one would ever dream of turning him down or saying no to him—not about anything at all.

She had not turned him down. She had denied him nothing—granted him everything. Everything he'd ever wanted of her...

Memory, hot and fervid, scorched within her. From the very first moment those hooded night-dark eyes had rested on her, assessing her, desiring her, she had been lost. Utterly lost! She had yielded to him with the absolute conviction that he was the only man who could ever have such an impact on her. That moment was imprinted on her—on her memory, on her suddenly heating body… on her heart.

Memory scorched again now, burning through her veins…

The art gallery was crowded with Rome's wealthy, fashionable set, and champagne and canapés were circling as Carla threaded her way among them, murmuring words of greeting here and there.

Reaching for a glass of gently foaming champagne, Carla knew that she herself could be counted as one of them. Oh, not by birth or breeding, but as the stepdaughter of multi-millionaire Guido Viscari she could move in circles such as these and hold her own and look the part.

Her cocktail dress in a deep blue raw silk had come from one of the currently favoured fashion houses, and it hugged a figure that easily passed muster amongst all the couture-clad females there. Her face, too, as she well knew, also passed muster. Her features veered towards the dramatic, with eyes that could flash with fire and full lips that gave a hint of inner sensuousness.

It was a face that drew male eyes, and she could sense them now—especially since she was there on her own. Unlike many of the other guests, she had a genuine reason for attending this private viewing other than simply being there to while away an hour or so before dining.

But she'd long got used to the constant perusal that Italian men habitually bestowed upon females. It had shocked and discomfited her ten years ago, when she'd been a raw English teenager new to Italian life, but since then she'd grown inured to it. Now she hardly ever noticed the looks that came her way.

Except— She stilled suddenly, the champagne glass halfway to her lips. *Someone was looking at her.* Someone whose gaze she could feel on her like a physical touch. Her eyes shifted their line of sight. Someone who was making her the centre of his observations.

And then, as her gaze moved, she saw him.

He'd just come into the gallery. The receptionist at the welcome desk was still smiling up at him, but he was ignoring her, instead glancing out across the room. Carla felt a little thrill go through her, as though somewhere deep inside her a seismic shock were taking place, and she noticed his gaze was focussing on *her.*

She felt her breath catch, seize in her throat. She felt a sudden flush of heat go through her. For the man making her the object of his scrutiny was the most devastating male she had ever seen.

He was tall, powerfully built with broad shoulders, his features strong...compelling. With a blade of a nose, night-dark hair, night-dark eyes, and a mobile mouth with a twist to it that did strange things to her.

Unknown things...

Things she had never experienced before.

The flush of heat in her body intensified. She felt pinned—as though movement were impossible, as though she had just been caught in a noose—captured.

Captivated.

For how long he went on subjecting her to that measuring, assessing scrutiny she could not tell—knew only that it seemed to be timeless.

She felt her lungs grow parched of oxygen... Then, suddenly, she was released. Someone had come up to him—another man, greeting him effusively—and his eyes relinquished hers, his face turning away from her.

She took a lungful of air, feeling shaken.

*What had just happened?*

The question seared within her...and burned. How could a single glance do that to her? Have such an effect on her?

Jerkily, she took a mouthful of champagne, needing its chill to cool the heat flushing through her. She stepped away, averting her body, making herself do what she had come there to do—study the portraits that were the subject of the exhibition.

Her eyes lifted to the one opposite her.

And as they did so another shock went through her. She was staring—yet again—into a pair of night-dark eyes. The same eyes...the *very* same.

*Night-dark, hooded, sensuous...*

That little thrill went through her again, that flush of heat moved in her body. The portrait's eyes seemed to be subjecting her to the same kind of measuring scrutiny that the man by the door had focussed on her.

She tore her eyes away from the face that looked out at her from the portrait. Moved them down to the brass plate at the side of the frame. She hardly needed to read it—she knew perfectly well who the artist was.

Andrea Luciezo, who, along with Titian, was one of the great masters of the High Renaissance. His ability to capture the essence of those who had sat for him—the rich, the powerful, the men who had controlled the Italy of the sixteenth century, the women who had adorned them—had brought them vividly, vibrantly, to life. Luciezo—whose dark, glowing oils, lustrous and lambent, infused each subject with a richly potent glamour.

Her eyes went from the name of the artist to that of his subject. She gave a slow, accepting nod. *Yes, of course.*

Her gaze went back to the man in the portrait. He looked out at all those who gazed at him with dark, hooded, assessing eyes. She looked at the powerful features, the raven hair, worn long to the nape of the strong neck, his jaw bearded in the fashion of the time, yet leaving unhidden the sensuous line of his mouth, the unbearably rich velvet of his black doublet, the stark pleated white of his deep collar, the glint of precious gold at his broad, powerful chest.

He was a man whom the artist knew considered his own worth high, whose portrait told all who gazed upon it that here was no ordinary mortal, cut from the common herd. Arrogance was in that hooded gaze, in the angle of his head, the set of his shoulders. He was a man for whom the world would do his bidding—whatever he bade them do...

A voice spoke behind her. Deep, resonant. With a timbre to it that set off yet again that low, internal seismic tremor.

'So,' he said, as she stood immobile in front of the portrait, 'what do you think of my ancestor, Count Alessandro?'

She turned, lifted her face, let her eyes meet the living version of the dark, hooded gaze that had transfixed her across the centuries—the living version that had transfixed her only moments ago and was now transfixing her again.

Cesare di Mondave, Conte di Mantegna.

The owner of this priceless Luciezo portrait of his ancestor, and of vast wealth besides. A man whose reputation went before him—a reputation for living in the same fashion as his illustrious forebears: as if the whole world belonged to him. To whom no one would say no—and to whom any woman upon whom he looked with favour would want to say only one thing.

*Yes.*

And as Carla met his gaze, felt its impact, its power and potency, she knew with a hollow sense of fatalism that it was the only word *she* would ever want to use.

'Well?'

The deep voice came again and Carla realised that she needed to speak—had been commanded to answer him. For this was a man who was obeyed.

But she would not obey immediately. She would defy him in that, at least.

Deliberately she looked back at the Luciezo, making him wait. 'A man of his time,' she answered finally.

*As you are not a man of your time.*

The words formed in her head silently, powerfully. No, the current Conte di Mantegna was *not* a man of the twenty-first century! She could see it in every austere line of his body. He carried his own ancient ancestry in the unconscious lift of his chin at her reply, in his dark brows drawing together.

'What do you mean by that?'

Again, the question demanded an immediate answer.

Carla looked back at the portrait, gathering her reasons for the reply she had made him.

'His hand is on the pommel of his sword,' she essayed. 'He will slay any man who offers him insult. He subjects himself to the scrutiny of one who can never be his equal, however much genius Luciezo possesses, simply in order that his illustrious image can be displayed. His arrogance is in every line, every stroke of the brush.'

She turned back to the man who had commanded her

to speak. Her answer had displeased him, as she had known it would.

There was a dark flash in his eyes, as he riposted, 'You mistake arrogance for pride. Pride not in himself but in his family, his lineage, his honour. An honour he would defend with his life, with his sword, —that he *must* defend because he has no choice but to do so. The artist's scrutiny is to be endured because he must be ever mindful of what he owes his house—which is to protect it and preserve it. His portrait will be his persona in his own absence—it will persist for posterity when he himself is dust.'

The night-dark eyes went to those in the portrait. As if, Carla thought, the two men were communing with each other.

Her brow furrowed for an instant. How strange to think that a man of the present could look into the eyes of his own ancestor… That, in itself, made *il Conte* entirely different from all those who—like herself—were simply cut from the common herd of humanity…who had no knowledge of their ancestors from so many centuries ago.

Her expression changed, becoming drawn for a moment. She didn't even know of her own more immediate forebears. Her father was little more than a name to her—a name reluctantly bestowed upon her when her mother's pregnancy had required that he marry her, only for him to be killed in a car crash when she was a small child. His widow had been unwelcome to her in-laws, and Carla had been raised by her mother alone until her remarriage to Guido Viscari when Carla was a young teenager.

*I know more about my stepfather's family than I do about my own father's!*

To a man like *il Conte* that very ignorance about her paternal forebears must seem incomprehensible, for he would know the identity of every one of his entire collection of ancestors for centuries—each of them doubtless from families as aristocratic as his own.

With such a heritage she could not be surprised by his immediate retort. Yet she had one of her own.

'Then it is entirely to the credit of Luciezo's mastery that he can convey all that with his portrait,' she replied, making her voice even. 'Without his genius to record it your ancestor *is* merely dust.'

There was defiance in her voice—and an open assertion that, however many heraldic quarterings the illustrious Conte di Mantegna was possessed of, none could compare with the incomparable genius of a great master such as Luciezo.

That dark flash came again in the depths of the Conte's eyes. 'Will we not all be dust in years to come?' he murmured. 'But until that time comes...'

Something changed in his voice—something that suddenly made the heat flush in her blood once more, as it had done when she had realised his gaze was upon her.

'Should we not *carpe diem*?'

'Seize the day?' Carla heard her voice answering. But inside her head she was registering that sudden change in the Count's voice, the smoothing of that low timbre. She could see, now, the change in his eyes. He was looking at her. Approving of what he saw. Sending that flush of heat through her again.

'Or, indeed, seize the evening,' he murmured again, with the slightest husk in his voice.

And now there was no mistaking the message in his voice. None at all. Those dark, long-lashed hooded eyes were resting on her, and the message in them was as old as time.

She pleased him. Her appearance, at any rate, even if her words did not. But their exchange had merely been the mechanism by which he had approached her—had given him the opening he desired, by which he would obtain the end he sought.

The end he now stated openly.

'Have dinner with me tonight.'

It was as simple as that. As straightforward. His dark, expressive eyes were resting on her, and Carla felt their impact—knew their message. Knew what reply she should make to this powerful, sensual man, who was displaying every obvious sign of his intent.

Her habit had always been to say no—the few relationships she'd had over the years had never been with Italians, nor conducted in Rome under the avidly speculative glare of the circles in which she moved. And never had she fancied herself to be deeply emotionally involved. It had been only friendship and compatibility that attracted her—no more than that. It was safer that way. Safer than yielding to any overriding sensual attraction that might ignite a passion that would be hard to quench.

After all, no one knew better than she what *that* might lead to. Hadn't it happened to her own mother? Falling for a man who, when he'd been faced with unintended pregnancy, had not wished to commit to her?

Although his father had cracked the financial whip and forced a marriage, there had been no happy ending. Her father had chafed at marriage, chafed at fatherhood—and had been on the point of leaving her mother when he was killed. Was it any wonder, Carla asked herself, that she was wary of making such a mistake herself?

So, for every reason of good sense, there was only one reply for her to make to this arrogant, sensual man who possessed the power to disturb her senses.

Yet she could not say the words. Could only find the means to give a slight, fleeting, demurring half-smile, and a self-protective sweeping down of her eyelashes to hide the all too revealing response in her eyes as she made an evasive reply.

'So…have you loaned any other paintings to the exhibition?' she asked.

Her voice sounded abrupt, even breathless, but she did not care. She met his gaze head-on, keeping hers quite limpid, though the effort was great—the more so since in his eyes was a look of knowingness that told her he had understood immediately why she had not answered him.

But to her relief he followed her diversion.

'Indeed,' he murmured, still with that semi-amused look in his eyes that was so disturbing to her. 'The Luciezo is, in fact, part of a triptych. The other two portraits are on display across the gallery.'

There was a discernible tinge of annoyance in his voice at the curator's decision as he indicated across the width of the gallery, towards an alcove in which Carla could make out two portraits.

'Shall we?'

The cool voice held assumption, and Carla found herself being guided forward. He halted, lifting his hand to the portraits they were now in front of.

'What do you make of them?'

Carla's trained eyes went to the portraits, immediately seeing the skill and artistry in them, seeing in them all the hallmarks of a master. Her eyes narrowed very slightly. But not Luciezo.

'Caradino?' she ventured.

She felt rather than saw the glance the Count threw at her. Surprise—and approval.

'Caradino,' he confirmed. He paused. 'Many attribute his few surviving works to Luciezo.'

She gave a slight shake of her head. 'No,' she said. 'There is a discernible difference.'

Her eyes ran over the portraits, taking in the brushwork, the lighting, the shadows. Her gaze went from appraising the technicalities of the portraits to the subjects themselves. And then, for the first time, her eyes widened as her gaze rested on their faces.

So unalike. So very, *very* unalike.

One so fair and pale. A married woman, clearly, as illustrated by the tokens in the painting—her pearl earring, the sprig of myrtle in her lap, the dish of quinces on the little table at her side—and yet there was about her, Carla could see, an air almost of virginity…as if with different garments and accoutrements she might have modelled for a painting of the Virgin Mary.

A crucifix was in her hands, glinting between her long, pale fingers. Carla looked at the woman's eyes.

Sadness. As if, like the Virgin Mary, she had in her gaze a foretelling of the great sorrows that were to come.

She pulled her gaze away. Let it rest on the other woman's face.

Another young woman. In this portrait the subject's hair was a lush chestnut-brown, lavishly unbound and snaking down over one bare shoulder. Her gown was a sumptuous red, not a celestial blue, and cut low across her generous bosom to reveal an expansive amount of soft, creamy skin. She held red roses in her hands, rubies gleamed at her throat and on her fingers, and her hands rested on her abdomen—its slight swell discreet, but undeniable.

Carla drew her eyes away from the telltale curve of the young woman's figure, moved them back up to scrutinise her face. Beautiful, in a sensuous way, framed by her rich tresses, her cheeks flushed, lips full and with a sensual cast to them. Carla's eyes went to the woman's eyes and held them for a long moment—held the unseeing gaze that looked out over the centuries between the two of them.

'Who *are* they?'

Her own voice cut short her perusal, and she drew her gaze away to look back at *il Conte*, standing at her side.

'Can you not tell?' he asked. He glanced back to the portrait of his ancestor, across the room, then back to Carla. 'His wife—and his mistress. He had them painted at the same time, by the same hand. Caradino stayed at my *castello* and painted them both—one after the other.'

Carla's face stilled. 'How nice for them,' she said drily. 'It seems your ancestor kept his mistress…handy.'

But the Count did not rise to her sardonic comment. 'It was quite normal in those times. Nothing exceptional. Both women knew and understood the situation.'

Carla's lips pressed together. 'Knowing and understanding are not the same thing as tolerating and agreeing,' she riposted.

The dark, hooded eyes were veiled. 'Women had no power in those times. And after all,' he went on, 'my ancestor's mistress was *very* lavishly looked after.'

'She's carrying his child,' Carla retorted.

She could feel an emotion rising up in her—one she did not want to feel, but it was coming all the same.

'An excellent way to secure the Count's protection,'

agreed Cesare. 'I believe they had several children, over the years. He was very faithful to her, you know. Surprisingly so for the times.'

Automatically Carla's eyes went not to the mistress of the former Count but to his wife. No sign of fertility there—and in the eyes only that haunting sadness.

Thoughts ran through her head, unstoppable.

*How did she feel? How did she cope? Knowing her husband was having children, openly, with his mistress? Yet presumably she, too, must have had an heir, at least, or the line would have died out—which it obviously hasn't?*

'But enough of my ancestors—have you seen the other paintings displayed here yet?'

The voice of the man at her side drew her back to the present. She turned towards him. Saw him with fresh eyes, it seemed. Her gaze went past him to the portrait of Count Alessandro, who had been so unconcerned as to have his wife and mistress painted simultaneously.

A shaft of female indignation went through her, as she brought her gaze back to the current Count.

'Not all of them yet, no,' she said. She made her voice purposeful. 'And I really must. I have fifteen hundred words to write up about the exhibition.'

She named the arts magazine she wrote for, as if she was aware that by stressing her professional interest she would diminish her personal one.

'And I must do my duty by all the paintings here!'

She spoke lightly but deliberately. She smiled. An equally deliberate smile. One that completely ignored the question he had asked her only a few minutes ago, making no reference to it.

'Thank you so much, Signor il Conte, for showing me

these fascinating portraits, and for giving me such insight into them. It's always enhancing to learn the origins and the circumstances of a portrait's creation—it brings it so to life! And especially since the artist Caradino is so seldom exhibited.'

She smiled again—the same social smile—signalling closure. For closure, surely, was essential. Anything else would be...

Her mind veered away, not wanting to think of the path she had not taken. The yielding she had not made.

Instead she gave the slightest nod of her head in parting and walked away. Her high heels clicked on the parquet flooring and as she walked she was intensely conscious of his following gaze, of how her shapely figure was outlined by the vivid tailored dress she was wearing. Intensely conscious of the urge overwhelming her to get away. Just...*away*.

As she walked, she sipped at her champagne again. She felt the need of it. Her colour was heightened, she knew—knew it from the hectic beating of her heart.

*He desires me—the Conte di Mantegna has looked at me and found me pleasing to him...*

Into her head sprang an image, immediate and vivid, conjured out of her ready imagination. That woman in the portrait—the brunette—working, perhaps, in her father's shop, or sweeping floors, or even toiling out in the fields in sixteenth-century Italy... *Il Conte* passing by, seeing her, liking her beauty, taking a fancy to her. Finding her pleasing to him. Lifting her with one beckoning of his lordly, aristocratic hand out of her hard, poverty-stricken life to dress her in a silk gown and place roses in her hands and jewels around her throat, and take her to his bed...

She felt the pull of it—the allure. Had to force herself to remember all that would have gone with it. The price that woman would have paid.

*To know that her place in his life was only ever to be his* inamorata—*never to aspire to be his wife.*

And as for the Count—oh, he would have had everything he wanted. His pale, subservient wife—his compliant, obliging mistress.

Having it all.

She dragged her mind away, making herself inspect the other paintings, consult her catalogue, interview the exhibition's curator, and then get a few words from the gallery's director, who greeted her warmly, both in her professional capacity and as the stepdaughter of the late chairman of a global hotel chain—a generous patron of the arts himself.

It had been her stepfather who'd first noticed her interest in art as a teenager, and it was thanks to him that she'd studied history of art at prestigious universities both in England and Italy. He'd encouraged her in her journalistic career. It was a career she found immensely satisfying, and she knew herself to be extremely fortunate in it.

Now, with all her notes taken, she was ready to leave. She'd spend the evening going through them, drawing up the article she would write.

As she made her farewells she found herself glancing around. She knew who it was she was trying to glimpse. And knew why she should not be. Cesare di Mondave was far too disturbing to her peace of mind to allow herself to have anything more to do with him.

He was not to be seen anyway, and she told herself she was glad. Relieved. Because to further her acquaintance with Cesare di Mondave would *not* be good sense at all.

Involuntarily her eyes went to the portrait of his ancestor—Count Alessandro, regarding the world in all
his High Renaissance splendour, his dark gaze compelling, arrogant. In her mind's eye she saw his wife and
his mistress. Two women, rivals for ever, their destinies
yoked to the man who had commissioned their portraits.

*Had they both loved him? Or neither?*

The question hovered in her head, its answer long consumed by the centuries that had passed. All she could
know, with a kind of ironic certainty, was that it would
not be wise for *any* woman to have anything to do with
the man in whose veins ran the blood of Luciezo's Count
Alessandro.

It didn't matter that his descendant could have an impact on her that she had never encountered before. That
his dark lidded eyes could raise her pulse in an instant…
that her eyes had wanted only to cling helplessly, hopelessly, to his sculpted, powerful features, that her hand
had yearned to reach towards him, graze the tanned skin
of his jaw, brush the sensual swell of his mouth… It didn't
matter at all.

Because letting herself get embroiled with the arrogant, oh-so-aristocratic Count of Mantegna would be
folly indeed!

She was not, and never would be, like the lush beauty
in the Caradino portrait, haplessly dependent upon the
Count's continuing desire for her, fearing its demise.
Her lips thinned slightly. Nor could she ever be like
the woman in the other portrait—oh, she might move
in Roman high society, but the Viscaris were hoteliers:
rich, but with no trace of aristocratic blood. Carla knew
without flinching that when *il Conte* chose a wife, it

would be a woman from his own background, with an ancestry to match his.

*I would be nothing more than an...an interlude for him.*

She walked out onto the pavement and into the warm evening air of Rome in late summer. A low, lean, open-topped car was hovering at the kerb, blatantly ignoring the road signs forbidding such parking. Its powerful engine was throbbing with a throaty husk, its scarlet paintwork was gleaming, and the rearing stallion on the long bonnet caught the light, glinting gold like the crested signet ring on the hand curved around the wheel.

The man at the wheel turned his head. Let his dark, lidded gaze rest on Carla.

'What kept you?' asked Cesare di Mondave, Conte di Mantegna.

# CHAPTER TWO

CESARE'S HAND RESTED on the leather curve of the steering wheel. Impatience was humming in him. He appreciated that she had a job to do—this woman his eyes had lit upon, drawn without conscious intent to her dramatic beauty, her voluptuous figure, the extraordinarily dark blue eyes that had a hint of violet in them—but for all that he did not care to be kept waiting.

He'd known who she was before he'd made the decision to approach her—he'd seen her about previously in society, even though the aristocratic circles *he* moved in overlapped only loosely with those of the Viscaris. The Viscaris were, to him, 'new money'—it was a mere handful of generations since the global hotel group that bore the family name had been founded at the end of the nineteenth century. They were newcomers compared to the immense antiquity of *his* family—and Cesare felt the weight of that antiquity upon him each and every day.

It was a weight that both upheld him and imposed upon him responsibilities to his ancestry that others could not understand. A duty that reached far back into the Middle Ages, stretching across all his estates from the high Apennine lands leased as a national park, to forests and vineyards, agricultural land and olive groves, and across all his many properties. Every *palazzo* was a historic monument, including the magnificent baroque Palazzo Mantegna here in Rome, now on loan to the nation and housing a museum of antiquities. And all those estates and properties came with tenants and employees whose livelihood he guaranteed—just as his ancestors had.

Yet at the heart of it all was the ancient Castello Mantegna, the heart of his patrimony. Within its mighty walls, built to withstand medieval warfare, he had spent his childhood, roaming the forests and pasturelands that one day would be his.

Was that something anyone not born to such a heritage could truly understand? The weight of inheritance upon him?

Or did they merely see *il Conte*—a wealthy, titled man who moved in the uppermost echelons of society, with a cachet that many would only envy? And which women would eagerly seek to bask in...

His dark eyes glinted. There had been no such eagerness in Carla Charteris, though he'd made clear his interest in her. He was glad of it—but not deterred by it. For his long experience of woman had told him immediately that the first flare of her violet-hued eyes as he'd addressed her had showed that she was responsive to him. That was all he'd needed to know—their barbed exchange thereafter had merely confirmed it. All that was required now was for her to acknowledge it.

He leant across to open the passenger side door. *'Prego,'* he invited in a pleasant voice.

He'd surprised her—he could tell. Had she really believed that walking away from him would discourage him?

He went on in a dry voice, 'It would gratify me if

you complied without delay, for the traffic warden over there—' he nodded carelessly along the street to where such an individual had recently turned the corner '—would so very much enjoy booking me.' He gave a brief sigh. 'I find that officials take particular pleasure in exercising their petty authority when their target is driving a car like this one.'

He smiled. He could see the conflict in her eyes—in those amazingly dark violet-blue eyes of hers—but above all he could see that same flare of awareness, of desire, which had been in them when he'd first approached her. That told him all he needed to know.

His expression changed again. *'Carpe diem,'* he said softly. His eyes held hers. Tellingly, unambiguously. 'Let us seize all that we may have of this fleeting life,' he murmured, 'before we are dust ourselves.'

His casual reference to her own comment in front of the Luciezo was accompanied by an exaggerated gesture of his hand as he again indicated the seat beside him.

His lashes dipped over his eyes. 'What is so difficult,' he murmured, 'about accepting an invitation to dinner?' His gaze lifted to hers again, and in his eyes was everything that was not in his words.

Carla, her expression immediately urgently schooled, stopped in her tracks on the pavement, felt again that incredible frisson go through her whole body—that shimmer of glittering awareness of the physical impact he made on her.

All around her the city of Rome buzzed with its familiar vitality. The warmth of the early evening enveloped her, and she could hear the noise of the traffic, the buzz of endless Vespas scooting past. The pavement was hot beneath the thin soles of her high heels. While in front of her, in that outrageously expensive car—as exclusive and prestigious as its driver so undoubtedly considered himself to be—the oh-so-aristocratic Conte invited her to join him.

As she had before, in the gallery, she felt the overwhelming impact of the man. Felt even more powerfully the impulse within her to give him the answer that he was waiting for.

Thoughts—fragmented, incoherent—raced through her.

*What is happening to me? Why now—why this man of all men? This arrogant, lordly man who is scooping me up as if I were no more than that woman in the portrait—scooping me up to serve his pleasure...*

Yet it would be for *her* pleasure too—she knew that with every shimmer in her body as she stood, poised on the pavement, feeling the weight of his lidded gaze upon her. That was the devil of it—that was the allure. That was the reason, Carla knew with a kind of sinking in her heart, that was keeping her here, hovering, just as he was keeping that monstrous, powerful car of his hovering, its power leashed, but ready to be let forth.

His words, mocking her, echoed in her head. *'What is so difficult about accepting an invitation to dinner?'*

His voice—deep, amused—cut across her tormented cogitations. 'You really will need to decide swiftly—the warden is nearly upon us.'

The uniformed official was, indeed, closing fast. But Carla's eyes only sparked deep blue. 'And you couldn't *possibly* afford the fine, could you?' she retorted.

'Alas, it is a question of my pride,' Cesare murmured, the glint in his eye accentuated. 'It would never do for *il Conte* to put himself in the power of a petty bureaucrat...'

Was he mocking himself? Carla had the suspicion he was not…

For a moment longer every objection she had made when he'd first invited her to dinner flared like phosphorus in her head. Every reason why she should give exactly the same kind of answer as she had then—evasive, avoiding the invitation—then walk briskly away, back to the comfortable, predictable evening she'd planned for herself in her own apartment. Making herself dinner, going through her notes in preparation for writing her article. An evening that had nothing, *nothing* to do with the man now waiting for her answer…

And yet—

Her own thought replayed itself in her head. *How dangerous might it be to light a passion that could not be quenched?*

But other thoughts pushed their way into her head. Thoughts she did not want to silence. Could not silence… *Desire and passion will burn themselves out! They cannot last for ever.*

Neither desire nor passion was love.

Yet both were powerful—alluring—speaking to her of what might be between them.

*Passion and desire.*

The same tremor went through her, the same flush in her skin as when he had first made his desire for her plain, calling from her an answering awareness. No other man had ever drawn from her such an overpowering response.

For a second longer she hesitated, hung between two opposing instincts.

To resist that response—or to yield to it.

The dark, lidded eyes rested on her—holding hers.

With a sudden impulse, impelling her way below the level of conscious decision, she felt her muscles move as if of their own volition. She got into the car, slamming the door shut.

Instantly, as if preventing her from rescinding her decision as much as avoiding the attentions of the parking official, Cesare opened the throttle, pulled the car away from the kerb—and Carla reached for her seat belt, consciousness rushing back upon her in all its impact.

Oh, dear God, what the *hell* had she just done?

*I got into his damn car just to save his damn aristocratic pride! So he wouldn't have to endure the ignominy of getting a parking ticket! How insane is that?*

Completely insane. As insane as letting Cesare di Mondave drive off with her like this—the lordly *signor* scooping up the peasant girl.

Her chin lifted. Well, she was no peasant girl! She was no poor, hapless female like the one in the portrait, trapped within the punishing limitations of her time in history. No, if she went along with what this impossible, arrogant man had in mind for her—*if*, she emphasised mentally to herself—then it would be what *she* wanted too! Her free and deliberate choice to enjoy the enticing interlude he clearly had planned.

But would she make that choice? That was the only question that mattered now. Whether to do what every ounce of her good sense was telling her she should not do—and what every heat-flushed cell in her body was urging her to do. To resist it—or yield to it. She turned her head towards him, drawn by that same impetuous urge to let her eyes feast on him. He was focussing only on the appalling evening traffic in Rome, which, she allowed, *did* need total focus. She let him concentrate, let herself enjoy the rush that came simply from looking at his profile.

Sweet heaven, but it was impossible not to gaze at him! A modern version of that Luciezo portrait, updated for the twenty-first century. Indelibly graced with features that made her eyes cling to him, from the strong blade of his nose to the chiselled line of his jaw, the sensual curve of his mouth. She felt her hands clench over her bag. Weakness drenched her body. What she was doing was insane—and yet she was doing it.

She felt her pulse leap, and a heady sense of excitement filled her. A searing knowledge of her own commitment. Far too late now to change her mind.

And she did not want to—that was the crux of it. Oh, the lordly Count might have scooped her up just as arrogantly as his ancestor had scooped up the peasant girl who would become his mistress, but it had been *her* choice to let herself be so scooped.

Rebelliousness soared within her—a sense of recklessness and adventure.

*I don't care if this is folly! All I know is that from the moment he looked at me I wanted him more than I have ever wanted any man—and I will not deny that desire. I will fulfil it...*

Fulfil it with all the ardour in her body, every tremor in her limbs. It was folly—reckless folly—but she would ignite that passion and burn it to the core.

'Take the next left here,' Carla said, indicating the narrow road in the Centro Storico that led down to her apartment, part of an eighteenth-century house. It was a quiet haven for her to write in, and to be well away not just from the buzz of the city but also from the tensions running across the Viscari clan.

Her mother, she knew, would have preferred her to stay on in Guido Viscari's opulent villa, but thanks to her stepfather's generosity in his will Carla had been able to buy her own small but beautiful apartment, taking intense pleasure in decorating it and furnishing it in an elegant but comfortable and very personal style.

However, her thoughts now were neither on the ongoing tensions in the Viscari clan nor on her apartment. There was only one dominating, all-encompassing consciousness in her head…

*Cesare.*

Cesare—with whom she had just dined, with whom she had conducted, she knew, a conversation that had taken place at two levels. One had seen him being the perfect escort, the perfect dinner companion, conversing with her about her job, about the arts, about the Italian landscape—of which he owned a significant proportion—and about any other such topics that two people making each other's acquaintance might choose to converse about.

He'd asked her a little about herself—neither too little to be indifferent, nor too much to be intrusive. He'd known who she was, but she was not surprised—she'd known who *he* was, though they'd never chanced to meet before.

But there'd been another conversation taking place as they'd sat there over a lingering dinner in the small, ferociously exclusive restaurant Cesare had taken her to—where he had immediately been given the best table in the house, and where they had been waited on attentively, discreetly, unobtrusively but with absolute expertise.

He had nodded at one or two other patrons, and her presence had caused the lift of an eyebrow from one group of women, and a penetrating glance, but no more than that. She had been acquainted with no one there, and was glad of it. Glad there had been no one she knew to witness the second level of the conversation taking place between herself and Cesare di Mondave, Conte di Mantegna.

The conversation that had taken place powerfully, silently and seductively—oh-so-seductively—between him and her, with every exchange of glances, every half-smile, every sensual curve of his mouth, every lift of his hand with those long, aristocratic fingers.

The light had reflected off the gold of his signet ring, impressed with his family crest—the same lion couchant that his ancestor had displayed on his own ring in the Luciezo portrait—and Carla had found herself wondering if it could be the very same ring.

Eventually Cesare's hand had crushed the white damask napkin and dropped it on the table to signal the end of their meal, and they'd got to their feet and made their way towards the exit.

Nothing so crude as a bill had been offered by the maître d'—nothing more than a respectful inclination of the head at their departure, a gracious murmur of appreciation from the Count, a smile of thanks from herself as they left, stepping out onto the pavement, where his car had been waiting for them.

Now, as they drew up at the kerb by her apartment, he cut the engine and turned and looked at her, an enigmatic expression visible in the dim street light.

Her consciousness of his raw physical presence seared in her again. She smiled at him. 'Thank you,' she said, 'for a lovely evening.' Her voice was bright, and oh-so-civil.

She realised she'd spoken in English. They'd gone in and out of Italian and English all evening, for the Count's English was as fluent as her Italian had become in the ten years she'd lived in Rome, though surely no Englishman could make his native language as seductive, as sensual as an Italian male could make it sound?

But English was the right language for this moment. Crisp, bright and utterly unseductive. The polite, anodyne description of something that had been so much more. She reached out her hand for the door release, her body still turned towards him.

A smile curved his mouth, long lashes dropping over his lidded eyes. 'Indeed,' he agreed.

She could hear the amusement in his voice, feel it catch at her, making her breathless, her pulse quicken.

'And after such a *"lovely evening"*...' his amusement was deeper now, his accented English doing even more to make her breathless '...there is only one way to end it, no?'

For an instant he held her gaze in the dim light, daring her to accept, to concede, to do what he wanted her to do—what he'd wanted of her from the first moment he'd set eyes on her.

'Like this,' he said.

His hand stretched out, long fingers tilting up her face to his as his mouth lowered to hers. Slowly, sensuously, savouring. With skill, with expertise, with a lifetime of experience in how to let his lips glide over hers, his mouth to open hers to his, to taste the sweetness within. As soft, as sensual as silk velvet.

She drowned in it. A thousand nerve endings fired as

he made free with her mouth, his long fingers still holding her. And when he had done he released her, drew back his hand, let it curve around the driving wheel.

He smiled. *'Buone notte,'* he said softly.

For a moment—just a moment—she was motionless, as if all the shimmering pleasure he'd aroused in her with only a single kiss had made it impossible for her to move. She could do nothing except meet that amused, lidded gaze resting on her like a tangible pressure.

Then, with a little jolt, she pushed open the car door. Swallowed. In a daze she got out, fumbled for her keys, found them and shakily inserted them into the lock of the outer door of her apartment building. Then she made herself turn to look back at him. Bade him goodnight in a voice that was no longer bright and crisp.

He said nothing, merely inclining his head as she turned away, let herself into the cobbled inner courtyard, shut the heavy outer door behind her.

She heard the throaty growl of his car as he moved off. On shaky legs she went up to her apartment, and only when inside its sanctuary did she feel able to breathe again.

Cesare strolled to the window of his Rome apartment and gazed unseeing out over the familiar roofline. The large plate glass window of the modern designed space was glaringly different from the richly historical interiors of his other properties, and it gave a wide view over the city even at this midnight hour. He did not step out onto the large adjoining balcony; instead he merely continued to stand, hands thrust into his trouser pockets, legs slightly astride.

Was he being wise? That was the question that was

imposing itself upon him. Was it wise to pursue what had been, after all, only the impulse of a moment—following through on a momentary glimpse of the woman who had caught his eye? Following through sufficiently to decide that it was worth spending an evening of his life in her company. Worth considering, as he was now considering, whether to pursue a liaison with her.

There were many reasons to do so. Uppermost, of course, was the intensity of his physical response to her. Unconsciously he shifted position restlessly, his body aware that a single kiss had only whetted the appetite that he could feel coursing through his blood. It was an intensity that had, he acknowledged, taken him by surprise. But was that reason enough to do what he knew his body wanted him to do?

Before he could answer, he knew from long experience that there was another question he must answer first.

*Will she understand the terms of our liaison?*

The terms that governed his life just as they'd governed all who had borne his ancient name and title. Had been hammered into him by his own dictatorial father who'd constantly impressed upon him his heritage, and yet who'd regarded him as favouring too much the mother whose outward serenity Cesare was sure had concealed an unvoiced regret.

Her husband had objected to her having any interests outside her responsibilities as his *contessa*, and she had confined her life to being the perfect chatelaine, the mother of his heir. His father had taken his son's sympathy for his mother as a reluctance to respect the demands of his heritage, and after his mother's premature death from heart disease, when Cesare was only nineteen, the rift between them had widened without her presence as peacemaker.

But when his father had died, some eight years later, he'd been determined not to neglect any aspect of his inheritance, dedicating himself to its preservation. If his father could see him now, half a dozen years on, perhaps his harsh judgement would be set aside.

The words that he had uttered only that evening, in front of the Luciezo painting of his sixteenth-century forebear, floated in his head.

*'Pride in his family, his lineage, his honour—all that he owes his house...'*

With the echo of those words his thoughts came full circle back to the woman to whom he had spoken them. Did she understand why he had said what he had about his ancestor—about himself? It was essential that she did. Essential that she understood that, for him, one thing could never change.

In his mind's eye two images formed—the other portraits in the triptych, the Count's wife and his mistress. Separate for ever, coming from different worlds that could never meet.

Four centuries and more might distance him from Count Alessandro and the women who made up the triptych, but for himself, too, his countess would need to share his own background. Not because of any heraldic quarterings she possessed, but because only a woman from the same heritage as himself could truly understand the responsibilities of such a heritage. That was what his father had instilled into him. He had even identified for him the very woman who would make him the perfect next Contessa...

His expression changed and he stared out over the

roofs of this most ancient city into whose roots his own ancestry reached. The lineage of a patrician of Ancient Rome was still traceable in his bloodline.

The woman who would be his Countess was well known to him—and she was not, nor ever could be, a woman such as the one he had embraced a brief hour ago, fuelling in him a desire for satiation that he must not yield to.

Not unless—until—he could be sure she accepted what could be between them. And what could not.

As, too, must he. That, also, was essential…

# CHAPTER THREE

CARLA STARED AT her screen. She still had six hundred more words to write for her article, and she was making heavy weather of it. She knew exactly why.

Cesare di Mondave.

*He* was in her headspace—had been totally dominating it, consuming every last morsel of it, since she'd made it into her apartment the night before, senses firing, aflame.

All through her sleepless night she'd replayed every moment of the evening over and over again—right up to that final devastating moment.

Cesare kissing her…

*No!* She must not let herself remember it again! Must not replay it sensuously, seductively, in her head. Must instead force herself to finish her article, send it into the impatiently waiting sub-editor at her office.

But even when she had she was unbearably restless, her heart beating agitatedly.

*Will he phone me? Ask me out again? Or*—a little chill went through her—*has he decided he does not want me after all?*

Face set, she made herself some coffee. She should not be like this—waiting for a man to phone her! She should be above such vulnerability. She was a strong-minded, independent woman of twenty-seven, with a good career, as many dates as she cared to go on should she want to, and there was no reason—no *good* reason!—for her to be straining to hear the phone ring. To hear the dark, aristocratic tones of Cesare di Mondave's deep voice.

And yet that was just what she was doing.

The expression in her eyes changed. As she sipped her coffee, leaning moodily against the marble work surface in her immaculate kitchen, more thoughts entered her head. If last night's dinner with Cesare was all there was to be between them she should be relieved. A man like that—so overwhelming to her senses—it was not wise to become involved with. She'd known that from the moment he'd first spoken to her, declared his interest.

But where was wisdom, caution, when she needed them? She felt her pulse quicken again as the memory of that kiss replayed itself yet again.

With a groan, she pulled her memory away. She shouldn't be waiting for Cesare di Mondave to phone her! Not just because she should *never* be waiting around for a man to phone her! But because she should, she knew, phone her mother—reply to her latest complaint about her sister-in-law's disapproving attitude towards her.

She gave a sigh. Her mother—never popular with Guido's younger brother Enrico and his wife, Lucia—had become markedly less popular after her husband's death, when it had become known that the childless Guido, rather than leaving his half of the Viscari Hotels Group shares to his nephew, Vito, had instead left them to his widow, Marlene. They had been outraged by the decision, and when Enrico had suddenly died, barely a year later, his premature death had been blamed on the stress of worrying about Marlene's ownership of the shares. Since then, Vito had sought repeatedly to buy them from Marlene, but Carla's mother had continually refused to sell.

To Carla, it was straightforward. Her mother *should* sell her shareholding to Vito—after all, it was Vito who was the true heir to the Viscari dynasty, and he should control the inheritance completely. But Carla knew why her mother was refusing to do so—her ownership of those critical shares gave her mother status and influence within the Viscari family, resented though it was by her sister-in-law.

Carla's mouth tightened in familiar annoyance. It also continued to feed her mother's other obsession. One that she had voiced when Carla was a teenager and had repeated intermittently ever since—despite Carla's strong objection. An objection she still gave—would always give.

'Mum—forget it! Just stop going on about it! It's never going to happen! I get on well enough with Vito, but please, please, just accept there is absolutely no way whatsoever that I would ever want to do what you keep on about!'

No way whatsoever that she would ever consider marrying her step-cousin...

Vito Viscari—incredibly handsome with his Latin film star looks—might well be one of Rome's most eligible bachelors, but to Carla he was simply her step-cousin, and of no romantic interest to her in the slightest. Nor was she to him. Vito was well known for liking leggy blondes—he ran a string of them, and always had one in tow, it seemed to her—and he was welcome to them. He held no appeal for her at all.

A shiver went through her. She remembered the man who *did*…who'd made every cell in her body searingly aware of her physicality. Who'd cast his eye upon her and then scooped her up into his sleek, powerful car effortlessly.

She felt the heat flush in her body, her pulse quicken. Heard her phone ring on her desk.

She dived on it, breathless. *'Pronto?'*

It was Cesare.

'But this is charming! Absolutely lovely!'

Carla's gaze took in the small but beautifully proportioned miniature Palladian-style villa, sheltered by poplars and slender cypresses, in front of which Cesare was now drawing up. It was set in its own grounds in the lush countryside of Lazio, less than an hour's drive beyond Rome, and its formal eighteenth-century gardens ideally suited the house.

She looked around her in delight as she stepped gracefully out of the low-slung car, conscious of the quietness all around her, the birdsong, the mild warmth of the late-afternoon sun slanting across the gardens—and conscious, above all, of the man coming to stand beside her.

'My home out of town…what is the term in English? Ah, yes…my bolthole.' He smiled.

He ushered her inside, and Carla stepped into a marble-floored, rococo-style hallway, its decor in white, pale blue and gold.

Into her head came a description for the house that was not the one Cesare had just given.

*Love nest*…

A half-caustic, half-amused smile tugged at her mouth.

Well, why *not* a love nest? It was a conveniently short distance from Rome, and so very charming. An ideal place for romantic dalliance.

Because that was what she was embarking on. She knew it—accepted it. Had accepted it the moment she'd heard Cesare's deep tones on the phone earlier that afternoon, informing her that he would be with her shortly. Taking for granted what her answer would be.

Was she being reckless, to come here with him like this? Of course she was! She knew it, but didn't care. All her life she'd been careful—never one to rush into passionate affairs, never making herself the centre of any gossip. Yet now, a little less than twenty-four hours since she had stood in front of that Luciezo portrait of Count Alessandro, she was going to do just that.

And she would revel in it! For once in her life she would follow the hectic beating of her heart, the hot pulse of her blood, and respond to a man who, like no other she had ever met, could call such a response from her merely by a flickering glance from his dark, hooded eyes. However brief their liaison was to prove—and she knew perfectly well that it could never lead to anything—she would enjoy it to the full until the passion between them burnt itself out, until her desire was quenched.

A man in late middle age was emerging, greeting the Count with respectful familiarity.

'Ah, Lorenzo,' Cesare answered, in a reciprocal tone that told Carla he showed full appreciation of his staff. 'Will you show Signorina Charteris where she may refresh herself?'

Carla was escorted upstairs, shown into a pretty, feminine bedroom, with an en-suite bathroom that had once, she presumed, been a dressing room. As she looked at herself in the glass, checking the careful perfection of her hair and make-up, retouching the rich colour of her lips, for just a second she felt a qualm go through her.

*Should I really go ahead with this? Plunge headlong into an affair with a man like this? An affair that can come to nothing?*

But that, surely, was why she was doing it! *Because* it could come to nothing! There could be no future with a man for whom marriage to her could never be an option, and therefore love could never be a possibility—never a danger. She would *not* follow in her mother's footsteps, imagining love could come from an affair.

*And that is all it will be—an affair. Nothing more than indulging in the overpowering effect he has on me, such as I have never, never known before.*

She could see the pulse beating at her throat, the heightened colour in her cheeks, the quickening shallowness of her breathing. All telling her one thing and one thing only. That it was far too late for any qualms now.

With a quick spritz of scent from her handbag, she headed back downstairs. A pair of double doors stood open now, leading through to a beautifully appointed drawing room with French windows. Beyond, she could see Cesare.

Waiting for her.

At her approach, he smiled, his eyes washing over her with satisfaction.

Yes—he had been right to make the decision he had. This would go well, this affair with this enticing, alluring woman. He had no doubts about it. Everything about her confirmed it. Oh, not just her sensual allure and her responsiveness to him—powerful as it was— but any lingering reservations he might have had about her suitability for such a liaison were evaporating with every moment.

All his conversations with her so far had been reassuring on that score. Though she was Guido Viscari's stepdaughter, she made no special claims on the relationship, which indicated that she would make no claims on the relationship that he and she would share.

Her cool, English air of reserve met with his approval—like him, she would seek to avoid gossip and speculation and would draw no undue attention to her role in his life while their affair lasted—or afterwards. She had a career of her own to occupy her—one that was compatible with some of his own interests—and intelligent conversation with her was showing him that she was a woman whose company he could enjoy both out of bed and in.

*She will enjoy what we have together and will have no impossible expectations. And when the affair has run its course we shall part gracefully and in a civilised manner. There will be no trouble in parting from her.*

*Parting with her...*

But all that was for later—much later. For now, the entirely enticing prospect of their first night together beckoned.

His smile deepened. 'Come,' he said, as she walked towards him.

A little way along the terrace an ironwork table was set with two chairs, and there was a stand on which an opened bottle of champagne nestled in its bed of ice. But Carla's eyes were not for that—nor for Cesare. They were on the vista beyond the terrace.

Once more a pleased exclamation was on her lips, a smile of delight lighting her features.

'Oh, how absolutely perfect!'

Beyond the terrace, set at the rear of the villa, a large walled garden enclosed not just a pretty pair of parterres, one either side, but in the central space a swimming pool—designed, she could see at once, as if it were a Roman bath, lined with mosaic tiles and glittering in the sun. Ornamental bay trees marched either side of the paving around the pool, and there was a sunlit bench at the far end, espaliered fruit trees adorning the mossed walls.

Cesare came to stand beside her as she gazed, enraptured.

'We shall try out the pool later,' he said. 'But for now...'

He turned to pour each of them a glass of softly foaming champagne. As she took hers Carla felt the faint brush of his fingers, and the glass trembled in her hand. She gazed up at him, feeling suddenly breathless.

His dark gaze poured down into hers as he lifted his glass. 'To our time together,' he murmured.

She lifted her glass, touching it to his. Then drank deeply from it.

As she would drink deeply from her time with this most compelling of men...

# CHAPTER FOUR

THE FIRE WAS burning low in the grate. The long, heavy silk drapes were drawn across the tall windows, cocooning them in the drawing room. Cesare's long legs extended with careless proprietorship towards the hearth from where he sat on the elegant sofa.

The evening had been long and leisurely. Champagne on the terrace, watching the sunset, followed by an exquisitely prepared dinner, discreetly served by Lorenzo in the rococo-style dining room.

Conversation had been easy—wide-ranging and eclectic—and Carla had found it both mentally stimulating and enjoyable, as it had been in the restaurant the night before. As it continued to be now, as she sat, legs slanting towards him, on a silk-covered *fauteuil,* sipping at a liqueur. Coffee was set on the ormolu table at her side... candles glowed on the mantel above the fire. An intimate, low-lit ambience enclosed them.

Their conversation wove on, both in English and Italian, melding Carla's expertise on High Renaissance art with Cesare's greater knowledge of the politics and economics of the time. And then at some point—she could not quite tell when—the conversation seemed to drain away, and she could not think of one more question to ask him.

Her liqueur was consumed, she realised, and she reached to place the empty glass on the low table at her side. As she released it Cesare stretched out his own hand. Let his fingers slide around her wrist.

It was the first physical contact between them that evening, and it electrified her.

Her eyes went to his, widening at the ripple of sensation that his long, cool fingers circling her wrist engendered. His eyes were on her, heavy and lidded.

Wordlessly, he drew her to her feet. Wordlessly, she let him. Still holding her wrist loosely, he lifted his other hand to her face. Those long, graceful fingers traced the outline of her cheek, her jaw. Faintness drummed in her veins and she felt her body sway, as if no longer able to keep itself upright.

Cesare smiled—a slow, sensual smile. As he had done in the car the night before, just before he'd kissed her. Kissed her as he did now—slowly, leisurely, with infinite sensuality, his mouth like velvet on hers…

'How very, very beautiful you are…' The words were a murmur, a caress. His gaze met hers. His mouth drew free. Her lips were still parted, her eyes still wide and clinging.

'Shall we?' he asked.

She did not answer. Did not need to.

She let him take her upstairs, into the bedroom she'd been shown to earlier, the house hushed around them. Then he was slipping the embroidered evening jacket from her, letting it fall to a chair, sliding down the zip of her dress, easing it from her shoulders. His mouth grazed the bare skin between the cusp of her arm and her neck, and she felt her head move to take in the luxury of his kiss. Slowly she stepped away from him a moment, to step out of her dress, drape it carefully on the chair.

As she turned back she saw that he had carelessly shrugged his own jacket free, and was loosening his tie, slipping the buttons of his shirt. Her eyes went to the smooth, hard wall of his chest. With an instinct older than time she stepped towards him, clad only in bra and panties, and the girdle of her stockings. She saw his eyes flare with male reaction. Felt her own fingertips reach to graze with infinite delicacy across the revealed skin of his torso. Saw his shoulders tense, his pupils become pinpoints.

Wickedly, oh-so-wickedly, she let the palms of her hands slide beneath his shirt, around the warm, strong column of his back, craning her head back to smile into his face with invitation and desire.

For one long, impossible moment he held fast, and still she smiled up at him.

Then, as if a limit had been reached, he gave a low growl in his throat and crushed her to him. His mouth came down on hers and now there was no slow, velvet arousing caress. Now there was only male hunger. Raw, insistent.

Fire flamed in her and her hands flattened on his spine, holding him against her as his mouth devoured hers. Arousal seared in her, her pulse soaring, skin heating. She felt her nipples crest, her breasts engorge—felt, with a fierce flare of arousal, his own arousal against her hips. Sensual excitement filled her…a mad headiness possessed her.

Desire, hot and tumid, took her over—took him over. Possessed them both.

He crushed her down upon the bed, upon the heavy satin covers, and the world was lost to her.

And more than just the world.

Carla twirled around her apartment, her body as light as air, her feet almost off the ground. *Cesare!* Oh, the very name, the very thought of him, filled her being, her mind, every synapse of her utterly possessed existence! How she thrilled to say his name, to see his face, his body— that powerful, sensual, perfect body!—in her mind's eye all the time...

She did not need to be with him to see him. He was there in her head, a constant presence, and every beat of her pulse was telling her what he had done to her.

Their first night together had set her aflame—caught her in a maelstrom of sensation and ecstasy that she had never known possible, that had set her alight with a flame that could not be quenched.

They had stayed at the villa for two days, and Carla had simply blotted out the rest of the world. She'd phoned in to the office the next day, on some pretext or other, to say that she was out of communication, and then she'd turned off her phone and given her entire and absolute focus to the man she was with. To Cesare—who had possessed her utterly, body and mind.

Cocooned at the villa, the only person they'd seen had been Lorenzo, for they had not ventured beyond the formal rooms that she and Cesare had occupied or the gardens beyond the terrace—and the joys of the sparkling Roman-style swimming pool. Where swimsuits had not been necessary...

And making love in the water, beneath the stars at

night, had been a revelation of sensual pleasure such as she had never, never anticipated. She had cried out in ecstasy as he'd held her, cradled her to him, and her head had fallen back, her hair streaming out into the water, her face lifted to the heavens, eyes wide with their reflected glory, as her body had shuddered, and shuddered again, in Cesare's strong possession.

Then, finally, as she'd let her head rest against his shoulder, let the water lap gently around them, he'd waded from the pool, wrapped her in the softest towels and carried her indoors and up to the bedroom—to make love to her all over again...

And again and yet again. Waking and sleeping, sleeping and waking, until the morning sun had streamed through the curtains and he'd been smoothing her tousled hair, smiling down at her.

'Breakfast,' he'd said. 'And then, alas, Rome. I have a lunch meeting I can't get out of.'

Carla had gazed up at him. 'And I must phone my editor.'

She'd smiled, lifting her hand lazily to graze the growth along Cesare's chin. If he grew a beard he'd look even more like his ancestor, she'd found herself thinking, amused.

But amusement had not been uppermost in her thoughts. There had been a stab of fear in the back of her mind—one that had returned as they drove back into Rome later in the morning.

*Will he want to see me again—or is this all I shall have of him?*

The stab had come again, almost drawing blood...

She'd hidden it, though—had known she must. Known with every instinct of her femininity that making any reference to that at all, asking any such question, would be the very last thing that would help to persuade him that he *did* want to see her again—*did* want more, much more, of what had been between them these last two incredible days.

And so it had proved. As he'd dropped her off at her apartment, he had casually wrapped his hand around her nape, drawn her to his mouth for a farewell kiss. But only farewell for the moment.

'I can't do tonight,' he'd said with a smile, his eyes washing over hers with warm intimacy, 'but the following night is clear. Tell me…how are you with opera?'

Carla had smiled in return, not letting the relief show in her face. 'Very predictable, I'm afraid. Verdi and Puccini, fine, Wagner and modern, not fine—'

He'd laughed and let her go. 'How about Donizetti?'

'*Bel canto* I can cope with,' she'd said in answer, and laughed too.

'Good. Can you meet me before the performance? I'll text you where. We can have a drink beforehand, eat afterwards. How would that suit you?'

*Anything—anything would suit me! Anything at all!*

The words had soared in Carla's head, but she had not spoken them. Again, instinct had told her otherwise. Instead, she had simply smiled.

'Lovely!' she'd said. And then she'd reached for the door catch, letting herself out of the car as it hummed by the kerb. She'd lifted her hand, given a little wave of farewell. 'See you then,' she'd said airily.

Without looking back again she'd opened the doors to the inner courtyard and stepped inside. Then, and only then, had she clutched at her key and given a crow of joy, of pleasure and relief.

*Yes!* Yes, he wanted to see more of her, wanted more time with her. Wanted her again… As she—oh, as she wanted him…

*Cesare! Oh, Cesare—*

His name soared in her head again—filling her mind, her being.

Him and only him…


'How's the article coming along?'

Cesare half twisted his head to call back into the shaded bedroom from where he sat, long legs stretched out in tan chinos, lounging out on the sunlit balcony, his city shirt swapped for a knitted polo, feet in casual, handmade loafers.

Beyond, the darkly glinting waters of Lake Garda hid their glacial depths, reflecting the encircling mountains. He flicked open the tab on the beer he'd just taken out of the minibar in the hotel room. As he sipped its cool flavour his sense of ease deepened. The leisurely weekend ahead beckoned him, and the prospect not just of taking his ease, but of spending it with Carla, bestowed a sense of well-being on him.

The time he spent with Carla always did that to him.

*I made a good choice in her. She's worked out well— very, very well.*

His eyelids drooped a moment as reminiscence played pleasurably in his head and anticipation of the night to come tonight did likewise. Carla might present a cool, composed front to the world, but when they were alone, when the lights went out… Oh, that was a different matter!

He felt his body quicken in memory. Like a struck match, when he reached for her she went up like a sheet of flame. Passion flared like phosphorous, incandescent and searing. Desire, unleashed, scorched between their bodies...

But it was not that alone—outstanding though it was—that had kept their affair going for so long. It had been six months now, and he showed no sign of tiring of her. But why *should* he tire of her, when passion still ran so strongly? And even when it was exhausted she was so very suitable for him—the ideal woman to have an affair with. She made no attempt to cling to him. Indeed, sometimes he found himself irked by her occasional unavailability, when she cited pressure of deadlines. But he respected her for it all the same. Made no demands on her when she was working.

His eyes shadowed for a moment. His father had shown no such respect for his mother—his mother's role had been to be a docile *contessa*, arranging her life only around the requirements of her difficult husband. Even the weakness of her heart condition had not made his father tolerant of what he perceived as any dereliction in her primary duty to be the chatelaine of his estates.

It was not an attitude he would take when he himself married. Of course his *contessa* would need to be completely willing to play her role as his wife, just as he himself would shoulder the myriad responsibilities of his position, but that did not mean she could have no life of her own as well. In fact...

He snapped his mind away. It was inappropriate to dwell on the qualities his wife would have when he was here with a woman who could never have that title.

And who would not want to.

Nothing about Carla Charteris gave him any cause for disquiet in that respect. And for that he was entirely appreciative. So if, right now, he was having to wait for her to finish her article, then wait he would—as patiently as his temperament permitted.

Some ten minutes later, as he was nearing the end of his can of beer, it was rewarded.

'Finished!' came Carla's voice from inside, with a sense of relief. 'All submitted.'

She lifted the laptop off her knees, closing it down, glancing out towards the darkening balcony. She'd been slightly apprehensive in booking this hotel, in case it did not meet Cesare's exacting standards, but its five-star rating was well deserved. Situated at the lake's edge, its luxury was discreet rather than ostentatious, and a weekend here—following on from her trip to Venice to cover the opening of a new gallery, which had conveniently coincided with Cesare's series of business appointments in Milan—should be extremely pleasant.

*Pleasant?* The mild word mocked her. The time she spent with Cesare was so much more than 'pleasant'! It was—

*Incredible—unbelievable—wonderful—unforgettable!*

Her expression softened. Had it really been six months since that first night at his elegant little villa outside Rome? Since then they'd stayed there frequently, recapturing each and every time the scorching intimacy that had swept her away then as never before. Could she have experienced such passion with a man who was *not* Cesare? Impossible—just impossible! He dominated her consciousness each and every day, whether she was with him or not.

Yet she tried hard not to show it—instinctively knowing that any sign from her of being possessive would be fatal. It was that instinctive awareness that told her to be sure never to make any assumptions about him, never to ask him when they would next see each other. Never to rearrange her life for him.

*I want to reassure him that he is safe with me. That I do not depend on him. That I have my own life, separate from my time with him.*

It was an odd thought, and the reasons she was thinking it were skittering in the back of her mind, trying to land. But she would not let them. Instead, she would enjoy to the max the times they *did* have together—such as this weekend.

She padded on bare feet to the minibar, drawing out a miniature bottle of wine and a glass, then headed out to the balcony, sliding her hands over Cesare's broad shoulders, squeezing lightly.

He turned his head, brushing the tops of her fingers with his mouth. The sensation sent familiar little tremors through her, but she only took a seat beside him on the other sundowner chair, gathering the loose cotton folds of the long printed sundress she'd changed into from her formal Venice outfit, and poured her wine.

*'Salute!'* he said lazily, and clinked his beer can against her glass.

She returned the toast and took a mouthful of chilled wine, turning to look out over the view. It really was spectacular, and she drank it in as Cesare was doing.

'It's good to see mountains again—though these are a bit too serrated for my tastes,' he heard himself observing, letting his fingers intertwine with hers.

As he spoke, he found himself wondering why he'd made such a remark to Carla. As a rule, he never talked about his own home—even if it was only to contrast the high peaks of the jagged Dolomites with the lower, more rounded Apennines that were the ever-scenic background to the Castello di Mantegna. The *castello* wasn't a place she would ever see, so there was no point mentioning it.

At the thought, a slight frown flickered across his eyes. He crumpled his beer can, tightening his fingers on Carla's.

'Shall we head down to the restaurant?' he said.

He got to his feet, drawing her with him. His eyes went to her. She looked good—but then she always looked good. Always immaculately groomed, with her fantastic figure on show. Wearing what she did now—that loose dress—she looked different somehow. Still a knockout— always that—but more...*medieval*. Her hair was loose too, waving lushly down her back.

A ripple of desire went through him, but he put it aside. That was for later.

They headed downstairs, Cesare carrying her unfinished glass of white wine for her, and in the dining room, which still caught the roseate glow of the lowering sun, they took a table overlooking the lake.

Cesare's sense of well-being deepened. This was good. It really *was* good. Being here, well away from Rome, from home, from responsibilities and social obligations, just having time to himself with the woman he wanted to be with.

*How long will I keep this going? This affair...this liaison?*

The question wound through his head as they got on with choosing from the menu. The answer came of its own accord.

*While it stays good.*

* * *

It had certainly stayed good for the rest of their long weekend together.

A sating, fulfilling night together, a slow, leisurely breakfast the next morning, before hiring a car to explore the lake's circuit, and the following day taking a private launch out onto the water itself, lunching on one of the little islands in the lake.

The weekend passed too soon. And it was with regret that he announced at breakfast on Monday morning that he must leave for Milan again.

Carla nodded. 'And I've promised my mother I'll spend some time with her. I've somewhat neglected her these past months.'

Cesare reached for his coffee. As ever, Carla had made no demur at their parting, and he was glad of it. After Milan he must go home—put in some time there, attending to his affairs. His agenda was crowded—the never-ending maintenance work on the *castello* itself, a controversial wind turbine proposal to evaluate, a reforestation project to check up on, a request for the loan of artworks to yet another exhibition to decide on.

Maybe he should discuss that last item with Carla—

He pulled his mind back abruptly. No, that would be a bad move. That might set seeds growing that he did not want to see taking any kind of root. Impossible that they should do so.

Quite impossible.

They drove down towards Milan. Cesare would divert via the airport to let Carla catch her flight back to Rome.

As they drew near, he remarked, 'What would you say to a visit to London?' he asked. 'I'll need to go next month.'

Carla considered. 'I'll have to check my diary,' she said. 'I'm not sure what I've got coming up.'

Cesare nodded. 'Let me know,' he replied easily.

'Will do,' she agreed.

She kept her voice neutral, though inside she felt the familiar flutter of emotion that came whenever Cesare indicated that she was included in his future plans.

*Short-term* future plans, at any rate.

No, she mustn't think like that. What they had was good. Very good. Incredibly good. Fantastically good. But—

*I don't know what the future will bring. I just don't know. I don't dare know.*

She felt a hollowing inside her as the thoughts rushed into her head. Disquieting suddenly, as they echoed again. *Why* should she not dare know…?

An unfamiliar emotion swirled within her, disturbing her by its very presence. And as her eyes went to him now, that hollowing inside her was still there—that disturbing, unidentified emotion that seemed to deepen, to make her gaze cling to his profile as he drove along the *autostrada*, his dark eyes focussed on the road.

As if aware she was looking at him, he glanced sideways a moment. Instantly she schooled her expression. Not noticing the sudden flicker in his eyes before he spoke.

'Do you *have* to be in Rome today?' he said. 'Why not stay in Milan with me? I'll be busy all day, but surely the charms of the *quadrilatera* would while away the hours away for you!' He spoke lightly, knowing that although Carla was always superbly attired, she was no fashionista obsessed with Milan's famous *haute couture* quarter.

'And, of course,' he added, 'there's always the Da Vinci *Last Supper* to look in on!'

That might tempt her more…

He caught himself—was that what he was seeking to do? Tempt her to stay with him now instead of heading back to Rome?

*Well, why not? Why shouldn't I suggest she stay with me tonight and head down to Rome tomorrow? It's a perfectly reasonable suggestion.*

But that wasn't the reason for his question to himself—he knew that perfectly well. The reason for the question was why he should object in any way to Carla getting back to her own life. Because he shouldn't object—of course he shouldn't. She was her own woman, with her own life, not in the slightest bit assuming that her life was melded to his—and that was very necessary. Essential, in fact, for their liaison to continue.

*So why should I need to remind myself of that?*

That question was displaced only when he heard Carla's answer. Her tone was a little more clipped than usual, the quick shake of her head infinitesimal.

'I can't, I'm afraid. I've promised my mother, and I don't want to let her down.'

Was there regret in her voice? Hesitation? As if she were reluctant to turn down his invitation to stay with him longer, issued on an impulse he did not wish to scrutinise beyond wanting their mutual enjoyment. If there was, Cesare couldn't hear it. Could only hear her turning his suggestion down.

Could only feel the nip of…of *what*, precisely? Merely annoyance that he was going to have to do without her until they next met up again in Rome? It couldn't be more than that—he would not permit it to be more.

Making himself give a slight shrug of polite regret, he nodded. 'Ah, in that case, then, no,' he murmured courteously.

The turning for the airport was coming up, and he steered off the *autostrada*. Yet after he'd dropped her off he was again conscious of a sense of displeasure. Even regret for himself, that Carla had not stayed with him when he'd wanted her to, despite her perfectly valid reason for not doing so. He would not wish her to neglect her mother for his sake.

Memory flickered in his mind, and he recalled his own mother. How she had always moulded herself around her husband's wishes, whatever they had been, always at his side, always compliant.

It was something he recalled again as, returning home after Milan, he busied himself with the myriad items waiting for him at the *castello*.

Passing the doors of the trophy room—one of a series of staterooms, including the *galleria* containing priceless artworks such as the Luciezo-Caradino triptych—he paused to glance inside. It was his least favourite room, despite its imposing grandeur, for the walls were thick with the antlers and heads of creatures slaughtered by his forebears and added to copiously by his father.

His own open distaste for his father's predilection for slaughtering wildlife had been frequently voiced to his mother, and he'd known she'd shared his disapproval, yet never had she criticised his father. She had acquiesced in that, as she had in everything to do with him, subjugating her views to his on all matters.

Her perpetually acquiescent attitude had both dismayed Cesare and exasperated him.

Cesare's mouth tightened as he walked on into the

more recent eighteenth-century part of the *castello*, where the family accommodation was. Every window of the magnificent enfilade of rooms looked out upon terraced gardens and dramatic views over the plunging river valley beyond, framed by the soaring upward slope on the far side that drew the eye to the stony peak of the mountainous summit.

Instinctively, his footsteps took him to the French windows of the drawing room, and he stepped out into the fresh air, drinking in the vista all around him. For a few pleasurable minutes he stood on the terrace in the breeze-filled sunshine, feeling the customary deep and abiding sense of possession of this landscape—this was his home, his domain, his patrimony. And, whatever the dissensions between himself and his father, he had done his best—would always do his best—to prove himself worthy of his inheritance, to shoulder his responsibilities and carry out all the duties of his title and estates.

Including the most critical of all—to establish his new *contessa*, so as to continue the bloodline that stretched far back into the past, to safeguard it for the future. When the time came to take that step—as come it must, one day—his choice of wife would be a wise one—that was essential.

Taking one last deep breath of the crisp, clean air, he went back indoors, made his way to his study at the furthest end of the enfilade. Although the windows gave out onto the same spectacular view he'd enjoyed from the terrace, he schooled himself to turn his attention to the stacks of paperwork neatly piled by his secretary on his desk.

Time to get down to work.

A swift perusal of the files and business correspondence enabled him to select his priorities for the morning, and he was just about to open his emails when his eye caught a glimpse of the handwriting on an envelope in the in-tray containing his personal correspondence. For the most part this consisted of social invitations he would sort through later. But the sight of the handwriting arrested him.

He pulled the envelope out of the pile. Stared down at it a moment. It bore an airmail sticker and a US stamp—and Cesare knew exactly who it was from.

It was from the woman he was destined to marry.

# CHAPTER FIVE

'DARLING, HOW LOVELY to see you—it's been such a long time!'

Carla's mother's embrace was reproachful, and Carla felt herself wincing guiltily. It *had* been a long time since she'd spent any amount of time with her mother. Their last meeting had been several weeks ago, and only for lunch while out shopping.

'Well, I'm here now!' she answered lightly, exchanging a careful cheek-to-cheek kiss with her mother. 'And I'm in no rush to leave!'

She would stay at Guido's villa for a few days—it would be at least a week before Cesare was back in Rome and she would see him again.

*But you could still be in Milan with him tonight if you'd said yes to him!*

The reminder was like a little stab. On the short flight down to Rome she'd replayed that brief exchange a dozen times—and a dozen times wished she'd not given him that short, cool answer. Yet at the time it had seemed essential to say what she had.

*I was trying to negate that sudden fear I'd had—fear about why I didn't dare think what my future would be with Cesare. Because I shouldn't feel that—I've always*

*known that there is no future with him. Known that I
mustn't care that there is no future.*

Known, too, right from the start, that if she wanted
any time at all with Cesare she must try not to cling to
him, try not to want him too much. He had to know she
would never have any expectations of him, never make
any assumptions.

Never want a future with him longer than he was prepared to give her.

Or she would have nothing of him at all.

Nothing.

The hollow feeling came again, like a crevasse opening inside her. A crevasse into which that same emotion flared again—more than disquieting, deeper than
disturbing.

*To have nothing of Cesare—how could I endure that?*

No—she tore her mind away. She must not think like
this! She was regretting not staying with him in Milan,
that was all! Regretting insisting on arriving today at her
mother's, even though she could, she knew, have postponed her arrival by a day. It would not have made any
great difference to her mother, and she'd have stayed on
a day longer to compensate.

*I turned down Cesare when I didn't need to.*

But she knew why she had done it.

*It was to show myself that I don't want to cling to
him...don't need to cling to him. To show myself how we
are simply having a relationship between adults that we
both enjoy, that suits us both. And that is all.*

'So...' her mother's voice interrupted her insistent
thoughts and she was glad of it '...how was Venice? Tell
me about this new gallery that's been opened. Where

did you stay? At the Danieli or the Gritti?' she enquired, naming two of the city's top hotels.

As she answered, telling her mother about her trip there and the article she'd written, Carla welcomed the diversion—welcomed, too, over dinner, letting her mother run on about her social comings and goings, knowing how much Marlene enjoyed her position in Roman society.

Only when all these had been comprehensively covered did Carla ask, casually, after any news of the Viscaris. Vito, she knew, had been on an extensive inspection tour of his European hotels, and was due back in Rome imminently.

'I do hope, Mum,' she ended, casting a significant look at her mother, 'that when he's back here you'll finally agree to sell him Guido's shares...'

The sooner that was done, the better. It had caused a significant rift in relations with her stepfather's brother's side of the family that had rumbled on ever since her stepfather had died.

But immediately her mother bridled. 'Darling, Guido entrusted those shares to *me*! And he had his reasons.'

Carla gave an exasperated sigh. 'Mum, please don't be stubborn! It makes far more sense for Vito to own the entire shareholding—'

The next moment she wished she'd never mentioned the wretched subject.

Her mother's eyes flared. 'Yes, and he could—very easily! Carla, darling, *why* don't you listen to me on this? It would make perfect sense—would be what I've always dreamt of! It would unite both sides of the family! *And* unite the shareholdings as well!'

Carla threw up her hands. Damn, she'd walked into this one!

'Mum,' she said warningly, 'don't go there! I know you've had a thing about it for ever, but please just accept that Vito and I are simply not interested in each other! Not in the slightest! And whether or not Guido left you his shares doesn't change a thing!'

She attempted to put a humorous note into her voice, to defuse the situation.

'Vito wouldn't look twice at me—I'm not blonde, which is the only type of female he ever falls for, and his flashy film star looks just don't do it for me either. I far prefer—'

She stopped short. But it was too late. Her mother pounced.

'Yes, that's *exactly* what I'm concerned about! Darling, are you *mad*?' She leant forward, her expression agitated. 'Cesare di Mondave of all men! I've been hoping and hoping it would just be a brief fling…or whatever you want to call it! But it's been months now and you are still with him! Have you *no* sense?'

Carla shut her eyes, then flashed them open again. Realising with a wash of angry dismay that giving her mother an opportunity to voice her obsession about her marrying Vito had been the least of it!

During the last six months she'd never mentioned Cesare to her mother—had deliberately kept their relationship out of any conversation. The fact that her mother doubtless knew—for Rome was a hotbed of gossip—was no reason to be open with her mother about it. And not just because it didn't play to Marlene's fantasy about finally getting her together with Vito. But because she knew her affair with Cesare would get exactly the reaction she was getting now.

Emotion stormed up inside her. Anger at her mother, and at herself for walking into this. The last thing she wanted was an inquisition.

'I'm twenty-seven years old—I can handle an affair,' she said tightly.

Her mother's eyes were piercing. '*Can* you?' she said. Her expression changed. 'Darling, it's you I'm thinking of! Affairs can go badly wrong.' She paused again. 'I should know. For me there was no happy ending. And that's what I fear for *you*! There can be no happy ending for you as Cesare di Mondave's mistress—'

Rejection was instant in Carla. '*Mistress?* Of course I'm not his *mistress*!'

Yet even as she rejected the term across her mind seared the memory of that triptych, and the sixteenth-century's Conte's mistress.

*I am not that woman—I am nothing whatsoever like that wretched woman! I am not Cesare's mistress, I am his lover, and he is my lover, and we are together by choice, of our own free will, and I'm perfectly happy with that. Perfectly!*

She could see her mother backing off, taking another breath. 'Well, whatever you call yourself it doesn't matter. All that matters to me is that you don't get hurt!'

She shook her head one more time.

'I know I can't stop you, but…' she looked worriedly across at Carla, holding her gaze '…promise me that, whatever happens, when it comes to Cesare di Mondave you won't go and do something unforgivably stupid.' She took a breath. 'Promise me that you won't go and fall in love with him!'

There was silence. Absolute silence. And then Marlene's voice again, sounding hollow now.

'Please promise me that, Carla—*please*.'

But Carla could not answer. Could not answer at all...

Emotion was pouring over her like an avalanche. Wiping the breath from her lungs. Suffocating her with a blinding white truth...

Cesare was out on the terrace, hands curled around the cold stone of the balustrade. Above the gardens and the valley the moon was rising, casting its silver glow over the world. His expression was studied.

*Francesca.*

Francesca delle Ristori—Donna Francesca—daughter of a *marchese*, granddaughter of a duke on her mother's side, daughter of one of his father's best friends, and ideally suited to be the next Contessa di Mantegna.

Ideally suited to be his wife.

He'd known her all his life. Known her and liked her. And what was not to like? She was intelligent—extremely so—sweet-natured, good-tempered, and, as a bonus, beautiful. She had a pale, ash-blonde beauty that would adorn his arm...that some of their children, surely, would inherit.

Into his head, memory pierced. His father talking to him...*at* him...shortly before the seizure that had killed him.

*'She'll be the perfect wife for you—if you've any sense at all you'll see that! She's serious, committed and would be an ornament in her role as your mother's successor!'*

It was impossible to disagree with his father's judgement. Francesca would, there was no doubt in his mind whatsoever, make a perfect wife, the perfect next Contessa di Mantegna and mother of the future Count.

When the right time came.

If it was to come at all.

His jaw tightened. That, he knew, was the meat of Francesca's letter to him. Was this long-mooted marriage of theirs to take place—or not? A decision was necessary. And very soon.

And that was the problem he had.

*It's come too soon.*

As the words formed in his head his inner vision blotted out the moonlit valley before him. He was seeing Lake Garda, sunlight bright on its deep, dark waters, the reflection of the jagged mountains in its surface, seeing his arm casually around the woman beside him as they leant against the stone balustrade on the hotel terrace overlooking the vista.

The memory burned tangibly in him—he could almost feel the soft curve of her hip indenting into his, her hand around his waist. More vivid memory came now, of the last time they had made love, her body threshing beneath his, her mouth hungry for his, her passion released, ardent and sensual, so arousing a contrast with her air of English composure when she was not in his embrace.

*I don't want to give that up—not yet.*

Oh, one day he would marry—of course he would—but his own preference would have been to postpone marriage for some time. For him there was no necessity to do so yet. But his marriage must be a partnership—with his wife an equal partner. Not for him a marriage like his parents'. His wife would not live the life of his mother, shaping herself around his father's wishes, giving up everything else in her life but her role as Contessa. No, Francesca would be very different—and that included her very understandable desire to marry when the time was right for *her*.

And that time seemed to be now.

He could not ask her to delay—not given the information she had shared with him in her letter. Whatever his reluctance to make that decision now, it had to be done.

He stared out over the valley one long, last time. Slowly, very slowly, his thoughts reached their conclusion. Slowly, very slowly, he exhaled, inclined his head.

Decision made.

In the bedroom that had been hers since her teenage days, up until the time she'd moved out to her own apartment, Carla lay in bed, sleepless, staring up at the painted ceiling. Her eyes were huge, distended. Words ran like an endless litany round and round the inside of her skull— like rats in a trap. Desperately seeking escape.

*I'm not in love with Cesare! I'm not! It's just passion— desire—that's all! The way it was from the very start! He makes my heart beat faster just looking at him—but that isn't love! I won't let it be love. I won't.*

But even as the litany was repeated she could hear another voice speaking.

*So why do you fear not knowing how long he'll want you? Why would you fear a future where you have nothing of him any longer? Why have you kept trying to prove to yourself that you have no need to cling to him, no need to want to be with him more than you are? Why did you make yourself turn down his invitation to stay longer with him today in Milan?*

She knew the answer to those questions—knew why she did not want to hear them, did not want to answer them. Did not want to face the truth of what had happened. Fear beat up in her, firing through her veins.

It mustn't be love—what she felt for Cesare, what she felt about him. It just mustn't…

*I'm not that stupid! Dear God, I'm not that stupid! To have fallen in love with Cesare di Mondave…*

But as the dawn came she knew, with a hollowing of her heart, that what her mother had feared—what she herself had guarded against, right from the start—had happened. And in her head, her mother's warning tolled like doom.

*'There can be no happy ending for you—'*

A fearful coldness filled her.

# CHAPTER SIX

CESARE HANDED THE keys of his car to the valet parker and headed into the restaurant. He was running late, and he knew why. Emotions spiked across his mind, troubling and unwelcome. Tonight was not going to be easy—but it had to be faced. He had to say what he had to say, do what he had to do. No escaping it.

*And take the consequences.*

Emotion struck again—powerful, like a leopard on a leash. His life was privileged—immensely privileged—but the responsibilities that came with it required a price. A price that he did not wish to pay.

He felt the leashed emotion tug again, bringing to his mind's eye the portrait of his ancestor, Count Alessandro, whom Luciezo had captured for posterity.

*You had it easier—you kept your privileges and did not have to pay for them at all!*

The triptych was testament to that. The Conte di Mantegna—flanked by his wife and his mistress. And he had kept them both—enjoyed them both. Had had to give up neither—give up nothing at all. Paid no price at all for the life he'd led.

Cesare's jaw tightened. Well, that was then, not now, and now, in this current century, no such arrangement was possible. Not with honour. To marry Francesca meant giving up Carla. No other option.

As he strode into the dining room he saw her immediately. Saw how her blue-violet eyes fastened on his, simultaneously felt another, different emotion seize him.

Her crepe dress in a luscious plum colour graced her full figure, her rich, brunette hair was coiled at her nape, and those lustrous eyes, the generous, sensual mouth, would draw male eyes from everywhere. But her attention was only for him. It had always been that way, and he was accustomed to it.

Yet into his head at that thought came another.

*I will have to see her lavishing that same unwavering attention on another man—another man who will have her to himself...*

The thought jabbed in his mind like a spike being driven in. As he reached her, sat himself down, he found himself lifting her hand and dropping a light kiss on it.

'*Mi dispiace*. I was delayed.'

Her smile was instant, and he could see relief in it. But as he looked into her face he could see more than relief. He could see a sudden veiling of her expression. As if she were hiding something from him.

A moment later, though, her expression was open again, her usual air of composure back in place. 'Long day?' she asked sympathetically, starting to skim down the menu.

'Long enough,' Cesare replied.

For the first time with Carla he was conscious of a sense of deceit—it was discomfiting.

He turned the subject away. 'How have you been? Did you visit your mother?'

She nodded with an assenting murmur, but said no

more. Cesare did not usually ask after her family—and she never asked after his family affairs. It was an invisible line she did not cross.

The sommelier was approaching, and Cesare turned his attention to him. There was a hollow feeling in the pit of his stomach that had nothing to do with hunger.

Or not hunger for food.

*I don't want to do this—I don't want to do it but I have no option. It has to be done, and it has to be done now—tonight.*

But not right now. Not over dinner. What he had to say required privacy.

*And, besides, I want one more night with her—one last night.*

He broke off such thoughts as the sommelier returned, filling their glasses. When he had gone Cesare lifted his glass. That hollow feeling came again.

'To you, Carla,' he said.

His eyes were dark, his expression serious. For a long moment he held her gaze. He saw her face whiten suddenly, her eyes distend. Then, like an opaque lens, he saw her expression become veiled.

Slowly, she inclined her head. 'To you, Cesare,' she replied. Her voice was steady, despite the whitening of her face.

She drank, taking a larger mouthful than she had intended. But right now she needed its fortifying strength. The tension from having waited for him so desperately, overwhelmed by the devastating realisation of what she felt for him, had made her feel faint. Emotion was knifing in her. She felt as if she were seeing him for the very first time.

*And I am—I'm seeing him with eyes that see what I*

*have refused to admit until now—what I have guarded myself from for six long months, and what has now overcome me. The truth of what I feel for him.*

Weakness flooded through her, dissolving her. Shakily, she lowered her glass to the table, hearing in her head the echo of his simple, devastating tribute.

*'To you, Carla...'*

That was all he'd said—and yet within her now she could feel emotion soaring upwards like an eagle taking flight from a mountaintop. There had been such intent in his gaze...such as she had never seen before.

*Can it mean—? Oh, can it mean...?*

For a second, the briefest second, she felt an emotion flare within her that she must not feel—dared not feel. She crushed it down. It was too dangerous. Too desperate.

Instead, she watched him set down his glass, saw the candlelight catch the gold of the crested signet ring on his little finger. He never removed it—never. It was there when he made love to her, when they showered, when they swam. It was as if it was melded into his skin. Given to him on his father's death, passed down generation to generation, one day it would be passed to his son, the next Conte.

She looked away, back at his face, unwilling to think such thoughts. Wanting only to drink him in as a thirsty man in a desert would drink in fresh water, feeling her heart beating heavily within her breast. The heart that had so recently, so devastatingly, revealed its truth to her. The truth that she *must* not show...

'So, how are things in the Viscari family?'

His casual question made Carla start. She dragged back her hectic thoughts. Collected herself. It was unusual that he was even asking, but she made her reply as casual as she could.

'Vito's heading back to Rome. He's been away for weeks, inspecting all the European hotels.' To her ears, her voice seemed staccato, but Cesare seemed to notice nothing about it. She was glad—grateful.

'Do you get on, the two of you?' Cesare's enquiry was still polite as he demolished the piece of bread roll he'd buttered.

He was not particularly interested, but it was a safe topic of conversation. And right now he needed safe topics.

She blinked, taken aback by his enquiry. Focussed on how to answer it. With a fragment of her mind she registered that Cesare, too, seemed on edge.

'Surprisingly well, really,' Carla answered, sounding, with an effort, more composed now. She made herself go on. 'Considering how my mother and his are usually daggers drawn. She and my mother never hit it off...' She gave a sigh.

'That's often the way between sisters-in-law,' Cesare observed drily. Their first course arrived, and he began to eat. 'Vito Viscari has had a lot to knuckle down to, given the successive deaths of both his uncle and his father. It can be tough. I vividly remember—'

He stopped. Talking to Carla about how he'd had to discover—rapidly—just how to fill his father's shoes after his fatal seizure was not wise.

But Carla did not seem to notice his abrupt cessation. She forked her seafood and nodded.

It was getting easier for her to sound normal, to get her hectic heart rate back under control.

'Because of his ridiculously gorgeous film star looks,

people tend to think Vito lightweight—but he isn't at all. I have considerable respect for him,' she said.

Cesare's eyes rested on her a moment. 'And he for you, I hope. After all, you had to contend with arriving in a new country, learning the language, adapting to a new way of life.'

'Vito was very kind to me,' she answered, her voice warming. 'Helped me settle in. Improved my Italian, took me about with him to meet his friends. Warned me off several of them!' she finished with a laugh.

The laugh had sounded quite natural to her ears, and she was again grateful.

Cesare smiled. But he knew it was something of a forced smile. There had been a fond note in her voice, and he had not liked to hear that. Nor did he like to examine *why* he had not liked to hear it.

'Would he have warned you off me?' he heard himself asking.

He'd kept his voice light, deliberately so, masking that slight jab that had come when he'd heard her praising her step-cousin so affectionately—yet he was aware that he had asked the question. *Why* he had asked it.

For all his light tone, he saw her face still. The expression in her eyes changed.

'He would not have needed to, Cesare,' she said quietly. 'I've always known the score with you. Credit me with that much, at least.'

His eyes shifted away, his jaw tightening. Then, abruptly, his gaze came back to her. She was looking at him, again with that veiled expression in her eyes. Impulsively he reached for her free hand, raised it once more to his lips. This was the last night of his life that he would spend with her—he would not stint on his appreciation of her. Of what she had been to him.

*What she can be no longer.*

He felt again that jab of regret that it should be so. More than a jab. Yet again the words sounded in his head.

*Not yet.*

But there was no point thinking that—none. He must part with her, and that was all that was possible now. That—and this one last, final night with her.

'I credit you with a great deal, Carla.'

There was emotion in his voice. She could hear it. And inside she felt again that sudden flare of emotion that she had felt when he'd raised his glass to her, let his gaze rest on her with such intent.

She returned his gaze now, as he let go of her hand and it fell to the table. Her breath seemed dry in her lungs.

Why had he said that? Why was he acting the way he was tonight? There was something about the way he was being that she had never seen in him before.

*What does it mean?*

She swallowed, feeling her cheeks flush suddenly. Dipped her head to resume her meal. Yet through her consciousness her mind was racing. That same swooping sensation was within her. Cesare was different tonight. She could see, could tell—knew with every instinct that something was changing between them. Something profound that would alter everything...

*Can it be—can it really be? After all, if I was in denial for so long, if I told myself over and over again I could not possibly feel love for him...could it be that maybe, just maybe, for him it's the same?*

The thoughts were barely there, barely allowed, barely shaped into words—for she dared not let them be. Dared not give in to the swooping, soaring inside her as their meal progressed, as emotions swirled and formed and dissolved within her.

How *could* she dare? How could she dare give in to the one emotion above all that she yearned to give in to?

How could she give in to hope?

*Hope that he might just feel for me what I now know I feel for him... That—despite everything—he's fallen in love with me too?*

'A miracle—a parking space!'

Carla's exclamation was heartfelt. To find a free parking space on her narrow street was, indeed, a miracle. Yet there it was.

*Is it a sign—can it be a sign?*

She almost laughed at herself for the notion, yet knew with a fragment of her mind that she was not joking at all.

As Cesare expertly parallel parked in the confined space, she could feel yet again her emotions soaring within her. For hope was a bird that, once released, could not be imprisoned again.

Throughout the evening, Cesare's air of particular attentiveness to her had been palpable, that sense of something different about him unmistakable.

Now, as they climbed out of the car and she opened the outer door to let them both into the inner courtyard, his closeness to her was even more palpable.

Upstairs in her apartment she went into the kitchen to set the coffee brewing. Usually when he stayed over with her he settled down on the white sofa, his long legs reaching out, and shrugged off his jacket and tie, happy to lounge with her while drinking coffee, and sometimes a liqueur, before arousal took them both and swept them off to bed.

Tonight, however, he followed her into the kitchen.

'Do you really want coffee?'

She turned. He was standing there, and in his eyes was an expression that wiped all thought of coffee from her mind—all thought at all. An expression that was all too familiar to her. Slowly she shook her head. For one long, timeless moment she did not move, and nor did he. Something flowed between them. Something that took her back to that very first night they'd spent together.

The villa outside Rome, Cesare's love nest, had seen much use in the months since then. But at this moment all she could think of was that very first night.

Warmth beat up in her. Suffusing her skin, flaring out from her core. He stepped towards her, curved his long fingers around the nape of her neck, drawing her towards him. But not into his arms. He held her in front of him while his other hand rested lightly around her waist. His dark, lidded eyes held hers, unfathomable, unreadable.

Turning her bones to water.

She felt emotion rise up in her like a sweeping tide, pouring through her. Her lips parted and there was a low, frail noise in her throat.

'Cesare—' His name was like a whisper in her mouth…an echo deep within her.

The knowledge of what she now knew she felt for him had ripped across her like a revelation and it trembled within her. It was making her tremble again now as the thumb of the hand at her nape reached forward to graze the cusp of her jaw, stroked the hollow below her ear in a soft, sensual caress that sent a thousand feathers fluttering through her veins.

'You are so, so beautiful,' he said.

Slowly, infinitely slowly, as if he were savouring every long moment of its descent, he lowered his mouth to hers. For one long, timeless moment, his kiss was nothing more than a velvet graze along her lips. Then, with a rasp in his throat, he tightened his fingers at her nape, his hand at her waist, and hauled her to him hungrily, ravenously.

As though she were the last meal he would ever eat.

Like a sheet of flame she went up in an inferno of sensation, of passion and desire, white-hot and incandescent. With absolute mastery he possessed her mouth and then, feasting his way down, he swept her up, clamping her against him as he strode from the kitchen, pushing open the door of her bedroom, coming down on the bed beside her.

Clothes were shed, bodies were arching, limbs twining, mouths meeting and melding. Bodies fusing.

Fusing with that same white heat, that same incandescence. She cried out over and over again, her body shaking. The ecstasy he wrought on her was unbearable, meeting for the first time the flood of emotion that poured through her, the knowledge of what it was he meant to her...

*The man she loved. Cesare—oh, Cesare—the man she loved.*

The knowledge of it, the certainty and the rapture of it, was a possession of her heart and of her soul even as she gave him possession of her body, took possession of his, giving to him all that was within her. It was a glory, a dedication of herself to him without measure, without reserve. An absolute oblation of herself...

And at the end, as wave after wave of shuddering ecstasy and love finally ebbed from her, she held him in her arms, crushing him to her. His dampened skin cooled, his hectic breathing calmed, and she wrapped herself around him, half cradled by him, their limbs tangled and exhausted. She knew, with certainty and utter conviction, that she had never known happiness until this moment. Never known until this moment what love truly felt like.

She held him close against her, smoothed the strong contours of his powerful back. Wonder filled her—and a gratitude beyond all things. He had cried out as the moment had possessed him, as if it had been the very first time they had made love. The intensity of it had shaken her, overwhelmed her.

It could mean only one thing—surely only one thing? His passion for her had been greater than he'd ever shown, his response more searing than she had ever known it to be, his fulfilment fiercer, more burning than she had ever seen before. And now, as she lay with him, his arms around her were tighter than she had ever known.

As if he would not let her go.

As if he would *never* let her go…

As if she were his and he was hers for ever now…

For ever…

Eyelids fluttering, she felt the great lassitude of her body sweep over her, and sleep took her.

She awoke alone. In the bathroom she could hear the shower running. For a few moments she lay, languorous, her mind in a dream state. Wonder still suffused her—like an underground spring filling the receptive earth. Happiness—rich, and full and glorious—ran in her veins like cream. She had never been happier in her life.

Because of Cesare—oh, Cesare, Cesare, Cesare! The world was new-made, new-found. Illumined by love, by joy, by glory.

The shower was cut off. A moment later Cesare was walking into the bedroom, a towel snaked around his hips. He walked quietly, as if not wanting to disturb her. She went on lying there, immobile, watching him through shuttered eyes only just affording vision.

She watched him dress swiftly, surely, fastening his cuffs, knotting his tie—all the tiny, familiar minutiae of the morning. She felt a vague disappointment, for clearly he had an appointment to get to. But then, *she* had to attend an editorial meeting that morning anyway, and a lunch afterwards, so she did not mind him leaving her like this. There would be tonight—and the night after, and all the nights thereafter. The future was stretching ahead of them. She was sure of it, certain of it.

How could it be otherwise now?

*Now that I know I love him.*

For now, with love pouring through her, she knew, above all, that she could dare to hope.

*Whatever it is he feels for me he* does *feel for me! I am more to him than I was! I know it—oh, I know it, I know it!*

*Give him time—just give him time. Make no demands, be as cautious and as careful as ever. But with time— oh, with time he will come to feel more for me. Whatever might happen...*

There were no certainties about him, but there *were* possibilities. Oh, that much she must have faith in. She must and she could—and she did.

Her mother's warnings seemed a thousand miles away—as did her own warnings, issued to herself all her life, all these months with Cesare.

*I can believe in my happy ending—I dare to believe in it! I dare to hope! To have faith in my heart...in his...*

Her love could make it happen—she needed only hope and faith. And both were streaming through her as her eyes drank him in, her heart overflowing with wonder and gratitude. With joy.

He crossed to the bed, sat down on it, his hand reaching for her shoulder as if to wake her. She opened her eyes—opened them and smiled, lifting her hand to catch his. For a second he let her, then her lowered her hand to the sheet, taking his own away. His face was expressionless.

Out of nowhere, like a knife sliding into her guts, fear gouged inside her.

'Carla, there is no easy way to say this...'

His voice was deep, with a tension in it that cut like a wire through flesh. His mouth was compressed, and she could only stare at him, motionless and frozen, while inside the fear widened into a chasm, swallowing her.

He took a breath, got to his feet. Stood tall and powerful, looking down at her. Remote and distant.

'This is the last time I can see you,' he said. 'In a few days I shall be announcing my engagement.'

He looked down at her. His eyes had no expression in them at all.

'I didn't want you hearing it from anyone else. Roman gossip is vicious.' He paused again, his mouth tightening yet more. 'I want you to know...'

And now, for the first time, there was something in his eyes—something that only plunged that knife into her yet deeper, with a serrated, twisting blade, eviscerating her.

'I want you to know how good these last six months have been. How...very good.'

He turned away. Reached her bedroom door.

'I'll see myself out.'

There was another pause, a whitening around his mouth.

'Look after yourself, Carla.'

Then he was gone, and she could hear him walking across her living room, reaching her front door. For a second, an infinity of horror, she froze. Then, muscles bunching, she hurled herself from the bed like a tornado, tore after him. Naked—completely naked. As naked as her soul.

Her eyes blazed like furnaces. A single word shot from her.

*'Why?'*

He turned. There was no expression in his face. It was tight and closed as the great oaken doors of his *castello*. Guarding him against all who might invade. He had not let *her* invade. Would not permit her to do so.

He answered her now, his voice steady, unemotional. As it had to be. As it was essential for it to be. He would tell her what he had had to tell himself. Rigid discipline held him to his course, as if he were urgently steering his car out of an aquaplane that would otherwise send him crashing down into a bottomless crevasse.

This had to be done. It had to be said—*had* to.

'You said yourself, Carla, that you've always known the score with me. As I said, I gave you full credit for that.' He took a breath. 'Full credit for understanding *"why"*.' His mouth thinned. 'I have to marry. I've always had to marry. I've always had an…understanding…'

Was there irony in his repetition? He was beyond irony—beyond everything right now except knowing that his only urge was to get away, not to see her standing there, her body naked—the body he had possessed. Still wanted to possess…

'An understanding,' he said, 'for many years. And whilst my…my fiancée…' He said the word as if it were alien to him, in a language he did not comprehend, had never needed to speak till now. 'My fiancée has shared that understanding, she has had her own interests to pursue till now. She's been living in America, but now she needs to decide whether to stay there…or come home. To fulfil the…the understanding…we have always had.'

He took another breath. Every word he was speaking seemed to be impossible to say. It was a clash of worlds and he was crushed between them.

'She's now made her decision, and it is to return to Italy. Therefore…' he swallowed '… I must part with you. I apologise that I could not give you more warning, but…' He took another heavy breath. 'She's flying to Italy tomorrow, to visit her parents, and naturally they will want to hear her decision. And then…' His expression changed again. 'Then they will all be visiting me at the Castello Mantegna, where our engagement will be formally announced.'

She stared at him.

Her eyes were stretched, distended. 'Do you love her?'

It seemed the only question she could ask. The only one in the entire universe.

Her voice was thin, like wire pulled too fine. It grated—grated on him. What place had 'love' in his life? None that he could permit.

A look of impatience, of rejection, passed over his face. 'Love is an irrelevance. Francesca and I are…well-suited.'

For a second—just a second—his eyes searched hers. He took a breath, forcing himself to say what he did not want to say, did not want to face.

'Carla, if you have ever fancied yourself to feel for

me anything at all...' His mouth tightened, his hand on the doorjamb clenching. 'You must know I never invited any such feelings from you—never consciously or unconsciously sought them. I never, Carla, gave you any indication whatsoever that there could be anything between us other than what has been. Acquit me of any accusations to the contrary. We had an affair. Nothing more. It could never have been anything more. You knew that as well as I.'

Long lashes dipped over his lidded, expressionless eyes—eyes that slayed her like a basilisk's lethal glance.

'I must go,' he said.

And he went.

Walked through the door. Leaving her. Closing the door behind him.

The noise seemed to echo in the silence. A silence that spread like toxic waste after the deadly poison of his words to her. That lasted until, timeless moments later, a strange, unearthly keening started in her throat...

'Carla! Open the door!'

Her mother's voice came on her voicemail. Continued loudly.

'I am not leaving here until you do. Just open it!'

Carla heard her, heard the sharp, demanding rap come again on her front door. Her mother would not go—she knew she wouldn't. Her mother's will was unbreakable.

She walked to the door, opened it, and her mother surged in.

Then stopped.

'Oh, dear God,' Marlene said, her voice hoarse.

She stared, horrified, at Carla, and Carla knew why. Her hair was unbrushed, she was wearing a tracksuit, not a trace of make-up. Her eyes were red, cheeks blotched. There were runnels running down from her eyelashes to her chin, where tears had been shed and had dried, shed and dried.

For two whole days.

Her mother's hand had gone to her mouth in disbelief, but now she lowered it.

'So, it's true, then?'

Carla looked at her. 'I take it the gossip has started already?'

Marlene drew in a breath sharply. 'Oh, yes,' she said. 'And *several* of my acquaintances have made absolutely sure I knew about it!'

Carla turned away. Tears had started again—but to what purpose? To what purpose was anything at all?

Her mother was speaking, her voice harsh, vicious, but she paid no attention.

*She warned me, and I didn't listen. 'No happy ending,' she told me—but I thought I knew better.*

She felt her face convulse, her throat constrict as if a snake were strangling her, its coils thrown around her body, tighter and tighter, crushing the life out of her, the breath.

She felt her mother's arms come around her, but what comfort could they bring? What reassurance? What help?

None. None, none, *none.*

Bitterness filled her, and self-hatred.

*No happy ending...*

She shut her eyes, resting her head against her mother's shoulder as her mother went on speaking, saying things she might say to a child, patting her back, rubbing it as if she could make her better. But there was no 'better', no happiness, no nothing. Only memories stabbing into her, over and over again, each one eviscerating her, taking out a little more of what she was made of.

*Dear God, I thought—I really, really thought—that he was being different that night in the restaurant because he was starting to feel something for me! I thought that there might be possibilities of his returning what I'd just discovered I felt. I actually started to hope...to believe in a future for us...to believe in love between us...*

Anguish clutched at her, its icy hand around her heart. Her stupid, stupid heart.

*Why did I have to go and realise what had happened to me? Why did I have to discover what I'd come to feel for him? If I hadn't—if I'd still thought it was only an affair and nothing more than that—I wouldn't be here like this now...destroyed...just destroyed.*

'You told me...you told me—*no happy ending.*'

She must have spoken. Words must have scraped past her lips. Her voice seemed to come from very far away, from polar regions where icy winds blasted her to pieces.

*No happy ending.*

She felt her shoulders taken, saw her mother step back from her, still holding her. Carla looked at her face, and what she saw made her stare.

'But what there *could* be,' Marlene said, biting out each word, her eyes suddenly as bright and hard as diamonds, 'is a *better* ending.'

She dropped her hands. The diamond brightness in her eyes was glittering now, her face as hard as crystal.

'There's only one way to do this, my darling girl. Only one! When a man does to you what that...that *swine*... has done to you, there is only *one* thing to do!'

She sat down on the sofa, patted the seat next to her.

'Sit down, Carla, and let me put something to you.'

# CHAPTER SEVEN

CESARE'S VOICE WAS warm as he greeted the guests being ushered into the drawing room at the *castello*—the Marchese and the Marchesa and their three adult children—Francesca and her younger brother and sister.

Francesca he'd already met up with, as she'd requested, on her own, when she'd arrived back in Italy. They'd talked, long and in detail, feeling their way forward, reaching a mutual understanding. Now she was here at the *castello* with her family to formalise that understanding.

Their greetings were cordial and affectionate. He'd known her family all his life, just as he'd known Francesca—though he'd seen little of her since she'd gone to the States to do her post-graduate studies four years ago. Only occasional meetings when he'd been out there on business and taken the opportunity to look her up, or when she was visiting Italy from time to time.

There had been no rush—no need to meet up more.

He'd hoped that he could go on like that for a while longer still.

Into his head stabbed an image—he thrust it from him. He'd been thrusting it from him for days now. It was essential to do so. Absolutely essential.

*Carla is in the past. I have made my decision. I will not rescind it. I cannot—*

Because it would be impossible to do so. Impossible now that Francesca was here, with her family, for the intimate gathering that would result in their formal engagement. The engagement he was entering into entirely of his own volition. His own preference. The engagement that had always been waiting for him. That would now be fulfilled.

Putting Carla behind him for ever.

Greetings over, he signalled that the champagne should be served. His staff were excited, he could see, for this was to be their new chatelaine—the new Contessa. They approved of his choice—and what was there not to approve of? Francesca had visited here often—with her parents, as a child, as a teenager and as an adult.

Now, as she sipped the vintage champagne, Francesca looked tall and serene in a Grecian style off-white gown that matched her ash-blonde hair, her pale, slender beauty—very different from Carla's full-figured, vivid looks.

Carla…whom he would now never see again—except perhaps on rare social occasions if their paths should cross in Rome. But never again would she be what once she had been to him.

*I wanted longer with her.*

The guillotine sliced down again. Sliced through the thought and the image that formed in his head of Carla at her most alluring. He must not think of her—must *not*. Francesca was saying something to him and he must pay attention to her, ask a question in return. Something about her work that he hoped was not too unintelligent. But her field of research was so rarefied he knew he could only stumble at its edges.

She smiled, giving him an explanation he could understand. Behind her, her father beamed proudly, and her mother bestowed a doting look upon her.

'A doctor of science!' her father said, with pride openly in his eyes. 'And achieved two years before it was expected!'

'Astrophysics!' breathed her mother.

Cesare shook his head ruefully. 'I'm humbled even by the thought of it!' he exclaimed lightly.

Francesca gave a laugh. 'Oh, Ces—you? Humble? You've never been humble in your life!'

'Before *your* intellect, how can I be otherwise?' he rejoined promptly.

His eyes rested on her. She truly was a remarkable woman—extreme intellect, glowing beauty and an ancestry that wound throughout the annals of Italy's history. *She will make an exceptional* contessa!

His father had been right—irrefutably right—in his judgement of Francesca delle Ristori. Only one aspect had he neglected—and that was what Francesca had needed to discuss with him so deeply.

Cesare had heard her out, given her all the assurances she required, let her choose entirely by herself whether she was going to do as she had now chosen—be his wife. He had assured her that of course there would be no question—none at all—of her having to focus solely on her role as his *contessa* as his mother had. She would join whatever research facility suited her field here in Italy, for as long as she wanted to, and find fulfilment both as his *contessa* and as a research scientist.

Francesca would *not* be the kind of wife his own

mother had had to be—of that he was completely sure. He didn't want that—and nor would Francesca have contemplated marriage to him on any other basis.

He drew her out a little over dinner, and she smiled and mentioned some possibilities of where she might work in Italy.

'I need to see how my doctoral research paper is received,' she said. 'Its reception may determine what offers I'm made, and by whom.'

'I'm sure they will be clamouring for you from all quarters!' he said gallantly.

Francesca laughed, and so did her parents and siblings.

The meal passed in similar convivial fashion. Everyone was pleased. Her parents were highly satisfied—for them, their daughter's marriage to him would ensure she stayed in Italy, and that was their preference. Francesca seemed pleased too, and he was glad of it. Her choice had not been made without inner conflict, but she had made it all the same. And in his favour.

And as for him—well, of *course* he was pleased. How could he not be? How could anyone not wish for Francesca as his bride, his wife, his *contessa*, the mother of his children, the companion of his life, his entire future...

Just as he'd anticipated, all his adult life...

The image he had banished earlier came into his head again, like a spectre haunting him.

*Carla*...

He sliced it off at source. Asked another question about astrophysics.

The evening ended.

Francesca and her family repaired to the guest quarters.

He would woo her later—do all that was necessary

between them to make her comfortable with him in that respect. Their respective pasts were irrelevant. With the decision made between them, all prior involvements would be severed. Terminated.

That guillotine sliced again.

Ruthless. Lethal. Permanent.

Because it had to be.

Carla stood, her back stiff, her face stiff, talking, sipping mineral water, refusing canapés, posing for photos. Her mother was entertaining—*fare uno mostro*—putting on a show, as she so loved to do.

This time it was for the director of a museum to which some of the choicest pieces of Guido's extensive collection were being donated. Her mother was in her element, Carla could see, being very much the gracious hostess, the generous patroness of the arts.

Across the large salon in her stepfather's opulent villa Carla could see her step-cousin, Vito, only that day arrived back in Rome from his tour of the European hotels, with his mother, Lucia. The latter looked icily furious, the former was visibly 'on duty'.

Carla had said very little to him during the evening. She was not in a talkative mood.

The reception went on and on. There were speeches— her mother's, in careful, laboured Italian, and then Vito stepping forward, clearly intent on representing the official side of the Viscari family. And there was posing for more photos, herself included, standing right next to Vito. The only saving grace was that she would not be writing this up—that would be too nepotistic.

Anyway, she hadn't been to work for days now. Citing a bug…a touch of flu.

Whether anyone believed her or not, she didn't care. She doubted the gossips did. They knew *exactly* why she was out of circulation.

Her mouth tightened.

Francesca delle Ristori—that was what Cesare's bride-to-be was called. The gossip columns were already full of open speculation. And after all, why not? What was there *not* to speculate about?

A vicious light glared in Carla's eyes.

*She's the granddaughter of a duke, the daughter of a* marchese, *a family friend from for ever—she has long fair hair down to her waist and she has a PhD in astrophysics! Dear God, is there anything she hasn't got?*

But there was only one thing she wanted Francesca delle Ristori *not* to be—only one.

Cesare's fiancée.

The knife thrust again into her guts. Eviscerating her. Her hands clenched at her sides.

People were leaving—finally. From her immobile position she saw her mother and Lucia go through a poisonous little ritual of one up-manship about the evening's success, then her mother was graciously inviting her sister-in-law and Vito to stay and take coffee with her, to hear all about Vito's recent travels. Adding, portentously, that they really must settle the business of Guido's shares…

Immediately, Vito tensed, Carla could see, and exchanged looks with his mother. Then promptly offered to escort his mother to her car, while he returned for coffee. The mention of Guido's shares—half the family shareholding—was a bait Vito would not be able to refuse. How could he? His determination to acquire the shares, giving him total control of the hotel chain as the sole Viscari left, was paramount. The shares her mother had adamantly refused to sell.

Now, walking with punishing stiffness, Carla followed her mother into the drawing room, taking up a stance behind her mother's chair. Vito strolled in, having said farewell to his mother—doubtless sympathising with her for the ordeal they'd both endured, with Marlene queening it over them as Guido's widow.

Well, she didn't care. Didn't care about Lucia's irritation, or Vito's frustration over the shares, or her mother's endless manoeuvrings. She cared only about one thing.

It burned inside her like hell's furnace. Her hand tightened, spasmed over the back of her mother's chair. Her mother was talking, but Carla wasn't listening. Vito was answering, but she wasn't listening to him either. The barbed exchange went on, but she paid it no attention.

Not until the moment came. The moment her mother had planned for, schemed for, hoped for, for so long now. The moment Carla had never in a thousand years thought she would collude with.

As she did now.

She heard her mother talking to Vito, her tone saccharine. 'What could be better than uniting the two Viscari shareholdings by uniting the two halves of our family? You two young people together!'

Silently, she watched Vito's reaction. Saw angry disbelief lash across his face. Didn't care. Didn't care at all. Saw his furious gaze snap to her, demand she answer—demand she shoot down immediately what her mother had just said. Refuse, outright, the preposterous notion Marlene had put forward.

She refused to think of the devastating, demolishing impact on her step-cousin.

The agonising pain of Cesare's brutal rejection had caused a consuming need to hit back at him, to claw around her raw and ravaged heart the tattered, ragged shreds of her own pathetic pride any way she could— no matter who paid the price for it, no matter how vilely it made her behave.

'I think,' she heard herself say, from somewhere very far away, where icy winds scoured all emotion from her, 'that's an excellent idea.'

The next days passed in a choking blur. Carla blanked everything and everyone. Refused to talk, refused to face what she was doing. She was like one possessed by an evil spirit, with the devil driving her.

Vito, getting her away from Marlene, had railed at her disbelievingly. Then he'd done worse than rail. He had realised why she was playing to her mother's obsession. His expression had said it all as the reason for her collusion with her mother dawned on him.

'So that's it—he's finished with you, hasn't he?'

Vito's pity had lacerated her, like thorns scraping her flesh. Then he'd poured acid on the wound.

'To speak frankly, it was always going to end that way. The Conte di Mantegna can trace his bloodline back to the ancient Romans! He's going to marry a woman who can do the same! He might have affairs beforehand, but he'll never marry a woman who—'

'A woman, Vito, who is about to announce her engagement to another man!' The words shot from her as from a gun.

Because that—*that*—was the truth of it! That was the poisonous salvation that her mother had put to her that unbearable morning in her apartment. *That* was how she

was going to survive what Cesare had done to her—what
she had done to herself. Falling in love with a man who
was marrying another woman. A woman so much more
*suitable* to be his wife than she was! A woman, so the
gossip columns were already saying, who was utterly
perfect to be the next Contessa di Mantegna.

As she herself had not been.

Worse than the words in the fawning articles had
been the photos of Cesare and Francesca delle Ristori—
smiling, elegant, aristocratic, such a perfectly matched
couple!

Worse again than that were the photographs of herself
and Cesare—taken, so she supposed in her embittered
misery, at any time during the last six months at restaurants and art galleries—or of herself alone, the photos
that accompanied her articles.

And the prurient, goading words that went with them,
contrasting her with Cesare's noble-born fiancée.

*One-time constant companion...*
*Another shapely beauty to adorn the arm of our*
*dashing, illustrious Conte di Mantegna...*
*Daughter of late hotelier Guido Viscari's English*
*wife, co-owner of the Viscari luxury hotel chain.*

Well, it was *that* that was going to save her! Save her
from the unbearable humiliation that crushed her, from
the mockery of the world—and herself.

*You fool—you pathetic fool! To have thought—to have*
*really believed—that that final night with him was the*
*start of something more! That he was feeling for you*
*what you had realised you felt for him! When all along...*

Her mind twisted away and the scorpion whips lashed

again. Wielded by the devil that was driving her now, along the desperate path she was taking. But she would take it all the same, and wouldn't care what she was doing to Vito, wouldn't care that he hated her for it, would not *let* herself care.

She would only forge on with it, frantic to cling to the only thing she *could* cling to—getting her own engagement announced to stop the pitying comments, the veiled sneers, the less than veiled gossip, targeting her as the discarded former *inamorata* of the noble Count now set on marrying his noble bride...

Because no one, *no one*, would pity her or sneer at her when she was the wife of one of the most eligible bachelors in Rome! When her husband was the multi-millionaire Vito Viscari with his film star looks, fêted and courted by all, a major European corporate player, and when their marriage had united the ownership of a global hotel chain!

Because if Cesare di Mondave could make a dynastic marriage—well, so could *she*! And her marriage to Vito would show Cesare she cared as little about him as his engagement to the beautiful Francesca delle Ristori showed that *he* cared about the woman he'd spent the last six months with! Show him that their time together had been nothing more than a pleasant interlude for *both* of them, before they'd *both* taken up their destiny—he to marry his aristocratic bride, she to unite the two halves of the Viscari family.

But she *had* to get her engagement to Vito announced formally! She had to make it happen—was desperate for it!

The devil drove her on, his reins steering her remorselessly, unpityingly.

Yet still Vito held out.

Balked at committing to her.

Wanted to reject her—just as Cesare had rejected her!

He had no desire to marry her—just as Cesare had no desire to marry her!

Desperation and despair possessed her, darkening her vision. She *had* to get Vito to publicly commit to her—by *any* means. Any at all—whatever it took.

Carla could see that as plain as day through the dark flames in her vision. Her mother saw it too. Took steps. Rumours flew—were Guido's shares for sale? If so, to whom?

The financial press ran with the story, just as her mother had intended. Rival hotel chains' names were speculated. Nic Falcone, his long-time competitor, was the front runner, keenest to snap up the oh-so-enticing Viscari shares. Yet still Vito would not agree to announce their engagement—now he was saying there was already a woman in his life, an Englishwoman he'd met on his European tour, whom he'd brought to Rome and who was staying at the Viscari Roma.

So Carla paid a visit there. Found the beautiful, long-legged blonde who was so clearly besotted with Vito. Told her that she was no one special—*like I was no one special to Cesare*—that Vito would have finished with her soon enough anyway—*like Cesare did me*—and with every stinging, bitter, galling truth, a knife went into her own heart, twisting in agony. And when Vito turned up, full of angry denunciation of what she'd said, she defied him to deny it—defied him to say she was *not* his fiancée. He could not—not if he wanted her mother's shares, if he valued them more than the tearful woman clinging to his chest, sobbing...

The blonde's despairing sobs tore at Carla, tore at her own throat, but she would not recant her words. Found justification for them in her own misery and torment.

*It's better she knows now what's important to Vito— and it's not her!*

Just as *she* had not been important to Cesare…

The devil's scorpion whip lashed at her again, driving her onwards as she dragged Vito away, forcing him on along the dark path she was treading, her eyes glittering with desperate fervour. Damning herself and everyone around her.

# CHAPTER EIGHT

Cesare stood in the massive fortified gateway that led to the walled courtyard of the *castello*, watching the Marchese's car wind its stately way down the hairpin road snaking into the valley below. Then he turned away, walked back into the *castello*.

The visit of Francesca and her parents had been a complete success, and now she was going with her parents to the family seat in the north of Italy before flying back to the USA to settle her affairs there.

There was no immediate rush for them to marry—the date was set for late summer, and Francesca's mother was intent on enjoying every moment of the lavish preparations. Also, Francesca wanted to see if she could secure a post-doctoral position at a physics department in Italy. When she returned from America, visited the *castello* once more, Cesare would start to take her out and about with him on prenuptial social engagements. Start his personal courtship of her, the woman who would be his bride.

As the woman he had set aside could never be.

Could never be in his life again in any way.

As it always did, the guillotine sliced down in his head. That subject was still not safe. With iron self-discipline— a self-discipline that he seemed to need increasingly now, but which, surely to God, would fade as time passed—he put aside the thoughts he must not have, the memories he must not recall.

He strode indoors, but as he did so, he glanced up the massive oak staircase that led to the upper floor of the staterooms. That floor was dominated by the full-length *galleria*, once the exercise space for the ladies of the house in bad weather, which now contained the bulk of the artworks here at the *castello*.

Including the Luciezo-Caradino triptych.

As if impelled, Cesare felt himself heading towards the base of the stairs. Then, abruptly, he pulled away. No, he would *not* go and look at it. To what purpose? He knew what it looked like. Knew why he wanted to go and look at it.

His expression steeled. His ancestor might have been born at a time when a man could 'have it all', but those times were gone. There could be no honour in thinking otherwise—not a shred of it.

*I have made my choice and I will abide by it. Carla is in the past now, and she must stay there. My future is with Francesca. And Francesca has made her choice too—she has chosen to be my wife.*

He walked into his study, sitting himself down at his mahogany desk, ready to catch up on work after several days of entertaining Francesca and her family. His eyes flickered. He had made his choice—Francesca had made hers. But Carla—Carla had not made a choice, had she?

For a moment—just a brief, flashing moment before that guillotine cut down again across his mind—he saw her that final morning.

*Naked, stripped bare of everything that she'd thought she had—everything she had presumed.*

The guillotine sliced down. Harsh thoughts sliced down with it. It was a harshness that was necessary. Essential. And not just for Carla.

Well, she should not have presumed! He had given her no cause to do so—none! He could acquit himself of that! He had never—not once—given her to think otherwise! And she hadn't needed any such reminder from him! She'd said she'd always known, always accepted the necessary limitations of their time together. That it would be…could only be…for a fixed duration.

*To our time together.*

That had been his very first toast to her. Right from the outset. And their time together had now ended. That was all there was to it.

Impatiently, ruthlessly, he switched on his computer. It fired up and he flicked to the Internet to check his emails. The home page of a leading financial newspaper sprang up, and there, in lead story position, was a headline that stilled him totally.

*He* had made his choice, Francesca had made *her* choice, and now it seemed that Carla Charteris, after all, was making hers…

*Marriage merger keeps Viscari Hotels in the family—Falcone's ambitions thwarted!*

He stared, seeing the headline. Seeing the photo that went with it.

Feeling the jagged emotion, like a serrated blade, knifing into him.

*The sonorous music swelled, lifting upwards to one last crescendo before falling silent. The hushed murmurings of the congregation stilled as the priest raised his hands and began to speak the words of the ancient sacrament in the age-old ceremony.*

*Inside her breast Carla could feel her heart beating like a hammer. Crushing all compunction about what she was doing—what she was making Vito do so bitterly against his will.*

*Emotion filled her and she felt a low, fine tremble go through her, as if her whole being were about to shatter as she stood there, gowned in white, her face veiled. Stood beside the man who was her bridegroom. Waiting for him to say the words that would unite them in marriage.*

*That would free her, finally, from the hell in which she lived.*

But there were no words. There was only silence.

At her side, Vito stood immobile. He had not touched her since she'd walked stiffly down the aisle, her back aching with tension—tension that had kept her in hell for weeks now. A hell she had dragged Vito into as well.

But she didn't care—could not care. Could only keep going with the desperate remedy her mother had offered her—a remedy that was, she knew with the last fragment of her sane mind, poisoning her.

She *would not* let Vito go. She could not—*dared* not. If she let him go she would plunge down into the abyss. She *had* to marry him—she just had to! She would not be safe until she did. Safe from everything that was devouring her.

*When I'm married to him I can be safe! I can be Signora Viscari and have a role to play, a person to be. Being his wife will give me protection.*

Her mother thought it was only protection from the

sneers of the world, the gossip and the jibes, that she wanted, but that was not the protection that she so desperately sought. She needed protection from herself.

*Without Vito's ring keeping me safe, keeping me here in Rome, keeping my days spent organising my wedding, without all that I'd be terrified...terrified...*

Cold snaked down her back. It was terror—the absolute terror that possessed her.

That she'd go to Cesare and beg him...beg him...

Beg him to take her back on any terms—any terms at all!

In her vision she saw again that damnable triptych— the lordly Conte flanked by his pure, perfect wife...and his lowly mistress.

Her stomach hollowed. Once she had thought herself far above comparing herself to the Caradino beauty. In this day and age there could be no such role for any woman. None.

How desperately wrong she had been.

*Love makes slaves of us. Strips everything from us. Craves only the object of our heart...*

She felt herself tremble again as she stood beside Vito, waiting for him to say the words that would keep her safe. Safe from all that tore at her.

Her mother's cruel description seared in her head. 'Cesare's mistress', she'd called her daughter. And there had been more words too...

*'No happy ending.'*

Except for Cesare. Cesare with his beautiful, clever, aristocratic bride—the perfect Contessa.

*'Do you love her?'*

The agonising question she'd hurled at him haunted

her, seared in her head now, as she stood rigid with tension beside the man she was forcing to marry her.

And in her head Cesare's reply came again.

*'Love is an irrelevance.'*

Her face convulsed beneath her veil. Words tumbled through her head, hectic and desperate.

*And it will be irrelevant for me too! I don't love Vito, and his emotion for me is only loathing and bitter hatred for what I've done to him, for the price I'm making him pay to get his family shares back. But when I'm safe—truly safe—I can let him go. In six months...a year...he can get on with his life again. I'll ask for an annulment and release Vito and then he can go and find that blonde of his if he really wants to. He can have it all—the shares, the blonde, everything... It won't be the end of the world for him, for her. They can sort it out between them if they really want to.*

As for herself—well, this time around it would be *her* choice not to be married! *She* would be the one to end it!

*I'll walk out with my head held high—no one will pity me! No one will think me scorned ever again! And Cesare and his beautiful, nobly born, terrifyingly clever, oh-so-damn-wonderful bride can go on having their wonderful life together and I won't care—I won't! I'll have shown him that I can do very well without him! That I've survived.*

As if surfacing from a deep, suffocating dive, she became aware that the silence was lengthening. That Vito was still not saying the words she needed to hear—the words that would rescue her from this hell she was in.

Her head jerked towards him, her eyes distending. Filling with urgency.

Then finally Vito was speaking. But it was not to the

priest. It was to her. His face stark, he was turning towards her. Saying words that drained the air from her lungs.

'I won't do this, Carla.'

She heard his words. But they came from a long, long way away. There was a roaring in her head...

'No, Mum—I said *no*!'

Carla's voice was like a knife. Her mother was arguing with her, trying to make her go back to Guido's villa with her. But she could not bear another moment of her mother's company.

Raging, shouting, almost hysterical, Carla sat in the vestry, on a hard bench, her nails digging into her palms.

'I'm going back to my apartment.'

How she'd got there she could not remember—one of the wedding cars, she supposed, waiting by the rear entrance to the church, had taken her away from the avid, buzzing speculation of the congregation. But now she was finally there in her bedroom, standing in her wedding dress.

Palest white, like the decor in her apartment. As if she might disappear into it...

A bead of hysteria bubbled in her throat. She fought it down. She must not let it out. She must keep it deep inside her. Must, instead, reach behind her back and with stiff, aching arms undo, hook by hook, the gown she had put on less than three hours ago at Guido's house.

*I was so nearly safe—so nearly! And now...*

She felt terror beat up in her—had to fight it down. Fight down the cold, sick feeling inside her that was running in every vein like liquid nitrogen.

*He jilted me. Vito jilted me. Turned me down. Rejected me. Refused to marry me... Refused, refused, refused...*

She felt the hysteria in her throat again, felt her eyes distend, felt pressure in her head as if it might explode. Felt her fingers tremble as the last of the hooks were undone and the heavy, beaded satin and lace gown plummeted to the floor.

She stepped out of it, twisted out of her shoes. God knew where her veil was—she'd torn it from her as she'd gained the vestry, with Vito's arm clamped around hers. If it hadn't been she'd have fainted on the spot. As it was she'd swayed, felt the church whirling around her, and heard a choking noise come from her throat.

She could be glad of that—glad that it had given her a lie to cling to.

'The bride is indisposed...'

Hysteria clawed again. Yes, 'indisposed'—that was what she was.

*Not jilted, not rejected, not spurned.*

Somewhere in the depths of her head she knew, with a kind of piercing pain, that she had only got what she deserved.

*I forced Vito to the altar—behaved shamefully...selfishly.*

*Desperately.*

She walked into the bathroom, yanking on the shower. She stepped under the plunging water, still in her underwear, her hair still pinned into its elaborate coiffeur, soaking herself in the hot, punishing water.

How long she stood there, she could not say. She knew only that it seemed to take an agony of time to peel off the underwear clinging to her streaming wet body—to free herself from the silken mesh of her stockings, push down her panties, yank off her bra, until she was standing there, a mess of lingerie in the shower tray, her hair covering her face, her back, standing there in the scorching hot water, shivering violently...

With shaking hands she turned the water off, pushed the dripping locks from her face, clambered out of the cubicle to seize a towel for her hair, for her body, her feet. She was still shaking, though her skin was red and overheated.

Somehow she made it to her bed. Somehow she thrust the wet towels from her, crawled under the covers like a wounded animal. Somehow, she curled her body, knees drawn up, arms wrapped about herself, her still wet hair damp on the pillow.

She felt the world recede and the blessed mercy of sleep came over her. The oblivion she sought.

# CHAPTER NINE

CESARE SMILED AT his hostess, greeting her with a kiss of her hand. He'd flown in from the USA that morning, back from a visit to Francesca—his first as her fiancé.

In America, seeing her for several days in her work environment, as opposed to seeing her as his guest with her family at the Castello Mantegna, she had seemed very...well, *American*...

There, she was not Donna Francesca, she was Dr Fran Ristori—the aristocratic honorific *'delle'* had been abandoned, he noticed—and she was clearly completely at home in the high-altitude intellectual freemasonry of her colleagues.

The conversation at the dinner party she'd given for him at her apartment on campus, to introduce him to her colleagues, had been virtually incomprehensible to him, excellent though his English was. It was his ignorance of astrophysics that had let him down...

But seeing her with her academic colleagues, speaking English with an American accent, so at home in the rarefied atmosphere of her subject, had made him think to ask her again if she were sure of her decision to marry him.

Had she hesitated? If she had, then her words had only negated that hesitation.

'Yes. You've assured me I can be both a *dottore di fisica* and Contessa di Mantegna. That was what I needed to hear. But…' Her clear blue eyes had rested on him. 'What of you, Ces?' She'd paused minutely, then spoken again. 'My spies tell me my arrival was something of an…an interruption for you.'

For the space of a heartbeat he had been silent. Then he had answered. 'What was interrupted is over, Francesca. Be very sure of that.'

Her eyes rested on him again. 'And are *you*?' she'd asked quietly. 'Are you very sure?'

He had felt the beat of his heart, the pulse of his blood. How many beats? Two? Three? More? Enough for him to exert the necessary control to say what he must.

'Yes,' he had answered. 'She is marrying someone else. I wish her well.'

In his head he had felt the serration of that same knife that had stabbed him when he'd learnt of Carla's engagement to Vito Viscari. He'd remembered the jab he'd felt that last night at the restaurant with Carla, when he'd heard that note of affection for her step-cousin in her voice.

*Is that why she's marrying Viscari—just as I am marrying Francesca? An old affection, born of long years of familiarity? A marriage of mutual convenience for them both?*

So how could he object? What justification was there for that knife blade slicing into his head as he told Francesca he wished her well? He would not permit it to be there. It served no function and had no cause. No justification. No place in his life. Just as Carla now had no place in his life.

Slowly, Francesca had inclined her head. Then, with

a little breath, she had changed the subject. Asked him something anodyne about his flight the next day.

Now, back in Rome, he was attending an evening party, accepting felicitations from friends and social acquaintances. His hostess, he realised with a slight frown, was Estella Farese, who had been present at the restaurant he'd first taken Carla to at the end of the previous summer.

The guillotine sliced down in his mind. He would *not* remember his time with Carla. Would banish it from his memory. Banish everything about it. Looking back was... irrelevant. Choices had been made, decisions taken. Irrevocable decisions—and not just for himself. Carla, too, had made decisions.

*Is she married already? Viscari would not have wanted any delay—would have wanted to get those shares safe in his hands as soon as he could.*

And that was good, wasn't it? Good that Carla had moved on. And if she'd decided to marry her step-cousin, with his film star looks let alone the fact that he came with a luxury hotel chain—to which *she* was contributing half shareholding—well, that only made Vito Viscari an entirely suitable man for her to marry. Entirely suitable.

So there was no reason—no *good* reason—why he should object to her marriage. Why his jaw should tighten, his eyes harden. Why that same spike of jagged emotion—that serrated blade—should flash across his mind, knifing into him now, as it had when Francesca had put her loaded question to him. The question she had had every right to ask and that he'd had every obligation to answer in the way he had. No valid reason at all. Except...

*Except that when I think of her and Viscari—of her and any other man—I want to find her...find her and—*

His hostess's voice cut across his thoughts as that serrated blade knifed into him again.

'*Cesare!* How lovely of you to be here!' Estella's greeting was warm. 'Now, do come and tell me—how is dear, *dear* Francesca! *How* delighted I am that you two are finally engaged! We've all had to wait *so* long! *Such* a brilliant young woman.'

She took Cesare's arm, guiding him towards the far side of the salon.

They passed a knot of women, avidly conversing with each other, and they suddenly paused, as if taken aback by his proximity, only continuing as he passed by. Their eager tones, though, penetrated his awareness.

'Jilted! Yes, my dear, I was there! I saw it all! He refused to marry her!'

A titter of unkind laughter followed.

'He wanted the shares, but not the stepdaughter!'

Another voice intervened. 'No, no, it was *she* who balked! She nearly fainted at the altar. He almost had to carry her away. It's my belief...'

The voice dropped, but not so low that it did not reach Cesare's ears.

'...that she couldn't accept Viscari when she might have had—' She broke off.

The first voice came again—spiteful and contemptuous. 'She never had a *chance* of that! How could she? Mantegna has been promised to the delle Ristori girl all his life! Just as their engagement now proves!'

Estella sailed on by, speaking a little louder than she needed to, as if to drown out the gossips' voices. She proceeded to quiz him about his trip to America, about the forthcoming wedding, about whether Francesca would continue with her research career afterwards.

Cesare felt himself go into automatic mode, giving responses almost at random. But inside his head a bomb was exploding in devastating slow motion.

*She didn't marry him.*

The words repeated in his head. Like a gunshot.

*She didn't marry him.*

They stayed in his head for the duration of the evening. Were still there as he left, exhausted by polite enquiries after Francesca, and how the wedding preparations were proceeding, and showers of felicitations and congratulations and well-wishing.

There had been no further tactless or untoward remarks about what was clearly sending the gossips into overdrive.

A jilting at the altar! A fainting bride! A mother in hysterics. *Two* mothers in hysterics! And all of Rome to witness it!

Back in his apartment, the words were still there, ricocheting around inside his skull. He strode across the room, pulled open the drinks cabinet. Fetching a bottle of whisky, he poured a hefty slug. He knocked it back in one.

*She didn't marry him.*

Then, with a rasp, he pushed the whisky bottle away, relocked the cabinet. He went into the room he reserved for his office. He needed distraction. He would check on his affairs.

Grimly, he turned on his PC, letting it fire up. So what if she didn't marry Viscari? What was it to him? Nothing—nothing at all! *She* was nothing to him! He'd made his decision—put her aside. Finished the affair. *Finished it!*

He'd had no choice to do otherwise. No choice at all.

*I could not have them both—those times are gone.*

His mouth contorted and he rubbed his hand across his face—a rough gesture, as if he could wipe out what was inside his head.

Two images formed in his vision.

Francesca delle Ristori—the woman he was going to marry.

Carla Charteris—the woman he had put aside to do so. *Carla...*

And, like a sluice gate opening, a dam breaking, all the images that he had kept out of his head since the moment he'd walked out of her apartment stormed in upon him.

More than images…worse than images.

Memories—vivid, tangible, indelible.

*Carla swimming with him at midnight in the pool at the villa in Lazio, their naked bodies glistening in starlight.*

*Carla, her limbs wound with his, spine arched as she cried out in his arms.*

*Carla smiling at him across the dinner table, telling him something about Luciezo, or Tintoretto, or Michelangelo—some detail of art history he did not know—while he set it in historical context and they discussed the implications of it.*

*Carla shaking her hair free as he drove along the autostrada towards the villa in Lazio, taking their time off together, looking forward to nothing more than easy, restful, peaceable days together—to sensual, passion-fuelled nights...*

Memory after memory.

Nothing more than memory now. Now and for ever—for the rest of his life.

*As it must be.*

Desperately, urgently, he made his thoughts fly across the ocean, back to where he'd left the woman who was going to be his *contessa*, his destined bride, the woman who was right for him in every way. But Francesca's image would not come—would not be conjured. Instead dark hair, blue-violet eyes, that rich, sensuous mouth that could smile, or kiss, or gasp in passion at its peak…all occluded his vision.

*She didn't marry him.*

The words came again—sinuous now, soft and dulcet, weaving in and out of his synapses. He felt his blood quicken, let memory ripen in his thoughts.

More than memory.

He shifted restlessly in his chair. It had been so long… so long since he had set her aside. Yet she was here—so close. Across the city—a kilometre or two…no more than that. How often had he gone to her apartment in those six months that had been their time together? How often had his hands closed over her shoulders, drawing her lush body to his as his mouth lowered to her parting lips, tasting the delectable sensual nectar of her kiss, deepening to heated arousal…?

Carla—with her blue-violet eyes, her rich mouth, her full breasts and rounded hips—with the dark, lustrous hair he'd loved to spear and tangle his hands in as he spread her body out on the bed for himself to caress, possess…to take and be taken while flames of passion had seared them both—Carla… Ah, Carla, who was only a dozen rooftops away…

Carla, whom he had set aside to fulfil his responsibilities to his name, his house... Carla, who could never be more to him than what she had been—and to have been that was...

Carla, who had thought to marry a man who was nothing to her! Merely for the reallocation of a handful of shares.

His mouth twisted. He had told himself she was entirely entitled to marry Viscari, had made himself applaud it—be glad of it. Glad that he could set her aside knowing she would be making a future for herself as her step-cousin's wife. Telling himself that her marriage made sense, was entirely suitable—just as his own was.

He could tell himself all he liked.

It was a lie. A barefaced lie to hide the truth of why she had taken such a step.

That was not why she'd walked up the aisle towards Vito Viscari! She'd done it for one reason and one reason only and he knew it—knew it with every burning fibre of his being.

*She did it to punish me—because of what I did to her. Because I put her aside...put her out of my life.*

That was the reason—the only reason.

Emotion reared up in him—savage, powerful. Fuelling the memories surging through his head. Impelling him from the room, from the apartment.

To one destination only.

Carla swayed, her body racked with pain. Her mind more so. Twenty-four hours—had it really been only twenty-four hours? Twenty-four hours since she had collapsed into the blessed oblivion that had blotted out the horrors of the afternoon before?

She clenched her hands, feeling her painted nails

digging into her palms. She welcomed the pain. She deserved it. Deserved it for being the cretinous, contemptible fool that she had been.

*To think I could get him to marry me! To salve my shattered pride! To let me outstare the world—outstare the man who threw me aside as if I was less than nothing to him!*

Mortification filled her—and self-contempt. And bitter, bitter remorse.

She deserved what Vito had done to her. Deserved his refusal to be blackmailed into saving her stupid, stupid face. Deserved everything.

She trailed into the kitchen, filled the kettle. She would drink tea and force herself to eat, despite the sickness in her stomach.

The future stretched ahead of her—empty and bleak.

She would leave Rome. She must. And her mother would be leaving too. No doors would be open to her now—Lucia Viscari would ensure that. For who would receive a woman who had sold her own husband's legacy—half the entire company—to his business rival, just to punish the man who had jilted her daughter at the altar? No, Marlene would leave for Spain and she would go with her. What else could she do?

The doorbell jangled, making her start. Dear God, not her mother again, surely? She had left only a few hours earlier, her fury at Vito's behaviour venomous, her vengeance upon him ruthless.

Carla had tried to stop her.

'Do you blame him, Mum? *Do* you? I behaved despicably to him! None of this was his fault, and yet I made him take the fall for it! And if you sell those shares to Nic Falcone you will have behaved as badly! Sell them to Vito—like he's implored you to do ever since Guido died!'

But Marlene had been deaf to Carla's pleas. Driven by maternal rage at her daughter's humiliation. There had been nothing Carla could do.

The doorbell came again—insistent now.

She put the kettle down, trailed to the door. Opened it.

Cesare walked in.

Shock, like a seismic wave in slow motion, detonated within Carla, hollowing her out, draining the breath from her body. Faintness drummed at her and she clung to the door frame for support.

He took it from her, closed it. Turned to her.

There was a blaze in his eyes. A black fire.

'Get out.' Her voice was faint, and very far away.

He ignored her, walked past her into her sitting room. His eyes came back to her as she stepped inside. She clutched her dressing gown to her, as if it might support her.

'I said get out,' she said again.

He looked at her. That black fire was still in his eyes. 'Were you really going to marry him? Did you truly intend to go through with it?'

'*Yes!*' she answered, her voice a searing hiss.

Emotion was knifing inside her. To see Cesare *here*, in her apartment, a handful of metres away from her...

His mouth tightened like the line of a whip. 'They can't decide, the gossips, quite what happened yesterday. Whether he threw *you* over or you him.' He paused. 'So which was it?'

She gave a laugh. A savage, vicious laugh.

'Which do you think, Cesare?' Her face convulsed. 'I should be used to it, shouldn't I? Being thrown aside!'

She took a shuddering breath. Lifting her chin, her eyes flashing like daggers, she clutched the material of her robe across her breasts, as if keeping him at bay. But she didn't need to keep him at bay, did she? He didn't want her…he would never want her again.

She slashed a hand through the air. 'So get out, Cesare! Get out of my apartment and out of my life—just *get out*!'

He stood motionless while she hurled her diatribe at him. Then, when all the fury of her words was spent, he stepped towards her.

'Get out…' she said again. Her voice was hoarse.

She should move…she should retreat. Flee. Barricade herself in her bedroom.

She could not move.

'You should not have tried to marry him,' said Cesare. His voice was strange.

There was a choking sound from her throat, but she had no words to answer him. He did not need any.

'When I saw that photo of you, that announcement in the financial press, I—' He stopped. Could not continue.

Emotion welled in him. Dark and blackening. Somewhere, far across the Atlantic Ocean, was the woman he was supposed to marry. While here…

'You should not have tried to marry him,' he said again.

From the depths of his mind he tried to conjure Francesca's face. But she was not there. He tried to say her name in his head, but he could not. That guillotine had descended across his mind, cutting him in half. There was a woman's name he needed to say—

The name of the woman who stood before him.

Her eyes were huge in her face, her hands convulsing on the silk of her robe. A robe he knew well. Raw silk, peacock-blue, shot with violet like her eyes. He'd said as much to her once as he'd slid it from her naked body, letting it pool on the floor.

He stepped towards her, reaching out his hand for the shoulder of her robe, letting his fingers slide over its silken surface. He felt her body shudder beneath his touch. Saw her close her eyes as if to shut him out, her long lashes wet.

*'Carla...'*

He said her name—the name he needed to say. Felt his hand fasten on her shoulder, his other hand graze down the edge of the material across her collarbone. Her delicate, intricate collarbone... The pale satin skin below yielded to his touch. And only to his.

*No one else's! No other man should touch her.*

His blood pulsed like a hammer in his veins. He could not do without her. Not tonight.

Memory drummed across his mind. *This* was why he was here. To make those memories real again.

He lifted her chin, cupping it with his fingers. Her eyes flared open. There was terror in them—and more than terror.

'Don't do this...' Her voice was faint.

He shook his head. 'Then tell me to go,' he said. 'You've said it to me over and over again. Say it to me now. Say it, Carla—tell me to go. To get out of your life.'

She could not speak. Could only stare.

'Tell me to get out, Carla.'

His voice was a harsh, raw husk, his mouth twisting as he spoke, his eyes spearing hers. A pulse throbbed at his throat and his long fingers plunged into her hair, indenting into her skull. Holding her for himself...*only* for himself...

'Tell me to get out,' he said again, one final time.

But she could not. She could do nothing. Nothing at all. Could only feel her lips part, helpless, hopeless as, with a rasp deep in his throat, he lowered his mouth to hers, grazing it, taking his fill.

'I want one last time,' he said, his voice still a husk, his eyes still burning with that black fire. 'One last time, Carla. One last time to show you why you should not have agreed to marry another man. *Any* other man—'

He grazed her mouth with his again, his hand slipping the silk from her shoulder, exposing a single breast.

'So tell me to go, Carla…or tell me to stay…or tell me nothing at all.' His hand moved, to cup the lush curve of her breast, so rich and ripe, to feel its crest peak and bloom within his palm,

And then the time for speaking was done. With a surge of his blood, he opened her mouth beneath his, his hand tightening at her breast, kneading the soft, aroused flesh.

A moan escaped her throat. Helpless. Hopeless.

She could not speak, could not protest. She could do only what every part of her body, her being, wanted… craved her to do.

Her hands snaked around his back, hauling him to her, crushing his hips into the cradle of her body, feeling her body surge, his body answer hers.

And then the black fire took them both…

Carla moved slowly, as if emerging from paralysis. Consciousness seeped through her. For a moment she lay there, motionless. At her side, his limbs heavy upon her, Cesare slept. His face was in repose, and for a long, timeless moment Carla looked upon it.

Behind her eyes, thoughts ran.

There was a sickness inside her.

Slowly, infinitely slowly, she began to move. He did not stir. Weak with gratitude for that one small mercy, she slid from the bed. Silently, desperately, she found clothes, crept from the bedroom, forced unwilling limbs into them, found her handbag, her keys.

The morning light was dim—dawn barely broken. Her heart was pounding…the sickness was overwhelming her. She stepped forward, as if impelled by a power she could not resist.

At the door of the bedroom she halted. Her eyes, stricken, went to the figure lying in her bed, sprawled across it, the strong planes of his muscled back delineated in the dawn light. Emotion, like a wolf, leapt in her throat to devour her. Her hand was pressed to her mouth, and a sound that might have been a sob was stifled before it could be born.

Then, as if it required all the strength in her body, she turned away.

Left the apartment.

Left the city.

Fled for her very life.

# CHAPTER TEN

THE SPANISH SUN was warm on Carla's bare arms and legs as she sat on the terrace of her mother's huge, newly purchased villa on this most exclusive stretch of the Costas. It seemed a lifetime ago since she had been in Rome. Yet only a handful of months had passed since she'd fled like a wounded creature.

A haunted expression filled her eyes. Then, deliberately, she picked up the newspaper at her side, turning, as she often did now, to the financial pages.

Her expression tensed. Yes, there was another news item—small, but immediately eye-catching to her—about Viscari Hotels. Something about yet another fraught board meeting, now that Nic Falcone was co-owner of the whole company and helping himself to the pick of Viscari Hotels across the world, dismembering Vito's inheritance piecemeal.

Guilt, familiar and shaming, fused through Carla. Guilt and remorse.

*How could I have done that to him? How could I?*

But she knew how—knew, even as the hot Spanish sun beat down on her, how her whole being had writhed in the torment of Cesare's rejection of her, in the humiliation of knowing that she had only been exactly what her mother had feared she was.

*Nothing better than his mistress. To be set aside the moment his aristocratic bride beckoned!*

She closed her eyes, fighting the emotion that swept up in her. What good was it to remember? Cesare had treated her by his own rules—and it had been she who had been the fool! A fool to fall in love with him—a fool ever to think she could have her happy ending...that Cesare could return her love for him...

She felt her stomach churn again. And the worst fool of all to have let him into her apartment that last, disastrous, fatal night after Vito's jilting of her. Fool upon fool!

And now...

Her hand dropped the newspaper, slid across her stomach to ease the nausea that bit there.

Dear God, how great a fool she was!

'Carla, darling, there you are!'

Her mother's voice was a welcome distraction as Marlene emerged out of the villa. She paused, surveying her daughter.

'How are you feeling this morning?' she asked carefully.

Carla stood up. 'I'm OK, Mum.'

'*Are* you?' Marlene's eyes worked over her, concern in their expression.

She was about to say more, Carla could tell, and she needed to stop her. She picked up the newspaper.

'There's another piece in here about Viscari and Falcone,' she said.

There was reproof in her voice, and she could see her mother's colour heighten.

She held up a hand. 'Mum, don't say anything—we're

never going to agree on this. But I did treat Vito appallingly.' She took a breath, saying what she had resolved. 'I'm going to go to Rome. I have to see him—to…apologise. And also,' she carried on, still not letting her mother speak, 'I want to put my apartment on the market.' She paused. 'I'm never going to live in Italy again, so there is no point owning it. And besides—'

She halted. She would not tell her mother that she intended to do more than merely apologise to Vito. Since her mother had profited hugely from selling Guido's shares to Vito's rival, she would make what amends she could by gifting the proceeds from the sale of her flat—bought, after all, with Guido's legacy to her—to Vito. He could use it to help fund his financial recovery. Pittance though it was, it was the only thing she could think of doing.

'Darling…' Her mother's voice was openly worried. 'Are you sure you want to go back to Rome? I mean—'

Carla shook her head. 'No, I don't want to—but I must.'

It was what she'd kept repeating to herself—right up to the grim moment when she bearded Vito in his office in Rome.

The ordeal was gruelling. From the moment she arrived she could feel eyes on her—curious…openly hostile.

Vito himself was stone-faced as she made her stumbling, tight-throated expression of her remorse.

'I'm desperately sorry, Vito, and deeply ashamed of myself. I let my own misery over Cesare consume me. It made me behave vilely to you—and…' she swallowed '…to…to your girlfriend.' She paused again, uncomfortable. 'I hope… I hope you were able to make it up with her after…well…since then.'

A bleak look passed across his face. 'That wasn't possible,' he said.

Carla felt guilt bite at her again. 'I'm sorry,' she said. 'Would…would it help if I…if I went to see her? Apologised for what I said…what I did?'

The bleak look came again. 'I have no idea where Eloise is. She's vanished. I've been trying to find her since—' It was his turn to break off.

'Oh, Vito, I'm sorry!'

Carla's voice was even more apologetic, her guilt ever deeper. There had been something in her step-cousin's voice that she recognised in herself—a bleakness that matched her own.

Her face twisted. 'I didn't realise she was so important to you… I mean, you usually—' She broke off again.

Vito looked at her, his eyes strained. 'Yes, I know. I *do* usually have some long-legged blonde on my arm,' he said, echoing the words she'd used. 'But Eloise—'

He broke off again, and now Carla *knew* she could see something in his drawn face that she recognised only too well. Vito's dark eyes looked at her with a nakedness in them that smote her.

'Eloise was different. I wanted so much to spend time with her—to discover if…if she was the one woman I'd ever met whom I could—'

He broke off again.

'And now I'll never know,' he said.

The bleakness in his voice broke Carla. Impulsively she stepped forward.

'Vito—let me help! Please let me help you find her. There must be a way—there *must*!'

He looked at her. 'How? She won't answer my texts or my calls. I don't have any address for her in London, where she lives, because she works as a nanny. I've had investigators checking nanny agencies, but nothing—absolutely *nothing*! She's vanished!'

Frustration and pain were clear in his voice. Carla felt her mind racing. An idea was forming in her mind.

'Vito—listen. Even if *you* can't find her—and neither can your investigators—maybe…maybe the press can!'

Vito looked at her blankly. Carla felt words tumble from her in her desperation to make amends—any kind of amends—to the step-cousin she had treated so shamefully.

'Vito, I'm a journalist—I know how the press works. What about this? I'm fairly friendly with the features editor on one of those glossy international celebrity magazines. She loves it that I know loads of the people she likes to put in it, especially you! I've always been very discreet, but this time—'

Swiftly she outlined her idea.

Vito looked at her. For the first time the lines around his eyes seemed to lighten. 'Do you think it has a chance?' he asked.

Carla looked at him. 'It's worth a shot, isn't it? A centre spread of you, with a glamorously romantic photo of you both, and a headline asking, *"Can you find my beautiful Eloise?"* Those glossy celebrity magazines have a *huge* readership!'

'Can you set it up for me? A meeting with this features editor?' There was sudden urgency in Vito's voice.

Carla smiled. The first time she'd smiled for a long time. If this was some way to make amends to Vito, however belated, she would do it.

'I'll phone her now,' she said.

Five minutes later she put the phone back on Vito's desk.

'She almost bit my hand off,' she told him.

She could see her step-cousin's eyes flare—fill with hope.

He got to his feet, came round to her. Took her hands. 'Thank you,' he said.

Emotion welled up in her. 'Oh, Vito, don't thank me! Not after what I did to you! I can never forgive myself— *never*! I was just so…so twisted up inside. So—'

She broke off again. Half turned away. But Vito did not let her go. Instead he put his arms around her, hugged her tightly. She felt tears prick at her eyes.

Then, abruptly, Vito stood back from her, looked at her with shock in his face.

'Carla—' There was disbelief in his voice.

Too late, she realised why. She stepped away, disengaging her hands.

*'Cesare?'* Vito's voice was hollow.

Colour stained her cheekbones. 'After…after you refused to marry me he…he turned up at my apartment. It was—'

'Does he *know*?' There was a steely note in Vito's voice.

Violently, Carla shook her head. 'No! And he mustn't! Vito—he *mustn't*!'

Vito's brows snapped together, giving him a quelling appearance. 'He must know *at once*!' he retorted. 'Before he goes any further with his engagement!'

Carla caught at his sleeve. 'No! Please, Vito! I couldn't bear it!' There was panic in her face.

For a moment his quelling expression held. Then, abruptly, it vanished.

'I understand,' he said. His voice changed. 'Carla, look…now that we've made our peace with each other I think we should show Rome that the family rift…is no more.'

He held up his hand decisively. 'I know that the gossips couldn't decide just why our wedding never took place, but I want to show them that whatever has happened since—' he did not spell out what her mother had done '—you and I, at least, are friends. So I think we should be seen out socially, while you're here in Rome, to confirm that.'

She looked at him uncertainly. 'If…if you want,' she said.

How could she refuse anything that Vito asked of her, given how badly she had treated him? Socialising in Rome might be the most gruelling ordeal she could imagine right now, but she must face it for Vito's sake.

*And if I fear I might see Cesare—well, why should I? Viscari circles don't usually overlap with his, and anyway Cesare's probably in his* castello *planning his wedding…*

She felt the nausea bite again—and something worse than nausea. Much, much worse.

'Good.' Vito nodded. He smiled. 'How about tonight?'

She paled. 'Tonight?' she echoed faintly.

Vito quirked an eyebrow. 'You have something more pressing?'

Slowly she shook her head, realised that in all conscience she could not refuse.

That evening, as she stood staring blankly at her reflection in the mirror, she knew the last thing she wanted was to go out into society—even though she owed it to Vito. So, ignoring the knots in her stomach, she threw one last glance at herself, reassured by the dark indigo evening gown, generously cut—nothing clinging or curvaceous now—and her immaculate hair and make-up.

Her phone buzzed to tell her that Vito was waiting for her in his car below, and she left her apartment.

She had spent the afternoon with estate agents and her solicitor, booking a removal company to transfer her possessions to her mother's house. She would tell Vito this evening that she was going to hand him the proceeds of the sale—it wasn't much, compared to the loss he'd suffered, thanks to her mother, but it was all she could do.

She paid little attention to where he was taking her, but as they walked inside an ornate *palazzo*, the venue for the fundraising reception for a *museo di antiquity* that Vito was attending, she suddenly froze.

Her hand clawed on Vito's sleeve. 'This is the Palazzo Mantegna!'

He glanced at her. 'I know,' he said. 'That's why I brought you here—Cesare will be here as one of the *museo*'s patrons.'

Desperately, Carla tried to pull away.

But Vito's hand clamped over hers. 'Carla—he has to know. He *has* to!'

A drumming filled her senses.

Cesare was talking to his fellow *museo* patrons, but for all his polite conversation he had no inclination to be there. His mood was grim.

Francesca was still in America, vacating her apartment, making ready to move back to Italy and become his *contessa*. He was glad of her absence. How could he face her after what he had done? Committing an act of folly so extreme he could not now believe that he had done it.

Folly? Was that what it had been? That final, self-indulgent, devil-driven night with Carla? The sour taste of self-disgust filled him. Of shame.

*I went to her with my betrothal ring on Francesca's finger! And yet I presumed to accuse her of being prepared to marry another man! As if she had betrayed me... spurned me for another man.*

In that one shameful night he had behaved unforgivably to the woman he'd undertaken to marry *and* the one whom he could never marry. Could never again possess. Could never again see, or have anything to do with.

*She is lost to me for ever.*

As he said the words, he felt something twist inside him, as if the point of a knife had broken off, stayed in his guts. It would stay there, lodged for ever. Scar tissue would grow around it, but it would remain for all his life. A wound that would not heal...

'Signor Conte—'

He was being called to the podium to make a short speech. The moment he'd done that he'd leave. Tomorrow he'd head back to his *castello* and ready it for his future bride.

He felt his mind veer away. Contemplating his wedding—his bride—was not what he wanted to do. Memory sifted in his mind. It had been a function similar to this—the opening of that exhibition he'd lent the triptych to—where he'd first had his interest caught by Carla Charteris.

He could see her now instantly, in his mind's eye, her figure sheathed in that cobalt blue cocktail dress, her svelte brunette beauty immediately firing his senses. Calling to him…

His gaze flickered blankly over the throng of guests milling around in the palatial hall of his ancestors' former residence in Rome.

Flickered—and stilled.

No—he was imagining it. He *must* be. It could not be—

Without volition he was walking forward. Striding. People were stepping aside for him.

She had seen him. He saw it in her paling face, her distended eyes. Her hand was clutching at the sleeve of the man with her.

*Viscari!* With an inner snarl that came from some deep, primitive part of him, Cesare felt jealous rage spear up inside him as he reached the couple.

He could see Vito Viscari step forward slightly, as if to shelter Carla, whose face was still bleached and stark. Then, with a little breathless sigh, she started to crumple.

There were voices—deep and masculine, angry and agitated—penetrating her brain. Her eyelids flickered feebly, and she became aware that she was perched dizzily on a chair in a small antechamber—and that Vito and Cesare were standing over her.

'Are you all right?' Cesare's demand was stentorian, his face grim. The question was directed at her—he was ignoring Vito totally.

But it was Vito who was answering for her. 'No,' he said tersely, 'she is not.'

Carla's heart was hammering, the blood drumming in her ears.

Cesare's gaze snapped to Vito. 'What is wrong?'

Vito started to speak, but Carla reached for his arm.

'Vito, no! *No!*' Terror was in her now. She had to stop him—she *had* to!

But the expression on Vito's face was one she'd never seen before. Angry—stern. He was squaring up to Cesare, who was glaring at him, his face dark and closed.

Vito's chin lifted. He paid no attention to Carla. 'Your marriage plans are going to have to be altered,' he said to Cesare. 'Carla is pregnant.'

Cesare's car speeded along the *autostrada* heading into the Lazio countryside. At his side, Carla sat silent. Memory was biting like a wolf in her mind. How she had sat beside Cesare like this that first weekend together as he'd sped her towards his beautiful little rococo love nest.

*I thought I could handle an affair with Cesare. A civilised, sensual affair, for the mutual enjoyment of both of us.*

How utterly, totally wrong she had been. How incomparably stupid. Folly after folly! All compounded by the single greatest folly she had committed.

To have fallen in love with him. Cesare di Mondave, Conte di Mantegna. A man who would never marry her.

Except—and that wolf bit again, in her throat now—now that was exactly what he was prepared to do.

The irony of it was agonising. Unbearable. As unbearable as the words she had heard her step-cousin uttering last night. And Cesare's explosive outburst… Vito's coldly terse assurance.

Both of them had ignored her until a moan had come from her lips, and then suddenly they'd both been there, bending over her.

She'd pushed them both away, struggling upright.

Cesare's arm had come around her instantly, but she'd pulled herself free. Her head had been pounding, her heart racing.

'Leave me alone! Both of you!'

A look had been thrown between Cesare and Vito. Cesare had said something to Vito she had not been able to hear, hearing only the grimness in his voice. Then Vito had nodded.

'Be sure you do,' he'd said, in that same terse voice.

Then Cesare had looked at Carla. His face had been unreadable. He'd seemed a thousand miles away. A million.

'All the necessary arrangements will be made,' he said to her. 'I will fetch you tomorrow. Until then—'

He'd exchanged one more look with Vito, and then he had gone. It had been Vito who'd seen her back to her apartment, talking to her—*at* her—all the way. She'd said nothing, her mouth tight, compressed. Right up until Vito had seen her into her apartment.

Then she'd turned to him. 'I am not marrying Cesare,' she'd said.

Vito had said nothing. And then—'He has given me his word that he will. For now, that is enough.'

He'd left her, and this morning Cesare had arrived. She'd seen his eyes moving around the apartment and had known that he was remembering the fatal night he'd forced his way in, daring her to make him leave.

*And now he's reaping the consequences.*

She'd wanted to laugh, hysterically, but had silenced herself. Almost wordlessly he'd ushered her down to his waiting car and she'd gone with him, her suitcase packed.

She'd wanted to go back to Spain, to her mother, and yet here she was, in Cesare's car, going back to the place that had once been a place of bliss for her. Now, it was evident, it was going to be the scene where Cesare di Mondave steeled himself to offer to marry his former mistress who'd so disastrously got herself pregnant.

'Is it cool enough for you? I can turn up the air conditioning.'

Cesare's voice interrupted her bleak thoughts. His tone was polite. Distant.

'Perfectly cool, thank you,' she answered, her tone matching his.

He drove on in silence.

At the villa, Lorenzo was there to greet them, as he always had been. Carla was glad of his presence—it insulated her from Cesare.

Yet as lunch was served, and Lorenzo departed, suddenly she was alone with Cesare again. She watched him reach for his wine glass. Then set it down, untouched. He looked across at her from the head of the table to herself at the foot. His face was still expressionless.

It hurt her to see him. Hurt her eyes to take in the features of his face, which had once been so familiar to her—so familiar that she could have run her fingertips over its contours in the dark and known it to be him out of all the men in all the world.

And now it was the face of a stranger. She could not bear it...

But bear it she must. Must bear, too, the words he now spoke to her.

'Would you have told me that you were pregnant had your step-cousin not intervened?' he asked. His words were staccato.

Carla looked at him. 'No,' she said.

Something flashed in his eyes, but all he said was, 'Why not?'

She gave a shrug—the tiniest gesture. 'To what purpose? You were engaged to another woman.' She paused. 'You still are.'

The dark flash came again. 'You must leave it to me to communicate with my…my former fiancée,' he said heavily. His mouth was set. 'You will understand, I am sure, that this will not be easy for her. This situation is nothing of her making and I must do all that I can to make it as comfortable for her as I can.'

She watched him pick up his wine glass again, and this time he drank deeply from it. His unreadable gaze came back to her.

'Once I have spoken to Francesca—and out of courtesy also to her parents—our betrothal will be formally announced. Until that time I would be grateful…' he took a breath '…if you would be…reticent about our engagement.'

Carla did not answer.

He went on. As if he were forcing himself. 'And for the same reason I would ask you to stay here, in the villa, until I am free to become formally betrothed to you.'

Her answer was a silent inclination of her head.

For a long moment Cesare let his gaze rest on her. Emotions were mounting in his chest, but he kept them tightly leashed. It was essential for him to do so. He watched her pick up her knife and fork and start to eat. She did not look pregnant. But then, she was scarcely into her second trimester.

He felt his insides twist and knot.

*She carries my child! A child she would never have told me about! I would have married Francesca—had*

*children by her, a son to be my heir—while all along
Carla would have been raising another child of mine,
born outside marriage.*

For a second—just a second—images flashed in his
head. His ancestor, Count Alessandro, flanked by the two
women in his life. His wife—the mother of his heir—
and his mistress, her body rich with his bastard child.

*That will not be me! Never.*

Inside, he felt his leashed emotions lash him, as if
trying to break free, but he only tightened the leash on
them. It was not safe to do otherwise. He must ignore
them, focus only on the practicalities of what must happen now. His world had just been turned upside down
and his task was to deal with it.

Blank out everything else.

Blank out the memories that assailed him of how often
he and Carla had retreated here to the villa to have private time together, relaxing away from their work, their
busy lives. Private…intimate… Enjoying each other's
company, in bed and out. Enjoying their affair.

An affair he had ended because it could no longer
continue—because of the commitment he had to make
to his family responsibility, to the woman who had expected to marry him all her adult life.

The commitment that now, because of his own insane
behaviour the night he'd gone to Carla's apartment, driven
by demons he had not known possessed him, he had to
set aside. A commitment overridden by a new, all-con-
suming commitment. To the child Carla was carrying.

*Only to the child?*

The question was searing in his head, but he must not
let it. Not now—not yet.

Once more he yanked at the leash on his emotions,

tightening his grip on them, and let his eyes rest on Carla, so pale, so silent.

Across the table she felt Cesare's tense gaze on her. How often had she eaten here with Cesare in the months they'd spent together? Taking their ease—talking, smiling, laughing—their eyes openly entwining with each other, the air of intimacy between them as potent as their glances.

Yet now it was as if they were each encased in ice.

*What can we say to each other? What is there to say? How can we ever speak to each other as we once did? Comfortable, companionable...*

'Are you well in the pregnancy?' Cesare's words, still staccato, interrupted her bleak, unanswerable questions.

'Perfectly,' she answered, her tone of voice echoing his. 'Some nausea, but no more than that. It will ease as I go into the next trimester.'

He nodded. 'I'm glad to hear it.' He paused again. 'I'll book an appointment with whatever obstetrician in Rome you choose. And perhaps it would be sensible to book you into a delivery clinic before long.'

'Thank you,' she answered. She tried to think of something else to say, and failed.

'Have you had an ultrasound yet?'

Another stilted question. Only highlighting the strain between them.

She shook her head, answering no just as stiltedly.

'Perhaps we should book one. Are there any other tests that need to be done?'

'I'll speak to the doctor, but it should all be very straightforward.'

He nodded. 'Good.'

*Good?* The word echoed in Carla's head, mocking her.

'Good' was a million miles from what it was. She felt nausea rising up in her throat and had to fight it down. She had just told Cesare she was coming out of morning sickness, but this nausea didn't come from her body, from her pregnancy.

It came from a source much deeper inside her.

Stolidly, she ate her way through the rest of the meal.

Painstakingly, Cesare kept a limping conversation going, talking about her pregnancy, asking questions she could scarcely answer.

When the meal was over they repaired for coffee to the terrace, underneath a shady parasol, catching the lightly cooling breeze. Out in the beautiful walled garden the sun sparkled off the water in the pool.

'How much exercise can you take?' Cesare asked.

'As much as I like, really. Swimming is the best— especially as I get closer to my due date,' she answered.

Her eyes went to the pool. So did Cesare's.

*Is he remembering too? Remembering how we swam stark naked beneath the stars?*

Emotion gripped her, like a knife sliding between her ribs.

Without thinking, Carla reached for the silver coffee jug, pouring black coffee for Cesare as she had done a hundred times before, handing him the delicate porcelain cup and saucer with its silver crested coffee spoon. He sketched a constrained smile of thanks and took it, sitting back in his chair, crossing one long leg over the other.

Absently, he stirred his coffee. Then, abruptly, he looked across at her as she poured hot milk into her own coffee.

'We can make this work, you know, Carla. We just

have to…to set our minds to it.' There was resolution in his voice, determination in his expression.

She lifted her cup to her lips, took a sip, then lowered it. She looked across at him. Her eyes were bleak. Negating his resolve.

'How can we?' she said. 'You'd be marrying your mistress. How can that ever work?' Her voice was tight—so tight it must surely snap, like wire under unbearable tension.

'You were never my *"mistress"*!' The words came from him like bullets. Automatic, instinctive. 'Do not paint yourself as such! We had an affair, Carla—a relationship. It was simply that—' He broke off.

She shut her eyes. Took a ragged breath. She would finish for him. Tell the truth that had always been there, right from the start—the truth that was not her fault, nor his, but that had always set the terms of their relationship.

'It was simply that marriage to me was never on the cards for you—and it still doesn't have to be, Cesare! I'm perfectly prepared to stay stashed away in Spain with my mother. I'll never show my face in Rome again! If you want to pay towards the child's upkeep, you're welcome—but I don't need your money. I'll sign any document you like never to make a claim on your estate, or your heirs.'

She fell silent. Breathless. Inside her there seemed to be a knot—a tight, hard knot that was getting tighter and harder every second. She kept her eyes on Cesare. Fixed. Resolute.

*I have to say this—I have to do this. He must hear from me that I do not want this marriage.*

She felt a crying out in her heart.

*Not a marriage like this! Oh, not a marriage like this!*

Across her heart a jagged knife seemed to be dragging its serrated blade. Had she ever had such insanely impossible hopes that he might be falling in love with her? That last evening of their affair, when he'd been so different, she'd thought—dear God, she'd really, truly thought—it might be because he was recognising what she had come to mean to him!

The jagged knife drew her heart's blood from her. But now all she was to him was a burden. An obligation. A duty he must fulfil.

For a moment—an instant—she thought she saw emotion flash darkly across his face. Then it was shuttered.

'That is out of the question,' he said.

He drank his coffee, jerkily lifting the cup to his lips, precisely setting it back down, as if every muscle were under tight control.

He looked across at her. 'Once,' he said, 'it might have been acceptable to have a…a second family, an informal arrangement.'

Into his head flashed that Caradino portrait of Count Alessandro's mistress, the mother of his illegitimate children, her swollen belly. He thrust the image from his head.

'But that is out of the question these days!' His voice was a snap—a lock to shut out any other possibility.

It did not silence Carla. Her violet eyes flared with emotion. 'It's just the opposite!' she retorted. 'There is no longer any social opprobrium in having children outside marriage. We don't have to go through a marriage ceremony just for appearance's sake! Not like—'

She broke off. A crushing sense of fatalism paralysed

her. Words, unsaid, scars inside her head, played themselves silently.

*Not like my parents had to...*

Cesare's shuttered expression did not change. 'No child of mine will be born outside marriage,' he said.

There were lines around his mouth, deep-scored. Carla stared at him, a stone in her chest. Then Cesare went on speaking, crossing his legs as if restless yet forced to sit still. Forced to endure what he was enduring.

'When we are in a position to formally announce our engagement,' he said, his voice coming from somewhere very distant, 'you will come to the *castello* and take up residence there. We shall be married in the chapel and—'

'No!' Once again Carla's defiant voice cut across him. Her chin went up and her eyes were burning violet. 'There will be only a civil ceremony. Nothing more. That way...' She took a ragged breath. 'That way we can divorce, without impediment to your future marriage.'

His brows snapped together. 'What are you saying?' he demanded.

'What has to be said! Oh, Cesare, if this is something we really have to do, then in God's name let us do it so that it does the least damage possible!'

She ran her fingertips over her brow. She was hot suddenly, despite the shade, hot and breathless. How could she sit here with Cesare in this dreadful mockery, this travesty?

Her voice dropped. 'Cesare, we can't do anything else. A civil marriage to legitimise the birth, and then a civilised divorce.'

He was looking at her. 'If you bear a son, he must be raised to his heritage,' he said.

She looked at him. 'Let me pray for a girl, then—

that would solve everything, wouldn't it, Cesare? A girl who can grow up with me and leave you free to marry the woman you want to marry and have your heir with. Wouldn't that be the best? *Wouldn't* it?'

He was looking at her, a strange expression on his face. She could not read it—but not because it was shuttered. Because there was something in it she had never seen before.

'Is the thought of marriage to me so repulsive to you, Carla?'

She dropped her eyes. She had to. What could she say?

*It would be unbearable! Unbearable to be married to you...loving you so much and yet being such a burden to you! Someone you don't want—who is forcing herself on you simply because she's carrying your child!*

She swallowed. That jagged knife was in her throat now. She forced her eyes back to his, reaching for her coffee, making herself drink it.

'No more than it is repulsive for you to marry me,' she said, her voice low.

His gaze was on her—that strange, unreadable gaze that she could not recognise.

'I don't see why it should be repulsive at all,' he said slowly, his eyes never leaving her. He took a breath. 'After all, our time together showed we are, in fact, highly compatible. Neither of us were ever bored in each other's company.'

As he spoke memory flickered in his head. Not of Carla, but of the dinner party with Francesca, in the USA, with all her physics colleagues talking about things he had not the faintest comprehension of. With Carla it had been quite different—

At the choking point of their leash, he could feel his

emotions straining to be free. Unleashed. One, at least, he *could* set free, granting him release.

His long lashes dipped over his eyes, clearing them, leaving them with an expression that Carla recognised only too well, that drew from her a tremor that was deep inside her.

'And sexually, of course, we are highly compatible.'

His gaze rested on her, only momentarily, but for long enough to send colour flaring out into her heated cheeks. She tore her gaze away, clattered her cup back on its saucer, stared out over the sparkling azure water of the pool, suddenly longing for its cooling depths.

The blood was beating in her veins, hot and hectic. Cesare was speaking again, and she heard his words, heard the sensual languor in them that only heated her blood the more.

'You must let me know, Carla, when it is safe for us to resume physical closeness. I know that in the early months it is not advised, but—'

She pushed back her chair, scraping it on the stone. 'I… I need to lie down!' Her voice was high-pitched, and even as she said the words she felt her colour mount.

He was on his feet too, his emotions back under control, back on their leash. 'Of course,' he said. 'You must rest.'

He glanced at his watch. Then back at Carla. Carla, the woman for whom, for all the complications and confusion and complexity, he felt one emotion that was very, very simple.

*Desire.*

He had desired her the moment he'd set eyes on her. He desired her still. That was undeniable—*that* was the emotion he knew he was safe with.

But not at this moment. Indulging it at this early stage of her pregnancy was out of the question, he knew, and for that one reason he must take himself off—let alone for all the other reasons assailing him.

'If you will permit, I will take my leave of you. I'm afraid I must return to the *castello*. I will be away, I fear, for several days. There is a great deal to be sorted out.'

Was there grimness in his voice? Carla looked at his shuttered expression. She was sure there was—and knew the reason. What else could it be for him but grim to perform the unwelcome task of telling his fiancée she'd been usurped by the extreme inconvenience of his former mistress becoming unexpectedly pregnant, requiring a swift marriage to satisfy the exacting terms of his sense of self-respect and familial honour?

She felt bleakness go through her. A sense of unreality. Yet this was real—all too real. That jagged blade drew across her heart again, sending a shot of agony through her. To have her heart's desire—marriage to Cesare—and yet for it to be like this was a travesty. An agony.

*How can I do this? How? Cesare is forcing himself to marry me—just as I tried to force Vito to marry me. Is that all I'm good for? Forcing men to marry me?*

A bead of hysteria bubbled in her throat. She swayed. Instantly Cesare was there, his hand strong under her elbow, steadying her. She felt his hand like a brand upon her.

'Are you all right?'

There was concern in his voice, and his eyes flickered to her abdomen, where only the slightest curve of her figure indicated her pregnancy. It was hardly visible yet—it had taken Vito's bear hug to reveal it to him, as he felt the swell below her waistline.

Vito, whom she had sought to use as a sticking plaster over her broken heart. Broken by the man her pregnancy was now forcing her to marry. Unbearable—just unbearable!

She turned her head to him, her eyes wild. 'Cesare, I can't make you marry me like this! I can't face another unwilling bridegroom! I forced Vito to the altar, using the threat of my mother selling his uncle's shares to Falcone, because I felt so…' She swallowed, finding a word that she could use to Cesare. 'So humiliated.'

She stepped away, taking a huge and painful breath, making herself look at him, her expression troubled, stricken.

'*So* humiliated, Cesare.' She watched his face close up, but went on all the same. 'I tried so hard while we were together—to be the woman you wanted me to be. I never pushed our relationship, never made demands on you.' She paused, remembering the dreadful, hideous moment when he had told her he was leaving. 'And I know you told me you'd never given me reason to expect anything more than what we had. But all the same, when you left me—'

She broke off, her throat thickening. Nearly—so nearly—she had blurted out what she must never, never tell him! What would be the ultimate humiliation for her. The ultimate burden on him.

*He must never know I fell in love with him! Never!*

He stepped towards her, then halted. There was something in his face again—that same look she had not understood before. Did not understand now.

'I was brutal to you that morning,' he said. There was reproof in his voice. Harshness. But not for her. 'Unforgivably so. But it was because—'

He frowned, and she saw him making his next words come, making himself hold her gaze.

'It was because I did not want to part with you,' he said. He shifted restlessly, altering his stance. 'I didn't want to end our relationship. But my hand had been forced. Francesca needed a decision—'

She saw his hand lift, as if he would reach for her, then drop again. She felt emotion welling in her, but did not know what, or how, or why.

'I had to give you up—and I was not pleased to have to do so. I knew I had to make the ending—swift. I never meant...' His eyes rested on hers. 'I never meant for you to feel what you said you felt.' His voice dropped. 'I never meant for you to feel humiliated by my rejection.'

He shook his head slowly, as if clearing it of things he had never thought about. His eyes fixed on hers again.

'I always respected you, Carla. Always. I still do. And if...' He took a heavy breath and she watched the breadth of his powerful chest widen with it. 'If I have seemed... distant, then think only that this has been a shock to me. Less than twenty-four hours ago...' his voice changed '... I saw my life, my future, quite differently from now.'

'I'm sorry,' she said, her voice low. 'So sorry for what has happened.'

'Don't be! It is not of your making. I take full responsibility! My behaviour that night—when I learnt you had not married Viscari—was unforgivable! No wonder you fled from me!' He paused for a moment, his face working. 'But if you had not fled before I woke, then perhaps—'

He stopped, as if silencing himself. His expression changed again. 'This is not the time for further talk,' he said.

He was finishing their discussion, she could see.

'We will have leisure for that ahead of us. For now—well, America is waking up, and I cannot in all conscience delay contacting Francesca.' He glanced at his watch, all businesslike now. 'So I will take my leave of you—for now. I will phone you this evening.'

She nodded wordlessly, and started to walk back indoors. Cesare fell into place beside her. Side by side—yet separate.

Her eyes went to the pair of elegant silk-upholstered sofas by the fireplace.

*That's where he first started to make love to me. The night that he carried me upstairs, began our affair. Made me his.*

But he was never hers. *Never.* Not even now, when he was forcing himself to marry her for the sake of the child she carried. The as yet unreal being who would become, as the months yielded to each other, so very, very real. Binding them to each other with an indissoluble bond, even if she were to divorce him and he was to marry—belatedly—his aristocratic Francesca.

*This child will bind us to each other for ever. With him wishing it were not so and me...me haunted by what can never be. I can never be the woman he loves.*

Into her head came the images on that triptych—the paintings that had catalysed their affair so many months ago. The Count flanked by the two women in his life. The peasant girl, gowned in red silk, who could never aspire to be his wife. And his pale, haunted wife, dutifully married, bonded for life, whether or not she had ever wanted to be.

*I've become them both. The mistress he kept for his bed and the wife he married for duty, for a legitimate heir. Neither woman was happy. How could they be?*

The bitterness was in her throat. Her heart.

They reached the cool, marbled hallway.

'Shall I see you up to your room?'

Cesare's voice penetrated her dark, bleak thoughts.

She shook her head. 'No—it's fine. I remember the way.'

She hadn't meant to sound sarcastic, and hoped she hadn't. Cesare did not seem to notice anyway. He only nodded.

He took her hands, holding them lightly but in a clasp she could not easily pull away from. His eyes looked into hers.

'Carla—I'm… I'm sorry. Sorry for so much. But however…however difficult things are to start with, you have my word that I will do my best—my very best—to be a good husband to you.'

His gaze held hers, but she found it hard…impossible…to bear it.

'I have said that we can make this work, and we can.' He took a breath. 'We can have a very civilised marriage. If we do divorce, at some later date—well, that is not for now. It is for then. And it may not come to that.'

For a moment it was as if he might say something more. She saw a tic in his cheek—indicating, she knew, that he was holding himself in strict self-control.

She drew back her hands. 'Cesare—go. There isn't anything more to say.' Her gaze slid away, not wanting to meet his. Heaviness weighed her down.

*Be careful what you long for.*

The warning sounded in her head. Once she had longed to become Cesare's wife—but not like this. Oh, not like *this*!

'Very well—I will take my leave, then.'

He did not make any gesture of farewell. Once, long ago, he would have dropped a swift, possessing kiss upon her lips, as if it were the seal of possession for their next time together. Now she was carrying his child, and that was seal of possession enough.

*Except that I am a possession he does not want...*

'Goodbye, Cesare.'

She did not say any more. What *could* she say? She'd said everything that could be said. Now they were simply bound to the motions they would need to go through.

She stepped back, waiting for him to leave. But suddenly, impulsively, he took her shoulders, dropped onto her forehead a brief flash of his lips. She felt his hands pressing on her shoulders, the shock of his mouth on her skin.

'We *can* make this work, Carla.'

There was intensity in his voice, in his eyes, pouring into hers. Then he was releasing her, striding away, throwing open the doors and moving out into the sunshine beyond to climb into his car and drive away.

Carla stood, listening to the engine fade into the distance. She walked forward to close the doors. Then slowly, very slowly, went upstairs.

How could they make it work? *How?*

*Impossible...*

# CHAPTER ELEVEN

WITH SURE, SWIFT STEPS, Cesare headed down the winding pathway through the ornamental gardens below the elegant south-facing frontage of the *castello*, down into the deep valley where the narrow river rushed noisily over the boulders and rocks in its bed.

His stride was purposeful. He knew he should be contacting Francesca, but he could not face it—not yet. Instead he was doing what he had so often done as a boy, when he'd been seeking distance from the father he'd never been able to get on with.

By the river's edge he settled himself against an outcrop of rock in the late-afternoon sun, overlooking the tumbling water, fresh and cold and clean. Here, so often in his boyhood, he had found refuge from his father's admonitions and reproofs in watching the wading birds darting, in lying back on sun-warmed stone, hearing the wind soughing in the forest trees. Feeling the deep, eternal bond he had with this domain—the land that was in his blood, in his bones.

How many other Mondave sons had done likewise over the centuries? Waiting to step into their father's shoes, to take over the birthright to which they had been born?

And now, already, another son might be preparing to be born.

Out of nowhere the realisation hit him. Stilling every muscle in his body.

*She carries my child! Perhaps my son—my heir!*

The arc of the sky seemed to wheel about him and he took a shuddering breath. She was not the woman he had thought he would marry. In a single night, with a single act of tumultuous consummation, he had changed his own destiny. He felt emotion convulse in him. Carla— *Carla* would be his wife. Not Francesca. Carla carried his child. Carla would become his *contessa*.

He could feel the blood beating in his veins. Memory flashed through him—memory after memory. All the nights, all the days he'd spent with her. The sensual intensity of her body in his arms. The casual companionship of their times together.

*I did not wish to part with her when I did.*

He had told her that truthfully. Admitted it to her— to himself.

Yet into his head came her bitter words to him. 'You'd be marrying your mistress.'

His expression stilled, becoming masklike. Distant.

*Is this what I want?*

But what did it matter? His own desires were irrelevant. They always had been.

He had changed his own destiny. And now he had no choice but to marry Carla and set aside the woman whom he had always cast in the role of *contessa*. In his inner vision, the portraits in the triptych imposed themselves. The two women—the mistress and the wife—flanking his ancestor. The ancestor who had never had to change his own destiny.

*He had them both—the mistress and the wife.*

His eyes, as he gazed back towards at the *castello*, were suddenly grave. His destiny was to continue the ancient lineage of this house.

*Always I've had to follow the path set out for me— first my duties to my inheritance, then my duty to marry Francesca, and now I am set by my honour to marry Carla, who carries my child. Choice has never been a possibility.*

Slowly, his expression still grave, he got to his feet, made his way back to the *castello*, let himself into the drawing room. Walking through it, he moved out beyond into the state apartments, up the great staircase to the *galleria* above. Knowing just where he was going—and why.

The triptych at the far end was waiting for him. He walked up to it, looked into the face of his ancestor. *Proud*, Carla had called him, and he had taken her to task for it. She had not liked him, his ancestor, had seen only self-satisfaction, an overweening consciousness of his own sense of superiority as a man above others, taking whatever he wanted from life and paying no price for it.

Cesare's eyes went to the pale blonde woman to his ancestor's right. The woman he had married. *Chosen* to marry. Fingering her rosary, she had her prayer book on her lap, a poignant air and an expression of otherworldliness. As if she longed to be elsewhere. As if the sorrows of her life were too great to bear.

His eyes slid away to the other portrait—the other woman, his mistress. *Chosen* to be his mistress. The rich satin gown, the heavy jewels draped over her, the roses in her lap, a symbol of passion, and the ripe swell of her belly. The expression in her eyes showed her consciousness of her illicit relationship with his ancestor.

His ancestor had been free to choose them both. To pay no price for either.

Again Cesare's eyes slid away, back to the portrait of his ancestor. Saw the long-fingered hand, so like his own, closed over the pommel of his sword. His eyes went upwards to the face that Luciezo had preserved for all posterity. For *him*, his descendant, to look upon and contemplate.

For the first time, as he stood there, so sombrely regarding his ancestor's face, he saw something in those dark, brooding eyes—a shadow around the sculpted mouth…a tightness. A tension. As if his gilded, privileged life had not been entirely to his pleasure. Not entirely what he'd wanted…

Across the centuries that divided them Cesare's eyes held those of his ancestor. As if he would divine his innermost thoughts. Drill across the centuries to see inside the man whose blood ran in his veins.

A tightness shaped itself around his own mouth—a tension.

Abruptly, he turned away. Walking with rapid strides, he moved back down the lofty length of the *galleria*, descending the stairs with clattering heels. He walked into the library with its vast array of shelves, its acres of tomes inset.

His archivist was there, working on some research project or other requested by some university's history department. He started as Cesare walked in, and got to his feet.

'Tell me, are there any personal diaries or journals from Count Alessandro—the one Luciezo painted for the triptych?' Cesare asked without preamble.

His archivist blinked. 'I would need to check…' he answered uncertainly.

'Do so, if you please. And anything that you find, have sent to my office. Thank you.'

Cesare took his leave briskly, wondering to himself what impulse had made him make such a request—wondering what he had glimpsed in his ancestor's impassive face.

He pulled his mind away. He had no time to brood further. He must phone Francesca. That could not be postponed any longer.

His brows drew together. Was this really something that could be said over the phone? Telling her that he could no longer marry her? His frown deepened. He owed her more than that, surely—more than a cursory phone call.

*I have to tell her to her face—I owe her that courtesy, that consideration, at least.*

He would be changing her expected destiny, just as his was now changed.

He gave a heavy sigh, sitting himself down at the desk in his office, calling up airline websites, seeing when he could fly out.

He would have to tell Carla what he was doing. She would understand. He would be away a handful of days—no more than that, allowing for time differences across the Atlantic. Then he would return and announce his engagement to Carla.

Carla lay in bed, listening to the dawn chorus. She had scarcely slept. She had spent the remainder of the previous day, after Cesare had left, lying on her bed, sleepless, and then restlessly going down to the pool, immersing herself in the cooling water.

As she'd worked her way up and down in a slow breaststroke she'd felt a kind of numbness steal over her. It had lasted through the evening, through dinner—served with Lorenzo's usual skilful unobtrusiveness—and even through the phone call that Cesare had dutifully made.

Conversation had been awkward—how could it have been otherwise?—and after enquiring how she was, and how she had spent the rest of the day, his voice constrained, he had informed her in an even more constrained fashion that he would be flying to the USA the next day to see Francesca.

She had been understanding of his reasons—but as she'd hung up she'd felt a wave of guilt go through her.

*He didn't ask for this! He didn't ask for me to present him with my pregnancy, turning his life upside down as it has!*

And the woman who'd thought she would be marrying Cesare—*her* life was being turned upside down as well. Ripped out from under her.

*By me—by my giving in and agreeing to marry Cesare. Who feels he has no choice but to marry me.*

Just as she had tried to force Vito to marry her. Making him do what she wanted. Ripping up his life. Ripping up the life he had been planning to make with that blonde English girl he was now so urgently seeking.

She closed her eyes in misery.

*Haven't I done enough damage to people? Do I have to ruin Cesare's life too—and his fiancée's?*

The knowledge hung darkly, bleakly inside her.

Silently, she ran her mind back, thinking of the father she could not remember—had scarcely known. For the first time she thought of how he must have felt, told that he had to marry a woman he did not love because she carried his child. Had he had other plans? Other dreams?

Dreams that had been smashed to pieces? Of a life he'd wanted to live and that had been barred to him?

Just as her pregnancy was barring Cesare from having the life *he* wanted. Requiring him to do his duty, take *her* for his wife instead of the woman he wanted to marry.

A cry sounded in her head.

*I don't want to force Cesare to marry me!*

She felt her heart constrict. Memory poured in around it.

*I had my happiness here—as much as I could ever have with Cesare. I knew from the start it was all I could have with him. That he could never be mine—not the way I came to long for him to be.*

She felt her eyes distend, looking back into the past, the days and nights she had spent with Cesare. Then looking into the future she had now committed herself to—becoming his wife, his *contessa*, but not the one he had chosen of his own free will.

*I can't do this to him.*

With a sudden impulse she threw back the bedclothes, her hand automatically easing across her abdomen as she got up. Inside—invisible, almost intangible—new life was growing.

She felt her throat close with sudden, overpowering emotion.

*This is Cesare's gift to me. Not his heart, but his child. And it will be enough.*

With swift, resolute movements she dressed, repacked her case, headed downstairs. She needed to find Lorenzo—needed him to summon her a taxi to the airport. Needed to do what she knew she must do—set Cesare free.

* * *

With heavy tread Cesare walked down the ornate stair-case to the *piano nobile* of the eighteenth-century section of the *castello*. He was booked on a flight to the USA, and his helicopter pilot was on standby now to fly him to the airport. He'd emailed Francesca last night, to let her know of his impending visit—but had given no indication of his purpose. It would be a shock to her, what he must tell her, but it was one he had no choice but to inflict.

Yet again, as it had done the previous afternoon, across his mind flashed the image of that Luciezo portrait. The ancestor who had had complete freedom of choice in his life. He ejected the image. What was the point of think-ing about his forebear? His own life afforded no such freedom of choice.

Abruptly he went into his office, snapped on his lap-top, dragging his mind back to the present and all the difficulties that enmeshed him. He must check to see if Francesca had replied to his email. She had—but it took him a moment to steel himself to open it. The enormity of what he was going to have to do to her weighed upon him. She did not deserve it.

*Yet nor does Carla deserve to have to marry me. She made it clear enough to me yesterday how reluctant she is!*

And he—what did *he* feel about it?

He veered his mind away. That was a path he did not wish to follow. Not now. Not yet. First he must smash up Francesca's life.

He clicked open her email. Made himself focus on what she had written. For an instant, her words blurred, then resolved.

He started to read.

My dearest Ces, your email has been a catalyst for me. I have something I can no longer delay telling you.

He read on, disbelievingly.

Then, as the full impact of what she had written hit him, he sat back, his chest tight. Slowly he reached to close down his laptop. He would reply—but not yet. For now he could only sit there. Taking in what she had written. Taking in the implications.

A discreet knock sounded on his office door. At his abstracted permission to enter, his archivist came in.

'The papers you asked after yesterday,' he said, placing a leather-bound folder in front of Cesare. 'This is Count Alessandro's private journal.'

Cesare thanked him, his manner still absent, his mind still elsewhere. Then, as if to shake his thoughts from him, he reached for the folder and opened it, bringing out a marbled notebook, its pages mottled with age, covered in thin, flowing script. Sixteenth-century Italian, difficult to decipher.

But across the centuries his ancestor's words reached to him. And as he read a frown started across his face. He read on in silence, his expression sombre. Then, at last, he lifted his eyes from the page, from the ink scored so deeply into the antique paper, as if reverberating still with the vehemence of his ancestor.

For a long while he sat. Feeling emotion swirl deep within him—turbid, inchoate. Making sense of what he'd read. Seeing, too, the printed words on his screen—Francesca's email—melding with the antique script in front of him.

Then, with a sudden intake of breath, he pushed back his chair. He needed to stand down his helicopter pilot. And he needed to drive back to Lazio.

He was halfway to the door when he felt his phone vibrate in his jacket pocket. He pulled it out, glanced at the screen.

A voicemail.

From Carla.

He stilled. Pressed 'play'.

And everything in his world changed again…

# CHAPTER TWELVE

CARLA WAS SWIMMING—slowly but steadily ploughing up
and down the length of the pool at her mother's villa. Had
it really only been a week since she'd made her decision
to set Cesare free?

As she climbed out of the water she felt a familiar
tightening of her chest—an ache of emotion burning
within her. Regret? Could it be that? Regret at having
walked away from the one chance she would have to be
part of Cesare's life?

No—marriage to Cesare like that would have been
unbearable! She had told him so, and it was true. True,
true, *true*. So that was what she must hold to—all that
must guide her now. However hard it was.

'Darling, are you all right? You mustn't overdo it.'

Marlene's voice was concerned as she hurried forward with an enveloping towel, draping it around Carla's wet back.

Carla smiled her thanks, taking a seat in the sunshine
while her mother fussed about her. Her mother had been
fussing…hovering…ever since she'd arrived back from
Italy. And as she'd heard her daughter out Carla had seen
the reaction in her face.

'He's offered to *marry* you?' she'd said.

Her eyes had worked over Carla. Then slid away into her own past.

'The decision must be yours,' Marlene had said slowly. 'But for my part I think it's the right one—the decision you've made.' She'd paused a moment before continuing. 'Marrying your father was the worst mistake I made. I'd hoped it would make him love me. But it did the opposite. He married me because of pressure from his father, who held the purse strings and did not want any scandal. But when his father died—you were only a toddler—he took off.' She'd paused again. 'When he was killed in that car crash there was a woman with him—and he'd just filed for divorce.'

She'd looked at her daughter, her eyes troubled.

'I ruined his life—and marriage brought no happiness for me either.' She'd taken a breath, exhaled sadly. 'No happy ending—for me *or* for him.'

*No happy ending...*

The words hovered in Carla's mind. Her mother's sorry tale only confirmed the rightness of her decision to leave Italy, to tell Cesare in that solitary voicemail that it was all she could face doing—that she preferred single motherhood to forcing him to marry her instead of the woman he wanted to marry.

*'Go back to her, Cesare, and make the marriage you have always been destined to make. I don't want to be the one to part you from her—not for any reason. She is the woman you chose for your wife, not me. The time we had together was very...very special to me. But it is over. I wish you well. This is my choice. Please do not try and dissuade me from it.'*

She had had no reply. Knew that she must be glad she

had not. Knew that she must be glad she had set him free. Must bear the pain that came with that.

*To have nothing of him... Nothing—just as I had when he left me—nothing of him.*

Yet as she sat sipping at her iced fruit juice, feeling the Spanish summer heat warm her damp limbs, her hand slipped to curve around the swell of her abdomen.

*No, not nothing. This is Cesare's gift to me.*

And memories—memories that she would never lose. *Never!*

Cesare reaching for her, taking her mouth with his, slow and seductive, arousing and sensual, taking his fill of her as her hands stroked his smooth, hard body, glorying in the feel of it beneath her exploring, delicately circling fingertips.

Cesare, his body melded with hers in the white heat of passion, desire burning with a searing flame, until she cried out, her body arching in ecstasy, the ecstasy of his possession...

A possession she could never know again.

She felt that ache form in her chest again, around her heart. An ache that would never leave her. Could never leave her. The ache of a broken heart that could never mend. She could never have the man she loved, loving her in return.

No happy ending...

Cesare walked up the wide, imposing staircase to the panelled, gilded *galleria*. Along the walls priceless Old Masters marched on either side. But he did not look at them. He went only to the far end of the long room. Stood before the triptych, letting his eyes rest on the three portraits, thinking of their tangled, entwined lives.

Once he had thought he knew them…presumed to know them…these three people from so long ago. Thought to know his ancestor, whose blood ran in his veins. The ancestor who had been free to choose, flanked by the women either side of him. The woman he'd chosen for his wife. The woman he'd chosen for his mistress.

*Free to choose.*

Abruptly, he turned away. Nodded at the two men waiting patiently at the entrance to the *galleria*.

'You can remove it now,' he told them.

Without a backward glance, he walked out of the room.

His expression was unreadable. But emotion was heavy within him. Weighing him down. In his head he heard, over and over again, as he had done since he had first listened to her voicemail, Carla's farewell to him.

*'This is my choice. Please do not try and dissuade me from it.'*

Behind him he heard the sounds of the triptych being taken down, dismantled. Packed up.

He walked on, face set.

Carla was breakfasting with her mother. The weather was cooler today now, and she was glad. Glad, too, that by the time she was in late pregnancy she would be cooler still.

As it did so often, her hand glided protectively over her abdomen. Her thoughts were full. She must stay calm, serene. Let no agitation break through—no emotion or trauma. She had chosen this path—single motherhood—over a tormented marriage to Cesare. It had been the right choice to make.

Her expression changed. Vito was appalled that she was not going to marry Cesare, but she remained adamant. She would not be swayed. And, for himself, Vito had finally found a ray of hope in his search for the woman she had caused to flee. She might have been located at last. She wished him well—hoped that he would find the happiness he sought.

As for herself—well, happiness was beyond her now. Cesare had accepted her decision. She had heard nothing more from him.

*I grew up fatherless, and my child will too. But it will have me, and my mother, and safety and love, and that is all that really matters.*

That was what she told herself. That was what she must believe. As for Cesare—well, he would marry his *marchese*'s daughter and live the life he had always planned.

*And I will have his child—his gift to me.*

It was more than she had ever hoped to have of him. She must be content with that. In time her battered heart would heal, and Cesare would have no place in it any longer.

A sliver of pain pierced her, but she ignored it. Soon, surely, it would cease. The ache in her heart would ease. It must.

It *must*.

'The mail, *señora*.'

Her mother's maid was placing a stash of post on the table, breaking Carla's painful reverie. Idly, she watched her mother sort it, then pause.

'This is for you,' she said, holding up a bulky envelope, her expression wary.

Carla felt herself tense—the stamp was Italian, the dark, decisive handwriting instantly recognisable. Steeling herself, she opened it, taking out several folded papers.

*It will be some sort of legal document I have to sign, foregoing any claim on his estate for the baby, or a contract making me a maintenance allowance or something.*

But as she unfolded them she gasped. It was neither of those things.

'Darling, what is it?' Marlene's voice was immediately alarmed.

Carla stared, then looked blankly across at her mother. In a hollow voice she spoke. 'It's from a secure art vault in Rome. It tells me...' She swallowed. 'It tells me that the Luciezo-Caradino triptych is now in storage. That it is being held in trust—for...for...'

Instinctively her hand went to her ripening abdomen, her eyes distending. She dropped the letter, seized up the piece of paper with Cesare's handwriting, and the third folded document.

'Mum, I—I—'

She could say no more—only got to her feet, stumbling slightly as she walked away, past the pool, to find the bench underneath the shade of the bougainvillea arbour, overlooking the beach.

She sat down with trembling legs. Opened Cesare's letter to read it. The writing came into focus, burned into her retinas—Cesare's words to her.

*I have made this bequest to you not only for the child you carry but as a token—a symbol of what is between us. To understand why, I ask you to read the enclosed. It is a typed transcript from the personal diary of Count Alessandro, who was portrayed by Luciezo.*

*Read it now, before you read more of this letter.*

She let the page fall to her lap, then unfolded the transcript with fumbling fingers. Made herself read it. The Italian was old-fashioned, with some words she did not know. But as she read she felt the world shift and rearrange itself.

Slowly, with a hollow feeling within her, she set it aside, picked up Cesare's letter again. Resumed reading.

It was brief.

*I will not make the mistake he made. Whatever decision you now make, know that I am not my ancestor.*

It was signed starkly, simply, with his name: *Cesare.*

Carefully—very, very carefully—her heart hammering in her chest, she put the papers back in the envelope. Then she went up onto the patio, where her mother was anxiously looking for her.

Marlene started to get to her feet, but Carla stayed her.

'I have to go to him,' she said.

Her voice was strange. Hollow. Her heart was filling with an emotion she could feel overwhelming her, drowning her.

The hire car ate up the miles, racing along the *autostrada* across the lush countryside of Lazio as she snaked ever upwards into the mountainous terrain, gaining at last, as darkness fell, the mighty stone entrance to the massive bulk of the Castello Mantegna.

*I will not make the mistake he made.*

Slowly, she made her way to the gate, looked at the walls of the *castello* louring over her. A postern door was set into the towering iron-studded gates, with an ancient metal bell-pull beside it. And a more modern intercom and surveillance camera.

She pressed the buzzer, giving her name. There was silence—complete and absolute silence. No response at all from within that stony fastness.

Her head sank. Defeat was in the slump of her shoulders.

*Fool! Oh—fool, fool, fool!*

The words berated her, like blows.

*'Signorina! Prego—prego!'*

The man at the now open postern gate was in the uniform of a security guard—which, Carla realised dimly, given the value of the artworks within, even without the priceless triptych, made sense. He was beckoning her frantically.

Heart in her mouth, she stepped inside, through the gate into the vast, cobbled courtyard within. The guard was apologising fervently, but her eyes were darting either side to the ranks of former stables, now garaging, and the old medieval kitchens, now staff and estate office quarters. Both wings were utterly dominated by the huge mass of the *castello* itself, rising darkly ahead of her.

Dusk was gathering in this huge paved courtyard, and security lights were coming on as she was conducted across it to a pair of palatial iron-studded doors that were being thrown open even as she spoke. Inside, she could see a huge, cavernous hall, brilliantly lit with massive candelabras. And across it, striding rapidly, came the figure of the man she had come to brave in his mountain fastness.

Cesare di Mondave, Conte di Mantegna, lord of his domain…

Faintness drummed at her. The effects of her early start that morning—after a night in which the hours had passed sleepless and tormented with confusion, with emotions that had pummelled through her mercilessly, relentlessly—the drive to the airport, the flight to Rome, the disembarking, the hiring of the car, the journey here. Exhaustion weighed her down like a heavy, smothering coat. Her nerves were shattered, her strength gone.

She sank downwards.

He was there instantly, with an oath, catching her. Catching her up into his arms, even though she weighed more now than she had ever done, as her body ripened with its precious burden. But as if she were a feather he bore her off. She closed her eyes, head sinking onto his shoulder. Feeling his strength, his warmth, his very scent...

*Cesare.*

His name soared in her head, fighting through the clouds, the thick mist that surrounded her. He was going through doorways, up a marble staircase, all the while casting urgent, abrupt instructions at those whose footsteps she heard running. There were anxious voices, male and female, until at the last she was lowered down upon the softest counterpane. She sank into it and her eyes fluttered. She was lying on a vast, ornate four-poster, silk-hung, and lights were springing up everywhere. Cesare was hovering above her, and there was a bevy of people, so it seemed, behind him.

'*Il dottore!* Get him here—now!'

There was command—stern, urgent—in that deep voice. Obedience in the one that answered it.

'*Si! Si!* At once—at once. He is summoned!'

She struggled upright, emotion surging through her

again, past the tide of faintness. 'No…no… I don't need a doctor—I'm fine… I'm fine.'

Cesare looked down at her. The room, she realised, was suddenly empty. There was only him, towering over her.

'He is on his way, nevertheless,' he said.

There was still command in his voice. Then his expression changed. His gaze speared into hers, and in his face Carla saw something that stopped the breath in her body.

'Why did you come? Tell me—*Dio mio*—tell me!'

She had never heard him speak like that—with so much raw, vehement emotion in his voice. She felt an answering emotion in herself, yet dared not feel it…*dared* not.

Her eyes, so deep a violet, searched his, still not daring to believe.

Slowly, falteringly, she spoke. 'When you wrote…*what* you wrote—I read… I read Count Alessandro's words… and then yours…'

Her voice was strained, her words disjointed. Her eyes searched his. She still did not dare to believe. This was the man prepared to marry her out of duty, out of responsibility. So how could he have written what he had? *Why?* Once before she had allowed herself to hope—hope that his feelings might be starting to echo hers…the very night he'd told her he was leaving her. Destroying her—

So how could she dare to hope again? *Could* she dare? She had to *know*.

'Cesare, why…why did you write what you did? That you would not make the mistake he did?' Her voice was faint, low. Yet her eyes were wide, distended.

That same vehemence was in his face—the same emotion that was stopping the breath in her body, that she had never seen before in it. It had not been there—not once—in all the time she'd known him.

His eyes burned into hers. 'You read his words,' he said. 'He married his *contessa* from duty, from expectation. Yet she never wanted to marry him. Never wanted to marry at all. Her vocation was to become a nun. But her family forced her to marry, to do her duty, to bear his children as a noblewoman should do. And he—Count Alessandro—he did as a nobleman should do: protective of his honour, taking pride in his ancient name. He did not love her, his *contessa*—that was not relevant.'

In Carla's head she heard again what Cesare had said when he had informed her he was intending to marry— that loving Francesca, his intended wife, was not 'relevant'. As she remembered, as she gazed at him now, still not daring to believe, she felt the same emotion that had brought her here, to his ancient *castello*, driven by an urgency that had possessed her utterly.

'And yet...' She heard the fracture in Cesare's voice. 'And yet there was a woman he *did* love.' He paused, his eyes still spearing hers. 'It was his mistress. The mistress he had taken from desire, whom he had never thought to marry. It was his mistress with whom he spent his hours of leisure. And it was the family he had with *her*—for babies were impossible to stop in those times, as you know—that he loved. Not the solitary son he had with his *contessa*—the son who grew to manhood hating the father who so clearly had no time for him, no love. Just as he had no time, no love, for the son's mother, the Contessa.'

Abruptly he let go her hand, got to his feet. Thrusting his hands into his pockets, he strode to the windows

overlooking the valley beyond. He spoke with his back
to her, gazing out at the night beyond the panes of glass,
as if he could see into it, through it, back into a past that
was not the youth of Count Alessandro's heir—but his
own youth.

'My father had no time for me,' he said.

His voice had changed. Thinned. He was speaking of
things he never spoke of. But now he must.

'He thought me oversensitive! Unlike him, I did not
think that being a brilliant shot, a hunter of game, of
wildlife slaughtered to hang as trophies on his walls, was
a worthy accomplishment, fitting for my rank. He despised me for what he called my squeamishness. Judged
me for it. Condemned me. Openly told me I was not up
to being his heir.'

He was silent a moment, and his lips pressed together.
Then he went on.

'When he died I determined to prove myself—to prove
him wrong. Oh, I still never took to his murderous love
of slaughtering wildlife, but I immersed myself in the
management of all the heritage that had come to me—
the enterprises, the people in my employ, the tenants and
clients, all those whom the estates support and who support the estates. I did my duty and beyond to all that my
name and title demanded and required of me. I gave his
ghost, the ghosts of *all* my ancestors, no cause at all to
think me lacking!'

He turned now, looking back across the room to the
figure lying propped up against the pillows on his bed,
to the swell of her body visible now in the lamplight
limning her features. He felt emotion move within him
as he spoke on.

'And the final duty for me to discharge,' he said, his

voice grave now, and his expression just as grave, 'was to marry. The final duty of all who bear my name and title is to marry and create a successor.'

His eyes shifted slightly, then came back to Carla. Her eyes were fixed on him, her face gaunt now.

Cesare took a breath. 'My father always approved of Francesca—always identified her as the ideal woman I should marry. She was suitable in every way—and he told me I would be fortunate indeed if she would agree to the match.'

He shut his eyes again, his face convulsing, then opened his eyes once more. Let his gaze rest unflinchingly on Carla.

'And so she would have been.' He stopped, his jaw tightening. 'If I had not met you.'

There was silence—complete silence.

'But when Francesca wrote to me, told me she had gained her doctorate earlier than she'd expected, she said she would need to choose between staying on in the USA and coming home to marry me.' He paused, his eyes looking inward, his mouth tightening. 'My first reaction to her letter should have told me.' His face twisted. 'Told me that I had changed profoundly. For my first reaction was immediate.' He paused. 'It was to cry out in my head, *Not yet!*'

His gaze came back to Carla.

'Instead—' He took a heavy breath. 'Instead I told myself how *ideal* marriage to Francesca would be. How entirely suited she was to be my wife…how well she would take on the role of my *contessa*. She knew all that it would entail and, unlike my own mother, who made being her husband's wife the sole reason for her existence, Francesca would continue her academic research here in Italy. When she gave me her decision I knew there was only one thing for me to do.' He paused again, and when he spoke his voice was heavier still. 'Remove you from my life'.

She had shut her eyes. He could see it—see how her fingers on the counterpane had spasmed suddenly.

His voice was quiet now, and yet she could hear every word as clearly, as distinctly as the space between them would allow.

'But there was a place I could not remove you from. A place I did not even know you had come to occupy.'

She could hear him now, in the darkness of her blinded vision.

'A place, Carla, where you will always be. That you can never be removed from. *Never!*'

The sudden vehemence in his voice made her eyes flare open. She could see his gaze burning at her.

'I did not know you were there, Carla! I did not know it even when I was filled with jealous rage—a rage I knew with my head that I had no right at all to feel. Yet it tore me apart all the same! When I heard that you'd become engaged to Vito Viscari—' His voice twisted. 'Madness overcame me that night I came to your apartment, blackly rejoicing that he had not married you.' His expression changed again, became gaunt and bleak. 'Even when Viscari told me that you carried my child—even then, Carla, when I knew we would marry, *must* marry, even then I did not realise.'

He stood still, hands thrust deep into his pockets, looking at her across the space that was between them.

'All I could think was how I'd never been permitted to choose—how first it had been my *duty* to marry Francesca, if she would have me, and then…' he took a ragged breath '…it became my *duty* to marry you instead.'

She shut her eyes for a moment, feeling the bleakness she had felt at knowing she was forcing Cesare to marry her. But he was speaking still, his voice changing yet again.

'When I came back here I found myself seeking out that Luciezo portrait—thinking how my ancestor had been free to choose whatever he willed, as I had never been. And yet—'

He broke off, his face working. Carla's eyes were on him again, wide, distended, and her throat was tightening.

'Yet when I read his journal…' He exhaled slowly, his eyes never leaving hers, filled with a darkness that chilled her suddenly. 'When I read his final words, then—'

When he resumed, his voice was raw.

'He cursed himself—cursed what he had done, the choice that he had made in marrying a woman he could not love. He had blighted his whole life—and the lives of both his wife and his mistress, condemning them all to unhappiness. It was a mistake that could never be mended—*never*!'

Carla felt her own face work, her throat close.

Words burst from her, pained and anguished. 'That is what I felt *I* would do if I married you! It would be as if I had become *both* those Caradino portraits—the pregnant mistress becoming the unhappy wife!'

Her fingers clenched again, spasming.

'I knew you didn't want to marry me! How could you, when you'd chosen another woman to marry, had set me aside as you had? How could I condemn you to a loveless marriage to me—condemn you to a marriage you'd never wanted?'

Her voice dropped.

'How could I condemn *myself* to it? Condemn myself to the kind of marriage my own mother made—and bitterly regretted. Just as my father regretted it. And…' Her throat closed painfully. 'Just as you would regret it too. Regret a loveless marriage—'

She broke off, emotion choking her voice. Her eyes closed, and it was as if she could feel sharp shards of glass beneath her lids. There was a sudden dip in the bed—the heavy weight of Cesare jackknifing down beside her. His hand closed over hers, stilling its clenching.

Her eyes flared open, diamond tears within.

Emotion was in his face, strong and powerful, sending a sudden surge to her pulse, a tightening of her throat. There was a searing in her heart against what he might say next.

'It would not be loveless.' Intensity infused his voice. 'It would *not* be loveless,' Cesare said again. 'When I read Alessandro's cry of despair and remorse for the mistake he had made, the mistake that could never be amended, I knew—finally *knew*—what I had blinded myself to! I realised, with a flash of lightning in my eyes, that I could leave you, or you could leave me, and it would make no difference—none at all. For you were lodged in that place from which you could never be removed.'

He paused. Eyes resting on her. The truth was in them, as he knew it must be now.

'In my heart, Carla. Where you will always be. *You* are the woman I would choose for my wife. Whether you carry our child or not.' He took a breath. 'I would choose *you*—because I love you.'

JULIA JAMES 179

She heard his words—heard that one most precious word that was more to her than all the world—heard it and felt her heart fill with an emotion she could scarcely bear. Did she see the same emotion in his eyes?

She felt Cesare's strong hand press down on hers. Another ragged breath broke from him.

'*That* is what I wanted you to know. *Needed* you to know. You may not love me, Carla, but I *needed* you to know my heart. So that whatever choice you make now— whether to marry me or not—you know that you are in my heart for all time. And that you always will be.'

He took a shuddering breath. Poured all that he was into his next words.

'The choice is yours—it always will be—but if you feel…if you *can* feel even a fraction of what I feel for you, will you accept my hand, my heart, my life, my love?'

Carla felt her hand move beneath his. Curl into his. Hold his fast. Those diamond tears were still glittering in her eyes and she could not speak. She started to lift her free hand and in an instant he had caught it. Raised it slowly to his lips.

She saw his expression change, grow sombre again.

'Alessandro is dust,' he said. 'As are his wife and the woman he loved. For them all, his regret, his remorse, came too late. But we—' And yet again he broke off as strong emotion worked in his face. 'We live *now*—and we can make our future what we will. We can seize it, Carla—seize it and make it our own!'

His hands pressed hers.

'My most beloved *preciosa*, will you accept my hand in marriage? Will you stand at my side all my life, as my beloved wife—my *contessa*? Will you give me the priceless gift of your heart, your love? Will you let the precious child within you be the proof and symbol of our love, our life together? Will you be…' his voice caught '…in one person, both my wife and the woman I love?'

His voice changed, became overwrought with emotion.

'Will you unite the triptych—not, as you feared, as an unhappy mistress becoming the unhappy wife, but in the way it *should* have been united? So that there is no division between wife and love—united in the same woman. United in *you*.'

She felt her heart turn over and fill to the brim with a joy she had never thought to feel.

*Cesare, oh, Cesare—my Cesare!*

He leant forward to kiss her tears away, then kissed her mouth. Her fingers clutched his as he drew away again.

'I tried not to fall in love with you,' she said, her voice low and strained. 'Right from the first, when we began our affair, I knew that that was all it could ever be. I knew all along there could be no future for us. That one day you would set me aside to make the kind of marriage I knew you must make. But I could not stop myself. I fell in love with you despite my warnings to myself. And when you ended it… I went into a kind of madness.'

Her face shadowed.

'I behaved despicably to Vito. I nearly ruined his life. That's why—' She took a ragged breath. 'That's why I realised I could not ruin your life when you did not love me. When you wanted to marry Francesca—'

She broke off, her expression changing suddenly.

'*Francesca!* Cesare—?' Concern was open in her voice.

He smiled. A wry, self-mocking smile. 'Francesca,' he said, 'has gone to California! It seems,' he went on, half rueful, half relieved, 'that she, too, did not wish to make a loveless marriage—or any marriage at all! She wrote to tell me that out of the blue she has been invited to join an ultra-prestigious research team on the West Coast, led by a Nobel laureate, and it is her heart's desire to take up the post. She is beside herself with excitement, and knows I will understand why she cannot marry me now after all.'

He smiled again, and Carla could see relief in it, as well as a self-deprecating ruefulness.

'Astrophysics is her love—not being my *contessa*!'

Carla's expression changed. 'Count Alessandro's wife wanted to be a nun…' she mused. 'That was *her* true calling.'

Cesare nodded, seeing the analogy. 'And scientific research is calling Francesca. For which—' he dropped a kiss on Carla's forehead '—I am profoundly grateful.' He smiled again. 'You will like her, you know, if she makes it to our wedding. But you will have to accept that you won't understand much of what fascinates her so.'

The wry look was back in his face again, and then his expression altered a little, and he frowned slightly.

'Maybe that was a warning to me—the fact that I found it hard to communicate with her about her work. Although I know she would always have discharged her responsibilities as Contessa, her heart would not have been in it. I think,' he said, 'it took our betrothal to make her realise that what she had grown up with—the expectation she'd always had of what her future was to be—was not, after all, what she wanted.' His voice grew sombre again now. 'Just as did I.'

He paused, his eyes holding Carla's. Then went on.

'I do not ask forgiveness for what I did to you—only

for…understanding. If you can bring yourself to give me that, then—'

She did not let him finish. 'I give you both, Cesare—I understand *and* I forgive! From my heart—believe me!'

Her voice was broken with the urgency of what she said.

His expression changed again, lightening now, and he slid the palm of one hand across her abdomen, catching his breath as he felt the ripening curve of her body. For a moment he closed his eyes, almost unable to believe that this moment had come. A great peace had come upon him, filling his every cell, suffusing his body—his mind and his soul.

He leant towards her, his lips brushing hers, and Carla met them, her eyes fluttering shut as if to contain the immensity of the joy within her. His kiss was warm and deep, and in it were the seeds for a harvest of happiness she would reap all her life.

'My dearest heart,' Cesare said. 'My dearest love.'

He kissed her again—tenderly, cherishingly—this woman he loved, whom he had so nearly lost. Who would now be at his side and in his heart all his life.

For a long, long moment they simply held each other, feeling the closeness of their hearts, feeling the peace of love envelop them. Unite them.

'*My* Cesare,' she whispered.

For now he *was* hers—truly hers—and all her hopes had been fulfilled, all her fears and losses had gone for ever.

Her fingers slid around the strong nape of his neck, splaying into his raven hair. She knew he was hers and she was his. For all time—now and far beyond mere time.

There was the sound of a knock upon the door, the door opening. Cesare's steward announced the doctor.

Cesare glanced at Carla. She had a look of dazed happiness on her face that made a smile curve at Cesare's mouth. Maybe the doctor was not needed. But the woman he loved carried a gift for them both that was infinitely precious.

After greeting the doctor, he left him to his examination and, out in the hall, gave instructions for the best vintage champagne in his extensive cellars to be fetched. Then, in time-honoured fashion he paced outside the bedroom door, until the doctor emerged.

'Well?' He pounced immediately.

The doctor nodded. 'Quite well,' he pronounced. 'Fatigue and an excess of emotion, that is all.' He cleared his throat. 'Would I be presumptuous,' he asked, his eyes slightly wary, 'in offering you, Signor Conte, my felicitations?'

Relief flooded through Cesare. He met the doctor's eyes. 'You would not,' he said decisively.

He spoke deliberately. His steward had returned, ready to show the doctor out. The words Cesare had spoken would be all his steward would require. Within ten minutes every person in the *castello* would know that a different chatelaine from the one they had been expecting would now be in their future.

His heart, as he went back into his bedroom, was soaring. Carla possessed the one attribute that was all he needed in his wife.

*She is the woman I love—and will love all my days.*

And he was the man she loved.

What else could matter but that? *That* was what his

ancestor Alessandro had taught him, through his own heart-wrenching regret.

*I will not make the mistake he made.*

The words seared in his consciousness again as he swept Carla—the woman he loved—into his arms.

'The doctor tells me all is well.'

His eyes were warm—so warm—and Carla felt her heart turn over. Could she really be this happy? Could she truly be this happy? And yet she was.

*This is real, and it is true—it is not my mere hopes and dreams!*

Wonder filled her, and then pierced even more as Cesare drew back and with a sudden movement did what she had never seen him do before. He took from his little finger the signet ring engraved with the crest of his house, which he *never* removed—not for bathing, or swimming, or for any reason—and then reached for her hand again.

His eyes went to her. 'For my *contessa*,' he said, and slid the ring, still warm from his skin, onto her finger.

Then he closed his hand over hers, knuckling her hand under his. He smiled.

'There's actually a signet ring specifically for the Contessa,' he said. 'My mother wore it always from her wedding day. But for tonight, my dearest love, as we celebrate this moment, wear my ring, which I have never taken from my finger since the day I placed it there—the day my father died.'

She felt her throat catch. So simple a gesture—so profound a meaning. She felt tears well in her eyes again. His hand tightened over hers.

'No more tears!' he commanded. 'I will not permit it!'

Her face quivered into tearful laughter. 'There speaks *il Conte*!'

'Indeed he does,' he agreed, patting her hand.

He dropped a kiss on her forehead, then started to draw her to her feet.

'If you feel ready, *mi amore*, can you face my household? My steward will now have informed everyone of our news, and I have ordered champagne to be served in the salon. One glass, I am sure, will not harm our child.'

He helped her stand up, and walked with her to the door.

'And then I am sure you will wish to phone your mother, will you not? I hope she will be glad for you now that she need have no fear that you are repeating her own experience of marriage, and now that she knows how much I love you.'

His expression softened, and Carla felt again that wash of bliss go through her.

Then another emotion caught her. She halted.

'Cesare—my mother is…controversial,' she said uneasily. 'When she sold Guido Viscari's shares after Vito refused to marry me, Lucia ensured she became *persona non grata* in Rome—'

'I think you will find,' replied Cesare, his voice dry and edged with hauteur, 'that as my mother-in-law, and grandmother to my heir, she will find *no* doors closed to her—in Rome, or anywhere else!'

Carla smiled. 'Thank you,' she acknowledged gratefully. 'Though I know she means to live in Spain now, which makes things easier all round.'

'She will visit here whenever she wishes,' Cesare ordained. 'Starting with our wedding. Which—' he glanced at her speakingly, his eyes going to the slight swell where their child was growing '—I would ask to be as soon as possible.'

She looked at him, her eyes glowing with love. 'I would marry you tonight! You need only send for your chaplain!'

His hand stilled on the handle of the door before he opened it. 'Before, you wanted a civil ceremony only.'

Carla shook her head vigorously. 'Cesare—now I will marry you in your chapel here—before God and all your ancestors. I want our marriage to last all our lives and for all eternity, for that is how long I will love you!'

She leaned into him, resting her head against his shoulder, feeling his strength, his presence, his love for her. Her hand entwined with his, the gold of his signet ring indenting her finger, their hands meshing fast, indissoluble. She felt his hand tighten in return, heard the husk in his voice as he answered her.

'And it is how long I will love *you*,' he promised her.

He took a breath, resolution in his stance as he opened their bedroom door. Beyond was the wide landing, the marble staircase sweeping down to the hall, and waiting there, he knew, would be all his household. Beyond he could see the salon doors thrown wide open, brilliantly lit, and champagne awaiting them all.

He stepped out with Carla, leading her to the head of the stairs. And as they paused for a moment, looking down, applause broke out below. He turned to Carla, raised her hand to his lips, then smiled at her, with a smile as warm as the love in his heart.

'Ready?' he murmured.

'Quite, quite ready,' she answered.

And at his side—as she would always be now—she went down with him to take her place as the woman he would marry, the woman he would love all his life—his wife and his own true love. One and the same.

\* \* \*

*The metre-thick stone walls of the* castello's *chapel seemed to absorb all the low murmurings of the small, select congregation, which stilled as the priest—Cesare's chaplain—raised his hands and began to speak the words of the age-old sacrament.*

*Inside her breast Carla could feel her heart beating strongly. Emotion filled her—and she felt a low, fine tremble go through her as she stood there, her cream lace gown moulding to the fullness of her ripening figure. Stood beside the man who was her bridegroom. Waiting for him to say the words that would unite them in marriage—as they were already united in love, each for each other, and both of them for the child who would soon be born to them, who would continue the ancient family of which she was now an indissoluble part.*

\* \* \* \* \*

# MILLS & BOON

## THE HEART OF ROMANCE

---

## A ROMANCE FOR EVERY READER

---

### MODERN

Prepare to be swept off your feet by sophisticated, sexy and seductive heroes, in some of the world's most glamourous and romantic locations, where power and passion collide.

### HISTORICAL

Escape with historical heroes from time gone by. Whether your passion is for wicked Regency Rakes, muscled Vikings or rugged Highlanders, awa[k] the romance of the past.

### MEDICAL

Set your pulse racing with dedicated, delectable doctors in the high-pressure world of medicine, where emotions run high and passion, comfort a[n] love are the best medicine.

### *True Love*

Celebrate true love with tender stories of heartfelt romance, from the rush of falling in love to the joy a new baby can bring, and a focus on the emotional heart of a relationship.

### *Desire*

Indulge in secrets and scandal, intense drama and plenty of sizzling hot action with powerful and passionate heroes who have it all: wealth, status good looks…everything but the right woman.

### HEROES

Experience all the excitement of a gripping thriller, with an intense romance at its heart. Resourceful, true-to-life women and strong, fearless m[] face danger and desire - a killer combination!

To see which titles are coming soon, please visit

## millsandboon.co.uk/nextmonth

# GET YOUR ROMANCE FIX!

Get the latest romance news, exclusive author interviews, story extracts and much more!